Blood on the
Siberian Snow

Also by C. J. Farrington

Death on the Trans-Siberian Express

Blood on the Siberian Snow

An Olga Pushkin Mystery

C. J. Farrington

CONSTABLE

CONSTABLE

First published in Great Britain in 2022 by Constable

1 3 5 7 9 10 8 6 4 2

A CIP catalogue record for this book
is available from the British Library.

ISBN: 978-1-47213-315-1 (hardcover)
ISBN: 978-1-47213-316-8 (trade paperback)

Typeset in Caslon Pro by SX Composing DTP, Rayleigh, Essex
Printed and bound in Great Britain by Clays Ltd, Elcograf S.p.A.

Papers used by Constable are from well-managed forests
and other responsible sources.

Constable
An imprint of
Little, Brown Book Group
Carmelite House
50 Victoria Embankment
London EC4Y 0DZ

An Hachette UK Company
www.hachette.co.uk

www.littlebrown.co.uk

For Xavier and Claire, as always

Prologue

Olga Pushkin struggled to her feet, fighting for breath and raising a hand in front of her, as if she could stem the choking snow-flurries that poured in upon her from every side. Her face was a frozen mask, her lips and nose scoured by the searching wind till they felt raw and scalded, while her scalp throbbed with a sharp, insistent beat, the remnant of a cowardly blow struck from behind.

She turned and looked backwards, gripped by a sudden fear that she'd been tripped on purpose – that her assailant was on her heels again, and might close in at any time to finish the job. Olga had foreseen death, a troubling vision of snapped limbs tumbling to earth . . . What if she had prophesied her own murder? But Olga's eyes, half closed against the dazzling whiteness, saw only a rough-edged rock upon the ground and, beyond, empty fields rolling on to the wooded horizon. Then the weather closed in again, a pale curtain falling to hide the prospect from view. Olga turned and headed into the wind once more, as if by choosing the hardest road she might earn the gift of sanctuary. But her faltering progress, leaning forward against the buffeting gusts, took her nowhere better than where she'd already been.

Olga couldn't shake the thought that she'd been there before – that there'd been another time when she'd walked in snow with pounding head and wheeling skies, and in danger of her life from some horror behind her. After a time – it could have been one minute or twenty in that barren, trackless waste – the memory came back to her, piercing the fog that lay upon her mind. It had been last winter, she realised, not even a year ago, when she'd fled for her life through a disused warehouse on the edge of Roslazny, the village in Western Siberia where she had spent most of her life. Vassily Marushkin had been there, too, but had fallen senseless to the ground with the other policemen, leaving Olga to tackle the monster by herself.

She'd avoided her demise then, but narrowly, as if a train had gone rocketing past and only brushed her shoulder. That was partly due to her own ingenuity, coupled with an obscure piece of local knowledge – but it was also because her brother, Pasha Pushkin, had come to find Olga lying unmoving in the snow afterwards, and had called for help in time to save her from hypothermia and death. But this time her brother was miles away, and Vassily, too; and there were no paramedics at hand, either, in the wilderness beyond Roslazny's sparse and feeble streetlights. Not even Nevena Komarov remained: her reliable, comforting presence had been swept up and lost in the bitter cold of the early snow, torn from Olga like a scarf whipping out of hand in a gale. No: no one good was coming. Olga Pushkin was alone, with only danger by her side.

The day wore on and the snow darkened from white to grey, but still she staggered forward in search of safety, the passing of time measured only by the crunch of ice beneath her sturdy winter boots. She knew now what the Mongolians meant by *zud*, the pitiless winter she'd read about in guidebooks and tourist magazines – a season so desperate that livestock would perish wholesale, a handful of the hardiest nomadic horses surviving only by eating each other's coats. *Zud – zud* . . . The word sounded like the swish of her waterproof trousers, long since soaked with sweat and melted snow. *Zud –* swish – *zud –* swish . . . The words mingled and overlapped like the snowflakes that tumbled so profusely from the leaden sky.

Olga stumbled and fell again, this time toppling all the way to the ground. She cursed, but was soon grateful for the jolt of agony in her leg and its rousing effect on her mind. She'd almost become delirious, she realised, and that would lead only to a frozen death on the plain. She lay on the snow for a moment to recover, then looked around. Whichever way she gazed, the ground seemed to fall away from her, as if she were on some peak or summit. The low skies cleared again, and she saw she *was* on a summit: she must have ascended a long, slow incline without knowing. She saw her fast-vanishing footprints behind her, interrupted by a line of small boulders that straggled downwards from a mound to her right. The stones looked familiar, somehow, but Olga couldn't work out why.

But then she gasped: she'd been there before, she acknowledged, and not long ago – earlier that same day, in fact, when she and Nevena Komarov had headed out into the cold and the dancing snow. Of course: Nevena had even remarked upon the mound and its train of toppled rocks, nodding towards it as if in deference, her raven hair darting and dancing around her neck in the ice-laden wind. What had she called it? Oh, yes, thought Olga: a *svyatynya* – a shrine. Those mounds were ancient temples to gods with forgotten names, Nevena had said, gods of

3

heaven and mountain and nature; in the old forgotten days Russians had honoured them by dancing circles around them. This was the origin, Nevena had said, beautiful eyes glowing, of the Siberian *khorovod* circle-dances that could still be seen, now and again, in the farther reaches of the *taiga*.

Circling. *Circling* – and hadn't this whole time, this whole experience, really been all about circling, about repeating and returning to where they'd started from? Russians, after all, were not averse to revolution . . .

Perhaps they should have turned aside to pay homage to the old gods, thought Olga. Perhaps then they could have stayed together and fended off the dangers that dogged them.

But Olga had had other concerns on her mind earlier that day when Nevena had told her about the circle-dancers. They'd been running from different terrors then, the fear of circumstances and systems beyond their control. But now, immersed in frozen solitude and untethered from any goal save that of survival, an older, circle-prompted memory came to mind – a recollection of her mother, Tatiana, telling her of childhood days spent in the Lodge at Astrazov, when the aged housekeeper, Lubov, would read to Tatiana from ode and tale and fable, books from the Tsarist days and before, and some that came afterwards, too.

Of all the writers whose books lay upon the mellow wooden shelves, Lubov loved Aleksandr Sergeyevich Pushkin best of all, little guessing the pain that would come to Tatiana from that surname in days yet to come; and she stood often on tiptoe in the library to fetch the second volume of his works from its lofty place. Then she would sit Tatiana by her side and read aloud from *Ruslan and Ludmila* by firelight. The scented wood-smoke surrounded them like perfume as Lubov recited the familiar words:

> *There's a green oak-tree by the shores*
> *Of the blue bay; on a gold chain,*
> *The cat, learned in the mythic stories,*
> *Walks round the tree in ceaseless strain:*
> *Walks to the right – a song it sings;*
> *Walks to the left – a tale it tells.*

Nevena's account of the ancient Siberians wandering circle-wise around their rustic shrines had reminded Olga of the cat, and how, as a girl, she had made her mother walk around the room to the right if she felt like music, and to the left for a story. And if it was a story that Olga demanded, Tatiana would laugh and bow to the ground with arms outstretched and tell Olga that she must sit still, that she must never move a muscle, or yet a hair, but instead sit motionless and listen to the chosen story just as Pushkin told it – just as her great-great-grandfather Pavel, indeed, had once heard it from Pushkin's own lips, in a grand Peterburgtsy house on Nevsky Prospekt! Olga must put herself in Ludmila's shoes, said Tatiana, and listen to the story with patience and imagination, as if she had herself been captured by the evil wizard Chernomor, and was awaiting rescue by the heroic Ruslan.

But if she were to become Ludmila once more, who would be her Ruslan, her courageous, all-conquering knight? wondered Olga. Would it be Vassily, the far-off policeman, as she'd long thought (or at least hoped) it might be? But Vassily was too distant to help her now, in every sense. Then she reflected that she'd already thought this thought, and that she was going in circles in her mind, just as she had meandered across the whitened fields.

She must find shelter, she told herself, or she would lie down, go to sleep and never wake again. She rose to her feet and reeled onwards, heading into the wind and battling her way downhill. As she reached the tussocky foothills, she caught her breath and stood motionless. What was that in the near distance, revealed by a passing lull in the blizzard? Her eyes had picked something out: a long, low shape rising from the snowy earth, overtopped with a thick white layer but underlain with the homely brown of carven oak. Olga gasped: with great good fortune she'd come across a country dwelling, a *dacha* belonging to some farmer in the desolate land between Roslazny and the outlying villages. Then she gasped again, realising she recognised the place – that she knew the very man who dwelled there: Erik Filippov, who eked out a hardy living from Yakutian cattle and shaggy-haired Mangalica pigs. But the windows were dark, and there was no smoke rising from the chimney: Filippov must be away. Nonetheless the *dacha* offered shelter from the storm, if she could break a window or a door-lock.

Just then she seemed to hear a noise behind her, bringing all her terror flooding back. She hurried forward, her legs swishing rapidly once more and her feet ploughing through the drifts as she staggered past a row of tied-up cows, head-down and miserable under ever-renewed snow-blankets. And there – was that a glimmer of light she saw, in the corner of the window nearest the door? Yes – yes, she said to herself, with pounding heart – yes, yes, it was! There must be someone there after all! Help, sanctuary, safety!

She almost tripped over a power line that ran from a petrol generator to the nearest outbuilding, but ran onwards until at last she reached the brightly painted door, its red and blue colours vivid and clear even in the growing darkness, and battered upon its surface until it quivered and opened outwards. She fell back, her eyes momentarily dazzled by the bright electric light that flowed out upon her, cast by a single powerful bulb that hung from a naked cord in the low corridor. Then, when her sight adjusted and she saw who was at the door, her face contorted in terror.

'No,' she whispered. And then, more loudly, her voice cracking in horror. 'No – you can't be here. You can't be here! I – I—'

But Olga's strength was wholly spent at last, and her eyes rolled upwards in her head. She fell forward into the open doorway and lay unmoving, with her legs, still outside, gathering snow like the cows under their winter mantles. A strong pair of hands reached down and drew her inside the *dacha*; then the colourful door slammed, and the fields were dark and silent once more, leaving only a few, rapidly disappearing footprints as evidence of her passing. Olga Pushkin, railway engineer (second class), aspiring writer and amateur investigator, was lost to the world.

Eight days earlier

1

Cold Calling

'*Tomorrow?*' said Olga Pushkin. '*Wednesday?*'

'Tomorrow – Wednesday,' confirmed a gruff voice on the phone – or so Olga thought: she could hardly hear a word over the TV blaring down the corridor. She pressed the receiver a little harder against her ear, trying not to think about Igor Odrosov's relaxed attitude to hygiene, and spoke once more into the grimy, chipped mouthpiece of the Café Astana payphone.

'Before the ceremony?' blurted Olga, dazedly, hardly knowing what she was saying. 'But – but I can't go before the ceremony! The mayor's coming to give Danyl Petrovich his medal. The whole of Roslazny's coming to watch him get it – Danyl's friends and family, too. They cleared the railway schedule for the whole morning – did you ever hear of them doing that before? And the Trans-Siberian's stopping at my hut, for the first time in history!'

'Oh, don't worry about that,' said the voice, permitting itself the luxury of a gravelly chuckle. 'You'll see the ceremony! Oh, yes, you'll see all that – the Mayor of Tayga, and Danyl's grand arrival, and the award ceremony with press from miles around . . . Well, the *Tayga Gazetteer*, anyway, and maybe the *Kemerovo Herald*, too. Only you won't be able to stay for vodka and *pirogi* afterwards: you'll be joining Danyl instead, back on the Trans-Siberian. He's carrying on with his shift after all the festivities, driving the service through to Ulan Ude – wouldn't take no for an answer. He's a real Russian, that one, a real *tovarisch*, even though he's got a ponytail . . . Can't imagine *him* trying to weasel out of anything unpleasant.'

'Well,' said Olga, ignoring the insinuation, and trying to think more rationally – to conjure up some bureaucratic barrier she could use to delay this rather hurried departure. 'Oh, yes – I mean, well, what about the visa?'

'Don't worry about that either,' said her interlocutor. 'It's all arranged. Obviously it's all been arranged, or I wouldn't be calling, would I?'

'Well, n-no,' stammered Olga, her heart sinking. 'No, I suppose not. It's just . . . it's just . . .'

'It's just what?' barked the voice, after a few seconds, making Olga jump. She'd been staring at one of Igor's dog-eared posters of old USSR space missions on the corridor wall, she realised, bewildered at the prospect of finally making her long-awaited trip, and sad, all of a sudden, to think that the hawthorn bush outside her bedroom window would turn to fragrant white blossom in spring, and she would not be there to see it.

'I – I was beginning to wonder if the exchange was ever going to happen, that's all,' she said at last. 'You know Russian Railways.'

'Of course, it's going to happen!' said the voice at the other end of the line, which belonged to Boris Romanovich Andreyev, foreman at the nearby Tayga depot and Olga's immediate superior. 'I told you already – I'm on first-name terms with Sotolmayr, the head of the Railway Academy out there.'

But you can't have known Sotolmayr all that well, given the delay since summer, thought Olga. Or perhaps she knew you all *too* well and was quite sensibly trying to avoid any further contact. In any case, Olga knew just what to say next.

'Well, my guidebook says Mongolians go by just the one name,' she said. 'They don't bother much with surnames, or patronymics. So, technically, isn't everyone on first-name terms in Ulaanbaatar?'

A brushing sound, like hair grazing against the mouthpiece, came to Olga's ear, which meant she'd succeeded in irritating Boris Andreyev. Like his predecessor Viktor, now languishing in Kemerovo jail, Boris prided himself on his extravagant, Stalinesque moustaches – moustaches whose tendency to dance up and down was a well-known sign, in Siberian circles, to run for cover till the storm had blown over.

This was no longer Olga's concern, however, since Boris's phone-call spelled the end of his influence over her for the foreseeable future. It spelled, indeed, an entirely new chapter in Olga's life. The arrival of her Mongolian visa at the Tayga depot, stamped at last by the consulate in Moscow, was like a railway signal switching from red to green. And now Olga herself, like a Novercherkassk VL85 pressed into service after months spent rusting in a siding, had to overcome her inertia and jerk at once into unexpected motion – unexpected, because the visa had been so long coming that Olga had begun to hope it might never arrive at all. It had been months ago – July, in fact – that she'd first received notice of her mandatory participation in a two-year exchange programme between railway academies in Outer

Mongolia and Irkutsk in Russia, whose Taygan satellite college boasted Olga among its graduates.

She well remembered the moment she had received the letter: a bright summer day of gently waving boughs, shimmering heat rising from the desiccated ground around the track, and a certain police sergeant, with untidy black hair, kind eyes and a crumpled cap, walking down the path towards her, envelope in hand. She'd resigned herself to her fate as soon as she'd read the message within – she'd resigned herself, that is, to the fate of all Russian women: to travel onwards, always onwards, to the ever-receding horizon, in the hope that some day they might reach it, and find upon its cusp an Eden of warmth and ease and merriment. To be alive, to live in Olga's skin, was to struggle onwards, onwards, ever unquestioningly onwards, whether or not you thought you'd ever reach anything really worth struggling for. And so, on that day in July, bathed in fierce sunshine and the reflected glare of shining track-metal, and armed, too, with the knowledge that Vassily Marushkin – the policeman with the crumpled cap – would never stop looking for his lost wife Rozalina, Olga had found herself able to accept her imminent departure.

But days and weeks and months had passed since then, dulling her accustomed sense of acceptance and raising that most dangerous of feelings, false hope; and now winter had come early to Roslazny, and it made leaving all the harder. The snow had only gone in March, and already it was back in September, concealing the village's frayed edges like a comforting, much-used throw. How could Olga forsake Roslazny at such short notice – and on the day of the much-anticipated ceremony, too, an unheard-of honour in Russian Railways history? She'd seen the Trans-Siberian service clattering past her hundreds, thousands of times, trundling to Tayga, Tomsk and beyond, to the ends of the earth; but it had never actually stopped at her track maintenance hut before – had never stopped at *anyone's* rail-side hut, so far as she knew, in the entire history of a network dating back to the days of Alexander the Second.

Admittedly, the great event wasn't taking place because of Olga. It was taking place, in fact, because of Danyl Petrovich, who'd started out at the very site of Olga's beloved hut in Roslazny, working his way up from trackside engineering – still Olga's principal task despite her recent promotion to track engineer, second class – to the increasingly lofty heights of locomotive maintenance, locomotive engineering, and then, at last, engine driving itself, the jewel in the railway crown. And since then he'd racked up more miles at the controls than any other driver in Russian Railways, somehow evading the mandatory retirement age of sixty-five and amassing enough by way of salary to buy outright a modern three-bed in the up-and-coming suburbs of Yashkino.

Some of the gossips at Tayga depot spoke knowingly of personal connections to Human Resources at Russian Railways, while others winked when his name came up, and hinted darkly at a deal with the devil, a Faustian pact giving Danyl all his worldly desires but at a terrible cost. But however Danyl Petrovich had managed to become Russian Railways' leading train driver, he hadn't stopped there. Quite the contrary, in fact: Danyl had also become something of a hero in the Kemerovo region, by virtue of saving a child from a burning house near the railway depot in Tayga earlier that year. The papers had painted quite a picture of the operation, describing how Danyl had plucked the toddler intact from the flames while his terrified father stood panicking outside. Danyl and his wife, Anoushka, had no children of their own, and one paper, the *Kemerovo Herald*, went so far as to suggest that Danyl should adopt the child he had rescued. *This particular driver may technically be past retirement age*, said journalist Sasha Tsaritsyn (who happened to be a school friend of Olga's), *but the* Herald, *at least, is glad Russian Railways can still boast a few real men among its ranks!*

They printed the story alongside a glossy, full-colour picture of Danyl next to his Trans-Siberian locomotive, standing tall and glaring into the camera with heroic demeanour, grey hair pulled back into a tight ponytail.

'If he wasn't a hero before, he is now,' Vassily Marushkin had said, when the paper came out in March, making Olga think once more of the power of the written word. Any stranger, happening across the *Kemerovo Herald* or any of the other papers that praised Danyl so highly, would believe everything they read about him – would accord him nothing but the highest accolades in their minds. Whatever Danyl had done before, whatever spectres he had in his past, were now surely banished – just as a single revelation of clay-formed feet, a single instance of wandering hands or casual accounting could eradicate decades of virtue and goodness. Yes, thought Olga, writers were like gods, with the power to elevate and destroy alike. (Or, at least, they were if they were published.)

And now the mayor of Tayga, Abataly Denisovich, would give Danyl Petrovich the Kemerovo Man of the Year Award – the highest civic honour in the whole province – in recognition of his achievements both on and off the track.

(There was, as yet, no Kemerovo Woman of the Year Award, but as her housemate Anna Kabalevsky had once remarked, mounting such an endeavour would be quite impossible. 'It's easy to find one man who's better than the rest,' she said. 'They stand out like sore thumbs. But try to pick out just *one* good woman . . . You'd be there all year, Olga! You'd be there all year.')

Yes: the unprecedented Trans-Siberian stop at Olga's hut was much more about Danyl Petrovich than it was about Olga Pushkin. Nevertheless, Olga tended to regard the hut as her own property rather than as a network asset, and as such she interpreted any compliment paid to it, however obliquely, as a compliment to herself. It was Olga who maintained the hut, wasn't it, and kept it spick and span all year, despite sun and ice and wind?

Anyway, until Kemerovo *oblast* did mount a Woman of the Year award alongside the men's shindig, the mooted ceremony was probably the closest Olga would get to regional glory for the foreseeable future. Besides, the unusual stop might also draw attention to Olga's faultless maintenance of the track and its surrounds, thus aiding her progress up the ranks and – in logical sequence – generate more money to put towards her dream of studying literature at Tomsk State University, the Harvard of Northern Eurasia.

But now all that was ruined, taken away by Boris Andreyev at the drop of an Ushanka hat. The trackside event would no longer serve as a red-letter day – a day for toasting by the track with strong alcohol and sharply pickled herrings, and for dancing, later on, to deafening, speaker-distorted Kazakh folksongs between (and perhaps upon) the tables in Café

Astana. Now the much-anticipated ceremony would serve only to mark her departure from the little hut she loved so much, and the people she loved even more.

Olga stood in the corridor of Café Astana, Roslazny's finest – and only – restaurant and shop, half listening to the instructions Boris was barking down Igor Odrosov's ancient payphone, and wondering how she would ever bring herself to leave.

'What was that?' she said, shaking her head to clear it.

'Oh, for God's sake,' said Boris, crossly. 'I said, get yourself down to your hut as fast as you can. I spent ages ringing round the village for you, and there's no time to waste. Why didn't you answer your mobile?'

'Reception round here—' began Olga, but then she cut across herself: 'My hut? My shift doesn't start for another hour.'

'So what?' said Boris. 'I've sent Galina out with all the paperwork for your trip. She's hitching a ride on one of the shunters. Give the boys a bit of a treat, eh!'

Galina was Boris's latest PA – he had a new one every two or three months – and since Boris recruited solely from the Tayga nightclubs, they tended to attract a certain degree of attention from the train crews.

'On a *shunter*?' said Olga, picturing Galina Ektov in her usual outfit of a skin-tight dress and sky-high heels against the backdrop of a deafening, oily locomotive cab occupied by two, or even three, leering railwaymen. 'Why didn't she just drive over – or take a cab?'

'Haven't you seen the forecast, Pushkin?' said Boris. 'The snow'll be coming down hard again in two swipes of a bear's paw, and that's on top of what we've already had . . . Already the taxi drivers are saying they won't risk coming out your way.

Can't say I blame them, neither – a one-track ditch like that's no joke in heavy snow. Good thing we've got proper snowploughs on the network! We Siberians know how to deal with a bit of *sneg*, eh? We'll probably have to get the mayor out in a four-wheel-drive tomorrow, if we don't have a unit available on the track . . . Anyway, you'd better hurry up, like I said, and get yourself down there. And it's not just Galina I want you to meet,' went on Boris. 'Just walk on down – right now. You'll soon see why! Oh, yes, you'll see why.' And he hung up with a crash.

Was Olga imagining it, she wondered, as she replaced her own handset, or had there been a touch of something nasty in Boris's tone – enjoyment, perhaps, or even delight? She hoped she *had* imagined it. Nothing that pleased an unpleasant person like Boris could itself be pleasant.

'Bad news, Olga?' called Igor Odrosov, as Olga emerged from the corridor into the dingy bar, and tripping, as she did so, over the half-empty paint cans that Odrosov had left lying around after his latest, quarter-hearted attempt at renovations.

'Not sure yet,' said Olga, forcing a reluctant smile, and feeling annoyed that she'd let her emotions show in front of Café Astana's proprietor – not to mention his customers, who now turned to look at her in search of fresh entertainment. Whatever else was happening in Olga's life, she had no desire to take the place of lunchtime soap operas for Odrosov's clapped-out regulars.

It was no wonder that Odrosov couldn't muster the energy to finish his renovations, thought Olga, looking around. After all, you could do up a place, but you could hardly do up the clientele. 'It's probably nothing, Igor,' she said aloud, speaking more briskly, as if speed alone could dispel the mix of anger and sorrow she felt rising within her at the thought of leaving even Café Astana's unpalatable patrons. 'Just – it's just some urgent track maintenance business, that's all.'

With a conscious effort, she made herself walk towards the door as if nothing had happened – as if she hadn't just been given her marching orders for a two-year exile abroad.

'Thanks for lunch, Igor,' she said, as she opened the door, waving a hand vaguely towards the pickled venison she'd started before the payphone had rung.

Igor called something – perhaps a belated request for payment – but the door had already closed behind her, and his words were cut off.

Olga blinked at the sudden blaze of pale sunshine – no sign of Boris Andreyev's fresh snowfall yet – and wrinkled her nostrils at the wall of freezing air, coldly refreshing after the warm fug of the café with its tang of pickle, stale beer spill, and paint fumes from Odrosov's corridor. Olga didn't really mind the paint – it reminded her of her brother Pasha and his enthusiastic, if slapdash, attempt to do up the house they shared with Anna and the children – but Igor Odrosov's three-day sweat was a different matter altogether.

She turned left, somewhat reluctantly, and headed north-east towards the railway and her little hut, taking the narrow road that divided Roslazny's meagre north from its equally meagre south. She trudged along, enveloped in the stillness that always seemed to fall upon the village in winter. Tayga's nearby hum of traffic and busyness floated over the fields and straggly trees as it always did, but softened in subtle ways by the weekend's early snow, as if heard through a filter.

Olga stopped for a moment opposite the tumbledown church, blessed now with the redeeming whiteness of Sunday's light snowfall. When she was younger she'd always longed to be away, far away, from Roslazny and its quiet, neglected alleyways. But now, she acknowledged, she'd miss these paths despite their disrepair. She'd miss these well-known walls and gable-ends, and even these derelict wrecks of abandoned buildings strewn across the village like so many forgotten toys. Yes, she would miss them, when she was far away in the vast concrete plains of Ulaanbaatar – oh, how much she would!

And she would miss the people who still clung to a life lived in Roslazny – Igor Odrosov despite the smell, and his daughter Svetlana; Fyodor Katin, the Dreamer; Alexeyev the mechanic, and Ludmila the waitress, despite her role in breaking up Anna's marriage; Gagarin the office-cleaner, Nonna the hotel maid, Popov the butcher and his wife Nadya, despite the sausages; and the Katins, the Sidorovs, and the Ilyins despite themselves ... Even accounting for her father Mikhail, her aunt Zia, and Mikhail's crony Vladimir Solotov – no more unpleasant trio could well be found anywhere in Western Siberia – there were more people in Roslazny she liked than otherwise. And that wasn't even reckoning with those she loved: her brother Pasha who now lived with her, tall and fair and gentle; her other housemate Anna Kabalevsky and her little boys, dear creatures in spite of the noise; and most of all, perhaps, Vassily Marushkin with the kind eyes, mangy golden ferret, and teenage son Kliment, the only permanent inhabitants of Roslazny's tiny police station.

Olga could see the station at that very moment: it lay down the pathway that peeled off from her road, heading due east past the old bathhouse. The crooked blue sign, reading *Politseyskiy Uchastok*, was clearly visible in the cool air. Olga even caught a distant glimpse of Vassily as he bobbed out of the front door to empty something onto the narrow road – probably the latest droppings created by Rasputin the ferret – before ducking back inside, his messy black hair and tattered fur hat vanishing from view once more. He wasn't stopping to sniff the air, Olga saw, or even smoke one of his beloved Belamorkanal cigarettes. Probably he was hard at work trying to track down the vandals who'd wreaked small-scale havoc on Roslazny and its surrounds in recent weeks – vandals who'd proved surprisingly difficult to track down despite Vassily's big-city know-how, gained during long, hard years on the trail of his lost wife, Rozalina. Vassily had already visited all the teenage tearaways in the district without success, sparing only his son Kliment, who would as soon put Rasputin out in the snow as do anything to disappoint his long-lost father.

Olga usually entertained rather ambivalent feelings towards Rasputin – ferrets loved eating hedgehogs, after all, including white-breasts like Olga's beloved Dmitri – but the thought of being parted even from Vassily's pet was enough to bring a lump to her throat once more. And as for Vassily himself – but no, no: she couldn't bear to think of him just then, or his boy, the lean, calm, bowl-headed Kliment, whom Olga had helped rescue from people-traffickers earlier that same year, and who'd become almost like her own son since.

She turned away from the police station, choking off a sob that threatened to burst out in the icy silence: you never knew who might be nearby. She'd already come perilously close to revealing her feelings in Café Astana, after her phone-call with

Boris Andreyev, and that would never do. She was her father's daughter in this one respect: her firm belief that showing emotion was a distinctly un-Russian thing to do. American girls were always weeping, in the dubbed movies and TV shows the Russian networks had started broadcasting in recent years – weeping, and sulking, and screaming, and beaming, and generally wearing their hearts on their sleeves for the whole world to see.

But that wasn't how Russians behaved, or how Russians *should* behave, anyhow. Russians carried on moving down the road, keeping their joys and sorrows to themselves. They had better things to do than indulge every emotion that passed through their heads, or their hearts. They had pigs to feed and *dachas* to maintain and *banyas* to feed with apple-wood that filled the air with fragrance.

But the tears came to her nonetheless, filling her eyes and distorting her view, taking the low-slung roofs and half-hidden wooden doors laid out in front of her and swinging them crazily, dancing and telescoping them in the wintry light as though she were a string-tied puppet tugged by unseen hands.

She shook her head, wiped her kaleidoscope eyes and carried on, pretending not to think of all the things that now appeared before her, and which tomorrow would be nothing more than dwindling dots on a far horizon. She told herself that feelings didn't matter, anyway – that what mattered was going to Mongolia as ordered. Then she could keep her job and pay the mortgage so that Pasha and Anna and the boys would continue to have a roof over their heads. She told herself that what mattered was working hard abroad to pay the bills at home, and saving a few roubles along the way for Tomsk, so that she could go to university and become a proper writer, an author in the lineage of Gogol and Bulgakov, Pushkin and Tolstoy. Hadn't she always wanted to travel, anyway, ever since those tales of far-off places voiced by her mother Tatiana? And wasn't going to the concrete outskirts of a modern city on a high-pressure, low-reward railway exchange just as good as exploring the backstreets of Paris, notebook in hand, or writing her next masterpiece on the stuccoed, shadowed terraces of Zanzibar? But telling yourself something was one thing, thought Olga, and really believing it was quite another.

As she neared the track, walking through the forest and brushing past the drooping, snow-heavy boughs that hung over the pathway, she first felt, then heard the heavy beat of an engine passing along the tracks. That must be the shunter Boris had promised, thought Olga – and that voice she could hear, carrying shrilly over the diesel's deep-throated roar – that voice must be Galina herself, instructing the railwaymen where to set her down, and in no uncertain terms. The engine noise died away amid a squealing of brakes, and Olga caught a glimpse through the trees of a busty figure dropping awkwardly to earth. She saw, too, that the new snow heralded by Boris Andreyev had begun to fall at last – just a few light flakes at first, floating in the air and seeming almost to rise rather than descend, like dust motes in sunlight; but then supplemented with a thicker wave of snow, and then another, until the daylight seemed visibly to increase with the pale reflected dots in their uncountable thousands.

The engine noise started up again, and though the trees now blocked Olga's view she imagined Galina staggering back to the shunter on her customary stilettos, picking her way through the track-side ballast with difficulty until she was pulled upwards by several pairs of oily and enthusiastic hands. Then she heard a loud blast from the shunter's horn and growling notes from the engine, generating a commotion that gradually died away as the shunter bustled back down the line to Tayga. But hadn't Boris said Galina would give her the necessary papers in person?

She must have left them by the hut, said Olga to herself, as she turned the corner and reached the track, twin lines of silver straightness amid the swirling white confusion. How typical of Galina, she thought, whose attitude to her professional duties resembled Popov the butcher's approach to hygiene – how typical of a Boris Andreyev PA, thought Olga, to leave important paperwork lying around outside in the middle of a snowstorm, with nobody but her little white-breasted hedgehog, Dmitri, to look after it!

She was half tempted to leave the papers where they lay. In time, she reasoned, the paper would become sodden, and then the ink would run. Soon, very soon, the papers would be completely ruined – her precious visa would become, in effect, un-stamped – and she would be forced, absolutely *forced*, to stay in Roslazny after all, with Vassily, and Kliment, and Anna, and Pasha, and all the rest!

But no, she said to herself, with a sigh. There was no point in putting off the inevitable. Postponing the trip would by no means cancel it: it would just mean more difficulty, more unpleasantness, and in the end more unhappiness. And anyway, Olga was the kind of person who ripped off a plaster rather than easing it off bit by bit. If there had to be pain – and it usually seemed that there *did* have to be pain, sooner or later, and of one kind or another – then it was better to get it over with.

And so she firmed her jaw, clenched her gloved fists, and made herself march forward once more, nearing the familiar outline of her hut, painted in faded green, and stamped with a peeling Russian Railways logo. For more than a decade, the hut had been her home from home – not just a miniature office but an ample haven for the soul, the place where she'd found Dmitri, the place where she'd encountered Vassily Marushkin once more after so many years, and the place where she'd begun her career as an author, writing on cast-off timetables and memos, piece by piece and page by page, until the manuscript of her masterpiece was completed – and a masterpiece, moreover, that was now under serious consideration by Lyapunov Books, an important Novosibirsk publisher (or so it said on their website). Soon, she hoped, *Find Your Rail Self: 100 Life Lessons from the Trans-Siberian Railway* by Olga Mikhailovna Pushkin would appear in bookshop windows from Tomsk to Nizhny Novgorod – a fitting tribute to the long years she'd laboured, as writer and engineer. By the time she returned, she could have sold a thousand copies, or even more. She could be at the top of the Kemerovo book chart – she could be a famous writer!

And it was important to stay positive about things like this, she reminded herself. It was important to have confidence in yourself and your ability to see things through, whatever else might be happening. She'd written as much in her book, and if she couldn't follow her own advice, who would?

Life Lesson No. 32: *Confidence gets us from A to B. Engine drivers need to have confidence, or trains would never get where they're going. A train driven by an unconfident driver would creep along at a snail's pace, so that the driver could keep checking the line for obstacles – for bricks or branches or missing ballast or breaks in the track that could derail the train. But a confident driver, like a confident person in general, keeps going as fast as possible and trusts to fortune. And most of the time the tracks are clear and unbroken, and almost always the train gets to its destination in one piece.*

Even if she had to leave now, she would return, Olga told herself. Everyone would still be here, waiting for her. Yes, she would return; and what was more, she'd come back with a new manuscript – a sequel inspired by her destination, Mongolia, by the wide-open spaces she'd read about in books and magazines, and the plains that countless nomads still called home. Ulaanbaatar might not be her first choice of destination, but she would make the most of it – just as her mother, Tatiana, had made the most of her low-budget life in Roslazny, or tried to. Olga had even come up with a provisional title: *Take the Next Steppe: 101 Life Lessons from Ulaanbaatar.* (A sequel obviously had to have more life lessons than the first book in a series, or readers would feel cheated.)

The thought of a triumphant return with a brand-new manuscript went some way towards displacing Olga's irritation at Galina's carelessness. But as she approached, she heard a loud, shrill voice raised in anger. Then the front door of her hut swung open and banged against the side.

'Shoo!' she heard, as the end of a brush appeared outside the hut, then swung inside once more. 'Shoo! Go on, get out of here!' Then, to Olga's horror, Dmitri the hedgehog came into view, wrapped up in her favourite patchwork teacloth, before being thrown bodily into the undergrowth.

'*Kagogo cherta!*' shouted Olga, running to pick up Dmitri, and striding up to the hut. 'Who's there – and what the hell are you doing in my hut?'

As she marched hut-wards she wondered if Galina had somehow jumped back off the shunter without Olga seeing, and had subsequently managed to enter the hut uninvited. Who else could it possibly be?

A sturdy figure stepped out into the snow, hands on hips, facing her squarely and bringing her skidding to a halt on the gravel that lay under the thin grass by the tracks.

'You're not Galina,' said Olga in surprise.

'No,' said a firm, female voice. 'No, I'm damn well not.'

2

Spectres at the Feast

Olga stared at the figure in front of her, thinking she looked familiar. Of course! Her stocky physique, trim hair and no-nonsense skirt and coat had brought Ivanka Kozar to mind – the *provodnitsa*, or carriage attendant, she'd got to know earlier that year in memorable circumstances. But there were differences, too, like this woman's thick, horn-rimmed glasses. (The medical reports had said Ivanka's eyesight was perfect.) There were also the stout wooden clogs this person had on her feet, as opposed to the Tomsk-bought leather boots Ivanka had always favoured for her shifts on the Trans-Siberian. Olga looked at the woman's stolid, clumpy shoes, painted yellow and decorated with a colourful arabesque, and hoped she hadn't used them to kick Dmitri.

'Oh, my Dmitri, my Dimi-*detka*,' Olga crooned to the little bundle in her arms, trying to help him forget that some monstrous woman had just bundled him up and thrown him into the undergrowth, like a load of old tea leaves. Poor little thing, thought Olga, with heightening indignation. Poor little thing, to be rudely plucked from his favourite position by the hut's miniature stove, lying on a pile of Olga's old jumpers and warming his prickles to the comforting sound of a bubbling samovar. Poor little thing, to be plucked from comfort and safety, and summarily ejected into the chill by unfriendly hands!

Olga reached inside her stained patchwork teacloth, feeling the sharp quills on the hedgehog's back still curled tightly into a protective ball, and her anger rose just as sharply inside her. 'Just who the hell do you think you are?' she said. 'And what gives you the right to kick poor Dmitri' – holding up the creature in his makeshift hammock – 'to kick poor Dmitri out of his only home?'

'His *home*?' snorted the woman. 'This isn't some sanctuary for re-housed animals! It's a workplace, though how anyone could work in that unholy mess is beyond me . . . B said the woman was a fool, but he didn't say she was untidy, too. There's a way I like huts to look, and this isn't it. There's no excuse for untidiness, don't you agree?'

'B?' said Olga, ignoring (for the sake of her blood pressure) the stranger's gratuitous insults about her hut-related house-keeping – gratuitous, and ridiculous: admittedly the hut was no showroom, but what did anyone expect of a rail-side hut in Western Siberia?

'Oh, sorry,' said the woman, flashing a quick, toothy and wholly unconvincing half-smile at her. 'B for Boris. Boris Andreyev, I mean. The foreman over at Tayga depot. He's an old friend of mine – his wife and I go to the same hair salon.'

Olga stared at the woman, wondering how any self-respecting hairdresser could charge for a cut like that. She frowned and was about to speak again – but as she opened her lips the woman stepped towards her and held out her hand. 'I'm

Polina,' she said briskly. 'Polina Klemovsky. I'm running track maintenance here, for the foreseeable.'

'Oh,' said Olga, shaking her hand with extreme reluctance and brevity, and clutching Dmitri to her with the other hand, the hedgehog retaining his curled-in shape for safety's sake.

'Yes, I'm here for as long as I need to be,' said Polina. 'B picked up the phone and gave me a call, said he needed a safe pair of hands to replace someone who was off to Mongolia on some junket or other, and no one else would do.

'It's like the old days,' she continued, leaning on Olga's doorframe in a familiar manner, 'when the hammer and sickle still flew across a good-sized part of the world – exciting days, if you ask me, when a good Russian worker, a labourer worth her salt, might be packed off at a moment's notice to Sevastopol, or Tashkent, or the Aral Sea! Well, who knows? Maybe those days will come again. Yes, I wouldn't be surprised if they did – for some of us, at least.'

'You sound like Fyodor Ivanovich,' said Olga.

'Who?'

'Oh, you'll see, soon enough,' said Olga, pleased to know something that Polina Klemovsky didn't, and amused, despite the situation, at the thought of an encounter between Polina and Fyodor Ivanovich Katin. Fyodor was a youngish, old-looking man with thick, greasy spectacles and lank, unwashed hair. The villagers called him Mechtatel – the Dreamer – for he was always working on some new scheme for Russian reform, which he would share on his blog, *Dead Square*, or elaborate in vast, sprawling, as-yet-unpublished manifestos that he composed, page after laborious page, on an ancient typewriter in his parents' attic. Like Polina, he hankered for the past – but for the Tsarist days, harsh yet magnificent, rather than the Soviet era with its conformism, hypocrisy, and ashen factories of death.

'Well, I don't know anyone around these parts,' said Polina, as if it was something to be proud of, looking around at the wintry trees with an air of distaste. 'Never been down this way before, and can't say I was missing much, either. I mean, holding a special ceremony for a *pridurok* like Danyl Petrovich, a nonentity promoted and promoted and *promoted*, just because he's a man . . . It speaks volumes, doesn't it? Honouring a man like Danyl, with the local mayor, and newspapers, and all that? Not how we do it back in Itatka – not how we do it at all. Lucky for me this is only a station along the way! I'm just going to do my job here and get out again, as far away as I can.'

'Well, if you hate it so much, and you're so friendly with *B*, why don't you ask him to send you somewhere exotic, too?'

'Oh, I will, in time!' said Polina Klemovsky. '*B* will be more than happy to send me wherever I want to go, believe me. But not yet. I've got some things to do first, you see.'

'What things?' said Olga. But Polina looked at her quizzically, as if she'd suddenly realised she might have said a little too much to a stranger like Olga.

'Oh, just some little side-projects,' she said, eyes glinting behind her glasses, and though she spoke in an airy, offhand manner, there was something in her tone – something almost threatening – that made the hairs on Olga's neck stand up. She stared at her, wondering if she had imagined it. But there was no time for introspection, as Polina carried on speaking in her loud, strident voice. 'Well, never mind about those – that's for the future! I've got to get the lie of the land first. I've never met the main track engineer here. B did say it was a woman, though – Volga something? Or was it Bolga?'

'It's *Olga*. Olga Pushkin,' said Olga, tight-lipped.

'Don't tell me that's you!' said Polina, reading her expression correctly.

'And why shouldn't it be me? Maybe you were expecting someone older – someone more like yourself.'

'Ha,' said Polina, and made to carry on, but Olga cut across her.

'And now I come to think of it, I thought they were going to replace me with someone from Mongolia, not some . . .'

She waved her hands vaguely in Polina's direction, trying to think of something that was insulting but not outrageously rude.

'Not some – not some *minion* of Boris Andreyev,' she said, 'who doesn't know Roslazny from Itatka, or Fyodor Katin from Sergeant Vassily Marushkin! It's an exchange programme with Mongolia, after all, so it's natural for me to expect a Mongolian to turn up – but, then, maybe you didn't know that. There seem to be a lot of things you don't know.'

'On the contrary,' said Polina, ducking inside the hut and emerging with a small package of papers. 'I've just taken delivery of these from Galina – that's B's PA. His *BA*, you might say,' she added, stretching her mouth into yet another grimace that (Olga supposed) might possibly be intended as a grin rather than an expression calculated to scar young children for life. 'And since they were handed to me in my professional capacity, I took the liberty of opening them.'

'You – you what?' gasped Olga. Even her father Mikhail, in the days when Olga used to share the family home with him, had never gone as far as opening her post.

'Yes – yes,' said Polina, waving a hand to dismiss Olga's protests. 'Oh, there's nothing personal in them. Just your visa, details of your home address, criminal record, marital status – single – and bank details. Oh, and your last medical check-up – clean bill of health, though looks to me like you could lose a kilogram or three – and travel documents to Mongolia, by rail. And there's a covering letter, too – seems the exchange part of the programme is optional for the Russian side. Not so much for the Mongolians – so they have to take our cast-offs, but we don't have to pay for some useless foreigner to travel over here. So I'm replacing you instead. Win-win. Maybe the old days aren't quite gone, after all!'

'Give me those!' cried Olga, striding forward and snatching the papers from Polina. 'I'll thank you to mind your own business, from now on.'

'Happy to,' said Polina. 'As soon as you send someone to get all your things from the hut, I'll stop going through them.'

'Oh, you wouldn't dare,' said Olga. But one look at Polina's face was enough to convince her that she would, and in fact already had. With a grunt of rage Olga barged past her into the hut. She put Dmitri down next to the samovar, grabbed one of the sacks she kept by the door for firewood, emptied it of twigs and splinters, and filled it with everything she could see that belonged to her: the box of old memos and schedules that she used for writing down life lessons and other ideas; the three rows of books, faded yet beloved, that had come to her from her mother Tatiana, long ago; the pile of teacloths and old jumpers that smelt of Dmitri, pickled beetroot and wood-smoke; and the photographs she'd printed in the Tayga post office and stuck up on the low wooden beams in the past few months – her brother

Pasha, her friend Anna Kabalevsky with her arms around her boys, and a third, favoured image of Vassily Marushkin and his son Kliment, captured on a sunlit, autumnal day only the week before, Kliment in motion with a smile lighting up his round head, and Vassily, standing still behind him, and beaming at him with a face full of pride.

With an expression of iron – she wouldn't cry: she *would not* cry, in front of a person like Polina Klemovsky – she gathered up the sack and flung it over her shoulder like an angry Santa Claus, before bending to pick up Dmitri once more. Then she marched out of the hut and past her tormentor, stalking down the path that led towards Roslazny without a backward glance.

'Yes, you'd better go,' called Polina, after her. 'There's no room for messy, workshy layabouts round here.'

'Oh, I'm going,' said Olga, turning to face her once more. 'But don't get too comfortable, Polina Klemovsky. I've a feeling you won't be staying too long. It takes a certain type of person to get by in Roslazny. You need a certain get-up-and-go.'

'Looks like the best ones have already got up and gone,' said Polina. She walked forward amid the snow, her clogs scraping on the gravel like maracas. Then she stopped and pointed at Dmitri, still cowering in Olga's free arm. 'You'd better keep that *thing* away from me in future, or into the pot it goes, spikes and all!'

Then she marched back to the hut, ducked inside, and slammed the door, dislodging a growing belt of snow from the sloping roof, and leaving Olga staring after her with a mixture of anger and disbelief. Leaving her precious hut in the hands of a stranger from abroad, or even some nobody from Russian Railways, was one thing, but this new creature was another kettle of *omul* altogether.

'You haven't seen the last of me, Polina Klemovsky,' she muttered, in the hut's direction. 'Not yet!'

Then she shouldered her sack of belongings once more and set off towards Roslazny, stamping the snow viciously with her boots as she went.

Olga didn't get far before – quite literally – running into other pedestrians warily braving the unexpectedly wintry weather. She had just breasted the slight incline that crowned the path's ascent towards Roslazny when she darted sideways to avoid one of the protruding roots – a hazard she passed daily, but for some reason always forgot. Burdened by her heavy bag of belongings, and unable to reach out a hand for support because of little Dmitri, she slipped on the wet snow and cannoned forwards, jogging for a few steps down the little path to regain her balance, and nearly knocking over an old man, and then a second, in the process.

'Look out!' one of them said. 'Can't you watch where you're going?'

'Oh, I'm sorry,' said Olga, avoiding a pirouette with difficulty, and finally managing to stand upright once more with bag, hedgehog and person intact. 'I didn't— Oh, it's you.'

'Who else did you bloody well think it was?' said Vladimir Solotov; and indeed, Solotov and his companion, Olga's father Mikhail, were hard to mistake once you saw them clearly. Mikhail Pushkin was wearing his usual tracksuit and denim jacket combo, though paired, in a nod to the unusual weather, with heavy working boots instead of his preferred slip-on plastic sandals. Solotov, meanwhile, was dressed in ancient cold-weather army fatigues, and with his bushy white beard and dancing eyebrows under a baggy skullcap he looked like a modern-day Tolstoy – until you heard him speak. Then his torrents of foul verbiage would soon drive any lingering resemblance to the author of *War and Peace* from your mind; and if you were unlucky enough to be an unchaperoned woman into the bargain, Solotov would soon add lecherous remarks and glances to the mix, until the kindly, smock-clad éminence grise seemed a thousand miles away.

On this particular occasion, however, Solotov was relatively restrained at first, confining himself to reiterating how Olga had betrayed Mikhail to the authorities earlier that year, and how bad it had been for him to be forced back into employment.

'He's working round the clock, thanks to you, and his heart in a bad way, too, despite what those government quacks say. It's no good, at his time of life – no good at all. Just look at him!'

Olga agreed that his appearance, upon close inspection, was not a recommendation for the life choices her father had made, but this did not go down well with Mikhail Pushkin.

'Don't you take that smart-arse tone with Vladimir, Olga,' he said, jerking a thumb at his acquaintance. 'I've had a lifetime's worth of your cheek, and we don't need any more now. And keep that little rat away from me!' He nodded at Dmitri's diminutive snout, just poking out of Olga's teacloth. 'Last thing I need is catching croup, or something.'

'He's not a rat,' said Olga, sharply. 'He's a white-breasted Siberian hedgehog. Not that I'd expect you to know about animals, or about anything that's not poker, *Pravda*, or Putin.'

'Is that so?' Mikhail replied, quite sharply, narrowing his eyes under his shaggy brows. 'Think you're so clever, don't you, tricking me like that? You and your precious friends, forcing old men out to work, as if it's some kind of glorious service to the nation.'

'She might think she's clever,' put in Solotov, 'but she doesn't know everything that goes on round here, do you, Devushka Pushkin? You didn't even know Boris Andreyev was sending you off tomorrow, did you? No, you don't know anything.'

'I prefer "Dama" to "Devushka",' began Olga, having recently decided to correct men who called her 'Miss', but Solotov rode over her.

'Neither does your precious friend, *Sergeant* Marushkin! Couldn't find his own nose in a blizzard, that one.'

'Ha!' barked Mikhail, slapping Solotov on the back. 'Well, he won't be around to bother us much longer.'

'What – what do you mean?'

Solotov grinned at her, a look of pure delight. 'Ha! Don't you know? You don't know?' He turned to Mikhail. 'She doesn't know! Well, well, I guess *damas* don't know a damn thing more than *devushkas*.'

'Just tell me,' said Olga, through gritted teeth.

'Well, he's on his last warning,' said Mikhail, all but laughing as he spoke. 'He hasn't got enough crimes on his book, has he? But that's not for lack of criminals. What about all those little jobs going on round these parts, all the vandalism and burglaries? I even heard the police station was robbed, and the Petrovs are out a bag of garden tools . . . And Marushkin's got nothing to show for it! But they know, up in Tayga and beyond – oh, believe me, they know! They'll shut him down faster than a fox shuts down a henhouse, and post him back to that inner-city slum he came from – Ekaterinburg, was it, or Novosibirsk?

'Anyway,' he went on, when Olga didn't deign to reply, 'we can't stand here talking all day in the cold. We're off to see your replacement.'

Olga stirred. 'Polina? You know her?'

'No – but I know her father,' said Solotov, pushing past her. 'We were in the army together. He called me up yesterday to say his girl was coming to replace someone being sent off to Ulaanbaatar – to replace *some nobody*! That's what he actually said! And I thought Mikhail might appreciate her company more than the last inhabitant of that little hut . . . Well, so long, *Devushka* Pushkin,' he called over his shoulder, still laughing as the two men set off towards Olga's hut.

'Enjoy the Mongolian camel's milk!' added Mikhail, before disappearing from sight.

'Should have guessed,' muttered Olga, thinking that birds of a feather flock together, and that leopards don't change their habits. No doubt Solotov and her father, Mikhail, had some scheme on the go, and wanted another recruit for their nefarious activities. Maybe her aunt Zia, who'd been one of Mikhail's closest cronies ever since her husband passed away, was getting too old for some necessary task, so that fresher blood – and specifically Polina's blood – was needed.

But that didn't really matter. Nothing really mattered, if Vassily was to be sent away. So that was why he'd been so jumpy in recent weeks . . . Olga had noticed a change in his behaviour – short answers to questions, smoking even more than usual, and a tendency to come down too hard on Kliment – but she'd put it down to fatherly anxiety. Kliment had been parted from Vassily at an early age, and Olga knew that Vassily worried about his lack of parenting skill, and all the challenges coming over the horizon as Kliment moved through his teenage years. But an imminent forced departure would be more worrying still, especially as Vassily, she knew, was trying his best to create a stable environment for his son.

What else could possibly go wrong? Olga asked herself. First, she heard she was to be sent away into exile, on a day's notice; then she discovered that her hut was to be left in the hands of the ghastly Polina Klemovsky, hedgehog-hater and Mikhail-and-Solotov associate; and now it seemed that Vassily might not even be here when she got back. Olga didn't think she could bear to leave, without the certainty of Vassily and Kliment and, yes, even Rasputin waiting for her when she returned.

Confidence was all very well to get you from A to B. But what if you didn't want to get to B? And what if B – or Boris Andreyev – was the problem in the first place?

She looked down at little Dmitri, still quivering in a tightly curled ball in her arms, then sideways at the heavy bag of belongings still cutting into her shoulder, and then upwards at the snow now streaming steadily from a gunmetal sky. The sensible course was to turn left, taking the shortest path home. That was the sensible thing to do, in this weather, with a heavy sack over her shoulder and a hedgehog in her arms. And so, of course, she turned right instead, and headed straight towards the police station.

'*Olga?*' said Vassily Marushkin, sitting forward and peering down the road through the thick snow-curtain. He dropped his cigarette at the foot of his chair, the chair he placed in the doorway of the police station every lunchtime, come rain, shine or snow, to sit on and smoke and see what might be seen. Then he pulled his fur collar up around his ears, and set off towards her, head bent low against the snow. It was falling more heavily now, its icy torrents slanted by a withering breeze until the world seemed to have tilted on its side, and piling up in new, deep drifts around the Roslazny police station.

'Oh, Vassily, there you are!' she said, as he appeared in front of her. 'Can you help . . .'

But Vassily had already taken the sack from Olga's hands and slung it over his own shoulder. Taking her hand in his, he kicked the chair out of the doorway and ushered her through. Then he barged the door shut with his shoulder and let the sack fall heavily upon the floor. Finally he stood facing Olga, both of them covered with slowly melting snowflakes.

'What's going on?' he said. 'Why have you come with all this stuff, with – with your books from the hut?' he went on in surprise, glancing down at the sack, which had spilled open to reveal Gogol's *Lost Souls* and the slim *Requiem* of Anna Akhmatova, each filled with old bookmarks and scribbled notes, and covering many more books underneath them. He looked back at Olga, staring closely at the writhing bundle in her arms. 'And is that *Dmitri*, too?'

'I'm leaving, Vassily,' she said heavily. 'Boris Andreyev rang me up and told me, earlier on. I'm off to Mongolia, after all – I've got to go tomorrow. And I've been kicked out of my hut – a terrible woman's taken it over, called Klemovsky, and I had to get all my things together in two minutes, just like when Father kicked me out . . . You've got to see if there's a police record on her, Vassily, you've just *got* to, and to hell with rules and regulations – and old man Solotov's already there, cosying up to her, and my father, too. And he said – he told me – oh, Vassily, he said you're leaving, too! Is it true? Are they going to kick you out? Can you really not find the vandals and the thieves, so that you can stay?'

Vassily Marushkin stared back at her, bewildered by the rush of new information, amid requests for even more. 'Er – well,' he began, then stopped. 'Look – you'd better sit down. Take that coat off and come and sit by the fire. You and Dmitri must be freezing! And don't worry,' he went on, as Olga cast a worried look around her. 'Rasputin's in his cage. Dmitri's quite safe.'

'Well, that's something,' she said, allowing herself to be led towards the police station's diminutive fireplace, and sitting on one of the armchairs that Vassily had salvaged from a nearby house.

'And that's better still,' said Olga, taking the mug of coffee that Vassily had poured from the saucepan he kept simmering on the station's gas stove, and drinking deeply from its pock-marked rim. Then she leaned towards the Soviet-era fireplace with missing tiles like a gap-toothed *babushka*, taking whatever heat she could, and carefully unwrapping Dmitri from his teacloth blanket to expose him to the grateful warmth.

Vassily sat down beside her. 'You're leaving *tomorrow*?' he said, shaking his head. 'But *tomorrow* . . .'

'That's what I said to Boris. Or B, as Polina Klemovsky says.'

'But you can't go – you can't go tomorrow!'

'It's set in stone, Vassily. I've got to go, or I lose my job. I've got a mortgage to pay, don't forget, and a house to maintain for some very important people . . . Did you know baby Ilya has nearly all his teeth now? And anyway, I've worked too hard, too long, to give up on Russian Railways now. God knows I'd like to. But – but—'

'But that's not who Olga Pushkin is,' said Vassily, slowly, looking at her with sad, earnest eyes.

'I wish it was,' said Olga, after a long pause. 'You have no idea. Oh, Vassily, you really have no idea!'

'Well, I just wish – I just wish you weren't like that,' said Vassily, after an equally long pause. 'And I wish you could stay. I wish you had a choice, so that you could stay here, in – in safety, and with your friends and, well, with those who care for you. All of us wish that – all the villagers.'

'Maybe not all,' said Olga, flashing a brief smile.

In his turn Vassily forced a nod and a bleak smile. He knew all about Olga's recent struggles with her family, not to mention the murderous secrets they'd uncovered together earlier that year.

Olga's smile faded. 'But, Vassily, are you going to carry on being a villager yourself? Or is it true? Are they really going to make you leave, if you can't get enough crimes on the book?'

'They might,' he said, setting his mug on the floor, and running a hand over his face, his fingers sibilant on his three-day beard. Yes, they really might, if I can't get some more criminals in the cells, and soon. It's the new regime, up at HQ in Kemerovo. You know, Arkady Nazarov and his crew. He's brought in a heap of new regulations – showing he means business, so he can campaign for re-election, and move up to the Duma, in time. And one of the new regulations is the local crime directive.'

'The local what?'

'Crime directive. How many crimes they think we should solve from each police station, depending on the local population. Oh, they used some government statistics to work it out, I suppose. They didn't bother telling me about that. They just sent me this letter' – Vassily pulled a dog-eared piece of paper from his inside pocket – 'and told me I was on course to miss the local target by three crimes, and I had till the end of the month to make good or I'd be on my way.'

'Oh, *Vassily*,' said Olga. 'But can't you find something to bump up the numbers? What about all the anti-social behaviour?'

As Mikhail Pushkin had mentioned, Roslazny had been hit by a wave of petty crime in recent weeks, with numerous thefts of sundry items, spray-painted obscenities on numerous walls, and even a few cases of small-scale arson.

'I don't know,' he said morosely. 'I really don't know, Olga. I've already questioned all the teenagers in the village – not that it took long! And that yielded nothing, nothing at all. Then there's the younger men – but can you imagine Alexeyev doing things like that between his shifts at the garage, or Artyom Grigorovich Petrov between shifts on the farm, or Fyodor Katin, between . . . well, between whatever it is he does to fill his time? No: it must be an outside job – but why would anyone travel to Roslazny to knock over crumbling walls and steal your aunt's washing? I'm completely at a loss.'

'Well, what about other things – other crimes you could track down? There's always Popov's horsemeat, or Odrosov's licences – and maybe Nonna's been shop-lifting again.'

'Yes, but three crimes in twenty days? No problem in Tayga,

or Itatka – in Leninsky, even. But here, in Roslazny? We might as well start packing Rasputin's mice now. Apart from the vandalism, the last thing we've got on the books was back at the end of August, and even then it barely counted as a crime. It was only Ludmila selling those knockoff handbags, you remember?'

Olga nodded. Ludmila's day job was waitressing at a café in Tayga, but she was always open to new opportunities, whether acting in low-budget adult films – as Anna Kabalevsky had discovered earlier that year – or selling imitation Pradas for a fistful of roubles apiece.

'I don't know, Olga,' Vassily went on, shaking his head. 'Maybe I'm losing my touch – maybe I deserve to be kicked out. But it's Kliment who worries me – his school, and his friends. It's all so difficult already. How much harder would it be somewhere else? Yes, it's Kliment who worries me. Well, Kliment and – and some others I'd miss.'

He looked so downhearted that Olga reached out a hand and gripped his arm. 'I believe in you, Vassily,' she said. 'And I know you'll find your crimes – I just know it. And—'

Her reassurances were interrupted by a sudden knock on the door, making both of them jump.

'Who can that be, in this blizzard?' said Vassily, irritably, yet getting up to answer all the same. He shifted Olga's sack carefully to one side, walked down the corridor that led to the door, and disappeared from view. Olga heard a female voice – an unknown voice, she thought, or did it have a faint ring of familiarity? – then Vassily's deeper reply came to her ears, but she could hear neither his words nor their visitor's. Maybe it was news of a crime. She hoped so, for his sake, but she was too drained after everything that had happened to get up and eaves-drop for details. Instead, she turned in her chair, and gazed out of the low window that overlooked the narrow road running past the station. Across the way stood a clump of Siberian larches, their branches bowed down with the weight of snow. As Olga looked, first one, then another, then a third and a fourth bent and snapped with their white burden, so that the snow fell in sluices to the ground.

Olga frowned. When had she seen that happen before?

Then she remembered: it had been earlier that year, when she was still sharing a house with her father Mikhail. She'd gone out one night to clear the snow from heavy-laden boughs, only for them to snap like limbs, one after another, until all of them lay in a splintered heap upon the ground. That collapse had presaged death, a brutal killing on the Trans-Siberian, with several more to follow. Now she shivered as the thought presented itself to her, unwelcome but insistent: did this new collapse also foreshadow terrible things? Was she connected to some supernatural realm – some sixth or seventh sense that called to her like a bat-squeak at the edge of hearing, telling of things that lay down the line, horrible yet unavoidable – things like blood and blows and death?

Olga didn't really believe in such things – she left that to her friend Anna Kabalevsky, who said prayers daily to fend off demons with the serried powers of angels and archangels, marshalling icons, incense and bells in her heavenly battles against foes immortal. Olga prided herself on a more rational approach to life. But despite all her strict self-reproaches, a question remained, circling in her mind – a dreadful question, filled with evil foreboding: *who would die this time?*

3

The Return of Nevena Komarov

'I've got to go, Olga,' said Vassily, stepping back inside the narrow corridor that led to the front door.

'Oh – what is it?' said Olga, straining to see past him. 'Or who is it?'

'Some *postoronniyya*,' said Vassily, shrugging. He had used the word Roslaznyans reserved for those unlucky enough to hail from anywhere else. 'Here on business, she says – but she happened to see an arsonist at work.'

'An arsonist? Again?'

'Exactly,' said Vassily, rubbing his hands. 'Same as last time – another useless, empty building gone up in smoke, except this time we've got an eyewitness. Wouldn't it be fantastic if she helped me track him down? Just what I need to bump up the statistics! But I suppose it'll be another dead end,' he went on, with a sigh. 'Like the time Kliment reported hearing someone issuing death threats on the phone, and it was just Alexeyev talking to a customer.'

(Koptev Alexeyev worked at the Pultarova garage in Tayga, renowned far and wide for its robust approach to customer service.)

'Still, I'd better go and investigate, all the same – I'll question the *postoronniyya* later,' said Vassily. 'It's one of the old dairies up on the north-west, she said. You don't mind letting yourself out?'

He turned to go, pulling on his police winter jacket and padded gloves – but then he stopped and looked back at Olga, sitting by the fire, her chipped, half-empty mug of coffee in her hands, and Dmitri finally uncurling amid the fire's gentle heat.

'Look,' he said, in a gentler tone, 'why don't we all get together at the café for a few drinks, later on? I mean, it's not every day we send off one of our own on a prestigious foreign exchange – an all-expenses-paid trip to Ulaanbaatar!'

'Well, I didn't have much choice,' Olga began, but then her face softened, seeing the sadness that lay behind his eyes. 'Yes, Vassily – yes, I think a few Rocket Fuels will be quite in order. A toast to my travels.'

'It's a date, then,' he said, turning towards the door. Then he stopped and turned back again, opening his lips as if to supplement or qualify his last remark. But in the end he merely nodded, stuffed his hat awkwardly onto his head, and stalked out of the door, pulling it half shut behind him. And though he hadn't spoken, his meaning was clear: yes, it was a date, but not of the romantic kind. It wasn't *really* a date – how could it be, when Vassily's lost wife Rozalina lay always between them, like a beautiful ghost, shimmering and scarcely visible in the daylight, but there nonetheless, a shifting, diaphanous barrier to the very possibility of their union? No, it wasn't a date: it was just an assignment between friends, an arrangement to mark a departure, and possibly two. It was just an agreement, a social contract to get somewhat drunk together, to laugh too loudly and spend too much money on the few indulgences that Café Astana offered, like little cellophane bags of *pelmeni* oozing with mushrooms and greasy, delicious onions, or *churchkhela* strings bursting with nuts, raisins and chocolate and dangling from hooks like Halloween fingers in green and orange and black.

Olga would have to be careful that night, though, she said to herself, gazing into the fire and gently caressing Dmitri's prickles. Four or five tots of Odrosov's blue-tinged, kerosene-like homebrew were par for the course, but much more than that and she'd be heading to Outer Mongolia with a hangover of steppe-like proportions – and Olga knew from experience that Russian Railways travel was rarely improved by headaches or nausea, above all in a *platskartny* third-class compartment in which you bumped up and down on unforgiving wooden seats, jostling cheek by jowl with burly, singlet-clad shot-putters and large families with small children and smelly lunches.

Better not to think of the details, she told herself, and instead to try to work up some big-picture enthusiasm for her impending adventure. It would be her first journey out of the country, after all, and surely that was a cause for some celebration. She might be leaving behind everything she loved, but she would at least have *been* somewhere – something her mother Tatiana had always longed to do, until her father Mikhail had married her and trapped her into a life of drudgery far from the fairy-tale Lodge at Astrazov.

Olga was just trying to imagine what it would really be like living in Ulaanbaatar – could it be true, for instance, that the Mongolians used some kind of smartphone app to organise their addresses with three randomly chosen words, and that her designated railway accommodation could be found at the unpromising location of massage.pound.parlour? – when a voice broke in upon her thoughts.

'Olga! Olga Pushkin – is that really you? But what on earth are you doing here?'

Olga turned towards the source of the voice, and clapped her hand unconsciously over her heart, which raced under her fingers as if she'd been startled by the phantom of Vassily's wife. The voice did not belong to Rozalina's ghost, however, but to a flesh-and-blood woman striding down the corridor towards her: a strikingly attractive woman of about forty, holding an Ushanka hat and a leather satchel, and with dark hair that flowed over a green noose of a scarf and fur-collared jacket, now shedding snowflakes that spiralled downwards in graceful arabesques. She reached Olga and stopped, staring down at her with puzzlement on her face.

'But – but – but it's me,' she said at last. 'Don't you remember? Nevena Komarov! You must remember – from the Institute?'

'Nevena Ivanovna Komarov! Do I remember?' cried Olga, jumping to her feet. 'How could I forget? Only – what a long time it's been! Is it ten years? No – less: I saw you at Valeriya's wedding in Leninsky. Did you hear she's divorced now? But no matter: give me a hug, for old times' sake! And join me by the fire.'

Nevena shed her coat, revealing a slender figure encased in the figure-clinging cut currently fashionable among younger Russians, and perched delicately on Vassily's chair. Olga offered Nevena a fresh mug of coffee, and she flashed a brief smile of gratitude, taking it with her left hand while Olga sat down. Then followed a slew of anecdotes, stories and rumours of those they knew in common, until Dmitri interrupted their flow by poking his nose out of Olga's jacket, making Nevena jump.

'Don't worry!' said Olga. 'It's only my hedgehog, Dmitri. I got him, or rather found him, a couple of years ago. But if hedgehogs make you jumpy, you should be glad Vassily's out,' she went on, stroking Dmitri's pincushion head. 'Sergeant Marushkin, I mean – because he loves showing off Rasputin to guests. That's his horrible ferret,' she explained. 'He's safely in the cells for now – down that corridor there. Vassily – Sergeant Marushkin – sleeps there, too, and his son, Kliment, when he's not at school in Tayga. Anyway, enough of all that. What brings you to Roslazny? Did you come merely to stop all our buildings burning to the ground?'

'Oh, no,' said Nevena Komarov, quite seriously. 'No – I just happened to see someone flitting into an old building, and flitting out again, and then I saw a little tongue of fire snaking out of a window, and thought I'd better report it straight away. And then someone directed me here to the station – a youngish woman in a short skirt, who was smoking outside the café. She didn't seem very interested—'

'That would be Svetlana Odrosov,' put in Olga, drily. 'The proprietor's daughter, and the world's most reluctant barmaid. She'd be interested if you were a man in a leather jacket, with money to spend!'

'—but I came anyway and knocked on the door. And then your sergeant answered, and then I saw you through the doorway, and came in. And that's all!'

'That's all? But what about the rest?'

'How do you mean?' said Nevena Komarov, fixing Olga once more with her earnest, unwavering stare.

'Well, you still haven't said why you're here in Roslazny, have you?'

'Oh – no, I suppose not! I never could put things together in a logical way – you remember? I work for Russian Railways – just like you! Only I'm on the HR side, reporting to the Kemerovo office. I joined last year – fancied a change from the dental factory. That's where I was working before this, up near Kislovka.'

'Near Tomsk,' muttered Olga, enviously.

'It's the same kind of job, though,' went on Nevena. 'You know, inspecting working conditions, onboarding new people, all that sort of thing, only now I've got to memorise train timetables instead of gum disorders! I go all over the place – I've been past Roslazny quite a few times recently, but never had time for a proper visit. You know what's it like: always on the clock, always racing to complete your assignments, and fired in two seconds if you don't . . . But I'm here today, to answer your question, Olga,' she went on, glancing at her with a dazzling smile, 'because they've moved someone new to the trackside hut – a Polina something-or-other – and I've got to fill out her paperwork.'

She patted the leather satchel by her feet. 'I'm a bit late, I know, but I can't always get to new people as soon as I'd like. Lots of cases up near Itatka, then back south, Kemerovo way . . . All over the place, but always by the track – always next to the line, wherever I am. Anyway,' she went on, in a livelier tone, 'did they just move you to Tayga, instead? I suppose you've graduated to driving engines by now?'

'No,' said Olga, somewhat curtly. 'No, I haven't. I'm still stuck on trackside maintenance, here in Roslazny. Didn't you realise it's me that Polina's replacing? I only found out today – they're sending me off on some ancient exchange programme. I think Boris Andreyev – you know Boris, the foreman at Tayga? I think he resurrected it on purpose, just for me. He's getting far too big for his boots. And they sent Polina on the same day he told me I was going – can you believe that?'

'Wait – Polina only arrived today?'

To Olga's surprise, a look of concern, or even anxiety, had passed over Nevena's face.

'You didn't know?'

'Oh – no, no. I'm – I'm sorry, Olga, I didn't,' she said, in troubled tones. She stared down at her mug of coffee for a long moment. 'Oh, but I could – I could just kill that Pavel up at Headquarters! You know Russian Railways – they never fill out the forms properly . . . They just sent me Polina's information and told me she'd started on the twenty-first of August, weeks and weeks ago.'

'Well, what does it matter?' said Olga, then immediately wished she could have softened her words. Nevena might well be worried about her job, after all, despite her elevation to HR and Kemerovo Headquarters – quite a coup, really, in Russian Railways terms. Nevena must have been an impressive candidate to land that job ahead of all the men who must have gone for it. But then Olga had to suppress a sharp twinge of jealousy: here was yet another person who, like Danyl Petrovich, had bypassed Olga on the fast-track upwards! But what was it Nevena had just said? Russian Railways would fire people in two seconds? Well, that was true enough, thought Olga, though she'd never heard of corporate types like Nevena getting the sack – and certainly not for getting dates mixed up, with no harm done.

Still, it went to show that you never knew what was going on in other people's lives or hearts or thoughts. You just never knew.

Nevena's reply shook her out of her thoughts. 'You're right, Olga,' she said, with a slightly forced grin. 'It doesn't matter at all. What's a couple of weeks, between friends? And I'm sorry for what I said about driving trains – about you driving trains by now. I – I – well, I didn't mean to imply that . . .'

Olga felt her heart warm as her friend stammered before her. How many people would worry about her feelings like this? She could count them on the fingers of one hand – so she hastened to reassure her, telling her that she'd been quite happy over the years, all things considered, in her little hut, and not to trouble herself about it at all. Polina Klemovsky, on the other hand, was definitely a concern for anyone obliged to come into contact with her, said Olga.

'I imagine she's pretty good on paper,' she went on grudgingly, nodding towards Nevena's bag, 'but just wait till you meet her, Nevena! Just wait till you meet her, and then tell me what you think!'

'Sounds like I've got quite an afternoon ahead of me,' said Nevena. 'But whatever I think of her, I've got to make sure she signs the PQ11 and RTX-46 by close of play, or Russian Railways will have my head on a platter. And then there's the Kemnik requirements . . .'

Nevena began to list all the bureaucratic boxes that had to be ticked by the end of the day, but after a moment Olga cut across her. A piece of vital information, ingested and stored at the back of her mind, had gradually made its way to the front, displacing any discussion of the clog-clad Polina with more interesting subject matter.

'Wait – did you say your name's still Nevena *Komarov*? So you – you never . . .'

Nevena laughed, a pleasant, musical and, above all, amused sound that compelled a sympathetic, answering smile upon Olga's lips. 'Women *can* keep their names when they marry, you know, Olga, but in my case you're right. I never married.'

'But I thought – I mean, all of us thought . . .'

Nevena laughed again. 'You thought I'd get together with Matvei, or Gleb, or Ilarion, or one of the Institute boys, instead of remaining a lonely, dried-up old spinster?'

'Well – no,' said Olga. 'I mean – well, first of all, you're no spinster, Nevena! And I never thought you'd end up with one of those idiots . . . You know what they were like about – well, about the *support* staff at the Institute.'

'I do,' said Nevena. 'In fact, Matvei told me himself one day: he said I wasn't good enough for him. He said he hadn't signed up for the Irkutsk Institute of Railway Engineering, Tayga College, to marry a *sluga*.'

A *sluga* could mean many things in Russia, from a gentleman's valet to a public official, but it could also signify *menial servant* – and it was clear from Nevena's eyes that Matvei had made his meaning perfectly apparent.

'Oh, I could kill that Matvei,' said Olga, angry despite the gulf of years between then and now. 'Why did you never tell me that? I thought we were friends.'

'We are friends!' said Nevena. 'Well, I hope we still are . . . Look, I know we lost touch a bit after Valeriya's wedding. And I know you called me up, once or twice, after the Institute years, but I didn't reply . . . You see, I was . . . well, I was embarrassed,' she went on, a red tinge creeping across her knife-edge cheekbones. 'Because he was right, wasn't he – Matvei, I mean? After all, look at you compared to me. You come from such a proud tradition. Your father Mikhail, on the railways all his life – or until his accident, at least. And you, only the third woman ever to attend the Irkutsk Institute of Railway Engineering, at either Tayga *or* Irkutsk! And even if you haven't made your way up to driving yet, there's no reason why you shouldn't, in time. We can all make new lives for ourselves, become different people in our lives or the lives of others, honouring those who've gone before. What was I saying? Oh, yes – a proud tradition. And there was I – just a cleaner. A *sluga*.'

But Olga shook her head. 'There's no proud tradition in my family. My father's just a layabout who pretended to be sick for twenty years, and I've been in Russian Railways for over a decade with nothing to show for it but a meaningless promotion. A second-class engineer, it turns out, is no nearer first-class than a third . . . And now look at you, an inspector based up in Headquarters at Kemerovo – outranking me by far. And, besides, you were never *just* anything, Nevena.'

She gazed at her long-lost friend. 'Matvei married Belka Ilyinichna Simonovich, did you know that? She owns a bakery now and has to be carried in and out of it, they say. All those honeyed cakes . . . And to think Matvei chose *her* when he could've had you. No, but look at you, Nevena! It's truly a wonder someone didn't snap you up before now.'

'Nonsense,' replied Nevena Komarov, before listing reasons why this was not the case – but it *was* a wonder: Nevena was beautiful, truly beautiful, beautiful in the way that could stop traffic, or a file of pigs if Nevena happened to walk past a farmhand at work in Itatka or far Leninsky or the dreary holdings on the outskirts of Tayga. She had blue eyes – and not the pale, wan, wintry blue of the girls from Kamchatka that Boris Andreyev so coveted, but a profound, lustrous blue like the depths of the ocean, a blue that shimmered against her raven hair and set off her high cheekbones – cheekbones like Olga's, but completed by curved, voluptuous lips that Olga had always envied, and all set above a lithe, energetic figure that Olga had never possessed. Nevena might have been born into poverty – the kind of poverty that could force a young woman to take up a cleaner's post at the Tayga Institute – but she could easily have earned herself a millionaire in any part of Ekaterinburg or Novosibirsk or Moscow. She could have gone to the cities, like all the pretty girls did, snared a wealthy owner of consortiums and conglomerates, and ended up killing time in an expensive downtown flat while her husband entertained a newer model in his *dacha* out in the sticks.

But clearly that hadn't happened. And, now that Olga thought about it, perhaps it was no surprise. Nevena was . . . well, she was different, somehow, from the other pretty girls. Perhaps it was the sheer potency of her beauty that marked her out – a gift from God, Olga's friend Anna Kabalevsky would have said, or maybe a curse, a cross to bear, a barrier between her and the rest of humanity, and men in particular. Olga could just imagine how the likes of Fyodor Katin would behave around her, mumbling about Russian history and showing her his schemes for dialectical reform and generally acting like a red-cheeked imbecile until she left the room.

Then again, maybe Nevena just didn't find men attractive, or the men thereabouts, at any rate. Olga found that easy enough to understand, when she thought of the specimens who ate and drank in Café Astana each night, or the men she saw lounging about in the staff canteen at the Tayga depot, smoking and swapping stories of their one-night stands or their souped-up, unsilenced car engines. A fitting match for someone like her would be supremely difficult to find in Roslazny, or any of the other villages that punctuated the *taiga* like living dots.

And even if a man could be conjured up to mirror her charisma, might she not end up pushing him away? Olga had always known her friend as a formidable character, a woman with inner strength to match her outer beauty; and perhaps she was simply happier to be left alone. After all, as a wise person had told Olga once, you're never really alone if you're by yourself. But wasn't it a little sad, after all, for a person so seemingly full of life to spend its glories only on herself?

'You're miles away, Olga!' said Nevena, returning her gaze with an earnest look. 'I swear you didn't hear a word I just said. And you were miles away when I came in, too. What are you thinking about?'

'Oh,' said Olga, slightly embarrassed. She searched for a topic other than the one that had been foremost in her thoughts, and landed on the nearest to hand.

'So you still wear the green scarf? In memory of Alyona – in memory of your mother?'

'Oh,' said Nevena, a little self-consciously, her hand travelling to her neck and patting down the richly virid silk draped around her elegant shoulders. 'Oh, yes – you remember that, too? What a memory you have, Olga!'

'Well, I always thought it was such a nice thing to do,' said Olga. 'I wish I had a scarf, or a jacket, or, well, anything really that I could wear and think of my mother having worn before me. But my father threw it all out when she died, and I was too young to stop him.'

'So easy to lose all we hold dear,' said Nevena, shaking her head. 'But I'm afraid I don't quite believe you, Olga.'

'You don't quite – what?'

'I don't believe you were thinking about my green scarf just now,' she replied, fixing Olga with her piercing sapphire eyes, and reminding her how hard it was to get anything past an old friend who knows you well. 'Like I said, you were miles away – and your eyes were sad.'

'Well,' said Olga, still not wishing to reveal her thoughts to Nevena, 'I *was* miles away, in a sense. You see, I was thinking about travelling – or, more precisely, about leaving. I'm . . . well, I'm going to Mongolia.'

'Mongolia? *Mongolia?* On holiday? Or – no – you said something about an exchange programme?'

'I'm afraid so,' said Olga, before updating Nevena on the system set up during Soviet times, and rejuvenated by Boris for his own purposes. But now, she saw, it was Nevena who wasn't listening, looking instead over Olga's shoulder in the way she'd always had, as if something more wonderful was there for the seeing.

'Oh, Olga – how *magical*,' she cut in, clasping together her elegant hands. 'To *travel* – to wander far afield . . . D'you remember how we used to talk about going away to – oh, to anywhere? D'you remember how we used to talk while the Institute boys skated on the ice-rink in Tayga? And how we always used to buy the same things whenever we had a few kopeks to rub together – magazines about far-off places, old books of journeys, even second-hand postcards?'

'Of course, Nevena,' said Olga, placing a warm hand over her friend's. 'Of course, I remember. How could I forget? The dancing, the ice-games, the fat men toppling over on their skates – and the mugs of *shiten* steaming hot and sweet, fresh from the samovars . . . And we swore we'd leave one day, and journey somewhere different, somewhere hot – places we'd seen in those postcards and books and magazines – but we never did. Well, I never did, anyway.'

'Neither did I, really,' said Nevena. 'Like I said, I've only been up around Tomsk – well, Tomsk and Novosibirsk, working for an office supply company, and then the dental implant factory, like I said. But now you can go to the land of the camels and the *gers*,' she went on, her deep blue eyes glowing in the pale light that flooded, ice-tinged, through the police-station window. 'The land of Chinggis Khaan and the nomads, the land of deels and shoe-sole cake and fermented mare's milk drunk from a gourd by a campfire under the glimmering stars. Oh, Olga! It's just what your mother would have wanted. It's what Tatiana would have done herself, given half a chance.'

Olga had almost forgotten one of Nevena's more endearing habits, which was her way of referring to Olga's mother Tatiana, who had died when Olga was only eight, as if she had known her personally, and as if Tatiana Pushkin, née Lichnovsky, was still a living memory of recent vintage, rather than a series of faded snapshots from Olga's childhood. Nevena had lost her mother, Alyona, at an even earlier age, she'd told Olga once, and had begun to wear her green scarf as soon as she turned fourteen by way of remembrance. But Nevena clearly hadn't wanted to say any more in those days – and Olga, who was more sensitive than most to parental challenges of various kinds, had declined to press her. Instead, she'd happily shared as many stories of her mother as she could remember, and willingly speculated, along with Nevena, on what Tatiana would say or do in a certain circumstance.

Who was Olga to object, after all? It was pleasant to hear her mother's name from lips other than her father Mikhail's, as if Nevena's complicity lent substance to the ethereal afterlife Tatiana enjoyed in Olga's mind, the frequent subject of question-and-answer, invented conversation, and vivid imagined looks on her tired, wistful, much-loved face, a soft, ongoing entanglement in the affairs of the living. And so she agreed with Nevena, and talked with her about her mother Tatiana Pushkin, née Lichnovsky, and imagined what she would have said and done and felt about Olga's unexpected journey to the far steppes of Mongolia.

'Well, I'd better get on,' said Nevena at last. 'I've got to meet this Polina Klemovsky and fill in these forms,' she went on, brandishing a clipboard, 'or I'll never hear the end of it from Kemerovo.'

'Are you staying around for a bit at least? Will you be here tonight?' said Olga. 'You don't have to rush off somewhere else? I know Russian Railways – always squeezing too many jobs into the day!'

'No, no,' Nevena replied. 'No, I don't have to slip away till first thing tomorrow, to get to another job in – in Sudzhenka, I think it is. But in the meantime I'm all yours. I've booked a room above that poky little restaurant – or is it really a shop? The man at the bar said I was lucky to get it – a last-minute cancellation on account of the weather, he said, though I didn't know whether to believe him or not. The rooms aren't all that great.'

'Café Astana?' said Olga, incredulously. She'd had to stay there herself, once, and found it hard to picture someone like Nevena in such drowsy surroundings. 'I'm not sure if lucky's the word – but I'm glad you're staying for a little while, anyway.'

And she really was glad, she reflected – it wasn't just the sort of thing one said sometimes to grease the social wheels. She was particularly glad, perhaps, because her good friend Ekaterina Chezhekov, a cigarette vendor at Tayga station, was currently away on personal business in Irkutsk, rendering her out of action for friendly farewells. Ekaterina had a complicated private life – her Irkutsk trip revolved around lawyers acting on behalf of her latest *amour* – and she wouldn't, Olga knew, be able to come back at short notice. Olga felt her absence deeply, and while Ekaterina would say her husky, smoker's-voice farewells on the phone, and while Olga would promise to call from Ulaanbaatar as often as she could, it wasn't the same as a fervent, bone-creaking, long-lasting, smoke-flavoured hug from her closest friend bar Anna Kabalevsky.

Olga didn't know Nevena Komarov anywhere near as well as either Anna Kabalevsky or Ekaterina Chezhekhov – how could she, when she hadn't seen her for almost a decade? – but her presence would be a comfort all the same, another friendly face to gaze on, steadily and lovingly, until the end.

'Well, I'll be at the café later on,' said Olga, 'to raise a glass with some friends, and to say goodbye. You see, it's tomorrow that I leave for Mongolia.'

'*Tomorrow?*' cried Nevena, a distressed look crossing her face. 'Tomorrow! So soon! Why didn't you say? Well, thank God I'm here tonight, at least.'

She shook her head and, after a moment, went on: 'But wait – there's something else you forgot to say. How long are you going for? Tell me it's just till Christmas, or the New Year.'

'Two years,' said Olga. 'I know, it's an age. But now I have one more reason to come back. Now I have you, as well as the rest. Come tonight, and you'll meet them all! And then you, too, will have a reason to come back, and we'll see each other again, like the old days.'

'Oh, Olga,' said Nevena, taking her hands, 'isn't it just like life, to find someone you've missed, and then lose them again? Isn't it just like life?'

It *was* just like life, thought Olga, later that day, as she sat with Anna and her brother Pasha, playing with the children in the house they shared together. Or, rather, it was just like *her* life, a life that seemed to gravitate towards the hardest paths as a matter of course, like a river or stream condemned to flow always uphill.

The news of Olga's posting came as an immense shock to Pasha and Anna, and to Boris and Gyorgy, two of Anna's boys, when Olga told them that afternoon. (Anna's third, baby Ilya, was too busy working on his new back teeth to take much notice.)

'You're leaving us, Olgakin?' Pasha had said, his thin face tinged with sudden pain. 'And for so long ... So long! Two years is two years too many, to be apart from such a sister. But of course we will visit – if we can.'

Anna, for her part, had been too overcome to speak, but her eyes had spilled over with tears and she'd clasped Olga to her as if for the last time. Boris and Gyorgy, for their part, had joined in with such enthusiasm that Olga thought she might collapse under the combined weight of their affection.

'Yes, yes, I'm leaving, but I'm not dying,' she'd said, laughing despite her sorrow, and finding, as she had at other times, that her own suffering was lessened by the sorrow of others. Their tears, after all, showed the depth of their love for her, and their love was a jewel without price or compare.

'You're right, Olga,' said Anna at last, jogging baby Ilya with one hand, and wiping away her tears with the other. 'We must be grateful for small mercies. You will come back to us, and then we will all be together again.'

Anna looked at Olga in that way she had, a gaze at once wise and kind, so that her face seemed somehow different – a face with features undeniably plain, yet lit from within by some inner radiance that transfigured them into loveliness. Olga's heart turned over within her, and as she looked from Anna to the children to her dear brother, gathered around her in the familiar surroundings of their shared home, it was all she could do to stop herself sobbing.

Olga needed self-control of a different kind when she prepared to venture out of the house later that day, braving the cascading snow to keep her Café Astana rendezvous with Vassily Marushkin – the final rendezvous this side of Mongolia – with Nevena Komarov joining for good measure. The problem was Anna's children, and more specifically an unfortunate incident involving a full nappy (courtesy of Ilya) and an unseen ball underfoot (provided by either Boris or Gyorgy, depending on whose account of events was accurate). Desperate to leave, Olga had hovered anxiously at the edge of the living room, making quiet clucking noises to express her impatience while Pasha and Anna tried to manage the situation. In the end, Pasha had insisted on sending Olga ahead while he helped Anna burn the carpet in an old, rust-holed dustbin outside the front door.

'Go, Olgakin – go!' he'd said, wrapping a scarf around his face. 'Send Vassily our regards. We'll be there as soon as we can. Go!'

Olga had nodded gratefully and taken her hurried leave, pulling her own scarf over her nose as she went in a vain attempt to mask the horrendous smell. But no sooner had she got outside into the crisp virgin whiteness than she began to feel guilty. It was just the kind of regret, she thought, that a clever child might experience if, having nagged a parent mercilessly, she finally received a longed-for toy, but one given out of exasperation instead of generosity.

Pasha was too kind, too perceptive – that was his problem. No stranger to distress, he had sensed her urgent desire to be away, and had ensured that she acted upon it as soon as possible. How many men would take the time to think of a sister's feelings while his hands were filled with the by-products of Ilya's digestive system?

But Pasha had suffered, of course. That was the key. He'd hidden his true self for years, decades even, until finally his secret was discovered in an army barracks in Crimea, preceding a swift – and disgraced – departure from his beloved regiment. The Russian Army might welcome gay soldiers in theory but, as Pasha had discovered, theory and practice were two very different things. And Roslazny, it seemed, was little different. Pasha's own father, Mikhail Pushkin, had instantly disowned him upon learning the news, while his aunt Zia (still unbeknown to Pasha) had said terrible things to Olga behind her brother's back. Olga could only imagine what the other villagers would say if they, too, learned the truth – old-fashioned men like Popov and Odrosov and Koptev Alexeyev – so she and Pasha had kept the news between them, telling the others that he'd been discharged for an indeterminate illness.

'That's probably what Putin thinks it is, anyway,' Olga had said. 'The villagers too, for all you know, Pasha. Trust me, sometimes it's better not to find out.'

And Pasha was little inclined to disagree – rather to Olga's relief, because even Anna Kabalevsky, dear soul, couldn't entirely be trusted on this specific topic. She was highly religious, and weren't religious people often rather (for want of a better word) *traditional*? And since Olga prized their hard-won domestic harmony above all things, the peaceful joy that had settled on the house she shared with Pasha and Anna and her children, she had reluctantly held back the truth from even her closest friends.

But was she now holding back a different truth from herself? Why *was* she so impatient to get to Café Astana? she asked herself. Was it just because she was desperate to see Vassily Marushkin, to snatch every fleeting moment with him before the digits of time, and the couplings of the Trans-Siberian, pulled her irrevocably from his side? Pasha appeared to think so: he'd asked her to send their regards to Vassily, and to no other. And of course he wasn't entirely wrong: she *was* desperate to see as much of Vassily as possible – time-wise, of course, she told herself firmly, not skin-wise — before she had to plod dutifully up the rusting steel steps to a third-class compartment and rattle away down the track to Ulaanbaatar, leaving Vassily Marushkin and his Belamorkanal cigarettes far, far behind.

But perhaps there was something else, too: something that hovered at the edge of her mind, but that had yet to take definite shape. What was it? Or rather *who* was it — for as soon as she asked herself the question in plain Russian she knew the answer. It had been there all along: it was Nevena.

What would happen, she'd asked herself earlier that same day, if Nevena should encounter a man to match her own attractiveness? But she hadn't thought to populate that abstract category with Vassily's tousled black hair, tractor-mechanic hands, and ragged, untidy, wholly disreputable pet ferret. She hadn't thought to, but why not? Vassily was attractive, engaging, kind, even dashing, in his own way. So Olga had seen him, anyway, standing at the foot of her bed while she'd recovered from a head injury earlier that year.

Vassily had come unexpectedly back into her life, years and years after their shared schooldays. Now Nevena had done the same, and Olga feared for Vassily's heart. He was only human, after all, and worse still, a man; and there in front of him was no insubstantial, shimmering shade, like the memory of his lost wife, Rozalina, but a living, breathing woman, and one with nothing uncanny about her but her unearthly beauty, heightened if anything by the thin, snowy light of premature winter. Olga had seen that exact light flooding through the police-station window earlier that day, landing upon Nevena's knife-edge cheekbones, sea-blue eyes, and raven tresses with breathtaking effect. If Olga had been so struck by her friend's appearance, might not Vassily have been the same, even doubly or triply so? Vassily, too, had seen for himself Nevena's public spiritedness, witnessed by her voluntary reporting of a case of arson. What better way could there be to a policeman's heart? And he must have met her again since, Olga knew, in the follow-up interview he'd promised her, before he'd rushed off to quell the flames. Yet more time to spend alone with Nevena, yet more time to fall under her spell . . .

Olga already found it hard enough to compete with Rozalina. How could she manage now, with Nevena Komarov on top?

Perhaps it was as well that night was falling, said Olga to herself, a little cattily. Perhaps Nevena's delicate beauty would appear less striking in the glare of Café Astana, lit not by the lambent glow of snowfall but by the garish hues of late-night TV chat-shows commingled with Odrosov's doubtful light bulbs.

Nyet, she said to herself, quite sharply. This was not how friends thought of each other! And if they did, they weren't really friends at all. In the end she just pulled her coat more tightly around herself, as if mimicking a forgiving hug from her absent friend, and resolved to think no more of the matter. If Vassily ended up with Nevena, so be it. What could Olga do? She would be far away, and for all she knew Vassily would be far from Roslazny, too, if he couldn't track down enough crimes to keep Mayor Nazarov happy in his plush Kemerovo office swathed in Russian flags, wall-mounted sabres, and framed photos of Putin at the Duma. Vassily could be far away from all this by the time she returned – far from all these sagging, abandoned houses, but maybe not so far from Nevena Komarov.

She turned and looked past the jumble of abandoned houses into the far distance beyond the village, a rolling, whitened landscape of patchwork fields guarded by tall, dark, icing-sugared trees in irregular clumps and copses. She could disappear into the falling dark if she chose, she reflected – just walk ahead and keep going, bypassing Tayezhnyy and Suranovo, pressing on until she faded from view in the dancing snowflakes, losing her own self and becoming part of the endless *taiga* about her.

But her feet were cold, her fingertips also, and the left-hand side of her face where the breeze played upon it, and she needed to keep her job so that Anna and Pasha and the boys would have a home, and she wanted to see Vassily and Nevena despite the complexities. She wanted, too, to raise a final glass (or five – but no more) of Odrosov's Rocket Fuel with Anna and Pasha and Fyodor Ivanovich Katin and all the others she loved in Roslazny, despite their failings; and so she didn't walk ahead and disappear into the vast, bottomless depths of Russia, but turned and headed along the pathway to Café Astana, to familiar window-panes that glowed with inner light, fretted with the fleeting, shadowed traces of beloved shapes as they passed to and fro within. She turned and went the way she was required to go, just as she would board the Trans-Siberian the following morning and take her leave of Roslazny, as Boris Andreyev had ordered. And what did it matter if she'd leave her heart behind?

4

Into the Storm

The next morning Olga picked up the phone again with an air of indifference, arising partly from her conviction that nobody would answer, and partly from her throbbing temples and the nausea, faint but undeniable, that served as a constant reminder of her overindulgence the night before. Hangovers were aptly named, she thought. What else were they but a shadow from the preceding day, hovering queasily over you and blurring the midnight boundary?

She'd woken early that day, as she always did when she'd drunk too much, lying in bed with a spinning head and listening to the sounds of early birdsong and a distant hammering and tinkling, as if some early bird was tackling a large and unusually metallic worm. Probably Koptev Alexeyev trying to resurrect another ailing Lada, she thought, but without any real curiosity, distracted by an unpleasant sensation of spiralling downwards – a feeling that she might sink into her bed, deeper and deeper, until the mattress closed over her and hid her from sight.

'Could do worse,' muttered Olga, pressing the corners of her eyes in a vain attempt to forestall the downward circling, and feeling that an unexplained disappearance into her mattress would solve a lot of problems. Her house might be a little run-down, a little damp in places, but she would give her right arm to stay in its warm confines for the foreseeable future, dilapidated or otherwise.

Her nose wrinkled. What was that chemical scent she could smell? Had Pasha been plying the paintbrushes again, in his ongoing – albeit frequently interrupted – attempt to make the house a little more presentable? He had taken over the renovations from Anna soon after they'd moved in, recognising that she had enough on her plate without joinery and decorating on top. But surely he hadn't been painting overnight, while she was sleeping? Pasha had a formidable work ethic, but even he needed a modicum of rest from time to time. Furthermore, he'd drunk at least as much as Olga, and would presumably have toppled into bed just like her, rather than ranging about the house, paint-can in hand, looking for faded surfaces to touch up.

But then a deeper and yet more intractable mystery presented itself to her befuddled mind. Someone had said something, she thought. And then, acknowledging that this was an idiotic thing to think – for many people said many things, all the time – she asked herself to be more specific, forcing her reluctant memory to yield further particulars. Someone had said *something strange* the day before, she realised at last – something she hadn't processed properly at the time, but which she had later registered, in her subconscious or even unconscious mind, as being odd, anomalous, not quite right. Sleep often worked that way, Olga had discovered – mining, agitating, and refining until something of interest emerged. But what was it – and who had said it?

Absently she caressed the side of her head that wasn't buried in her pillows, as if the gentle action could massage the truth from her unwilling memory. Then she cast her mind back over the previous day, hour by hour, in search of unsettling strangeness. At one point she was on the brink of remembering: a curious phrase, an atypical or even uncanny set of words all but formed themselves into tangible shape, and with them a face, a specific cast of features with their own distinctive character. But then they receded, like a man walking backwards into heavy fog, before dissolving into the frustrating incompleteness of a half-remembered dream.

There was a barrier between her and reality, she thought: a blue-tinged vat of alcoholic liquid called Rocket Fuel. A glass or two fired you up and made you energetic; a bottle had the contrary effect, dropping a veil over the sharpest of cognitive faculties; and now Olga found herself utterly thwarted in her mental explorations.

She stared up at the ceiling, noting for the twentieth time the place where a crack zigzagged neatly into the centre of the moulding around the light bulb, and fell into uneasy, shifting memories, allowing her mind to drift through unwise hours spent at Café Astana's sticky, uneven bar the night before, ensuring she spent as much time as possible with those she would miss, and as little time as possible near the table occupied by her father Mikhail, old man Solotov, and her aunt Zia. Aunt Zia, at least, had had the decency to avoid her gaze, staring down into her glass whenever Olga approached. Mikhail and Solotov, by contrast, glared at her in a manner almost triumphant, as if daring her to do her worst, in some unidentified way. Olga had already reminded Vassily to keep an eye on them, paying particular attention to any links between Solotov and Polina Klemovsky, whom Olga was more than willing to suspect of criminal tendencies. Vassily had duly promised to do so; but he also told her that the pig, once burned, doesn't approach the fire a second time, and that Mikhail and Solotov had been on their guard against him ever since Mikhail's conviction for fraud earlier that year.

Olga had nodded, sadly reminding herself that Roslaznyan crime no longer fell within her jurisdiction, and that she should concentrate instead on trying to enjoy her last night at Café Astana for many months to come. Nevena had been on particularly good form, Olga had thought, showing a surprising willingness to eat, drink and be merry despite her slender frame. She can't eat this much all the time, Olga remembered thinking, or she'd look more like me and less like her. And she can't be this lively all the time, either, or she'd run out of energy within the week – she particularly recalled Nevena's ruthless impression of Danyl Petrovich, whom she'd seen in the local papers following his heroic, medal-earning deeds, and to whose grey-haired ponytail Nevena had apparently taken violent exception. The laughs had come easily, and so had the Rocket Fuel top-ups.

But none of the others had to hitch a ride on the Trans-Siberian the morning after their vodka-fuelled festivities; none of them had had to go home as soon as the drinking was done and stand in their bedroom with a swimming head, before packing up their clothes, their belongings, their entire lives into a suitcase and a couple of frayed canvas bags, prior to moving to Ulaanbaatar at a day's notice.

In their defence, the others had at least helped Olga home, with Nevena going so far as to find Olga a walking-stick to help her navigate the rising snowdrifts. (The snow had continued to fall during their festivities, and indeed had started coming down yet more heavily during their meandering journey home.) Parts of the evening were still hazy in Olga's mind, but she definitely remembered Nevena thrusting something into her bare hands, her gloves having gone missing at some point during the festivities. But then Nevena had laughed.

'No, no,' she'd said, wresting the pole from her grip and casting it aside, 'it's too long for you! Try this stick – it's a bit shorter. Yes, much better! Now let's get you home, and watered, and into bed.'

Nevena swore by three large glasses of water as a pre-hangover cure, followed by as many hours in bed as possible. Olga had followed the first part of her remedy, overseen by Vassily, Pasha and a disapproving Anna as well as Nevena, but there'd been no time to spare for an extended lie-in the morning after, spinning head or no spinning head. Before long, Anna interrupted Olga's reverie by barging into her bedroom and helping her to get up and ready, tutting at Olga's excesses at Café Astana and reminding her that she had packing to finish and phone-calls to make. And before Olga had time to blink, she found herself sitting in the middle of their shared living room, staring at her luggage and finding it hard to believe that the day after tomorrow – for it was a two-day journey by rail – would find her marooned in Outer Mongolia.

Russian writers had, of course, been exiled before. Dostoyevsky had written *The House of the Dead* in an Omsk prison-camp, while her nearly-but-not-quite-ancestor Aleksandr Sergeyevich Pushkin had finished *Eugene Onegin* after being parcelled off to his family's estate at Mikhailovskoye. And perhaps it had been the making of them, Olga reflected. It was a cliché, but maybe one with some truth in it, that all the greatest writers had had some adversity, some immense difficulty to overcome – some struggle without which their work would lack the unmistakable ring of authenticity.

Olga hadn't told Nevena about her literary longings, but in a way she hadn't needed to. Just like one of Tatiana's imagined responses, she knew just what Nevena would have said: 'Oh, Olga, how wonderful! To be exiled – just like Gogol, and Nabokov, and Pushkin, and like, oh, like all the best writers, I'm sure. Just think what Tatiana, your dear mother, would say, if she could have known! How romantic she'd find it! She'd have waved you off with tears in her eyes and pride in her heart.'

Maybe so, Olga imagined herself responding. Maybe so, but Gogol hadn't written self-help books for young to middle-aged women, and Nabokov hadn't written books about lessons learned from a life of drudgery in a little hut by the side of the Trans-Siberian route from Moscow to Ulan Ude and beyond. And as for Tatiana, Olga thought she might not be so delighted, after all, to see her daughter shipped off against her will to a country where few people spoke Russian, without a firm commitment from Lyapunov Books, ostensible publisher of *Find Your Rail Self: 100 Life Lessons from the Trans-Siberian Railway* – without even a promise of mutual regard: for Olga had only recently dared admit, even to herself, that she loved Vassily Marushkin, and was desperately afraid of losing him. Yes, she loved him, but in the way the Earth circles the Sun: from afar.

And she loved him even more, if that were possible, now that she'd seen him become once more a present father to his son,

Kliment. Against the backdrop of Olga's experience with her father Mikhail, who had bullied her for years before unceremoniously kicking her and Pasha out of the family home, the sight of a kindly, loving man straining every sinew to care for an equally kindly, equally loving teenage boy was one calculated to win her lasting affection. But Kliment's very presence, the very way in which Vassily cared for him, was like a dagger in the night. For his fortuitous reunion with Vassily was a perpetual reminder of another that had yet to take place – a meeting that would overshadow even the astounding beauty of Nevena Komarov.

Rozalina . . . Rozalina . . .

The name haunted Olga like the distant sound of an engine on the tracks outside her rail-side hut, whispering at first and barely audible, as if the train might still be diverted onto another track, another route entirely; but then, as the service approached, passenger or freight or maintenance, the noise would increase, the ground would shake underfoot, and soon Leviathan would heave into view, swaying from side to side as if it would topple, but moving always undaunted onwards, rending the air with penetrating horn-shrieks and, at night, sending blinding bars of light from powerful headlamps through the darkness that lay ahead.

Just like the train that kept on moving, Olga knew that Vassily Marushkin would never stop looking for his lost wife Rozalina, and that the path to his soul would always be barred by the large, soulful eyes that stared out of the only image Vassily had of her: a crinkled, faded photograph taken in Berezkino long ago. It rested now in a plastic frame, placed on a shelf in the vacant prison-cell that Vassily called home, his lost wife gazing out of the frame as if she were keeping watch over him day and night, near or far, waking or sleeping, and weaving herself somehow into his life and doings as if she had never really left at all. Her name circled Olga's thoughts at night and her musings by day, as if the woman herself were calling to her in ethereal tones, telling her name over and over, heralding her own return like a train gliding towards her on gleaming silver rails: *Rozalina . . . Rozalina . . . Rozalina . . .*

'Hello?' came a voice on the telephone.

Olga jumped. 'Oh,' she said. 'Yes,' she said. Who was she calling again, she asked herself amid the morning-after miasma that filled her mind, and why? She had already called Ekaterina Chezhekhov and said her goodbyes, receiving the expected husky tears in return – but who had she called after that?

Her eyes flicked to the calendar that she, Anna and Pasha kept above the little table in the kitchen, ran down the column of Wednesdays, and saw LYAPUNOV in her handwriting, circled in red. Of course! Lyapunov Books, and the never-ending stream of financial demands that had yet to culminate in progress towards publication. No sooner had Olga replied with enthusiasm to their first letter in August than she'd received a barrage of legal documents to guarantee her exclusivity with Lyapunov Books; and no sooner had she dealt with these than she received another slew of unexpected letters, this time mentioning unforeseen (and rather costly) marketing expenses arising in connection with envisaged publicity for *Find Your Rail Self* – and could Devushka Pushkin please send the requested amount by cheque or bank transfer at her earliest convenience? It was all rather worrying (and expensive), and for the sake of her equanimity – and her equity – Olga wanted to settle things as soon as possible, one way or another.

'Yes?' said the voice impatiently, belonging, Olga imagined, to a woman in her fifties with grey hair, horn-rimmed glasses, and a utilitarian dress of Soviet cut and colour.

'Er – well, is Maxim Gusev there?' asked Olga, naming her main point of contact to date.

'*Nyet*,' came the curt reply. 'Out today.'

'And—'

'And tomorrow, too. All week, in fact.'

'Well,' said Olga again, 'could I – could I speak to someone, please, about my book? And I prefer to be addressed as Dama, not Devushka. I've been in correspondence with Maxim, but—'

'If you've been in touch with Maxim, then it's Maxim you'll need to speak to,' said the woman at the other end. 'Why don't you write? We prefer it when people write.'

'I could email—'

'Don't email,' snapped the woman. 'We don't have time to read it! Write a letter to Maxim. Goodbye.'

'But I *have* been writing . . .' started Olga, and the line went dead. 'But I have been writing to Maxim, all this time,' she went on, into empty space. Publishers, she reflected, were strange, unpredictable creatures: warm and eager one moment, and coldly standoffish the next – very like spring, in fact, that most untrustworthy of seasons. Winter, by contrast, had the great virtue of decisiveness, especially in Siberia. There was seldom much doubt when autumn was over, in Siberia. People didn't waste time debating whether it was or it wasn't: they just got up, realised their outbuildings were colder than their fridge-freezers, and pulled out their furriest hats and their warmest pair of underpants. Why couldn't publishers be more like Siberian winters? she asked herself. Then at least she'd know where she stood, even if it was in a puddle of freezing sludge.

She gazed at the calendar, which had been distributed free of charge by a local agricultural supplier, then got up and flipped the page to the month before, which showed a series of other LYAPUNOVs next to little sketches of envelopes (for planned letters) and telephones (for intended calls). She let the page fall again, and stared morosely at the picture for September, which portrayed an industrial slurry tank with several men in overalls. The men were leaning on its edge and staring into its depths; and as if following their gaze, her eyes slid down to the note she'd made to call Lyapunov Books. All at once she felt a yearning, a desperate longing to be once more the hopeful, clear-eyed person who'd written the schedule on the calendar some weeks before, rather than the headachy, nauseous person who'd read it that morning. Back then, everything was different. Whereas now—

'Don't worry, it might never happen,' said a cheery voice.

'Oh, Pasha,' she said, turning to see her brother, who had just come into the kitchen. 'But it already has.'

'Nonsense!' he said, reaching out a strong arm and pulling her to her feet. It was more than six months since he'd been dishonourably discharged from the army, but Pasha Pushkin still had a military bearing, standing tall, slender and flaxen-haired in the pale winter light, and looking fondly down on Olga as he always had. 'You aren't dying. You're just going away for a bit, that's all.'

'I felt like I was dying this morning,' she said, rubbing her head and smiling ruefully up at him.

'Well, who can blame you for having one too many?'

'I think it was a bit more than one too many.'

'One bottle too many, I meant. Now, look, you followed Nevena's orders last night by drinking all that water. But I know the only real cure for a hangover – fresh, cold, Siberian air! Come on, let's go for a walk. I know you're packed up already – Anna told me,' he went on, jerking his thumb towards the rear of the house, where loud crying and crashing suggested that Anna was getting her children dressed for the day. 'She's taking the boys tobogganing, out Tayga way – you know, that field near the Tembalovsky farmhouse. And then she's got Nonna coming to look after them, when it's time for the ceremony. Thoughtful of Anna, to give you a bit of quiet on your last day. And I think we should make the most of it! We could walk down to the railway in peace, one last time – it'll be too busy for you to catch your breath later on, with the mayor, and the ceremony, and all that. What do you say?'

'Have you looked outside, Pasha?' she said. 'It's still snowing. I don't think it's stopped all night.'

'You've never let the weather put you off before,' he replied.

'That's true,' said Olga, after a pause. She was reluctant, for some reason, to admit to Pasha that she was trying to ignore the whitened cascades streaming from the heavens – that it made her heart ache to think of exchanging them for the arid expanse of the Mongolian steppe.

'All right, then,' she said, after another pause. 'But I don't want to go past the hut, Pasha – that awful Polina woman will be there! Dmitri's still recovering from last time,' she added, nodding towards the kitchen, where she'd taped together three cardboard boxes as a makeshift hutch for her hedgehog. 'So am I, for that matter.'

'Let's go the northern way, then – up past the Petrovs' place on the far side. As if we were still after their honeyberries.'

Olga smiled despite her heartache at the thought of leaving Dmitri behind, remembering how she and Pasha used to sneak up to the Petrovs' garden wall in days gone by, gathering handfuls of the sweet purple berries and pocketing them to make into jam later, or eating them there and then, the risk of discovery by the irascible Artyom Petrov adding extra savour to the tiny bell-like fruit.

'All right,' she said again, rubbing her forehead and getting to her feet, rather gingerly. 'But we'd better go carefully. You remember who else lives up that way? Our dear father!'

'How could I forget?' said Pasha, his habitual smile momentarily disappearing. 'But you know, Olga, I've spent a lot of my life hiding from him, one way or another. One more hour won't hurt.'

In the event, they managed to skirt both Petrov and Pushkin unseen, and after battling through a low fringe of thorny brambles they emerged, somewhat warm and dishevelled, onto the narrow verge that ran along the track. As Olga had observed, it was still snowing – and snowing hard, too. Her eyebrows lifted at the height of the drifts over the track, rising to two or three feet of virginal white, or even more in places where the ground ascended in swelling waves towards the scrub and forest that marched along the route.

'You'd think they'd have sent the snowploughs through this morning,' she murmured to Pasha. 'It must be worse elsewhere. Well, I just hope Danyl Petrovich had the sense to have a snowplough fitted on his locomotive. Otherwise they'll struggle, Trans-Siberian or not.'

The track was quiet and devoid of murmurings from trains either coming or going, and the hum of any nearby roads was deadened by the innumerable snowflakes that filled the air. Pasha watched his sister looking up into the sky, ignoring the flakes that melted on her cheeks, and turning to look first one way and then the other, as if committing the scene to memory. He knew better than to break the peace.

Olga took out her phone, an elderly Nokia model that she had bought from Ekaterina Chezhekhov for a few hundred roubles the year before, and began to film the scene, starting northwards and turning slowly to the right, until she was facing southwards in the direction of her hut, out of sight around the bend. But then she frowned and lowered her phone, staring intently down the line with narrowed eyes.

'What was that?' she said.

'What was what?'

'I thought . . . well, I thought I saw something moving,' said Olga. 'To the right there – by that clump of trees behind the signal relay. Something shuffling back under cover, or – or just a smudge of darkness.'

'I didn't see anything,' said Pasha. 'Maybe it was one of those little deer you see sometimes.'

'I thought it was bigger,' said Olga. 'But it could have been a deer, I suppose,' she went on. 'They're always coming up to my hut and nibbling at the paintwork! But I suppose they aren't my problem now, are they? And it's not really my hut any more, either.' She stared again down the line, looking so desolate that Pasha hugged her.

'Olga, it's just for now,' he said, 'and then you'll be back, and it'll be like you'd never been away. We'll look after Dmitri, and the deer will be waiting for you. And we'll get your hut back, too. I'm sure of it. I'll *make* sure of it!'

She nodded up at him, then looked back down the track, blinking away her tears and forcing a smile onto her face.

'Oh, Pasha,' she said at last. 'Thank you! I needed to come and say goodbye in my own way, but I didn't know it till you dragged me out here.'

Pasha nodded. 'Sometimes we just need a little push to see what's been in front of us all along.'

Olga hugged him again. 'I wish *this* were in front of me for ever,' she said, gazing at the twin tracks threading their way around the corner. 'Oh, how I wish it were.'

Pasha looked down at her and opened his lips to speak, but then he closed them again and merely stood with his sister, looking down the line as the snow continued to fall.

Later that day, Anna Kabalevsky shouted two or three final instructions to Nonna and closed the door to the house, while Pasha shouldered Olga's bags and stooped to pick up her suitcase. They turned to Olga, who'd gone a few steps on from the house before standing still, looking around her and breathing in the cold, damp air as if for the very last time. Then she closed her eyes as if she could imprint the scent of Roslazny upon her mind: the soft, cool smell of snow, the distant savour of fatty meat cooking under someone's grill, a tang of oily steam from their neighbour's home-made heating system, and the earthy fragrance of the house's little garden, dead leaves and crushed herbs peeping out from the steep walls of mounting snowdrifts.

'Come on, Olga,' said Anna, gently, walking forwards and putting her arm around her friend. 'You'll feel better when we get to the tracks.'

'Will I?' said Olga, turning to her.

'Of course,' said Anna. 'Lots of people will be there to see you off. Shame about Nevena having to go off to Sudzhenka this morning – she seems so nice.'

Nevena Komarov had bidden farewell to Olga and the others the night before, since she had to leave first thing for another personnel mission on the far side of Tayga, and so couldn't attend the ceremony.

'She swore to you, Olga,' said Anna, 'though you probably don't remember, as you were so – so *tipsy* . . . She swore to keep in touch, to call and message and email while you're in Mongolia, and to meet up again as soon as you're back. So that's something. And Vassily's meeting us on the way down to the track,' went on Anna. 'He told me so himself, last night. So that's another thing,' she added, squeezing Olga's arm.

'And it won't be long until you're on the train,' said Pasha, from behind her. 'No – I know that sounds bad. But when you're in your compartment and meeting your travel companions and the *provodnitsa*, buying snacks and filling your little *podstakannik* with hot water from the samovar, well, you'll be moving, you see. You'll be setting out on your adventure, at last. It's right now that's the most difficult part of all. Now, when you're still here, but not really here. But soon you'll be *there* instead, and you'll feel better for it – take it from me.'

Olga nodded, trying to concentrate on what Pasha was saying about his many deployments with the army, and trying, too, to ignore the hint of wood-smoke hanging upon the still air like a loved one's perfume – a scent so delicate, so faint and far-off, so spindrift light that it all but broke her heart to abandon it. But she didn't say so: she just flashed a smile at Pasha, took Anna's arm, and walked forward at last, forcing herself to leave the house behind, step by heart-breaking step.

How hard it is to leave a beloved place on foot, she thought. What a blessing it would be if she could be whisked away in a helicopter, the familiar sights wheeling and dropping from view in minutes, or even seconds. In contrast, this was no way to depart, with each reluctant step bringing new and well-loved vistas into view, and with each moment bringing the thought that she could turn back – that she could simply stop walking away from home, and instead rush back into her house, run a bath, and pick out a book from the sprawling, untidy shelf that Pasha had installed above the TV upon her request. But she knew she wouldn't – couldn't – do that. To do that would be to put her own interests above those of others.

No, she told herself, as she turned the corner at the end of the path leading to her house. No: some choices simply can't be taken. Some choices, in fact, are not really choices at all, and therein lie the sorrows of this life. And the low-hanging clouds, as if in mute accord, unfurled their wings once more and released their pent-up burdens in ever-growing weight, draping Olga and the rest in new clothes of white, and shrouding the village from view. Yet still they walked on – on, on, ever onward: for Olga had an appointment with the Trans-Siberian, and the Trans-Siberian is late but seldom, wonderfully seldom, in its comings and goings.

Vassily Marushkin met them as arranged, at the place where three paths meet.

'It's nice to see you, Vassily,' called Olga, as they battled their way through the blizzard. 'And you, Kliment,' she added to Vassily's lean, round-headed son, who nodded and grimaced at her with the awkward sorrow of teenage boys.

'They closed the high school as well, then – for the snow?' said Anna Kabalevsky, prompting another soundless nod from Kliment. 'Sensible,' she said approvingly. 'I was worried they'd force you in. And then how would you say goodbye to Olga?'

'Nice to see you in civvies for once, Vassily,' put in Pasha. It was indeed unusual to see Vassily out of his police uniform, but in honour of Olga's departure he'd taken a rare day off and dug out some of his normal clothes: dark jeans tucked into heavy-duty boots, a thick red woollen jumper, and an ancient waterproof jacket that he'd brought with him from Novosibirsk, finished with an Ushanka crammed over his unruly black hair.

But Vassily wasn't interested in discussing his outfit. 'Look, are you really going to go in this weather, Olga? Surely they can delay it for a few days – seems a bit risky to me.'

'No, Vassily,' she called to him, stepping forward once more. 'It's got to be this way. I've resigned myself. It's—'

She slipped, her snow-boot slithering sideways into a rock, so that she fell towards him. Instantly he caught her. 'I've got you,' he said, looking down at her, his eyelashes traced in white snowflakes, and his breath warm on her cheek. 'I've got you,' he said again. She allowed herself to stay still, just for an instant, asking herself what it would be like if Vassily were always there to catch her when she toppled sideways, and wearing clothes like a regular person instead of a police uniform, like a responsible sergeant-in-charge. But then Anna and Pasha came up behind them, and she pushed his arm gently away, forcibly suppressing her warm imaginings.

'No,' she said, struggling to her feet. 'I mean – I mean, thank you, Vassily, but I can't turn back now. I've got to go, as long as the network can take me,' she continued, dusting the snow off her jacket, and picking up her luggage. Her face took on a determined look that Vassily knew well. 'Yes – I've got to go on.

'And I don't want to be late for my own train,' she said, turning to Pasha and Anna, and putting on her forced merriment once more. 'Pick up those bags, you two – no slacking!'

'*Da, tovarisch*,' said Pasha, but biting his lip, while Anna merely shook her head without speaking, her tears mingling with the snowflakes that danced around her eyes, as if silence were the best response, after all, to impending loss.

'Come on, then!' cried Olga, ignoring Anna's tears to forestall the appearance of her own, and marching one last time down the narrow path that led to her beloved rail-side hut. She knew every inch, every bramble and knotted root and twisted tree-trunk; every step felt like a betrayal, a cruel abandonment, a heartless leave-taking from all she held most dear – and a leave-taking, moreover, that had to be disguised with all the enthusiasm she could muster, a heartiness in spite of heartache, lest the other villagers should know what was passing through her mind, for that was the Russian way.

As Olga approached the railway with the others close behind, she realised she wasn't breaking virgin ground, as happened most days on her way to work, but, rather, walking in the footprints of several others. Then she tutted to herself. Of course! How could she have forgotten? A ceremony was taking place that day, with the mayor coming from Tayga, and a delegation of journalists, well-wishers and relatives of the man to be honoured, Danyl Petrovich, who would soon arrive at the helm of the train that was to bear Olga away to Mongolia.

Half the village was coming, too, from what she'd gathered at Café Astana the night before. Even Olga's suspects for unspecified crimes, her father Mikhail and old man Solotov, were scheduled to make an appearance at the ceremony, with their frequent associate, Olga's aunt Zia, who always liked to witness local events (if only to spite those who thought she was too old to get there). And now, as she neared the track, Olga caught a diagonal glimpse of the little stand the railway had erected for the day's festivities: a low wooden platform to the north of her hut, made of rough, unvarnished planks adorned with Russian Railways logos, and covered – somewhat ironically in the circumstances – with a tiny corrugated-iron roof in case of inclement weather, now completely swamped with thick snow.

But weren't the footprints rather fewer than Olga had expected? And shouldn't she be able to hear the buzz of excited conversation by now? She'd turned the second-last corner expecting to see a small but respectable crowd, but she saw instead only a handful of people sheltering under the trees. There were Popov and his wife Nadya, Igor Odrosov (but not his daughter Svetlana), and Fyodor Katin, the Dreamer, plus the dreaded Mikhail, Solotov and Aunt Zia, her hair pulled into a bun so tight that smiling was quite excluded – but where were all the rest? Where was the promised audience for her final send-off – and where was Mayor Denisovich and his usual retinue of lackeys, assistants and camera-festooned journalists? She stopped, wondering if something had gone awry, or even if she had the day wrong, like the time she'd turned up to a funeral in Itatka only to find the body already six feet under. But no: Boris had definitely said today. And Olga had seen the date written in black and white on the paperwork she'd snatched from Polina's hands in the hut.

Seeing her standing and staring in puzzlement, a short, powerfully built man called to her from his sheltered place under the trees. 'You're here for the ceremony? Well, the plan's changed.'

'The plan's changed? What do you mean?'

'Mayor can't get here,' said the man. He walked out of the undergrowth, like a bear emerging from its lair, his fur-hatted head hunched down against the keen wind and its snowy burden. 'So his assistant said, anyway, when she called through to the café this morning, and then Igor Odrosov told me. Can't come by rail, she said – all the snowploughs needed elsewhere on the network, they say, and he's too chicken to come without. And his official car's too fancy to get here in the snow, since he had the suspension lowered, like a gangster. But we got here well enough, didn't we? It's only three bloody miles, after all!'

He reached out a gloved hand. 'Ludis Kuskov,' he said. 'I'm Danyl Petrovich's nephew.'

'Olga Pushkin. And this is my brother, Pasha, and my friends—'

Ludis Kuskov cut her off. 'Ah, yes – the hut woman,' he said, ignoring the others and focusing on Olga. 'I heard about you up at the café this morning. Well, I'll tell you what's happening: the train's still coming to pick you up, but from the other direction, of course, so it can't help the mayor even if he wanted it to, which he clearly doesn't. So it'll be me giving Uncle Danyl the medal, not Mayor Denisovich. It'll be nice to give Uncle Danyl something, for a change! All the journos cancelled, as soon as they heard there'd be no more photo ops. And it's not even the Trans-Siberian Uncle Danyl's on – they've cancelled that, too, on account of the snow. But they found a freight train with a snowplough that he could drive instead. He'll take you on to Krasnoyarsk, they said, on a jump seat in the driver's cabin. God knows what you'll do after that! A bus, perhaps, or maybe an army tank. . . You're going to Mongolia, I hear?'

'I am,' said Olga, looking at the man, and thinking that she wouldn't want to cross him: he spoke clearly and lucidly, and in a calm, matter-of-fact tone, but his fur hat overshadowed fierce, glittering eyes, which in turn were set above a sharp, determined mouth surrounded by a dark halo of bristling stubble. Nevena, Olga recalled, had said something interesting about Danyl Petrovich at Café Astana the night before – something about local heroes always having nasty little secrets buried somewhere or other. But Olga wouldn't be surprised to learn that nephew Ludis had a few of his own, too.

There was no time for further reflection on this or any other issue, however, for now a distant horn blared in the distance, heralding the approach of Danyl's train; and as if it were a hunting-call foretelling a long-awaited kill, the train's sounding now drew a few more people out from under the sheltering branches, some familiar to Olga, and others less so. They headed down the trackside towards the wooden platform, taking the wandering, frequently overgrown path, whose overhanging boughs, when touched by a stray hand or hat, eagerly released a fresh load of snow upon unwary walkers. Olga had taken that way a thousand times and been snowed upon nearly as often.

But there was something wrong this time. Olga could tell as soon as she rounded the final corner that led to the railway clearing in the woods, a huge vertical scar cut through Siberia's endless forest. As she approached the snow-covered tracks and skirted the edge of the ballast, she felt the quivering of a heavy mass approaching through the soles of her boots. So far, so familiar – but this time was different. There was a subtle change in how the vibrations came through the ground, the way the whispers sounded upon the rails; and in her heart, in her railway-woman's intuition built up over nearly two decades, she knew the change promised nothing good.

Olga stood still, staring northwards, towards the place where she and Pasha had walked that morning, and straining to hear the approaching train. The others stopped, too, as if they sensed her fear. But then the noise of the locomotive came to their ears, and they relaxed a little, and even smiled, for the noise they heard was the standard throaty roar of a diesel, accompanied by another blast of the horn as Danyl Petrovich caught sight of his reception waiting by the track.

Polina Klemovsky put her head out of Olga's hut and glared up the track at the approaching locomotive, as if trains really shouldn't make such a racket. Some of the spectators and well-wishers began to clap and smile and cheer; one or two even ventured out upon the rails to wave Danyl on, or point out his wife Anoushka, sitting beside him in the cab.

But Olga wasn't smiling. She started walking towards the train as it approached, slowly at first but then more quickly. Finally she broke into a run, desperately ploughing through the snow, waving her arms and shouting something at the onrushing locomotive. Only scraps of words came back to the others, borne on the wind like so many snowflakes: 'Stop – wrong – danger—'

But there was no way for Danyl Petrovich to hear her. He must have thought she was yet another well-wisher, they said later – one who'd had too much vodka at Café Astana that morning, perhaps, and who wanted to celebrate in her own way by running towards the train like a madwoman, blizzard or no blizzard. He must have decided to placate her, or maybe to warn her, for the horn sounded again and again – but still Olga ran forward, screaming now, more and more desperately, as if the driver could hear.

But she was too late, too late by far; and now a new sound came to the well-wishers' ears, neither the deafening booming of the locomotive horn nor the rumble of its powerful engine, but something else – something deeper, something that reso-nated within their chests, like a great cathedral organ, a tremor of the very earth beneath them. And then, to their uttermost horror, they saw a sight that matched the sound: the great loco-motive, now drawn near them, quivering on its mighty wheels, lurching from side to side, the driver and his companion alarmed now and darting from window to window in the engine cab; and then, at last, with the inevitability of a found-ering ship, they saw the great train sink to one side and dig its snowplough nose deep, deep into the unyielding ground.

Aghast, the spectators watched as the engine stood high upon itself, dragging the foremost wagon up, up, up until its cargo of steel girders rained down on either side, like spillikins. But the two-thousand-ton juggernaut could not be stopped so easily, and the wagon after the foremost rammed through the girder-bearing steel as if it were made of melting ice, knocking the locomotive down upon its roof and riding over, then pushing the locomotive off the tracks entirely with a great grinding of metal that sent sparks flying into the snowy forest, until friction brought the wagons to a halt at last, and silence fell upon the devastated scene – a silence broken, after a horrified few seconds, by the shrieks of well-wishers and relatives of those in the cab who had surely perished, crushed under hundreds of tons of steel.

Olga ran to the front of the locomotive, with the others following close behind. She stared up at the hideous, steaming mockery of the machinery they'd seen operating so effectively just moments before. Then she reached out to something that dripped from the locomotive buffers: something deep crimson and viscous to the touch, something that – she now noticed – had fallen also in globular spurts upon the snow, spreading out in the close-pressed flakes like red dye. Could it be oil, or hydraulic fluid – or coolant, perhaps? But then Olga jumped backwards, pressing her hands into her stomach as if to cleanse them, for she knew, instantly and with deep conviction, that she had just touched the liquid heat of fresh-shed blood.

Vassily Marushkin came running up, and as he did so his walkie-talkie burst into life. He turned to the side, plucking it from his jacket pocket and raising it quickly to his head. He listened intently and spoke briefly once or twice, then listened again for a long time, his ear pressed against the crackling speaker; and then at last, after a curt '*Da*,' into the mouthpiece, he turned back to them, tight-lipped and white-faced.

'Was that the authorities? Did you tell them what's happened?' said Ludis Kuskov, speaking thickly, barely able to get his words out.

'Yes, I told them,' said Vassily. 'But they can't send any help. They can't send anything. The bridge to Tayga's collapsed – overloaded lorry that skidded on black ice – so they've closed the roads.

'And the railway's shut both ways, too,' he went on, turning to Olga and speaking rapidly, breathlessly, and not – Olga thought – merely from his exertions. 'They had crashes at Suranova *and* at Anzhero-Sudzhensk,' he continued, 'because of the snow. Once-in-a-lifetime event, they're calling it. So all the snowploughs are useless – they can't get anywhere on a shut-down network. And there's no chance of air support, either – all the army helicopters are grounded. And as for us, well, we've still got power, thanks to those new lines they laid in the summer, but the phone lines are down, and the mobile masts, too. So we can't broadcast out . . . I can't even reach Tayga on this,' he continued, brandishing the walkie-talkie. 'That was one of the constables. He made it halfway towards us, but can't get any further in the snow – piled too high. Said he's been recalled now, because there's so much going on in Tayga. He won't be able to try us again until everything's put back in working order.'

'So you mean . . .' began Ludis.

'That's right,' said Vassily, after a pause to catch his breath. 'We're on our own.'

5

Hoedown

Olga stared at the stricken locomotive, gaping at the sight of human blood running down the curved metal panelling of the Peresvet 3TE25K2M locomotive, its deep velvet shade clashing with the cheery signal red of the Russian Railways livery.

'That's blood,' she breathed to Vassily, her voice sounding like another's in her ears, still ringing from the screech of tortured metal and injured stone. He nodded but didn't speak, enveloping her, instead, in a bear-like hug to hide the horrific sight from her eyes.

It crossed Olga's mind that once again she was close to Vassily, as she'd longed just minutes before, but the thought came to her in a fleeting, intellectual manner, far distant from the passionate yearning of normal times. How could she think of love, of *romance*, at a time like this? Two people were dead! Two living, breathing beings – creatures she'd seen moving inside the cab just moments before – had now been crushed into the nothingness of inanimate matter. Enveloped in Vassily's arms, she could no longer see their blood dripping down the fly-speckled engine, but she didn't need to: she would always remember the sight, she knew, just as she could still see in her mind the American tourist she'd found dead earlier that year, his throat cut from side to side and his mouth stuffed with ten-rouble coins. The dead haunted the living, whether or not you believed in ghosts. They hovered over you, like a hangover from the life before, causing not nausea or headaches but troubles of a deeper kind, a chill presence that could neither be ignored nor confronted head-on.

A chill presence . . . Olga looked around her at the swirling snowstorm that encircled them, drifting already around the wrecked locomotive as if to claim it for its wintry own. Had the weather in some way contributed to the derailment? Surely not, she replied to herself. The Peresvet locomotive was fitted with a heavy-duty snowplough, capable of punching through even the deepest drifts. And snow on the tracks was neither here nor there to a train that tipped the balance at two thousand tons or more.

The streams of blood – still warm – dripped down upon the encroaching waves of white snowflakes, as if mounting a futile attempt to melt away cold nature with the remnants of mortality. But soon, Olga knew, the icy wind would freeze the blood as it ran, while the sinister ruby colour would disappear beneath layer upon layer of chilled Siberian snow, at once preserving it and hiding it from view.

I'm hidden, too, thought Olga, if only for the moment. I can't be plucked up and sent on my way, she reflected, while this dismounted juggernaut bars the way. And it wasn't just the derailment: there was also the bridge into Tayga, the line closures in both directions, the inaccessibility that had turned Roslazny into a frozen parody of a tropical island. Yes, the weather had saved her, if only for now. What was it she'd said to herself, when the snow had first begun to fall? That it was like a long-lost friend? Yes, and the best kind of friend at that – the friend who clings so tightly that departure is impossible, just as Vassily was embracing her now.

But then she stopped herself. She was on the point of clasping her hands in joy, she realised, while standing mere feet from the victims of a tragic accident. Twice in a year now death had come by rail to Roslazny, and she was clasping her hands for joy? What kind of a person did that make her? And wasn't it strange, now she came to think of it, that both these tragedies had occurred just outside her very own hut? Mightn't people begin to wonder, even to whisper and speculate, whether Olga herself had in some way brought these deaths upon them? Could a person become a railway Jonah, a track-bound curse bringing bad luck and ill fortune?

A harsh voice cut across her thoughts, while at the same time echoing them.

'What have you done?' said Polina Klemovsky.

Polina had come out of her hut as soon as she heard the freight train approaching, and then, when the train derailed, had run up the track as fast as her wooden clogs allowed, with most of the few villagers and well-wishers in attendance following in her wake. Now she stood with hands on hips, surveying the scene with a nonchalant air, as if she were inspecting the arrangements for a birthday party rather than the bloodied remains of a locomotive cab.

'I said, what have you done?' said Polina again, this time waving her arm at the smoking, twisted freight wagons that lay scattered about the track.

Vassily released Olga from his embrace, and allowed his eyes to follow the direction of Polina's gesture – but then they narrowed, as if he'd seen something of interest beyond the wreck.

'The smoke,' he muttered to her, before darting off to the side of the tracks, and heading back up the line.

'Which bit of smoke?' said Pasha to Anna, while watching Vassily leave. 'There's smoke everywhere,' he went on, nodding at the acrid pyres that rose from the remains of several wagons.

But Anna didn't answer: she merely stared straight ahead with her gloved hands over her mouth as the snow whirled around her and the distraught well-wishers surged past, her eyes filling with tears and then, as she shook her head in dismay, spilling over her cheeks until they reached her scarf below.

Standing beyond her, Olga emerged from a state of dazed horror to a keen awareness that unwelcome words had been addressed to her, and in Polina's harsh, unpleasant voice at that. What was it she'd said? *What have you done?*

Olga turned sharply towards her. 'What the hell do you mean by that?'

'Well, you do track maintenance on this stretch, don't you? And hasn't this train' – she stepped forward and kicked a wrenched-off piece of metal with a resonant clang – 'hasn't this train just derailed? That's health and safety, Roslazny style, I suppose.'

'Have some respect,' said Pasha, waving a hand at the battered remains of Danyl's train. 'This is no time for jokes!' But Polina only rolled her eyes.

'*She's* responsible for this, you say?' said one of the strangers, stepping forward to Olga and placing his substantial body squarely in front of her. He was a man of medium height in his late sixties, with a round, mostly bald and fast-reddening head.

'So you – you brought down the train? You brought down Danyl and – and – and *Anoushka*?'

His voice began to break, and he blinked, clenched his fists and bit his lip, turning back to Polina and saying again: 'So she brought the train down?'

'I don't know for sure,' said Polina, shrugging. 'I only took over yesterday – haven't had time to do my usual inspections. But I've never seen a train derail without some pretty serious track maintenance issues, that's for sure.'

'So it *is* her fault, then,' said the man, grasping Olga roughly by the shoulder – only for Pasha to knock his hand angrily away.

'Get your hands off her!' he cried.

'Mind your own business,' snapped the stranger. 'That's my neighbour in there! Thirty-two years I've been friends with – with *Danyl* Petrovich, and now he's dead, murdered by incompetence, by this country bumpkin from Russian Railways! Such a loss for the world! A more loving, better-natured person – man – you'd be hard pushed to find. And his wife, too – Anoushka . . .' He stopped, bowed, and put a finger and thumb to his eyes as if to quell his tears. 'Better people you'd be hard – hard pushed to find,' he went on, his voice trailing off as he shook his head in grief.

'Look, I'm sorry they're dead,' said Pasha, 'but that's my sister you're standing in front of. And you'd better watch who you call incompetent, or you'll have me to answer to. She's just about the best track engineer this side of the Urals.'

The villagers standing behind Pasha – Igor Odrosov, Koptev Alexeyev, Nikolai Popov and the others – nodded and murmured in assent. Olga might be a little eccentric, from time to time – she might get involved in criminal investigations, for example, or adopt hedgehogs, or even buy her friend a house on a whim – but she was one of them: a Roslaznyan, born and bred. And quite apart from all that, Olga was known to be a good engineer: the villagers knew there hadn't been a crash on Olga's stretch since well before her time.

'It's all right, Pasha,' said Olga, casting a hurried glance over her shoulder for Vassily, but only glimpsing the top of his hat – a little askew as always – as he disappeared behind the wrecked locomotive, walking up the track. Where *could* he be going, thought Olga distractedly, and why would he leave her at a time like this? But then another angry voice cut across her thoughts.

'Don't you dare threaten my husband like that,' it said, in a shrill, hectoring tone. Olga turned, and saw that the voice belonged to a short, grey-haired woman who had stepped in front of Pasha. She had large eyes, parchment-coloured skin, and hands with short, stubby fingers, one of which bore a large, aggressively gold wedding ring presumably placed there by the bald man in his sixties.

The woman now employed a different finger to tap Pasha aggressively on the chest. 'Gennady's quite right: someone's responsible for this disaster, and who could it be but Russian Railways? Danyl Petrovich, gone – gone . . . And Anoushka Petrovich is in there, too – Danyl's wife! Didn't you realise? I've known her my whole life, nearly. Such a – such a powerful, strong, good-hearted man – woman, I mean. At least all their suffering's over now. But that's only because he's – I mean she's – she's . . .'

The old lady's voice began to waver and break, as her husband's had a moment earlier, and she turned towards Gennady, who enveloped her in a hug while she sobbed on his shoulder.

Now a third *postoronniy* stepped forward – Ludis Kuskov, the short, dark-haired man Olga had spoken to at the fringe of the forest before the train had approached.

'You must forgive them,' he murmured to Olga and Pasha, while also bowing courteously to Anna Kabalevsky, who had now lowered her gloved hands to reveal a face that was deathly pale. 'They're old, Taisia and Gennady. They lived next door to Uncle Danyl for thirty years or more, and the elderly can't handle things the way we can, *nyet*? Sure, I'll miss Uncle Danyl – but he got around, in his time. He was no bear cub! And he'd want to go out that way, if he had a choice, at the controls of one of his precious engines.'

Olga looked at Ludis curiously. His tone was light-hearted, yet it jarred with what she sensed of his underlying mood. It wasn't that Ludis conveyed the levity of a nihilist or a narcissist, or even the general thoughtlessness of the comparatively youthful. No: his underlying mood exuded the serenity that comes only to the relieved and the delivered. Yes, that was it precisely: Ludis Kuskov had the air of someone who'd been saved from an unpleasant fate by a stroke of luck: a stroke of luck so unexpected that he could not, or would not, command his voice or his words to display the feelings appropriate to bereavement.

Or – or – and Olga could hardly bring herself to think it – or could Ludis be relieved because a murderous scheme had finally come to fruition? Could Ludis really have waited, medal in pocket, for a ceremony he knew would never take place? Could a man really kill off his uncle in cold blood, and stand barefaced by the tracks to revel in his success after the event had taken place?

There was no time, however, to reflect on Ludis Kuskov's inner world, for the old lady had begun to speak once more. Her hearing was clearly more effective than Ludis had suspected, for she disentangled herself from her husband's embrace and launched an attack upon the nephew of Danyl Petrovich.

'How can you say that, Ludis?' she said, in her falsetto tones, reedy yet piercing. 'How can you say that, at a time like this? And how dare you call us old? Have some respect for your elders – and for the dead.' She stared at him in thin-lipped anger, as if she'd like to fetch him a clip around the ear, but instead she merely said once more: 'How can you *say* things like that?'

'Because you know it's the truth,' said Ludis, flatly.

'I know nothing of the kind,' replied Taisia, clamping her lips together once more.

Ludis almost smiled, an ironic twitch of his mouth. 'You know nothing? *Da*, then we're in agreement.'

Taisia's husband Gennady Aristov, who'd been staring, blank-eyed, at the rivulets of bloody snow, now stirred, realising that Ludis was on the brink of insulting his wife. He sighed, turned from the engine, and began instructing Ludis on conversational etiquette harshly but, Olga thought, a little mechanically, as if he were carrying out a necessary duty while his heart and mind were busy elsewhere.

Taisia gestured at them without speaking, and glared at Olga once more, as if to say: Look at what you've done – look at the commotion you've caused!

'Listen, I'm sorry,' began Olga, but now a fourth stranger stepped forward. He hushed them all with flapping hands and uttered calming words – words that echoed his priestly appearance, for he was dressed all in black, surtopped with a stovepipe *kamilavka* hat above piercing eyes, a snub nose the colour of sliced beetroot, and a bushy, salt-and-pepper beard that had seen better days.

'Quiet, quiet, my children,' he said, making soothing noises with his lips, so that his straggly moustache buckled and hinged like a hairy caterpillar. 'It's not good to speak angry words near the bodies of the departed. We should be praying instead!'

The old lady looked up at him. 'Pastor, I don't think . . .' she began, but he spoke over her, prising her from her husband's grip and taking both her hands in his, so that she had to wipe her tears awkwardly away on her shoulder.

'Taisia Aristov,' he said, in a deep, resonant voice. 'Taisia Aristov, have I ever let you down, in all the time I've known you?'

'Well, it's only been a year or so . . .' began Taisia, but he spoke over her again.

'And in that time have I ever let you down? Or your good husband here – dear Gennady? Or our friend Danyl, or his wife Anoushka, now tragically departed?' He waved towards the smoking wreck behind them. 'No? Then let me speak now, my lady.'

'What's it got to do with you, Loktev?' said Ludis.

'*Pastor* Loktev,' he replied, with a pained expression. 'And haven't I myself lost loved ones in this disaster?'

'Not really,' said Gennady Aristov, sharply, and for the first time Olga found herself agreeing with the bald-headed stranger. A pastor or priest might get to know his congregation over the years, of course, and some more than others – this presumably explained his invitation to today's ceremony – but a churchman could hardly regard all his parishioners as his own loved ones, or mourn them as such, unless he desired to fill all his years with sorrow.

Besides, while the Aristovs displayed all the signs of bitter loss, Pastor Loktev seemed as unperturbed as Ludis Kuskov by the gory scene in front of them – a scene considerably worsened, to Olga's mind, by the fact that the true horrors still lay hidden behind the cracked, blood-stained engine windows. Perhaps it was Loktev's sense of divine providence, his inner certainty of the inexorable unfolding of a grand strategic plan against whose benevolent magnitude two individual souls were as nothing – perhaps that was what it was, but whether it was or not, Olga couldn't shake the impression that he was somehow *satisfied* by the wreck of Danyl Petrovich's train, just as Ludis seemed relieved.

But Gennady Aristov was still talking, or rather shouting. 'None of you has lost what I've lost!' he boomed, flecking the nearby Pastor Loktev with spittle. 'And it's all on *her*,' he went on, pointing a finger angrily at Olga. 'She did this, with her – with her negligence! I'm not familiar with these parts, but back in Yashkino we know how to deal with this kind of thing.'

'Not again,' muttered Pasha, massaging his knuckles as if preparing for a barrack-room brawl, and prompting Olga to put a restraining hand upon his arm. She looked around for Vassily, her eyes searching ever more urgently but equally in vain. Worse still, her gaze alighted instead on Polina Klemovsky, whose toad-like features now betrayed a fleeting look of relish. She quickly altered her expression to one of grave concern, but it was too late to fool Olga. Was her ghastly replacement taking some kind of repulsive pleasure in the trackside disagreement? Or was something still worse at play – something deeper and darker at work behind those broad spectacles and wide, toothy grin? Could Polina have taken a hand in the crash herself? wondered Olga. Was her recent appointment just a means to murderous ends? But she raised this possibility only to dismiss it: what kind of idiot would deliberately derail a train the day after taking responsibility for maintaining the track?

Olga's mind, already stultified by the hammer-blow of the crash, reeled from the strain of considering so many suspects at the same time, and strangers into the bargain. But once again there was no time for exploring unpleasant possibilities, for at that moment Gennady moved decisively towards her, prompting Pasha to step forward and block his way. They began shouting at each other, both men drawing on a colourful array of highly expressive vocabulary and threatening to inflict an impressively creative range of injuries upon each other. Olga began to worry that there might soon be yet more casualties by the rail-side, and in Vassily's absence she supposed she would have to step in herself.

'LISTEN,' she screamed, above the melee. 'Listen – listen! Listen, you're right,' she went on, in a slightly quieter voice, as the others turned to her. 'I *am* responsible for this track – or I was until yesterday, anyway. But I've been over this whole section with a fine-tooth comb. I even did an extra check three days ago to make sure everything would be fine for the big event today.'

'Well, you didn't do a very good job, did you?' shouted Ludis Kuskov, but again – thought Olga – with a subtle air of artifice, as if he were play-acting at grief. But the other *postoronniye* didn't seem to notice: Taisia Aristov cried something in agreement while Pastor Loktev shook his head and uttered ineffectual noises – ineffectual, for Gennady was soon pushing forward against Pasha once more, his face distorted by a mix of anger, grief and vindictiveness.

Olga looked around desperately for additional help, but there was only Polina Klemovsky, standing back with her arms crossed, and beyond her Anna Kabalevsky and the other villagers, most of whom were useless in anything approaching an emergency: Igor Odrosov and Nikolai Popov were sparring weakly in mid-air as if they would love nothing better than to get involved in a fight, if it weren't for their cricked back and gammy leg, while Fyodor Katin, the Dreamer, was actually wringing his hands. Anna Kabalevsky, meanwhile, was crossing herself repeatedly, clearly hoping for divine intervention of some kind or other.

No: there was no help coming, and Olga had just opened her mouth to speak again in her defence when she heard a loud, authoritative voice boom into life behind her.

'What the hell's going on here?' cried Vassily Marushkin.

Olga sighed with relief as he strode up to the group of well-wishers, took one quick glance at the scene unfolding before him, and stepped in front of Gennady Aristov.

'Step back, sir,' he said firmly, holding up a large and forbidding hand. 'Sergeant Marushkin, Roslazny Police,' he went on, forestalling Gennady, who had already opened his lips to enquire. 'And we don't want any difficulties here, do we, Grazhdanin?'

Gennady bowed and stepped back, recognising Vassily's tone as well as his use of the formal state term for 'citizen', which – in many parts of Russia – often precedes severe legal difficulties for said citizen. The others, too, calmed down, despite Vassily's plain-clothes appearance, and Taisia Aristov,

Pastor Loktev and Ludis Kuskov all joined Gennady in adopting a more conciliatory appearance and retreating a foot or two from the policeman who now stood between them and their prey.

But the prey was more interested in the policeman in front of her.

'What's that on your hands, Vassily?' she said, but he shook his head, a minute motion that only Olga could see, while simultaneously wiping his hands on the back of his ageing waterproof.

'*Pozzhe*,' he muttered to her. *Later.* And then, speaking more loudly, he addressed the others – the bereaved family and friends standing close by, and the villagers a little farther off. 'Attention, everyone – please. Attention! Thank you. I have a request to make to all of you, and it's a simple one: please don't tamper in any way with the scene behind me. There'll be a full investigation in due course, and it's my job to ensure it's got the best possible chance of success, so that tragedies like this don't happen again. In the meantime, I'm afraid we're all confined to Roslazny, as I said a few minutes ago. I think that some of you stayed at Café Astana last night? Well, I'm sure Igor Odrosov will be happy to put you up once more – *nyet*, Igor?'

Igor Odrosov, who had remained standing a little way off throughout, lifted a heavy hand to illustrate his consent, before adding, in his guttural croak, that he even had an extra room, since one of the *postoronniye* had left early that day, before the roads closed. 'The pretty one,' he added. Olga nodded: she knew already that Nevena Komarov had taken her leave that morning.

'A second night, in those horrible rooms above the shop floor?' said Taisia Aristov, in horrified tones. 'Above a bar whose drinkers don't even start leaving till midnight? I hardly think that's an appropriate suggestion for bereaved friends of the departed – is it, Gennady?'

'What? Oh, well, no – no, perhaps not,' said her husband, looking as if nothing would suit him better – as if, having been denied the chance to vent his anger upon Olga, he could hardly wait to drown it instead in some weapons-grade alcohol.

'There must be some more suitable place we could lodge,' went on Taisia. 'Some lady who lets rooms in her house, perhaps.'

Olga instantly glanced at her aunt Zia, still hovering at the back of the small crowd. Aunt Zia had rented rooms to her and Pasha in her faded green-and-white palace earlier that year, before the final and irrevocable rift had occurred between them. She thought of Aunt Zia, and almost pitied Gennady Aristov despite his anger: a man suffering from acute grief, as Gennady plainly was, would be far better served by Igor Odrosov's rough-and-ready hospitality than Zia's fussy intolerance. (And wasn't it strange, she thought in passing, that his grief *was* so intense – and his wife Taisia's, too? One would hardly expect next-door neighbours to feature high on the list of distraught mourners – any more than one would expect mere acquaintances to travel far in a cold September for a rail-side ceremony.)

Pastor Loktev, it seemed, agreed with Gennady. 'Well, let's not be too hasty,' he said, rubbing his beard, and nodding at Gennady rather than Taisia Aristov. 'It would be convenient, wouldn't it, to be close to hot food at all hours, in this weather? Bars are much more reliable in that regard than guesthouses, or so I understand. And – and one must be in contact with sinners, after all, to have any hope of saving them.'

Nobody saw fit to grace this remark with another, and after

Loktev fell silent, the four well-wishers looked at each other in one of those silent conversations where pursed lips, raised eyebrows and sniffs take the place of words. After a moment, they inclined their heads in tacit assent and shrugged their shoulders, as if to say, What else can we do? We came to see the mayor give away a medal, and what did we get instead? No medal, no mayor, and our loved ones meeting a bloody end in a benighted village cut off from civilisation by snow, fallen bridges and wrecked trains. Really, said their unspoken glances, it was too much – too much altogether.

The silence was broken by Pastor Loktev. 'It's all right if we go now, is it, Inspector?' he said. 'There's no sign of any let-up in the weather,' he continued, glancing up at the clouds that loomed low over the disastrous wreck, their grey, undulating bellies like folds of a blanket snagged on the stark tree-tops, and snowflakes tumbling like feathers from torn fabric in a helter-skelter dance of flickering whiteness. But Vassily stood unmoving amid the flurries.

'I'm not an inspector, only a sergeant,' he said, raising his voice to be heard above the wind. 'And haven't I met you before somewhere?'

'I don't think so, Sergeant Inspector,' said the pastor.

'Just sergeant,' said Vassily again. 'Well – well, yes, you can go, but not far, even when the weather clears. I'll probably need to speak to you all again, very soon. For the – for the accident investigation, I mean,' he added, but in a curious tone that made Olga stare at him. Any woman worth her salt knew when a man was lying, and Olga would have bet her savings, even the special sums she'd put aside for the honours literature course at Tomsk State University, that Vassily was lying now.

'I'm afraid the bodies will have to be autopsied as a matter of course, even though we know what's happened,' Vassily went on, in a more normal voice. 'And there'll be the usual coroner's inquest – you'll all be called as witnesses, probably. So, like I say, don't go too far. Popov, Alexeyev, perhaps you can lead our visitors back to the café? Thank you,' he went on, as the butcher and the mechanic turned towards the village – glad, thought Olga, of a chance to get out of the weather and back to the warmth of Café Astana.

The rest of the villagers followed suit, looking at Vassily and the others as if seeking permission to leave, then flocking grate-fully back to their homes. Polina Klemovsky, meanwhile, cast one more glance over the crash, muttered something about inefficiency, and walked towards Olga's hut.

'That's Polina Klemovsky for you – out for herself at all times,' said Olga to Pasha, watching her replacement as she walked away. 'I told you she was up to no good – and here she is, the day after she arrived, taking advantage of a tragedy and framing me for incompetence.'

'It's all because of the Americans,' said Fyodor Katin, who had sidled up to the group now there was no danger of physical conflict. He nodded vigorously, and sneezed as a snowflake blew up his nose. 'Sorry. What was I saying? Oh, yes – it's these new systems they've copied from America, tracking what people do so that everyone can be blamed for something. Convenient for the bosses and their yes-men, and women, like that Polina, but not so good for the workers. It's just not ice hockey.'

'Never mind all that now, Fyodor,' said Vassily, with a touch of asperity. 'Olga's perfectly capable of taking care of herself.

I'm more concerned about finding the person responsible for *that*.' He jerked his thumb at the wreck behind him.

'Well, everyone seems to think it's my fault,' said Olga. 'Maybe you should just arrest me for criminal negligence, and get it over with!'

Vassily shook his head, his face stern as he stared after the disappearing well-wishers. Then he leaned towards the others until they followed suit, first Pasha, then Anna, Olga and Fyodor Katin in turn. He granted them a glimpse of his hands, black and greasy with ash.

'The smoke,' murmured Pasha, prompting a muttered '*Da*,' from Vassily.

'I saw flames away from the tracks,' he went on, speaking softly and jerking his thumb towards the line that led to Suranovo. 'I followed the smoke and found the remains of a fire a few hundred feet up from here, and a few feet away from the line. Just ashes left, mostly, but I raked through it and found an old pickaxe, burned to hell, and a cold chisel, dark and scorched, and also the remains of a garden hoe, just a bit of metal and the end of a handle – enough to get a print, maybe, though then again, maybe not. And then I looked behind me, towards the track, and I saw a big pile of stones – some larger, some smaller, laid out higgledy-piggledy by the lines. Did you ever see any mess, any untidiness on Olga's stretch of track – any of you? Of course not! It wasn't the remains of some half-finished job, carelessly abandoned by Olga. No. It was—'

'It was the ballast,' breathed Olga, talking half to herself, while Vassily nodded in confirmation. 'They took the ballast from under the sleepers, so the train would topple.'

Fyodor gave a low whistle. 'So, it wasn't negligence,' he said, glancing behind him with unbelieving eyes, as if in wonderment that a few simple tools could bring down such a juggernaut.

'No, Fyodor,' said Vassily, grimly. 'It wasn't negligence. It was stone-cold murder.'

'And we're cut off,' said Pasha. 'The roads are closed, and the fields are six foot deep in snow. So the murderer—'

'Is probably still with us,' said Olga, shivering, and looking around her amid the whirring blizzard's whiteness. Somewhere nearby, somewhere beyond the snow-shrouded trees that surrounded them, was a madman who'd taken a pickaxe to the tracks and brought tragedy and ruin to Roslazny once more. How could this be happening again? Was all of Kemerovo *oblast*, all of Siberia and Russia and the world beyond, so filled with evil that murder should come twice in a year to their doorstep? And . . . and . . . She hesitated to ask herself, but what of her premonition, the four branches that had snapped and fallen to earth under the unaccustomed September snow? Two had died already: Danyl and Anoushka Petrovich. Yet what of the third – and the fourth?

She stirred and looked straight into Vassily's eyes, their mutual gaze continually interrupted by the pale, crystalline dots that danced between them like frozen fireflies.

'Look on the bright side, Vassily,' she said. 'Solve this, and you'll stay in Roslazny – you and Kliment and, well, Rasputin, too, I suppose, though it's hard on the rodents hereabouts.'

'We just wish you could stay, too, dear Olga,' said Anna, with sorrowful eyes.

'Well, you never know,' said Olga, with a jauntiness she did not feel. 'You just never know!'

But Anna merely hugged her in response, her body thin and angular beneath her winter clothing, and poignant, somehow, in its weakness. Sometimes a lie could be a kindness, said Olga to herself, looking over Anna's shoulder at the snowy wastes beyond. A lie could be a kindness, but only if the other was truly deceived. And there was no deceiving the oldest of friends – was there?

6

Third Wheel

I should have known, thought Olga, on the evening of the following day, staring sightlessly at the guttering blue-orange flames of the gas heater in the corner of her bedroom. I should have *known*!

It was inevitable, really, when she looked back. It was as inevitable as Danyl Petrovich's train careering from the tracks once the ballast had been removed, or (as Fyodor would say) the Bolshevik uprising following the serried stupidities of the tsars, who'd had so many chances – so many chances! – to avoid the bloodshed and disaster of revolution.

What was it she'd said to Anna? 'You never know.' But she had known, really, at some level, hadn't she? Perhaps we always know what's really going to happen, and just don't let ourselves acknowledge it. Perhaps it's a form of self-defence, she told herself, designed to stop us going mad with the impossibility of our desires coming true – from the secret knowledge of iron causality, of stern immutability, of cold, ruthless, relentless inevitability that walls us round, with never a gate or opening or even a window to peer through.

But it didn't *seem* inevitable, when she turned up at the Roslazny police station on Thursday afternoon, the day after the derailment. If anything, the opposite was the case. She'd expected something else entirely when she'd pulled on her snow-boots, left the house she shared with Anna Kabalevsky and her brother Pasha, and trudged through the heavy snow to knock on Vassily's door. Her thoughts had touched upon Nevena Komarov, yes – she'd thought of her with sorrow, in fact, regretting her unavoidable need to leave Roslazny for Sudzhenka on the morning of the crash. But she'd also felt a kind of relief, the lightening of spirits one might feel when newly safe from some external threat to one's health or happiness. With her gone, Olga at least had Vassily to herself for now – as much as she could, that is, against the ghostly light shed by the distant spectre of his lost wife, Rozalina.

But then she knocked on the collection of splintered planks that served as the police-station door, and as if Olga had cast in her mind some summoning spell of ancient power, a woman came out into the snow, tall and stately, and with raven hair that spilled over her elegant green scarf and her shoulders in compelling disarray.

'Nevena!' cried Olga. 'What on earth are you doing here?'

'I can't believe you didn't know Nevena was still with us, here in Roslazny,' said Vassily, leaning forward to strike a match on some exposed brick by the fireplace. 'I mean, if Odrosov so much as installs a replacement toilet-bowl it's all over the village by nightfall – so how did you miss that particular bit of news?'

Olga shrugged. 'It's like I said. Pasha and Anna marched me straight home after the crash – they said I needed to rest after the trauma – and then we stayed put for the whole night, and most of today, too. Pasha wanted me to rest, and Ilya's still got an upset stomach, so it's all hands on deck at home. I hardly felt like heading out again, anyway, after what happened.'

She shook her head, as if she could shake off the memory of the viscous red liquid running down the locomotive panelling. 'The crash . . . I can't help wondering if – if it was somehow – if I could have done something differently.'

'Olga, no!' cried Nevena, who was sitting beside Vassily and smoking a borrowed Belamorkanal. She rushed to Olga's side and flung an arm around her shoulders, while somehow preserving the delicate column of ash on the cigarette in her left hand. 'Olga, you mustn't *ever* think like that! Someone came along and dug out the ballast with a hoe. What could you possibly have done to prevent it, short of making your bed by the track?'

Olga darted a glance at Vassily: clearly he'd wasted no time in bringing Nevena up to speed with the murder investigation, just as he'd apparently wasted no time in asking her to join him at the police station that day. Nevena herself had just told her, quite innocently, how Vassily had popped into Café Astana just after breakfast to check up on the Petrovich well-wishers, and to see if Nevena was fully recovered from her recent ordeal – an ordeal that had started with her dutiful departure from Roslazny on foot and on time on Wednesday morning, and had ended with her lost for hours in a total white-out.

'If it hadn't been for that man – Alexeyev, isn't it, Vassily, the mechanic with the dyed hair? – if it hadn't been for that man coming along in his ATV after the train crash, I'd still be there in the snow,' Nevena had said. 'And it was just in time, wasn't it, Vassily? I heard them saying this morning he's had to put his ATV away – that the snow's too thick for it now. I'm a lucky woman!'

She'd then told Olga how Alexeyev had summoned Vassily, who'd enlisted Fyodor Katin to help him half walk, half carry Nevena back to her recently vacated room at Café Astana, Popov following with her baggage; and then she'd told her how, after a good night's rest and a hearty breakfast of fried *omul* from Igor Odrosov's kitchen, she'd insisted on joining Vassily's investigation and helping him to track down the murderer.

'Vassily told me how he and the others had taken the bodies from the train after you left, still dripping with blood,' she'd gone on, shivering as she spoke, 'and put them in the butcher's freezer, to keep them safe for the post-mortem. So *horrible* . . . I just *had* to offer my help, when Vassily asked. After all, humans are my speciality – that's what human resources deals in. It sounds a bit gruesome, doesn't it? But you know what I mean. We see *through* people, I always think. We know how to find out what they want, and then usually – in Russian Railways at least – find a way not to give it to them. So we can just apply the same logic here. What does the murderer want? He wants to get away scot-free. So I'm going to find a way to stop that happening.'

Olga had looked at Nevena as she spoke, wondering why Vassily had taken her into his confidence while keeping other strangers at bay – and the Petrovich well-wishers in particular: Danyl's nephew, Ludis Kuskov; his neighbours, the Aristovs; and the clergyman, Pastor Loktev. But then again, Nevena wasn't really a stranger: she was, as Vassily well knew, an old and dear friend to Olga. And there were other reasons, too, why Vassily might desire her involvement in the investigation. Nevena really was an HR specialist, and Olga knew – from some unpleasant experiences in the past – how well, and how clearly, HR people could delve into the dark recesses of the psyche when they had to. Her investigative nous might well be a worthy addition to the team.

And on top of that – did she need to spell it out again? No, she told herself, glancing to her left and watching Nevena tap her Belamorkanal so that the ash, released from the tip, circled precisely down into the fireplace. As she inhaled and blew an artful jet of smoke towards the low police-station ceiling, Olga was struck once more by her almost incredible beauty, like a model in a bus-stop poster, or an old-time film-star killing time in a black-and-white station café. And from Nevena her eyes were drawn inevitably to Vassily, who – Olga saw – was looking intently at Nevena as she inhaled a third time, deeply and voluptuously.

Olga sighed with irritation as she saw that Kliment, Vassily's bowl-headed teenage son, was also looking in Nevena's direction – though in his case with an unabashed, slack-jawed gaze that typified, for Olga, the unfiltered male response to physical stimulus.

She tutted, rather more loudly than she'd meant to, and suddenly found three pairs of eyes looking directly at her – four, if she counted the beady eyes of Rasputin, glittering in the darkness underneath Vassily's desk.

'Yes, Olga?' said Nevena. 'Is the smoke bothering you?'

'Oh – no, no,' said Olga, rubbing her cheek to conceal the reddened tinge that threatened to spread across her face and reveal her embarrassment. 'No – I smoke the odd one myself, you know, but I mostly gave up when I moved in with Anna. You know what she's like. Anyway, I was just thinking what a shame it is that Kliment has to miss school, because of the weather.'

'Are you kidding?' said Kliment, bursting into a raucous peal of laughter. 'Best thing that's happened this year. Apart from you finding me at the farm and bringing me to Papa, of course.'

'I think Kliment wishes it was still the holidays, when his only concern was helping me get the place tidy,' said Vassily, to a vigorous, if inarticulate, sound of agreement from his son. 'Painting doors and sweeping out cells in your oldest clothes beats geometry and Dostoyevsky, right, Kliment?'

'Is that what you call it – tidy?' said Nevena, glancing beyond Vassily to the jumble of papers on Vassily's desk, then downwards to the halo of straw and rodent remains that extended for several feet around Rasputin's cage. Vassily saw the amused smile playing on her lips and responded in kind, while Kliment shrugged at his side – but Olga had stopped listening. Vassily's mention of paint had reminded her of the scent that seemed to haunt her bedroom despite Pasha's denials, and – in turn – of another mystery: the conviction that someone, some time, had said something strange, something unsettling, something *wrong*. It flickered in her consciousness like a will-o'-the-wisp, and just as elusively. Again she felt she was on the verge of recalling the words that haunted her, and again they slipped away at the last moment, taunting her with their skin-prickling oddness and utter irretrievability within the dark recesses of her own mind.

How frustrating it is not to know what we don't know, thought Olga, and how liberating it must feel to be stupider. But then one wouldn't have a cleverer self to compare oneself to.

She shook her head once more, forcing herself to concentrate, to listen to what Nevena was saying to Vassily – something about the difficulty she found in getting rid of old clothes, since she always became so attached to them. Vassily uttered some truism in response, while Kliment, she saw, had reverted to his open-mouthed staring.

Olga tutted again, more quietly this time, and unceremoniously cut across their pleasantries. It was high time, she thought, that they got down to business.

'So,' she said, 'everything's still down?'

She leaned backwards, thinking to balance her interjection with a nonchalant look and a swinging, airborne foot – but then she leaned forward again as the rickety chair gave a warning creak.

'Everything's what?' said Vassily.

'All the usual networks, I mean,' said Olga. 'The police systems – the things you need for tracking down suspects.'

'Well, yes,' said Vassily, stubbing out his cigarette in the tin-lid that served as his ashtray. 'Everything except power. So, no internet, police intranet or phone lines. There's only the walkie-talkies left and, like I said yesterday, they can't reach Headquarters at Tayga. We can listen to radio, but the Kemerovo stations have got a whole region to cover, so there's not much going on about our little corner of Siberia – or not yet, anyway. I doubt they'll announce the train wreck until the high-ups come and see it for themselves. But the main point is this: we've got no access to criminal records, or bank statements, or employment history – none of the things we usually start with when we're screening suspects.'

'No fingerprint scanner either, then – for the handle of that hoe, I mean, if there's anything on it?' said Nevena Komarov, to an answering shake of the head from Vassily. He had, of course, bagged up all the tools he'd found in the trackside fire, but without the police's usual forensic capabilities they were currently useless as evidence.

'And that's why I thought of getting Nevena's input,' said Vassily, seeming to address Olga and speaking, perhaps, just a shade more quickly than normal, as if embarrassed or uncomfortable about something. 'After all, murder victims usually know their killer – and as nobody in Roslazny knew Danyl or Anoushka personally, it made sense to start with the well-wishers, with their neighbours, relatives, and their spiritual guide, or whatever Loktev is. And Nevena's spent more time with them than any of us, while staying at Café Astana. And, like she said just now, she knows people.'

'Yes, it all makes sense,' said Olga, in a flat tone that gave nothing away but her desire to appear unemotional.

'Well, as I was telling Vassily earlier, they're a strange lot,' said Nevena, after a pause. 'A creepy vicar, an angry young man, and a drab old couple. They've had a shock, of course, but even accounting for that they don't speak much. I think Igor Odrosov's found them hard going, and I get the impression he doesn't give up easily.'

'You think they're hiding something, maybe? Some secret they all share?' said Olga, her enthusiasm for the idea overcoming her carefully curated coolness. 'You don't think – you don't think they might all have been in on it? That they might have got together and conspired to put an end to Danyl by bringing his train down?'

'Unlikely,' put in Vassily. 'For one thing, derailment's a very uncertain means of murder, isn't it? I mean, I'm no engineer, but surely if the train had come off the tracks differently Danyl and Anoushka could have survived, or one of them, at least. And it's hardly an anonymous way to do it, is it? The only people in Roslazny who knew Danyl and Anoushka stick out like broken balalaikas!'

'But they didn't know the weather would get so bad,' pointed out Olga. 'And they must have expected more well-wishers to come, so they'd be less unique. Maybe more *would* have come, if it had been a normal September day – as well as the mayor and his entourage, and the journalists. Just imagine that all four of them had some kind of grudge against Danyl or Anoushka – maybe even the *same* grudge – so they devised a clever plan: bring down the train at whatever cost, and rely on the crowd to disguise their alliance.'

'It would have to be quite a grudge!' muttered Nevena.

'But the weather turned,' said Olga, ignoring the interruption, 'and nobody else cared enough to make the trip, and then they were marooned . . . Marooned, like all of us, only our island's a village, and we're surrounded by snow instead of seawater.'

'Sorry, but it's just too far-fetched, Olga,' said Vassily. 'We're not writing a detective show for TV! We've got to be systematic, rather than just guessing. Almost anything's possible, but not everything is likely or provable. And we haven't got much time, either: soon enough the snow will melt, and unless we can charge someone, *all* our suspects will disperse as fast as the ice, when the thaw comes.'

Instead of replying to Vassily's well-argued points, Olga got up after a moment and walked to the blackboard that hung on the wall opposite the doorway – a hangover from the pre-computer era, when Vassily's father, a long-ago incumbent of this station when Vassily and Olga were still at school together, had logged each new inmate by hand.

The others watched as Olga wiped the board clean with her sleeve, then dug out an ancient piece of chalk from its base and scraped four lines crosswise and four more vertically. One by one she wrote the names of the four well-wishers next to each crosswise row: Ludis Kuskov, Taisia Aristov, Gennady Aristov and Pastor Loktev. Finally she wrote a single word above each of the three columns: *Motiv, Sredstva* and *Vozmozhnost'*.

'Motive, means and opportunity,' said Nevena, nodding approvingly.

'There's just one thing missing,' muttered Vassily, looking across at her. *'Dokazatel'stvo.'*

'Proof – yes, indeed, proof!' laughed Nevena. 'Where would we be without it? But in the meantime, don't we already have *Sredstva* and *Vozmozhnost'* pinned down? I mean, we know they used a handful of tools to break up the ballast, before committing them to fire – that's the means. And we know they did it after your last track inspection, Olga, but before the train came yesterday morning, in the middle of nowhere, and in the middle of a snowstorm, too – and that's our opportunity. It doesn't really rule anyone out, though, does it? In other words, almost anyone could have done it! So it's only motive we need to bother about.'

'That's probably true,' said Vassily, but in a distant tone with which Olga was quite familiar. He was listening with less than half his mind, she knew, while most of it was focused on something else – something potentially more interesting or valuable. Presently, she knew from experience, he would reveal his thoughts to them – but in the meantime Nevena was still talking.

'Are you sure we want just those four names, and no others?' she said, gazing up at the blackboard.

'Well, who else would you put up?' said Olga, a touch more sharply than she'd intended.

'Oh, I don't know,' said Nevena, leaning back and swinging an elegant ankle to and fro as Olga had tried – and failed – to do. How on earth, wondered Olga, did she manage to make *snow-boots* look dainty?

'I don't know,' she said again. 'Maybe some local Danyl had ripped off, or cuckolded. He was quite a good-looking man in his way, wasn't he, despite his ponytail? Or maybe it was a colleague he'd offended. What about Polina Klemovsky? She's in Russian Railways, too.'

'True,' said Olga. 'And now that you mention it, she did call him a *pridurok* the other day – but she'd hardly time a train wreck to coincide with her first day on track maintenance!'

'You're right, Olga Pushkin,' broke in Vassily, unexpectedly. 'I think we must discount Polina Klemovsky, however much you – we – might long for her guilt.'

Olga saw that now, at last, Vassily was ready to share his inner reflections. '*Motiv*,' he murmured to himself. '*Motiv* . . . It's not just a motive for killing, is it? It's not just that someone wanted either Danyl or Anoushka dead—'

'Or both of them.'

'Or both of them. It's not just that. No, it's like you said, Olga: the plan was to bring down the train – to derail it. But that's what I can't understand. Why would you try to kill anyone *in that specific way*? Like I said earlier, death would be far from certain. The more I think about it, the crazier it seems.'

Vassily then pointed out that if the original plan had taken place, with the Trans-Siberian instead of a freight train, tens or even hundreds of people could have died instead of just two. 'It would be mass murder,' he said. 'And you don't come across that often, even here.'

'But that's the clever bit,' said Olga. 'Don't you see? If you kill two people at the same time as two hundred, nobody would be any the wiser.'

'Clever?' said Nevena, gazing intently at her. 'Yes, perhaps. But maybe *committed* would be a better description. A person committed to a course of action – something there's no going back from.'

'Well, let's just be grateful Olga's not a murderer herself,' said Vassily, drily, 'or I'd never have a day off. But we're getting off topic here – what was I saying? Oh, yes. That derailment isn't a certain way to kill somebody.'

'But maybe death wasn't necessary,' put in Nevena. 'Maybe they just wanted to— Oh, I've no idea! Maybe they wanted to humiliate Danyl, to show that he wasn't the great local hero everyone thought he was and, what's more, to do it with his pride and joy, his beloved trains. Everyone knows how much he loves – loved – driving. And if he was seriously injured in a crash, at his age? No more driving . . . Or maybe it was to give Anoushka a serious fright, to show her that her husband couldn't protect her from – from an enemy, or something. Oh, I don't know – it could be anything! I'm just trying to think like the killer might have thought – to get into their way of seeing the world.'

'That's a good way to do it,' said Vassily, nodding. 'You're already proving your worth, Nevena! Well, how about this?' he went on, grasping Olga's cast-off bit of chalk and scrawling two words on the board, before turning to stare at them in triumph.

Pochemu ballast.

'What do you mean by that, Vassily?' said Nevena.

'Isn't it obvious? Think about it. *Why the ballast?* We've been talking about why anyone would derail a train. But why, specifically, did they choose to derail the train by dislodging the ballast? What kind of person would even think of that?'

'I've never heard of it happening before,' said Olga, 'and that's in more than fifteen years on the railways. So if nobody does it, how can we guess what kind of person would?'

'I suppose – I suppose it could have been an engineer of some kind,' said Nevena, slowly. 'Someone who knows how track works – and how it can be made to stop working!'

'A track engineer, to be precise,' said Olga, a trifle sharply, so that Nevena turned to look at her.

'Oh, not *you*, Olga,' she said, laughing in her musical way. 'A woman devoted to her family and friends – devoted to a white-breasted hedgehog, even – and with no grudges against anyone, suddenly deciding to kill a Russian Railways colleague and his wife and maybe hundreds of others into the bargain? It doesn't bear thinking about.'

'Of course it doesn't,' said Vassily, quickly.

'Well, putting Olga aside,' said Nevena, getting up and taking the chalk from Vassily, 'and assuming that we're counting out Polina for now, can you imagine any of these four' – tapping the blackboard with the chalk – 'any of these four knowing how to do it? Which of Ludis Kuskov, Taisia or Gennady Aristov, or Pastor Loktev could have the skill and knowhow to bring down a train, armed only with a few simple tools? Can we guess?'

Silence fell upon the police station, broken only by the ticking of Vassily's ancient fireplace as it expanded with warmth and, outside, the mournful whistle of the wintry wind as it barrelled and twisted past the crooked timbers of the station's exterior.

'Not really,' ventured Olga at last, 'though it's hard to say without knowing more about them. Though I suppose – well, Ludis Kuskov, maybe. Like I told you, he looked almost contented at the track, as if he were relieved about something. Relief that he'd managed to pull it off, maybe? I think he's the strongest of the bunch, too.'

'You think so?' said Nevena. 'I reckon Pastor Loktev is wirier than he looks. Younger, too.'

'Don't forget Gennady Aristov,' put in Vassily, leaning back and perching on the desk. 'He might be an older man, but Pasha says he's still got plenty of power left in his arms – and Pasha knows what he's talking about, after a couple of decades in the army. And Taisia Aristov . . . She looks frail, I know, but I've seen *babushkas* do incredible things, if the motivation's strong enough. Taking apart some aggregate, and burning the tools afterwards, would be child's play in comparison.'

'So any of them could physically have done it,' said Nevena, shrugging. 'This isn't getting us anywhere.'

'All right,' said Vassily. 'Let's say any of them could physically have done it. Anybody in general could have done it – not just those four. But why *would* they? That's the key to motive. There's got to be a reason why they – the killer or killers – wanted Danyl and/or Anoushka dead. But what's the reason? We've mostly been focusing on the suspects, but we've got to think about the dead, too. What reason could anyone have for killing off a clapped-out train driver and his wife?'

'Love, revenge, jealousy, blackmail, passion, a piece of dangerous knowledge, money, politics,' intoned Olga, as she counted them off on her fingers, dipping into her extensive knowledge of TV detective dramas and reeling off all the standard plot-fodder for Saturday-afternoon viewing.

'Very exhaustive, Olga, but now we're just speculating again,' murmured Vassily. 'We need to go person by person until—'

But Vassily's words were cut off by a frantic knock at the door.

'Vassily!' shouted Fyodor Katin, barging his breathless way into the police station. 'You'd better come and see this.'

'See what, Fyodor?' said Vassily, a touch irritably. 'We're a little busy just now.'

'It's the bodies,' he said between pants.

'What bodies?'

'The train driver and his – his wife, Danyl and – and Anoushka,' said Fyodor, red-faced now, and bending to put his hands on his knees. 'Oh – this is – the problem – with modern life. No exercise! It was different – in the old days.'

'Never mind the glory days of serfdom,' said Olga, impatiently. 'What about Danyl and Anoushka?'

Fyodor stood up again and wiped the sweat from his brow. 'It's the freezer, at Popov's. They're— It's Danyl and Anoushka! They're on fire!'

Olga smelt the bodies long before she reached them, the charnel-house stench wafting on the air like some obscene barbecue. She felt her insides lurch as they approached the site of Popov's freezers, and all but turned aside to bury her face in her scarf, or take refuge in one of the houses they passed on the way. She would certainly have done so, indeed, had Nevena not been there. But Nevena's sudden elevation to investigative partner had made Olga determined to match her in every possible way – to show Vassily that she, too, could bear terrible things. If Nevena could stand it, so must she – and Nevena's face, though slightly paler than usual, was filled with the calm, resolute and almost satisfied determination of one who must see an unpleasant task to completion. Olga hadn't turned aside earlier that year when Vassily had been languishing, falsely accused, in his own jail – she hadn't turned aside then, though in mortal danger from one who'd killed many times, and she wouldn't turn aside now, either.

They rounded a corner and saw that Popov's vast industrial freezer was utterly ruined, the shimmering stainless steel of its heavy-duty doors now blackened and twisted. But worse, far worse, were the once-human remains within. Olga could hardly bring herself to glance at the horrors inside, far less recount them later: a second death, an earthly hell, a scorching pit of fire inimical to all things dead or drawing breath alike.

Popov the butcher was there, staring at the scene with mute disbelief, while his wife Nadya, openly weeping, was being comforted by several other villagers amid the swirling clouds of white flecks that encircled them, snow and ash commingled.

Vassily, however, wasted no time in mourning those who had already died, but instead sprang into action. He seized hold of the rusty pitchfork that Popov used for lobbing fresh meat into the freezer, and with Fyodor Katin's help he snagged the bodies and pulled them from the inferno, first Danyl and then Anoushka, until a terrible hiss came to Olga's ears as the flaming corpses met the freezing snow that surrounded them in steep-walled drifts. Nevena stood and stared at the gouts of steam that gushed upwards into the fast-falling darkness, while Olga, overcome at last, rushed aside and emptied her stomach upon the ground.

Vassily, glancing up from the bodies, came to her and put a strong arm around her shoulders until at last she came to the end of her heaving and gasping. Then he took off his jacket and draped it around her, the gentle pressure of his hands a living comfort amid the deathly horrors.

'Who would do such a thing?' gasped Popov, between coughs, wafting the smoke from his face with a chubby, charcoaled hand. 'Who would ruin a perfectly good freezer like that, for no reason?'

'How will you store your meat now, Nikolai?' wailed his wife Nadya. 'And thirty joints – sixteen whole lambs, seven Mangalica pigs, bought special from Erik Filippov – all ruined! Ruined!'

'And two *humans*, Nadya,' said Vassily, angrily, to no response. But Nadya's shrill complaints at least served to rouse Olga from her dazed sickness, and she turned to help Fyodor, who was beating out the remaining flames on the corpses as effectively as he could while simultaneously averting his eyes. Vassily joined them, though Olga noted that Nevena hung back a little. And who was Olga to blame her? Nevena, unlike Olga, had not encountered the dead bodies at the crash, and Nevena, again in contrast to Olga, had not met face to face with industrial-scale murder earlier that year.

'What's this?' said Vassily, after the flames had been extinguished, bending over the remains of Danyl Petrovich, his voice muffled by the thick scarf he'd wrapped around his face to protect against the smell. 'Something in a side-pocket . . . a piece of paper, I think. Or – wait . . .'

'Oh, let me help, Vassily,' said Nevena, stepping forward at last. 'You'll never get it out with those gloves! Just show me where – it'll be cool enough now, I'm sure.'

Somewhat reluctantly, Vassily moved sideways a little, and pointed with a gloved finger at a tattered fragment of the donkey jacket Danyl had worn under his high-vis vest. Nevena bent down, and with the delicate fingers of her left hand she threaded her way into the pocket and retrieved a crumpled, smoke-stained and heavily scorched piece of paper.

'Aha!' she said, grinning at Vassily in triumph. Then she stood up, turned the paper, and Olga realised they'd been looking at the reverse.

'It's a photograph,' she breathed.

'Let's get some light on this,' said Vassily, pulling a Maglite from his pocket and directing its snow-flecked beam onto the image in front of them.

'A woman,' said Nevena, after a pause. 'A woman from the past – just look at those clothes. So stylish then, weren't they, in spite of all the restrictions? And – and that hairstyle! But those eyes . . . They'd be just the same today, wouldn't they? So brave, staring out like that – so defiant and strong. They'd be just the same today as if she'd never – as if she'd never aged a day.'

Olga was surprised to see tears come into Nevena's eyes, but then she felt her own eyes, too, come alive with moisture, and not from the smoke that wreathed them still in its grey, hideously aromatic tendrils. She knew that Danyl had died, of course: his body was there in front of her. Her conscious mind was fully aware of that unpleasant fact. But that photograph, that small, shabby, ruined artefact of a life lived with feelings and affections – that image of a presumably beloved woman that he'd kept for looking at in odd moments, grasping it with greasy, engine-driver fingers, then returning it to the little pocket – it somehow tore at her heart, too.

'Can't be Anoushka,' said Vassily.

'No, I don't think so,' said Olga, automatically glancing aside at what remained of Anoushka's face, then looking back again as fast as possible. 'This woman was tall, I think, though she's sitting down. Tall and intelligent. And she's . . .'

Olga frowned, took the photo from Nevena, and held it sideways, as if that would help her memory – for she had suddenly been struck by the conviction that the woman's face was familiar, despite the image's poor quality and blurry, sepia tint. But, as with the elusive scent of paint and the flickering, will-o'-the-wisp piece of uttered strangeness, she could not quite express *why* the woman's face seemed known to her, frozen in time all those years ago in a single instant of the photographer's work. She sighed with frustration: what had gone wrong with her? Her nose, ears and eyes had detected unsettling, inexplicable things, and yet her mind – contained in the same scrap of humanity – could not process them.

'Of course it's not Anoushka,' said Nevena, abruptly, cutting across Olga's thoughts, and glancing down at Danyl's remains with a look that seemed cold, almost contemptuous in its scathing survey: clearly Nevena had little sympathy for men who carried torches for women other than their own wedded wives. Olga saw Vassily looking at her, his expression unreadable in the dim light. Was he thinking, perhaps, that he'd need to be careful himself, if he ended up with Nevena Komarov?

Then Nevena glanced sideways at Olga. 'That photo's forty years old, I'd say, or more – don't you think? Those faded colours . . . And the lady in it, she must be almost forty. How old was Anoushka? Seventy, maybe? The numbers don't add up.'

'Well, could it be his mother?' said Olga. 'Or his sister?'

On a whim she turned the photograph over, holding it up close to her inspecting gaze. Then she gasped: there was a minuscule faded scribble on the back, spelling the name *Zlata M.*

'Zlata . . . Zlata M . . . M, not P for Petrovich,' she mused. 'Probably not Danyl's mother, then, or his sister, unless she married and changed her name – but there's no wedding ring on her finger. But Zlata – it's an unusual name. I've never heard of a Zlata in these parts, M or otherwise. Have you, Vassily? Or you, Nevena?'

The skin around Vassily's eyes crinkled slightly in the faint reflected torchlight – a movement so fleeting that Olga wondered if she had imagined the narrowing of his eyes. For then he shook his head, and glanced at Nevena, who was still staring at the photo as if she could conjure the identity of its wearer by sheer willpower. She stirred, looked up, and slowly shook her head in turn.

Then her eyes, robbed of their shimmering blueness by the monochrome night, flicked their gaze beyond Vassily and Olga and back towards Popov's freezers, where a small group of newcomers had arrived to inspect the commotion and see what was to be seen.

It was the well-wishers, Olga saw: Taisia Aristov, headscarf drawn tightly around her greying hair like any *babushka* worth her salted cucumber, and beside her Gennady, her husband, staring at the blazing ruins with a despondent air. There, too, was Ludis Kuskov, elbow on knee and foot on tree-stump, staring impassively at the sparks that danced into the air, heedless of their sombre cause; and, nearby, Pastor Loktev was digging with his boot-tip at some debris that had fallen into the mud-stained sludge on the pathway.

Olga looked back at Vassily, and opened her lips to speak – she was going to tell him he should make a note of the name on the photo, and run it through his systems as soon as they came back online – but then she saw his closed-off eyes and troubled, corrugated brow, and shut her mouth without speaking. He had once more adopted the grave solemnity that came upon him whenever the sergeant of police displaced the jovial beet-farmer with unruly black hair.

So she turned to Nevena instead, and once more opened her lips to speak – this time to urge the platitude that at least Danyl and Anoushka were old rather than young, and had already lived long and purpose-filled lives before their untimely deaths – when Vassily stepped forward and, with a gentle hand, urged Olga away from the smouldering bodies where they lay in the snow.

'Come, Olga,' he said, in a voice that matched the soft pressure of his spade-like hand on her shoulder. 'Come.'

'Where are we going, Vassily?' she said. But he stayed tight-lipped, touching a finger to his nose-tip and glancing ahead to a place beyond the end of Popov's street – a narrow grove where some unknown person had planted a row of limber aspens in the days of the *sovkhoz*, the state farm that had once supported Roslazny through lean winters and arid springs.

Olga knew the grove well – in her teenage years she had often strolled under the elegant boughs on summer days, book in hand, dreaming of green oak-trees by blue-bayed shores and gold-chained cats that circled left, and right, and left again in song and tale and poem, and wicked sorcerers named Chernomor and heroes called Ruslan. And now, with blazing autumn colours half hidden by early snow, the slender trees looked more delicately beautiful than ever – and she was walking there, too, with Vassily Marushkin, his hand straying at times upon her shoulder as if to catch her should she fall, his gentlest touch like the jolt of a live wire, or the cold-hot burn of a molten pan handle.

He stopped her after a hundred yards, and turned to her.

'Olga,' he began, and then, after a pause, he said again, 'Olga . . .'

'Yes, Vassily?' she breathed. What was happening? Did she sense a momentous phrase or question coming, a foreshowing that took her heart and made it seem to stop and race at once?

'Yes, Vassily?' she said again, when he didn't speak, mirroring his hesitant beginning.

His kind eyes looked down at her; but then they hardened, anticipating the words that would run through Olga's mind that night as she stared into her bedroom's guttering gas-fire.

'Olga, you must leave the investigation,' he said.

'I – I— What?'

'You have to go,' he said, more firmly now, as if – like Pushkin's gold-chained cat – he'd finally decided which way to walk around the tree. 'I – we – don't need you any more.'

'We? You and – you and *Kliment*?'

She knew this wasn't what he meant, but she couldn't bring herself to speak what was in her heart.

'No. Me and – me and Nevena. It's – it's like I said, Olga, it's better this way. Safer. She's a specialist – she knows what she's doing. She can be a real help to me – speed things up. Whereas you—'

'Whereas I'm just a track engineer?' she said.

'I – I didn't say that.'

'You didn't have to. And have you forgotten so soon, Vassily Marushkin, who found the killer earlier this year, while you sat and scratched your nails on a prison wall? Have you forgotten who saved you and the others in that warehouse, and who – and who . . .'

Her voice failed her: she loved Vassily's son Kliment too much to append his name to a list of debts incurred. She swallowed, and breathed out slowly, closing her eyes and opening them, repeating the action, as if wishing that Vassily might disappear when she did so, and reappear in more familiar guise. But he was still standing there in the same unfriendly stance, with those eyes that she had thought so kind, but which had clearly been enchanted by Nevena's unearthly beauty, and those hands whose touch had so thrilled her, but were clearly meant to hold another.

Then she tutted once more – not with irritation as before, but with all the bitterness of the fooled and the unfairly undone – and stared at this man who had so deceived her. She should have known that a man like Vassily Marushkin could not possibly be in the same village as a woman like Nevena Komarov without falling in love with her. Vassily was a match for her, where Olga had thought there could be none. And, of course, once he had fallen in love, the last thing he'd want was Olga hanging around like a bad kopek, getting in the way and demanding his attention. Yes: she most assuredly should have known.

She stared so long at him that eventually he spoke again: 'Olga . . .'

But she was unwilling to allow him the last word. All along she had thought to tolerate Nevena's involvement in the investigation as a favour to an old, half-forgotten friend – had even welcomed her participation, since the more people helping Vassily, the more likely he would be able to solve the requisite number of crimes and stay in Roslazny. But now that all was revealed – now that she saw through his plain exterior to the subtle, cruel desires that lay beneath – she was determined that he, at least, should not set the terms of the parting.

'You go, Vassily,' she said. 'Nevena's waiting, and there's a murder to solve – two murders. One for each of you. You take Danyl, and she can take Anoushka.'

She stepped forward, until their coats were almost touching, and gazed up into his dark eyes. 'You go – I won't stop you. I'm only sorry I slowed you down for so long. But don't worry! By the time you solve it, I'll be safely on a train to Ulaanbaatar, and you'll have Nevena – and Roslazny – all to yourself. Go, Vassily – go! Go.'

She turned away, and gazed up at the trees under whose swaying arms she had so often walked in former times, until even she didn't know if her eyes had filled with tears or snowflakes.

When she turned a few minutes later he'd already set off back towards the village, and she stood, watching him, as his figure retreated slowly down the wooded avenue, with cascading snow taking the part of autumn leaves. Just before he disappeared into the twilight, he stopped, and half looked around – Olga could just see a pale glimmer from his face, and a darker wave above that was his tousled hair. But then he turned and walked forward again, till the pale-dotted darkness swallowed him and he was gone.

7

Out on a Limb

Friday began as Thursday had done: misleadingly.

Yes, thought Olga, when she looked back later: it had all begun so innocently that Friday morning – light-heartedly, even, if one was prepared to ignore the ever-present threat of a nearby killer or killers unknown, complemented for good measure by extreme weather, a comms blackout and, as Nevena had recently demonstrated, the near-impossibility of escape from the towering snowdrifts that now surrounded Roslazny, not to mention the desperate heartache caused by Vassily's cowardly betrayal.

'You don't deserve him, Olga Pushkin!' Fyodor Katin had said, quite passionately. 'Oh, no – I mean, he doesn't deserve you, of course. Just – just have an egg or two, or even three. You deserve it.'

Fyodor had come round early that morning with eggs from his mother's chickens. He had named each of these after a different literary heroine, and whether by chance or because of Fyodor's conscious shaping, the most generous of these – as generous in eggs as her namesake was in everything – was Tolstoy's greatest heroine, Natalya Rostova. But for once Fyodor had not come to speak of *War and Peace* and its hints of Decembrist reformism, but because he had heard of Vassily's treachery on the village grapevine.

For the news to reach Fyodor Katin's garret in his parents' house on the far edge of the village, it must have spread far and wide indeed – yet Olga hadn't mentioned it to a soul, and she could hardly imagine Vassily doing so either. But she had seen this happen before. It was just as Vassily had said: someone like Popov the butcher would catch a glimpse of something unusual, and later he'd mention it over a pickled bear's claw or a bit of smoked venison to Igor Odrosov at Café Astana. The two men would dissect the information, overheard by Igor's daughter Svetlana, and come to a fairly shrewd conclusion in the end.

Then Svetlana Odrosov would call her friend Ludmila, and as Ludmila stood outside on her break she'd bump into someone like Ekaterina Chezhekhov, Olga's best friend in the world apart from Anna Kabalevsky. Ekaterina knew everybody, everywhere, Roslazny included; and as soon as she heard a piece of news from Ludmila she'd take out *her* phone and call Olga, Pasha, Anna, Alexeyev the mechanic, Nonna the chambermaid, and everyone else she could think of – except Mikhail Pushkin, of course, or Olga's aunt Zia or old man Solotov: anyone who'd been unkind to Olga was Ekaterina's enemy for life. But anyone else she could think of would hear the news as soon as possible, interspersed with the sounds of enthusiastic puffing – Ekaterina sold cigarettes at Tayga station, but smoked at least as many as she sold – and ear-puncturing horn-blasts from the shunters on the tracks.

Things were a little different now, of course, with Roslazny in snowy lockdown. There was no internet or phone signal, for one thing. It was physically harder to get around the village, for another: four-foot snowdrifts, rising to six or seven feet against walls and gable-ends, presented significant obstacles even to the fleetest of foot. And Ekaterina Chezhekhov, the region's top lightning conductor, was far away in Irkutsk. Nevertheless, here was Fyodor Katin, bringing old news and new eggs to Olga's doorstep at nine o'clock on Friday morning.

'Oh – well, thanks, Fyodor,' Olga had said, in response to his stammered words of praise. 'And thanks for the eggs, too. I'm sure the boys will—'

But the older two of Anna Kabalevsky's boys, Gyorgy and Boris, had already carried the eggs off to the kitchen in triumph, and danced around Pasha Pushkin shouting, '*Yaytsa, yaytsa,*' until he gave in, grinning, and set to work at the stove.

'Ssh, Boris! Ssh, Gyorgy! You'll wake Ilya,' said Anna, nodding fiercely towards a cot with a muslin cloth clipped over its upper regions. And then, more pleasantly, she said to Fyodor: 'Thank you, Fyodor! It was kind of you to bring the eggs.'

'The least I could do, Dama Kabalevsky,' said Fyodor, bowing deeply.

'Oh, just Anna, please,' she replied, blushing a little. 'You can call me Anna, Fyodor. I've told you before.'

He bowed more deeply still, descending so low that his glasses fell off. 'Not every man in Roslazny is an unreconstructed *obyvatel*', you know,' he said, picking them up. 'Though I'd forgive you for thinking so today,' he went on, nodding at Olga.

'She deserves better,' called Pasha, from the kitchen, pan in hand and cigarette dangling from his lips, like any father who'd learned to multi-task.

'Of course she does!' said Anna, hotly, as if Pasha had

disagreed with something she'd said. 'Of course she does. But you know, Olga, I'm a little relieved, too.'

'Relieved?' said Olga. 'Relieved about what?'

'It's just . . . Well, it's nothing, really,' said Anna, taking her hands and leading her to one of the well-stuffed, sagging armchairs that adorned the living room of the house they shared together, indicating to Fyodor that he should do the same. 'It's just . . . Well, isn't it a bit dangerous, getting involved in police investigations? I mean, look what happened to those poor men back in February. I couldn't bear it if anything like that happened to you, Olga.'

'So it's men's work, is it, Anna, investigating crimes? Women shouldn't get their petticoats dirty with real problems, you're saying. We should just leave it to our lords and masters, while they move us around like – like pawns on a chessboard?'

'Bit of a cliché,' muttered Fyodor, quietly – but not quietly enough.

'Oh, spare us the literary critique, for God's sake, Fyodor,' said Olga, fiercely, while, beside her, Anna crossed herself to ward off the blasphemy. 'I'm sorry I can't come up with brilliant wordplay while I'm – while I'm stuck here without a hut to call my own, without a future in my own village, and without – without – without Vassily!'

Olga broke down in tears, and Anna enveloped her in her arms, simultaneously shaking her head at Fyodor, who had started from his seat in horror at the effect of his words, and Pasha, who had perilously balanced his pan on the corner of the stove in preparation for coming to his sister's aid.

'Olga, I'm – I'm sorry,' muttered Fyodor, rolling his woollen hat in his hands while Pasha frowned at him through the hatch that led to the kitchen. 'I shouldn't have said that. I shouldn't have—'

But Olga cut across him. 'No, Fyodor,' she said, emerging tousled from Anna's embrace, and wiping the tears from her eyes. 'You said nothing wrong – nothing at all. It *was* a cliché, and I should avoid them, shouldn't I – I, of all people?'

'You of all people?' said Fyodor, his puzzlement clear behind his greasy spectacles, and Olga suddenly remembered that Fyodor didn't know about her book – that nobody knew about her literary activities at all, except Anna, Pasha, Aunt Zia and, of course, the elusive Maxim Gusev at Lyapunov Books.

'Oh, well,' stammered Olga, 'It's because – because I've got to go to Mongolia, I mean. Did I tell you I've got to teach a class on track engineering at the Railway Academy there? So if I'm appearing in public, I'll have to mind my Ps and Qs, won't I? I can't just spout a heap of well-worn platitudes.'

'I suppose so,' said Fyodor, eyeing her with the residual suspicion of the unpublished writer towards a potential competitor.

'Oh, you'll have no trouble over there, Olga, no trouble at all,' said Anna, warmly. 'You know all about engineering, and railway tracks, and signalling, and – and all kinds of things. They're lucky to have you!'

'Vassily'd be lucky to have her too, on the investigation,' called Pasha, from the kitchen. 'I mean, who else round here's got first-hand experience of murder inquiries?'

'Ssh!' said Olga, glancing out of the window. 'Nobody knows it's a homicide case yet, remember, Pasha!'

'*Da*, Olgakin, *da*,' said Pasha, waving a deprecatory wooden spoon through the hatch. 'Don't worry – I can see the garden from here, remember? There's nobody outside. Anyway, even if

Vassily was only looking into an accident instead of a couple of murders, he'd still do well to get you aboard. Like Anna says, you know all about the track, and the locomotives, and all that. And you've also got the imagination of a wr—'

Olga glared at him, and he immediately pretended to cough, necessitating the start of another, safer, sentence. 'You've got all the imagination of a teacher at the Mongolian Railway Academy, too.'

Fyodor again adopted a suspicious air, but Olga was no longer looking at him or Pasha. She was thinking, instead, that Pasha was absolutely right: Vassily *would* be lucky to have her. After all, she didn't only bring the facts and figures of engineering knowledge, like how much ballast someone would have to remove to topple a train. (About a third of a ton, she thought, which would take a man about an hour and a half to shift with a pick and a hoe.)

No, it wasn't just that – for Olga could also think in the way that engineers thought, weighing resilience against time, and strength against corrosion, and structural integrity against the remorseless devouring energy of forces beyond the control of man or woman. This was a valid perspective, surely, in the fight against murder – just as valid, in fact, as Nevena Komarov's much-vaunted human resources expertise.

And didn't Olga bring something else, too, as Pasha had all but spoken aloud, something Nevena surely lacked – the imagination of a writer? Olga knew, from the various detective dramas she watched when Anna's children were asleep, that intuitive leaps were just as important as dogged legwork when it came to solving crimes – and who better to make such bounds than a woman whose entire livelihood might eventually depend on the fruits of her own imagination? And hadn't she herself demonstrated the value of such intuition earlier that year, when she'd helped Vassily out of some very sticky situations by virtue of very clever guesswork?

Her mouth firmed as she ground her teeth together, like Baba Yaga herself: no, Vassily Marushkin didn't deserve her. But then her face lightened as another thought came to her: might Vassily himself have realised this?

Just then, and not for the first time, Pasha Pushkin demonstrated the uncanny convergence of his thought with his sister's. 'He's just jealous of you, Olgakin,' called Pasha through the hatch, his right elbow planted squarely on the crosswise plank that functioned as a serving-station. 'Vassily, I mean. Or maybe he thinks you'll show him up in front of Nevena Komarov, eh? Find the murderer before he does and make him look like a *durak*?'

'Well, if I haven't yet, I will soon,' said Olga, in a decidedly determined tone.

'Olga,' began Anna, speaking with the air of a person familiar with a friend's tendency to engage in imprudent or even reckless behaviour, 'Olga, I don't think—'

'Anna, Anna,' replied Olga, laughing, 'you don't even know what I'm going to suggest!'

'I know it'll be nothing good,' said Anna. 'You've got to watch your step, you know – that's no joke. You can't go around doing your own investigation, like before, and just expect Vassily to turn a blind eye. He's a policeman first and foremost, don't forget, and a friend second. You've got to watch your step.'

'It's not just me who's got to do that,' pointed out Olga. 'It's all of us. We've always had to watch our step in Mother Russia.'

'You sound like Fyodor!' said Anna, looking at him with laughter in her eyes, and prompting a shy chuckle from Fyodor in return.

'No, but it's true, isn't it?' replied Olga. 'First we had the tsars, who'd boil you in oil or tie you to sleighs and run you into freezing water at any opportunity. Then there were the Bolsheviks, who did the same thing, but on an industrial scale, and while pretending not to. And now there's Putin – and what's really changed? Journalists poisoned, opponents made to disappear, anti-war protesters arrested . . . The world hates us, says our *glorious* president – but didn't we hate ourselves first?'

She shook her head. 'I thought we were safe here, in Roslazny. I thought we had a man on the inside to help us,' she went on, thinking of Vassily's figure walking down the tracks towards her in the summer heat, 'but clearly I was wrong. And now he's got other fish to fry, and other people to fry them with.'

'*L'ogok na pomine*,' said Pasha, staring with narrowed eyes out of the kitchen window. Speak of the devil indeed – for when Olga went to look out, there was Nevena Komarov standing in front of the door and about to knock.

She slid the window up and stuck her head out. 'Nevena Komarov! What brings you here?'

Nevena smiled at Olga – a little nervously, she thought, which was understandable in the circumstances – and nodded at the others, who now peered out of the living-room and kitchen windows: Pasha Pushkin, Fyodor Katin, Anna Kabalevsky and her boys. Then she lifted her head in a slight yet unmistakable gesture: Olga was to come out and talk to her in peace, away from prying ears.

She made her apologies to Anna and the rest, Anna nodding but with a troubled look in her eyes, and Pasha shrugging so that the ash on his cigarette tip fell across the pan of sizzling eggs. Olga ignored the resultant outcry of Boris and Gyorgy, who were watching Pasha's culinary efforts with expectant greed, and walked quickly around the boxed-in kitchen to get to the front door, hastily grabbing Anna's coat from a nearby hook and pushing her feet into Pasha's snow-boots.

'Olga, I'm here to tell you all I know,' said Nevena, breathily, as soon as she opened the door. 'But not here. Come – come,' she went on, stepping quickly away from the house and back along the path that led through Olga's little garden and towards the village. Together they rounded the house's shoulder and disappeared behind the outreaching branches of the Siberian privet that encircled its northern flank. Then at last, when Boris and Gyorgy's shrieks had died away, and the sizzling of Pasha's frying pan with them, Nevena turned to Olga and told her all Vassily's secrets.

'We went to the train,' she said, 'to see if there were any clues. We even went inside.' She shuddered at the memory, and sketched the scene in only the briefest of sentences. 'Oh, it was horrible, Olga,' she concluded, 'horrible . . . Frozen blood all over the place. I was so glad when we got out again, and went on to the café. Vassily wanted to see if any of the strangers knew the woman in the photograph.

'But none of them recognised the photo, Olga,' she said, shaking her head in accompanying negation. 'Neither the Aristovs, nor Ludis Kuskov, nor Pastor Loktev. Vassily was so frustrated! He was sure that one of them, at least, would recognise the mysterious Zlata M.'

'But none of them did,' said Olga, staring into snow-whitened space and bringing the crumpled photograph to mind: a sepia-tinted woman dressed in old-fashioned clothes, striking somehow despite the gap of years, and familiar, too, in some unfamiliar way. Olga had also expected one of the *postoronniye* to have recognised the image. Danyl Petrovich, after all, must have carried the photo for some reason – and as the woman in it was unlikely to be either Danyl's mother or sister, the reason might well be connected to his demise in some way or other. And weren't the well-wishers the chief suspects?

'No, none of them did,' echoed Nevena. 'But I noticed some interesting things, nonetheless, when Vassily came to Café Astana. Taisia Aristov, for one thing, seemed very – well, she seemed very *happy*, for an older woman trapped in a low-key hostel for the duration. Or maybe happy's the wrong word. Relaxed, perhaps, or relieved? Yes – relieved. As if she thought something worse was coming out of Vassily's pocket, and was pleased to see that crumpled old photo.'

'Taisia – relieved?' said Olga, frowning. Relieved, as Ludis Kuskov had looked, just after the train wreck? What could Taisia Aristov have possibly been concerned about, that the photo of Zlata M was such a pleasant alternative? Could Taisia's drab, frumpy outfits hide more than varicose veins – and could that faded, once-crimson headscarf cover a head filled with hidden schemes and evil intent?

Olga had little time to reflect on this, however, for Nevena was still talking, telling her of how Vassily had questioned each of the well-wishers about the photo, cleverly framing it as if it were quite the last thing on his mind – as if it were the merest trifle, next to the all-consuming business of working out what had gone wrong with the track or the train to cause the accident.

'He said "accident" so many times that I thought they'd tumble to his game,' said Nevena, putting an arm on the sleeve of Olga's coat, and laughing her infectious laugh until she couldn't hold back a smile in response. 'He saw me smiling – I couldn't help myself – and I think he nearly grinned, too. Quite an achievement, I'd say, to make a sergeant of police smile on duty! But, then, look who I'm talking to – I'm sure you've done that, Olga, in your work together . . . Oh, yes, Vassily told me all about it. Anatoly Glazkov, and Lieutenant Colonel Babikov, and Ivanka Kozar the *provodnitsa*, and Vassily in jail – it all sounds so exciting!

'But, Olga,' she went on, a note of regret, or even urgency, entering her voice, 'I am *so* sorry that Vassily made you leave our little team – and so soon after it was formed! I know he thinks I'm somehow better suited to finding the murderer than you and, of course, I could hardly say no. If it got back to HR in Kemerovo, I'd be in serious trouble for obstructing the authorities. I'll be in enough trouble as it is for missing that job in Sudzhenka. . . But I know, too, how much your friendship means to me, and I would hate to think of Tatiana, your dear departed mother, ever coming to know that I had supplanted her daughter, even if it was by accident, Olga – oh, believe me, so very much by accident!'

Nevena's beseeching eyes fixed Olga's own with such gleaming intensity that she could hardly fail to grasp her hands in fervent accord, and to assure her that of course she completely understood, that it was out of Nevena's hands, that her mother, Tatiana, would have understood, that there were no hard feelings.

149

'Well, it's very noble of you, Olga – very noble, indeed. It's no wonder you're descended from the Lichnovskys, on your mother's side. No wonder at all. You can judge a book by its cover, I always say – you just can. And Vassily would agree – you should have heard him going on about Pastor Loktev.'

'Loktev? What did Vassily say about him?'

'Oh, just that he thought he'd seen him before somewhere.'

'So what?'

'Well, Vassily's hardly a churchgoing man, is he? He's unlikely to have seen him at the nine o'clock service. And—'

Nevena broke off, her large liquid eyes swinging round northwards, in the direction of Café Astana and the centre of the village. She broke off because she had heard a noise – a noise familiar to Olga's ears: it was Vassily, whistling through the side of his mouth in that way he had, low yet piercing, and guaranteed to summon Rasputin from the farthest, darkest reaches of his jail-cell hidey hole for a choice rat or two. And now he was using it to call Nevena Komarov?

Olga frowned, gripped at once by indignation and jealousy: indignation that Vassily had seen fit to summon a woman like Nevena with the same whistle he used to call his ferret, as if she were some kind of unusually large and elegant pet; and jealousy, for she found herself wishing that it was *her* he wished to recall, not the beautiful friend from whom she had been for so long parted. There was, too, a faint hint of contempt in Olga's eyes, arising from Vassily's apparent unwillingness even to draw near to her house. Was he afraid to meet her – or ashamed?

'I'd better go, Olga,' said Nevena, turning back to her. 'Vassily's waiting for me. I told him I just wanted a moment to gather my thoughts – that I found the investigation a bit intense, and wanted to smoke a cigarette by myself for a bit. I didn't tell him I was coming here – I think he'd be angry. He just wants the two of us in the investigation – me and him, I mean. And he's always there, nearby – I'm not sure how often I'll be able to come and give you news. I'm sorry, Olga, really I am! I didn't mean—'

Again Olga heard Vassily's whistle, but nearer this time, and Nevena Komarov, after darting a quick look of concern at Olga, grasped her hands and squeezed them, turning to go.

'Nevena,' she said, and then, as her friend turned back quickly, and a touch impatiently, she went on, 'just – oh, don't worry about me. Vassily might want only the two of you in the investigation, but there's always room for three – even in the far reaches of Café Astana.'

Nevena opened her mouth to speak, anxiety written plainly upon her face – but then Vassily whistled a third time, and, with a whispered injunction to Olga to take care of herself, Nevena disappeared behind a low-hanging, snow-clad bough, with only dinted footprints to trace her passing.

'And that was it,' said Olga, to Anna and Fyodor, sitting facing her like panellists at a job interview, as she recounted what Nevena had said. In the kitchen, Pasha had just finished cooking the eggs Fyodor had brought, and was dishing them up to Anna's boys on the low table next to the telephone, to the accompaniment of loud cries of culinary delight. Then he came through, lit another cigarette, and perched next to Olga on the arm of her settee.

'And that was what?' he said. So Olga told him what Nevena had said, and how Vassily had called her away again.

'Good of her to come, under the circs,' he muttered, through a cloud of smoke. 'But what Vassily's getting up to, I've no idea. What is he thinking of, avoiding you like this?'

'Not just avoiding,' said Fyodor, 'but positively abandoning!'

Anna silenced him with a look and a shushing movement of her hands, but Olga spoke over her. 'Yes, Fyodor, yes. Abandoning . . . That's the key.'

'What are you talking about, Olga?' said Anna.

Olga didn't answer. Instead, she got up and walked over to the kitchen, standing on tiptoe and rummaging through the units that hung precariously over the sink. And then, while Anna, Pasha and Fyodor stared at each other in mystification, she walked back into the living room and towards the old store cupboard that led off from a little door by the back wall.

'The Mishka Prazdnestvo . . .' they heard her muttering. 'Yes, yes, the Mishka Prazdnestvo . . .'

'Olga, what are you talking about?' said Anna again, beginning to wonder if her housemate – and landlady – had begun to suffer from delayed shock following the Petrovich derailment. 'What's the Bear Festival got to do with anything?'

The Mishka Prazdnestvo Festival, named after the Eurasian brown bears that had once teemed in Siberia, was a highlight of Olga's year, as it was for everyone else in Roslazny. Come the third Friday of each October, Popov the butcher would first source and then sell as many pickled bear claws as he could lay his hands on, Igor Odrosov would concoct special vodka cocktails in Café Astana, and whichever children still remained in the half-abandoned village would put on their Mishka costumes and parade up and down the narrow streets while the adults pretended to chase them. And then, when night fell, the villagers would make a huge bonfire in the old churchyard of St Aleksandr, bring vast quantities of food and vodka from home, and stand around the flames, wreathed in fragrant wood-smoke, talking and eating and drinking and laughing as the stars winked into life in the vast coldness above, until the fire died down at last and it was time to go home and await the festival's return another year.

'Don't you see?' said Olga, coming back into the living room with dust on her jumper and cobwebs on her hair. 'We've begun stockpiling already, haven't we, saving things up for the festival? Just like everyone else – and I bet you have, too, Fyodor? Perfect, then,' she went on, as he gave her a puzzled nod. 'It'll be easy. It's just like the proverb says: a person's bag is like a person's heart. That's what they say.'

'Do they say that, though?' said Anna, who knew that Olga dearly wished to make her own additions to the Russian language, crafting masterpieces of pithy wisdom that would join those of Tolstoy and Turgenev in the canons of literary fame. To her certain knowledge, Olga had invented at least six so-called proverbs in the past two months alone, with many more – she was sure – to come in the future.

'They do,' Olga replied, quite firmly. 'Or at least,' she continued, in a more tentative tone, 'they will. Yes, they will! But first I've got to make everyone look the other way.'

'You're speaking in riddles today, Olga Pushkin,' said Fyodor, scratching his head.

'I thought you said it was clichés?' said Olga. 'But never mind all that now. Lead me to your parents' house! And, Pasha, you come too. Yes – and bring a sack.'

153

'A sack?' said Pasha, frowning.

'And what will that reveal about Pasha's heart – according to the proverb, I mean?' said Anna, mischievously.

'Why, that – that he has much to receive,' said Olga, with growing confidence. 'Yes, that's what they'd say. An empty sack is like an open heart: ready to be filled with love.'

'No wonder that proverb has lasted so long,' said Anna, smiling at her. 'It's just like you, Olga – just like you. It's *ot dushi*. It's from the soul.'

'Yes, Anna, yes,' said Olga, 'of course it's from the soul! But you know,' she went on, her smile dying away, 'I don't think my soul on its own will be quite enough. I'll need a healthy dose of luck, too. After all, you can lead a horse to water . . .'

'. . . but you can't make it drink,' said Pasha, nodding sagely until his cigarette ash teetered and fell once more – this time all over his egg-stained singlet.

'Another cliché,' muttered Fyodor Katin, but so quietly that Olga would not hear.

To use another well-worn phrase, getting the right people to look the other way was child's play. All Olga had to do was walk around the village with Pasha in tow, tramping up familiar pathways and knocking on familiar doors, and then, when the owner's face appeared in the resulting crack between handle and frame, somehow entice them into parting with at least some of the goods they'd laid up against October's bear festival.

'It's to bring us all together, Nikolai,' she said to the butcher, Popov. 'To bring us together during this horrible lockdown, and help us forget about the weather, and the crash, and poor Danyl Petrovich and his wife, and your freezer, too. Yes – this afternoon! At the old church hall.'

But just as Olga thought she was making progress, his wife Nadya appeared at his side in her dressing-gown with her hair still in curlers, and launched into a tirade against Olga: 'If it wasn't for you and your policeman we'd still be in business! If it wasn't for that Vassily Marushkin putting those – those *corpses* where they didn't belong, we'd still have our spanking, brand-new freezer to store our top-class meat – you can forget what they say about horses and dogs and goats and what-have-you. And he still doesn't even know who set fire to poor Nikolai's pride and joy – I heard him say so earlier. Hopeless!'

Olga tried to interrupt, but Nadya rode dauntless over her stammered words. 'So no, Olga Pushkin, you can't have anything from our Mishka cupboard. *Podi proch'!* I've got enough to do here without you and your deadbeat brother bothering me. And don't blame me if the others feel the same. It's not just our meat we lost, you know!' And with a violent movement she pulled Popov back into the house – no mean feat given his size and weight – and slammed the door in Olga's face.

'*Yey-Bogu*,' said Pasha, disbelievingly. 'This might be a bigger job than we thought, Olga.'

Luckily, however, things turned out otherwise on this particular occasion. As Fyodor Katin said later, with all his characteristic pedantry, a sufficiently large number of villagers disagreed with Nadya Popov to a sufficiently large degree to part with a sufficiently large quantity of material to enable a sufficiently large number of eyes to turn in the wrong (or, rather, right) direction. Accordingly, Olga and Pasha returned to headquarters not just with one, but with three sacks whose hessian fibres bulged with hard-angled boxes of *kozuli* biscuits, glugging bottles of vodka (Rocket Fuel and otherwise), and countless tins of preserved reindeer meat, venison and *pelmeni* bought from Tayga behind Igor Odrosov's back.

Anna's eyes widened upon their return, as did her boys', and Fyodor Katin's. He was still – Olga observed – sitting quite close to Anna in the living room, having begged off their philanthropic outing on account of his weak chest. (Not so much a weak chest as a weakness of the heart, thought Olga.)

'Well, you saw me the other day, Olga,' he said once again, as if feeling obliged to excuse once more his cosy residency by the Pushkin-Kabalevsky hearth. 'I've got no stamina – none at all. I've got five, maybe ten minutes of puff, and then' – he clicked his fingers – 'gone! I descend into a wheezing wreck.'

'Well, don't worry, Fyodor,' said Pasha, standing upright and rubbing the small of his back. 'It's not far to the church hall.'

'But, Uncle Pasha, are you going to take away all the food again?' said Boris, Anna's eldest, in a worried tone. 'All of it? Even the *kozuli*?'

'Don't worry, Boris!' laughed Pasha. 'You can come and eat it yourself at the church hall. Auntie Olga is planning a little – what did you call it, Olgakin? Ah, yes, a little gathering. I'll be there, and you'll be there – and the whole village will be there!'

And so it was: the church hall hadn't looked so busy, so alive and vibrant, for many a long winter. It had lain vacant and mostly unused in the years since the state farm had been shut down, first decimating, then halving and more the number of viable churchgoers in the village – churchgoers, that is, who could not only physically get to services during the snow-bound months but also furnish a few kopeks for the collection-box. Of course, there had been exceptions to the rule, lively, bright-lit intervals in the long sleep of the dormant building – like when Anna's estranged husband Bogdan had opened it up for filming adult movies earlier that year, following his ejection from the old bathhouse. But for the most part it had remained darkly silent since the priests left – a darkness that made the current festivities seem yet livelier by contrast. As Pasha had said, the whole village was there – or, at least, everyone who had given anything to Olga for the lockdown gathering, plus a few others for good measure.

Olga had been very careful to avoid calling the event a party, or anything suggesting happiness or joy: the well-wishers were still in Roslazny, after all, and still grieving, presumably, for their recently deceased neighbours, relatives and parishioners. In the event, however, she needn't have worried: Pastor Loktev was seen heading out from Café Astana towards the hall, tipped off about the event by Igor's daughter, Svetlana, followed by the Aristovs, Taisia and Gennady, and behind them Ludis Kuskov and the rest of the Café Astana clientele. And soon enough there flowed from the rest of the village a host of familiar faces – some welcome and others less so, like Olga's aunt Zia Kuznetsov. But all alike came to the church hall, drawn by the promise of free food and drink, some impromptu music – Fyodor Katin had brought his vintage balalaika, and Ludmila had a good voice – and the prospect of forgetting about their snowy isolation for an hour or two. Everything had been set up perfectly, for Olga's purposes.

But then there was Igor Odrosov, a wily operator who was not only temperamentally inclined to suspect hidden agendas behind any sudden outbreak of jubilation, but was also financially programmed to place the interests of Café Astana ahead of any personal benefit he might encounter. There he was, still standing behind the bar, though there was nobody to serve, and polishing glasses with a wary, circumspect air.

Yet Olga had a plan for him – a plan that drew on these very strengths, these very sources of resistance to her subtle manipulations. 'I hear, Igor,' she said, leaning close to him in the now-deserted café, 'that a certain newcomer is planning to set up a rival to your operation.'

'A rival?' he said, stopping his polishing. 'Who's that, then?'

'Well, who can you think of who's arrived recently? Someone formidable – someone you wouldn't like to cross?'

'That Ludis, you mean?' said Igor, tilting the glass he was holding towards the door. 'Can't see him running a restaurant.'

'No – not the well-wishers! I mean someone closer – well, closer to your own age, who wears *wooden shoes* . . . Maybe she wants to give you a good kicking with them.'

'That Polina, you mean?' said Igor. 'Polina Klemovsky, with the yellow clogs? But she's just—'

'Just what? A track engineer, Igor? So am I – but it didn't stop me solving those murders and getting Vassily out of prison earlier in the year, did it? Setting up a café's nothing compared to that! And just the other day I heard Polina saying . . .' Olga paused, consulting her writer's imagination for a plausible piece of dialogue '. . . just the other day I heard her asking Popov what he charged to supply sausages, and making enquiries about the old Kabalevsky Hostel that Anna left when Bogdan took off. And what was more,' she added, leaning closer still to Igor Odrosov, 'I heard Polina saying she didn't mind a bit of *cat-meat*, if it helped with the prices.'

Igor stared at her. How had a stranger like Polina worked out the origin of his Tuesday sausage special? Wordlessly he put down his cloth, nodded at Olga, and made his way out of the café.

Olga walked quickly up behind him and peered out of the window by the door, seeing Odrosov stalking down the snowy path in search of rivals, and other villagers around him, all streaming towards the church hall, their figures sharply illuminated against the bonfire that Pasha Pushkin had set in the nearby churchyard of St Aleksandr. By screwing up her eyes, Olga could see Boris and Gyorgy standing next to Anna and Pasha. There was Odrosov, too, and his daughter Svetlana – and wasn't that Pastor Loktev, standing next to her? And there, she noted with a sudden lurch in her chest – or was it a dagger? – there was Vassily, tall, strong and tousle-haired, and next to him his bowl-headed son Kliment, and next to *him* the unmistakable Nevena Komarov. She was laughing, Olga thought, her long mane of hair rippling over her fur collar as she threw her head backwards. And then, in a movement of unconscious grace, she moved forward again and touched Vassily's arm with her thin, gloved fingers.

Olga turned away by a galvanic exercise of will and forced herself to walk back through the café, wending her solemn way through empty tables, abandoned chairs and half-finished snacks before reaching the foot of the narrow staircase that traced a devious, twisting route around the bar and up, up, up into the café's dubious heights. She wouldn't look back, she told herself – she wouldn't look back and see Nevena steal Vassily's heart with those elegant hands, while Kliment looked on in awe. And neither would she sneak home, cowed like any other ruminant that sought safety from the storm. Threats lay all around her, building like snow in a drift: the weather itself, the imminent loss of Vassily's affection, the looming necessity of exile, and – above all – the disquieting knowledge that a murderer lay close by, so close that she might have walked past him that very day, that very *hour*, and been none the wiser.

It would have been easy to scuttle for cover, but that was not Olga's way. No: she would take the other path, the path that led upwards to discovery and danger, spurning the easy lies of the lazy and the half-hearted.

She reached the top of the stairs, her footsteps unnaturally loud in the unusual silence. Normally Café Astana was filled with booming voices and clinking shot-glasses until Odrosov turfed out the last regular with his brush at one or two – and even then there was still the TV blaring away until Odrosov went to bed an hour or so later. The TV was still on, but now there was nobody to watch – or was there?

Olga shook her head to dismiss the thought, but if it was nonsense, what was that sound that came to her ears? A faint rustle, or was it the silvery ring of fabric brushing past an empty vessel?

No: it was nothing, she decided, after a long moment spent standing still, and shrinking into the dark doorframe of Nevena's room. It wasn't the stealthy whisper of a killer drawing near: the bell over the door hadn't tinkled, after all. No. It was just the wind whistling through the cracks in Odrosov's Soviet-era façade, or a stray dog helping itself to some of Popov's cast-off horsemeat. It was nothing, she told herself, but she'd leave with nothing, too, if she didn't hurry up – free food would only keep the regulars away from Café Astana for so long, and once the first few shots of Pasha's vodka had gone down the hatch they'd soon realise that the old church hall was draughty, and ill-lit, and unheated, and lacking in modern audiovisual equipment designed to funnel ice hockey and soaps to their eyes at all times of day and night. And as soon as that thought had sunk into their Rocket Fuel-pickled brains, back they would come to Café Astana, and all could be lost.

She moved more quickly now, delving first into the room shared by Pastor Loktev and Ludis Kuskov, then proceeding to the slightly larger, though no more luxurious, double occupied by the Aristovs. The well-wishers were in her thoughts, as she dug through their belongings, dancing before her mind's eye as if they were there beside her: the cleric who seemed more like a sly drunkard and the bluff, dark-hued Ludis; and then Taisia Aristov, her *babushka*'s headscarf covering undoubted complexities, and her husband Gennady, whose vivid moods seemed equally hard to read. Olga found nothing on Gennady – nothing at all – but she couldn't say the same for his wife Taisia, or the two men who shared the twin.

The things she uncovered there made her heart race – something to go on at last, in this most opaque of cases – but despite her elation she found herself cursing Odrosov as she went, damning him to hell for the unholy racket his floorboards made underfoot. Things had already been bad when she'd stayed there earlier that year in a time of straitened circumstances, together with Pasha, Anna and the boys, but they'd clearly got much worse even since then. Olga was almost inclined to take the noise personally: the physical demands of her job kept her trim and, by any reasonable standards, she was hardly overweight at all, but anyone listening to her movements from below would suspect a baby elephant was trundling around the limited confines of Café Astana's first-floor guestrooms. Some of the creaks were so loud, she thought, that they could well disguise sounds from below – sounds like the bell over the front door . . .

She was distracting herself from this unsettling possibility by imagining how Vassily and Nevena might react when she announced the murderer to the whole village, when a different kind of sound reached her ears. It wasn't the tinkling of Odrosov's bell, but the sound of a foot treading on a floorboard in a Café Astana guestroom on the first floor. And there were only three guestrooms, *and only two storeys* . . .

Olga was seized by a cold-hearted fear that froze her to the spot, like one of Popov's discarded, prematurely icicled carcasses. The murderer . . . The murderer was still in Roslazny! In the excitement of arranging the afternoon's festivities, she'd almost forgotten the mortal danger that hung over them all, like a lowering sky. Might she now pay for this levity – for this literally criminal levity – with her life?

Could the killer himself be next door, in Nevena's room? Olga hadn't yet poked her head in there, and had hardly thought to – but didn't that just mean that somebody could have been there all along, as yet undiscovered but standing, breathing, looking, listening, *waiting* . . . Just as someone had stood breathing, looking and listening before Danyl Petrovich's train came, waiting for it to topple over on unsupported rails.

She held her breath, standing behind the Aristovs' open door and peering out of the crack into the dimly lit vestibule. Was that a shape coming out of the twin room shared by Loktev and Ludis Kuskov? Was that a group of shadows taking human form, a spidery mass of limbs knitting themselves into the shape of a man who crept out of the darkness, weapon in hand and evil in mind?

The shape moved into a narrow bar of reflected light from downstairs, and Olga could now see it clearly: a man who moved with slow, skin-crawling steps, inching towards her position and miraculously avoiding – she noticed – the worst of the floorboards as if by second sight.

Olga didn't hesitate, but in one fluid movement kicked the door away from her, grabbed a dimly seen implement, and dashed towards the intruder with a scream issuing from her furious, wide-open lips.

'Olga!' cried the intruder, ducking and holding up a hand. 'Olga Pushkin! It's me!'

'Igor?' cried Olga, withholding her intended blow with great difficulty, and realising in the same moment that the fearsome weapon she'd seized in the dark was in fact a knitted soft toy of a Chutotka Siberian moose, one of a collection that Igor kept, for obscure reasons, on a rickety chair on the landing.

'Who else?' said Odrosov, rather testily. 'This is my establishment, you know! What the hell are you playing at, jumping out at me like that? The children are playing downstairs, if you want to join in, Pushkin. And what are you doing up here, anyway? You know it's off-limits to regulars when there's paying guests in.'

'I don't know how you can charge people for rooms like that,' began Olga, hoping to deflect his attention from her unauthorised presence upstairs. 'And as for your floorboards—'

At that moment, an unseen hand thrust Olga into Igor with such force that they measured their length on the protesting floor together, while a third, hitherto unsuspected, person pushed past them and ran down the stairs, taking them two and three at a time.

'Who the hell was that?' roared Odrosov, leaning up on his elbows. Rather than staying to speculate, Olga got up and gave chase downstairs – but though she ran until her heart raced she saw only the door closing with a tinkle of the bell.

She drew it aside with force and stepped out into the snowy evening, staring each way with fierce, wide-eyed abandon – but there were only empty doorways and snow-clad eaves to greet her and, on the ground, the countless footsteps caused by her Mishka party at the church hall.

The thought drove her eyes back to the hall, and there, standing and staring at her from the gate at the entrance, was Vassily Marushkin, standing next to Nevena Komarov. Was it her imagination, acting at a distance, or was Vassily's face distorted with strong emotion – with distaste, and indeed with fear, that he then disguised as soon as he saw her with a grimace of a smile? But then he turned and walked back into the hall with Nevena, and Olga was left alone – or as alone, at any rate, as anyone could be at the door of Café Astana when the villagers had begun to get cold, returning first in their ones and twos, and then in larger groups, until Odrosov's takings at last began to show signs of recovery.

But Olga stayed outside, staring up at the leaden skies for a moment, then walking home with strong, energetic steps. For she knew some things that she was sure Vassily did *not* know – pieces of knowledge that compensated, somehow, for all his disdain and unexpected cruelty – knowledge that could even overcome it, by showing him she could beat Nevena Komarov at her own game, proving a track engineer superior to an HR rep after all.

But knowledge alone was insufficient: to win Vassily back she needed proof, and for that she needed to do a little more work. She must go just a few more steps down the road that led towards the horizon, the horizon that receded even as she travelled towards it. But soon, surely, she would reach it, and then all would be well. Soon, soon . . . Surely it would be soon. Wouldn't it?

8

The Ghost of Danyl Petrovich

'You know who the *murderer* is?' cried Anna, later that day. 'And – and was it them who burned the bodies, in Nikolai's freezer?'

'*Ssh*,' said Olga, glancing towards the window, a black canvas now that night had fallen, with an uneven line of fresh-fallen snow across the bottom. 'You never know who could be listening!'

'Olgakin,' said Pasha, the 'kin' falling away dismissively like the wave of an unbelieving hand, 'Fyodor's the only visitor we've had for days, apart from Nevena Komarov – so who else d'you think's out there, hiding behind the drainpipe and freezing their *yaichki* off in the snow?'

'*Pasha*,' said Anna, casting him a furious glance and indicating Boris, her eight-year-old, who was playing by their feet. She didn't say any more, but shook her head sternly in a warning to Pasha to keep his anatomical descriptions to himself from now on.

'Well, frozen whatsits or not, you just never know,' said Olga. 'And best to stay on the safe side of the tracks, till we get the killer safely locked away in prison.'

'Uncle Fyodor says we're all in prison already,' said Boris, looking up at them from his floor-bound toys with wide, earnest eyes. 'Because of capitism, and the president, says Uncle Fyodor. Because of capitism and the president and the – and the BSF.'

'*Capitalism*, and the FSB,' corrected Anna. 'And it's past your bedtime, Boris,' she went on, but distractedly, still staring at Olga and trying to make sense of her startling claim to have got on the trail at last. 'But, Olga, do you really think you know who derailed the train – and just by looking around Café Astana?'

'That's not quite what I said, Anna,' replied Olga. 'And I don't yet know who burned the freezer. All I said was that I found some things that – well, things that you'd only hide if they were somewhat incriminating.'

'But whose things are you talking about?' said Anna.

'I bet it was that Gennady Aristov,' cut in Pasha. 'You remember he tried to attack you by the wreck – twice?'

That's true, thought Olga. How had I forgotten that? Gennady Aristov *had* tried to attack her when Danyl's train had come off the tracks, only to be restrained first by Pasha's muscular presence, and then by Vassily's return. So he had a temper . . . Could it have been Gennady who'd pushed past her in Café Astana earlier that day?

But she asked herself the question only to dismiss it. The figure had moved quickly, lithely, youthfully. It hadn't felt like a lumbering old man who had pushed past her and Igor Odrosov and rushed down the stairs ahead of them. Or was she just telling herself the interloper was athletic because she was angry that she'd let him slip away into the falling night?

Either way, she'd decided not to mention the mysterious figure to Anna, Pasha and company, swearing Odrosov to secrecy in exchange for a promise of a substantial investment in his next delivery of smoked bear-meat. The last thing Olga needed was yet more fussing and worrying from Anna Kabalevsky, let alone her brother.

But Pasha was still talking.

'That's just what a killer would do, to cover his tracks,' he was saying, nodding sagely. 'Try to attack you, I mean. Because who'd suspect someone like Gennady Aristov, especially after he'd had a go at you? A tubby old man with a comb-over, seemingly overcome with grief, and lashing out at the nearest target from rage or stupidity or both . . . A murderer would never do that: it would look too suspicious. So if he really was the murderer, well, it would take some acting, wouldn't it, to pull that off – but isn't that just what murderers are? Actors? They can hardly go round with *Ubiytsa* tattooed on their foreheads, can they?'

'*Pasha*,' hissed Anna for a second time, nodding down at Boris – who was, however, still playing unconcernedly with his large-scale model of a Lun-class ekranoplan. 'You'll give him nightmares!'

'*Yerunda!*' said Pasha, sitting back and crossing his legs at the ankle. 'He's heard worse than that, haven't you, Boris? You remember Auntie Olga's exploits earlier this year? Well, then,' he said to Anna. 'An old man like Gennady Aristov's nothing compared to the monsters Olga snared.'

'Well, actually, Pasha,' said Olga, 'Gennady Aristov's the only one I've counted out, despite his anger by the tracks. I found nothing on him – nothing at all. His belongings were as immaculately boring as any sewage salesman, or whatever he is, could hope for.'

'He's a retired aggregate vendor,' announced Anna. 'I heard him telling someone at the church hall – Alexeyev, I think, or was it Popov? You know, Olga,' she went on, her brow lowering in a troubled frown, 'I hope we did the right thing, wasting all those supplies on a – on a party, when we're all stuck in the village for who knows how long.'

'Well, *I* enjoyed it, and so did everyone else,' said Pasha, pulling out his cigarettes and lighting one. 'What's more, it gave Olga the time she needed to prove that I'm right about Gennady.'

'What? I just told you I found nothing on him!'

'Precisely,' cried Pasha in triumph, sitting forward and almost stepping on Boris's monstrous seaplane in his excitement. 'That confirms it,' he went on. 'What was it you said – a person's bag reveals their heart?'

'It's what they say,' nodded Olga, blithely.

'Well, what could be more suspicious than to have spotless belongings, with nothing strange, or untidy, or questionable at all in any way?'

Olga frowned. 'I think you had too much free vodka at the church hall, Pasha,' she said. 'By your logic, we should suspect anyone with tidy baggage of being a murderer and a burner of bodies.'

'Well,' said Pasha, shrugging as if conceding a minor point, and sitting back once more against the amalgam of mismatched throws, second-hand cushions and discarded scarves that covered Olga's threadbare settee. 'Well . . . all right, but what about the others, then? You said you'd counted Gennady out. What about his wife, Taisia Aristov? Or Danyl's nephew? Not to mention that priest, or vicar, or whatever.'

'He's a pastor,' said Anna, shaking her head. 'Pastor Loktev. Did you know that anyone can call themselves a pastor – any

Tomas, Dik or Garri off the street? Not like our own holy fathers, in the old rite – and it's not the same, whatever any of these modern churches say.'

'Maybe not,' said Olga, 'but the things I found on Loktev were nothing to do with any of that. Nothing to do with religion at all, in fact. I can't quite make him out. But he's got strange papers in his briefcase, that's for sure – printouts of websites selling cheap liquor, and thick rope, and opiates from China, and – and *ammunition* for pistols. Now, why would a pastor, or even a priest,' she added, with a nod to Anna, 'have that kind of thing in their bag?'

'And then there's Ludis Kuskov,' she went on, before Anna could respond. 'Ludis Kuskov, nephew to Danyl Petrovich, and proud owner of a rucksack stuffed with unpaid bills! That's a man who needs money, and fast – and what better way to get a little windfall than to make sure a favoured uncle falls first? No wonder he was relieved at the scene of the crash. And I wouldn't put much past him, either,' she went on, bringing his glowering, forbidding presence to mind – dark-haired like Vassily, but lacking his genial kindness.

'And finally,' said Olga, 'there's Taisia Aristov, in whose suitcase I found a photo of Danyl Petrovich . . . Danyl was sitting behind the wheel of a car, laughing and smoking, and holding something I couldn't quite make out – I had to get out of there before Odrosov discovered me.'

'So you found a photo of Danyl. So what?' said Pasha, somewhat rudely. 'They were neighbours, weren't they? Why shouldn't she have a photo of him?'

'It wasn't the photo itself so much as where I found it,' said Olga. 'It was hidden in the bottom of her case, underneath the fabric – so it was something she didn't want Gennady coming across. And think back to the crash – remember how upset she was! I think she might've been having an affair with Danyl, but maybe he broke it off, and this was her revenge . . . If she couldn't have him, nobody could.'

Silence fell upon the living room, broken only by the faint crackling of the apple-wood fire and Boris's high-pitched imitation of eight giant turbofans in flight over the Caspian Sea.

'Will you tell Vassily about all this, Olga?' said Anna, after a moment.

Olga snorted, a single, bitter noise devoid of mirth. '*Nyet*,' she said decisively. 'How could I? He thinks I did it!'

She told them how she'd seen Vassily Marushkin staring at her with distaste and fear as she emerged from Café Astana, a look that could mean only one thing: a deep and growing suspicion in Vassily's mind that Olga had been involved in the derailment.

'I'm the track engineer responsible for that bit of track, after all! Polina Klemovsky had only just arrived when the train went down – and she didn't waste any time casting suspicion on me, either.'

'But why would Vassily think you wanted to kill Danyl – or Anoushka?' said Anna.

'And what's more,' said Pasha, 'why would he have thrown you out of the investigation, if he suspected you? Surely he'd keep you involved, so he could keep an eye on you.'

Olga shrugged. 'I don't know,' she admitted. 'Maybe he's concerned about keeping Nevena safe – protecting her from me, or something.'

'I can't believe that Vassily would ever think you could be

involved in something – something *nasty*,' said Anna. 'Not our Vassily!'

'He's not our Vassily any more, though, is he?' said Olga, trying – and failing – to keep the sadness out of her voice. 'He's Nevena Komarov's, now.'

Anna shook her head, but didn't voice any denial, reasoned or otherwise – a telling silence, thought Olga.

Pasha, looking between them, broke in with a somewhat forced jollity.

'So what's the plan from here?' he asked. 'Another diversion, I suppose? Only now we've used up all the Mishka beers and pickled venison.'

Somewhat to his surprise, Olga nodded at him, quite earnestly. '*Da*, Pasha, *da*! By solving our first problem we've created another. But I've thought of a way around that – a plan to get me face to face with our suspects at last. There's three people – at least three people – who need to answer a few questions.'

'But, Olga,' began Anna, her face twisted with anxiety, 'don't forget that one of them's probably a murderer! It's far too dangerous for you to go around talking to them – *cornering* them! Think of us, think of the children – think of Dmitri!'

Olga laughed, despite the serious look on Anna's face. 'Don't worry about Dmitri, Anna! He's quite cosy and safe in his new lodgings – aren't you, Dmitri-Dima-*detka*?' she crooned, calling across the room to Dmitri's cardboard kingdom – a call that went unanswered, however, by any hedgehoggian snuffling. 'You see? Sleeping soundly. He's a clever little white-breast, aren't you, *detka*? He remembers what happened in February – how I faced great danger, and yet survived. He knows his *mamochka* will always come back to him, even if she were sent to Ulaanbaatar for a thousand years.'

But Anna looked at her doubtfully. 'Well, I'm just glad Pasha will be going with you – won't you, Pasha? Yes, of course you will, and Fyodor Katin, too, if he can be found – safety in numbers, you know.'

'I'm sure you'd be delighted to track Fyodor down, Anna,' said Olga.

'Nonsense!' she said, but her tired, red-rimmed eyes twinkled with the faint, yet tangible, beginnings of inner joy.

Like all the best plans, Olga's strategy for Saturday morning was clear, simple and straightforward – and it might well have succeeded were it not for the machinations of Anna's children, and Boris in particular.

Olga's plan – like Roslazny itself – centred upon Café Astana. First, she and Pasha would casually approach Odrosov's establishment, as if they were merely out for a lockdown stroll and fancied a tot or two of blue-tinged Rocket Fuel to help cut through their over-indulgence of the day before. But Olga would first wipe the snow from the windows and check that neither Vassily nor his newly acquired shadow, Nevena Komarov, were inside. If they were, Olga and her brother would continue on their way as if they'd changed their minds, before circling back later. But if Vassily and Nevena were busy investigating elsewhere, Olga would give Pasha his orders to stand outside, in a suitably sheltered location, while Olga delved within. Then Pasha could see if Vassily or Nevena came along, upon which he could rush inside and warn Olga that her interviews with Ludis, Loktev and Taisia should come to a precipitate end. (The last thing Olga wanted was an embarrassing incident in front of Nevena Komarov and the collected regulars of Café Astana.)

Yes, the plan was ready – but then Boris, Anna's eldest, was sick in the middle of Friday night, the delayed result of too much Slavyanka cake at the church-hall lockdown party – a different kind of hangover from that brought on by Odrosov's Rocket Fuel, but no less unpleasant for those who had to deal with it.

Boris was still unwell in the morning, and as Gyorgy was also looking decidedly green around the gills Anna pleaded with Pasha to stay, and with Olga not to go alone – but Olga obtained her freedom by promising to go straight to Café Astana and nowhere else, and to come straight back again.

'It was like a teenager pleading with her mother to go to a party, Mamochka,' said Olga when she finally escaped the house, speaking to the fresh Siberian air as if the dancing snow-flakes it contained were something more than mere crystalline parcels of frozen water. 'It was like – it was as if you'd been there with us yourself, and I was a teenager, and had to persuade you I was going somewhere where no danger lurked.'

Tatiana Pushkin had not, of course, been there when Olga had entered her teenage years. She had passed away when Olga was only eight – dying in part, Olga was sure, of a heart broken by the relentless grind of Roslazny life in the days of the *sovkhoz* – so Olga's ascent to womanhood had taken place without a motherly hand to guide her. There had only been her aunt Zia, sister to her father Mikhail – and while Zia, in those days, had at times been capable of a kind of rough tenderness, any lingering humanity in her system had long since evaporated, scorched away by her grief over the death of her well-loved husband Ippolit, and by the need to survive in the difficult times that followed.

Aunt Zia had opened her doors to Olga when Mikhail had thrown her and Pasha out earlier that year, but reluctantly, and only in exchange for a preposterous amount of roubles, paid in cash on the round table by the foot of the stairs – a table that Zia swore had come from the house of Yakov Yurovsky, the Tomsk-born executioner of Tsar Nicholas the Second. (Zia made no secret of her love for the Bolsheviks, though thanks to Ippolit and the Kuznetsov fortune she owned by far the grandest house in Roslazny.) But after that – well, what happened after that had not showed Zia in a flattering light, ending with yet another change in address for Olga and her brother.

How could Zia have done that? Olga asked herself once again. How could her own flesh and blood have kicked her out into the snow? Admittedly, Zia was a Pushkin rather than a Lichnovsky, but still. And when Olga thought of what Zia had said about Pasha behind his back . . .

Olga was working herself up into an enjoyable mood of righteous indignation, with correspondingly quickened foot-steps that brought her rapidly to the gap-toothed wall that ran around the churchyard, when a shrill voice of protest brought her to a sudden halt. She looked up and, to her astonishment, saw that she had almost walked into Aunt Zia – as if Olga's inner murmurings had conjured her up, like Chernomor himself! (On reflection, though, Olga was unsure whether the great sorcerer from *Ruslan and Ludmila* would trouble to summon a spectre like Zia, with her poker nose, sour expression, and a bright red coat that jarred with both.)

Like Olga, Zia had been trudging along lost in thought, or she would have tried to avoid Olga, just as she had ever since Olga and Pasha had moved out earlier that year. That kind of avoidance was possible in normal circumstances: you could always cross the road or turn and go back, as if you had forgotten something. But it was harder to maintain that pretence when you were following a narrow path through the snow in lockdown conditions, any more than the Trans-Siberian, following a network snowplough, could circle back upon itself – so Olga's Aunt Zia Kuznetsov was obliged to look her in the eye as they passed.

'Aunt,' said Olga, nodding primly and edging past the churchyard wall.

'Olga,' grunted Aunt Zia, nodding in just the same way, and doing her best to shuffle past Olga without touching her estranged niece. But then she stopped, waited for her laboured breathing to return to normal, and spoke.

'I've just come from the café,' she said. 'That Vassily Marushkin was there with his son.' Her face distorted itself with an unpleasant smile. 'And with someone else, too. I suppose you wish you were there instead of her, working by his side – take your mind off your trip abroad, *da*? But it isn't you. It's his new bit of skirt.'

Zia meant Nevena Komarov, of course, and had referred to her like that to exacerbate Olga's jealousy – had halted her onward progress, indeed, to make sure she drove home the hurtful barb as effectively as possible.

'Asking questions, taking statements, pushing their noses in where they aren't welcome,' went on Zia, shifting into the whining register so familiar to Olga's ears from previous years. She had temporarily forgotten, Olga thought, that she'd stopped to make Olga jealous. Olga might be persona non grata, but she was still a person Zia could complain to – and complaining was one thing that certainly got easier with age.

'That Vassily,' Zia continued, 'hanging around those poor friends of the Petroviches and digging up what's gone, dead and buried . . . The train fell off the tracks, *nyet*? What else is there to say? What's the point of annoying that young one – Ludis, is it? – and asking all about the problems with his son? I told Vassily he was only annoying him, and making him upset – what's the use of that, when he can't get home to look after his little one? Yes, I told Vassily he was wasting his own time and that woman's, too – his new piece. I left him there just now, still at it. A waste of taxpayer roubles – that's what it is.'

Olga had certain knowledge that Zia's husband Ippolit had specialised in tax avoidance in the days of the *sozhkhov*, so she ignored Zia's faux-outrage about Vassily's supposed inefficiency and focused instead on the crumbs of information Zia had let fall by chance – something about problems with Ludis's son. Was that why Ludis had had so many unpaid bills? Perhaps his son was sick – or was he paying child support to a demanding mother? Most people would do anything for their flesh and blood. Not her father Mikhail, of course, or her aunt Zia, but most people. Had Ludis been pushed to extremes by worry about his little boy?

Olga opened her lips to question her aunt further, but Zia had clearly had enough of chit-chat in the withering cold of an early Siberian winter – and chit-chat, Zia suddenly remembered, that was being conducted with a forbidden niece.

'I shouldn't have been talking to you,' she said again, echoing the wind with her shrill, plaintive tones. She pulled her coat tighter around her and set off in the direction of her faded lime-green palace at the centre of the village. But then she stopped and waved a crooked finger at Olga. 'You tricked me! You tricked me into talking to you. Your father's right: you *are* wicked. Rotten as any winter apple – and sad as a dried-up rose in spring. It'll be good riddance when you go off to China or – or wherever it is. Don't expect the snow to save you! It only turns into sludge – and sludge always melts!'

Zia turned once more and shuffled homewards, Olga watching as the red-clad figure receded into the swirling white pointillism that flooded upon them from every side, leaving her in a silence broken only by the soft susurration of numberless flakes of ice, individually minuscule yet collectively potent, like a line of ants in the jungle – and biting just as viciously on the skin.

Snow doesn't save, she thought. *It only turns into sludge.* That sounded like something she could turn into a proverb for inclusion in her next book, *Take the Next Steppe: 101 Life Lessons from Ulaanbaatar.* But the chuckle she produced was forced and hollow, and it came and went without troubling her eyes.

To hell with Aunt Zia, she thought, as she reached the tracks. Hadn't Olga suffered enough from her vicious words already that year, without the universe conspiring to give the old woman yet another opportunity to stick the knife in?

She knew what Anna would say: the Lord has sent your aunt to you as a trial, and you have to rise above her mean-spiritedness and cleave to a higher mode of being – or rather Being. But Olga lacked Anna's otherworldly assurance, and in its absence she sought other, earthier, modes of consolation. There was no point in going to Café Astana if Vassily and Nevena were there – she couldn't get any questioning done with them looking over her shoulder and, besides, she had no desire to see Kemerovo province's latest detective duo in action. What was it Nevena had said, when she'd come to see her the other day? *Vassily's always near* . . . Of course he would be, with someone like Nevena to stare at.

Men . . . She'd hoped that Vassily would be different; she'd apparently hoped in vain.

No Café Astana, so instead she took herself to the place where, for the past fifteen years of her life, other troubles had seemed quieter, smaller, easier to manage – the place where she'd found Dmitri, and the place where she'd written almost all of her first book, *Find Your Rail Self: 100 Life Lessons from the Trans-Siberian Railway*. She took herself, that is, to the tracks, the snowbound silver streaks that pushed round Roslazny's north-eastern shoulder like the hem of an enveloping curtain.

She couldn't go into her hut, of course – her little haven had been off limits since Polina Klemovsky had arrived on Tuesday. (Tuesday! It seemed like months ago, thought Olga.) She peered around the trees that marked the end of the path from the village and, with a pang of longing, saw the familiar faded walls of her hut and, above, ascending wisps of smoke that betokened the dread presence within. Beyond the hut lay the wreckage of Danyl's train, dimly visible through the gently blizzarding snow, and softened now by an ever-thickening blanket of purest white, making the shattered engine and twisted wagons look no different from the other discarded vehicles that littered the outskirts of Roslazny.

Shaking her head inside her fur-lined hood, Olga dismissed thoughts of Polina's wooden clogs resting on her beloved bookshelf, and turned in the other direction, heading away from the hut in the direction of Tayga, and thinking that Aunt Zia's words were harder to dismiss than Polina Klemovsky's. She'd found this before: her words were barbed, carefully designed to stick in the mind, like a hook in the mouth of a fish, and just as hard to dislodge.

I bet you wish you were there instead . . . Take your mind off your trip . . .

Was that why Olga was throwing herself into the investigation, she asked herself – not out of some burning desire for justice, or even the urge to show Vassily he'd picked the wrong partner, but a simple, childish wish to stick her head in the snow and pretend she wouldn't have to go away after all? Was she trying to ignore the unpleasant fact that finding the killer would make no difference whatsoever to the machinations of Boris Andreyev and the slow, relentless, and utterly indifferent grinding of the Russian Railways machinery?

Maybe there was something in that, she admitted to herself as she pushed on through the heavy snowdrifts. And as she'd hardly thought about Mongolia for the past few days, perhaps it was working . . . Her mind had been completely taken up with a multitude of conflicting clues: the discarded hoe, the burning of the bodies, the photograph of Zlata M, and the well-wishers' belongings – not to mention the untraced scent of paint in her bedroom, and the haunting conviction that someone, sometime, had said something unsettling and strange . . .

Deep in thoughts of murder, it took Olga a few moments to realise she wasn't also knee-deep in snow. Coming back to the present, she found she was stepping in footprints rather than forcing her way through drifts. Had someone just been that way, ahead of her? And the air – could she detect a tang of smoke hiding between the snowflakes? But the hut, and Olga's poor stove, was far behind . . .

Olga caught her breath. There, hovering by that dark column of a larch trunk – wasn't that the shape of a person? A woman, in fact – short, partly hidden from sight, and blurred by the shimmering iridescence of dancing whiteness, but a woman nonetheless, hunched into the sheltering crook of the tree with a headscarf pulled tightly around her. A hand darted out and back again, leaving a thin grey signature in the air, and the source of the smoky scent was revealed. But what woman would have troubled to walk so far for the sake of a private cigarette, in the midst of a record-breaking, season-disrupting lockdown?

Olga stole forward, hardly daring to breathe, and utterly declining to broach with herself the precise reasons for drawing near to the unknown woman – or, worse still, the much more numerous reasons for *not* drawing near: the killer could, after all, be a woman, not a man. But what would happen if nobody ever took a risk? she said to herself, as convincingly as possible. What would happen if everyone turned back when they saw something suspicious on the fringe of a village paralysed by ice and shot through with murder?

The reward for her courage came quickly: the woman's cigarette was soon discarded in a fleeting snow-top sizzle, replaced by a flash of silver, or rather two: a pair of scissors that

Olga glimpsed between the boughs, and that the woman now raised to her headscarf. What on earth could she intend?

Olga's curiosity overcame her caution at last, and she flung herself forward through the snow and overhanging branches to see Taisia Aristov's face gazing up at her, gooseberry eyes wide with shock, and scissors in mid-air between hair and ground.

Olga stared at the wisps of hair at her feet, and then at the hacked-off ends on Taisia's head. Despite the intervening snow-filled air she caught wind of another distinctive scent – the acrid, skin-crawling scent of burned human hair – and at last she understood.

'The freezer,' she cried, stepping back in fear and dismay. 'The fire at the freezer – it was you!'

It *had* been her, Taisia frankly admitted. She could hardly do anything else, with Olga standing over her and staring at the scorched remnants of greying hair below her right temple, where – she said – an errant tongue of flame had caught her as she lit the petrol with her lighter. She looked a most unlikely arsonist, thought Olga. She looked, in fact, much more like Olga's image of an eccentric writer or grumpy librarian. But it was what Taisia said next that really surprised Olga.

'Yes, I did it,' she said. 'But you've got to understand that it – oh, it was for Danyl's sake! Yes, for his own dear sake – for his memory. You see, he drank. He drank so much . . . *too* much. More than even a Russian should! And I couldn't let Russian Railways find that out . . . They always find that kind of thing out, don't they, when there's been a crash?

'I found out when I popped over to borrow some sugar one night,' she went on, 'and found him lying on the sofa, an empty bottle beside him. Anoushka was upstairs asleep: that was how much she cared! So I stayed and put a blanket over him, and sat with him, and talked to him till he went to sleep. It was no burden, really. I mean, alcoholic or no, he was a fine man. Not that I had designs on him myself – *romantic* designs, I mean. He had a ponytail, for one thing, and you can never really trust a man with a ponytail.'

In the midst of her hurried reflections on Taisia's words, Olga allowed herself a brief, private smile, thinking that here was another woman who – like Nevena Komarov – could not abide a ponytail. But, really, there was no time for joking. Olga had to decide if Taisia's apparent selflessness could be trusted – that was the bottom line.

What was it Pasha had argued? Murderers had to be good actors? Olga thought back to the scene by the tracks when Danyl's train had derailed. What had Taisia said then? That Anoushka was a good and strong-hearted woman? Something like that. Yet now she was saying that Anoushka hadn't cared for her husband. Olga knew that killers often caught themselves out by contradicting themselves. But how could this particular paradox be explained?

Perhaps, thought Olga with quickening heartbeat, Taisia had expressed such emotion by the track because she was really talking about *Danyl*, not Anoushka – in which case Olga's hypothesis about his photo could be right after all. Taisia could have kept the photo because she was in love with Danyl – a love as secret as her suitcase picture. And perhaps Danyl had abandoned her, bringing their affair to an end and prompting

Taisia to wreak her horrific revenge by toppling his train to the tracks, then burning his body afterwards to wrap things up in a tidy package of evil-doing.

But it soon became impossible for Olga to maintain any such interesting theories. In the end, Taisia wore her down with an account of Danyl's professional life that was so extended, and so punishingly detailed, that Olga soon found herself shifting from suspicion to boredom. Standing there in the icy wind, she wished Taisia would stop telling her about Danyl's efficiency, his concern for the safety of others, his commitment to the job – and all this despite his ongoing alcoholism.

'If it had been different, I'd have told someone, wouldn't I?' she said, staring up at Olga with her round eyes. 'But, then, well, Danyl had been drinking quite a bit more, recently,' she went on. 'You've seen his picture – the one in that local paper – when he saved that child from the burning house? They framed it in the local café. Well, he looks so strong, so *sturdy*, in that picture, but he was nothing like that – not really. I've got a picture of him that shows a different view . . .'

'Ye-es?' said Olga, her whole attention – her whole being – focused on Taisia's eyes, as if by concentrating on them she could prevent herself from betraying that she already knew of the photograph in question.

'Oh, I had to swipe it from a packet of photos before Anoushka saw it!' said Taisia. 'Someone had taken a snap of him with a bottle in his hand – sitting behind the wheel of a car! Can you imagine what'd happen if the press or Russian Railways got hold of that? *Da*, I had to take it, for his own safety. But he noticed it missing, later, and got so cross with Anoushka – said it was typical of her to lose things. He was a difficult man, in his own way – a whole *matryoshka* doll, with layer after layer you could peel off, and never find the man inside.'

I could say the same about you, Taisia Aristov, thought Olga. Here I was, thinking you were having an affair with Danyl, but all along you were just his friend – and a good friend into the bargain. You hadn't hidden Danyl's photo as a romantic aide-memoire, but to protect him from Russian Railways! And you hadn't burned the bodies in some strange act of posthumous revenge upon Anoushka, but again to protect Danyl – to keep his reputation safe after his untimely death.

Olga drew in her breath with the air of a woman gathering her strength for a final assault. The time she had spent with Vassily over the past several months had taught her never to give up until the end, that even the end might not yet be the real, final, irrevocable end, and to keep on until you were really sure it was, beyond any possible doubt. Taisia Aristov might not have been Danyl's secret lover – and therefore she was also unlikely, in the absence of other motives, to have been his secret murderer – but she might still know something that could help uncover the real killer. And so it proved – by a long and winding road.

'So he was a *matryoshka* doll, and you had to peel off the layers – but what might you find on the way?' Olga spoke as casually as she could – probing for something, anything, that Danyl might have done to provoke his death, in case Taisia, having admitted to burning the freezers, might shed some light upon the derailment. But once again Taisia's next words were far from what Olga had expected.

'Well, there was his ghost, to start with,' she said. 'But there were other things too – like the way he always went on about the sins of his youth.'

'Hang on a minute,' said Olga. 'His ghost? What do you mean?'

'What I said,' said Taisia, shrugging. 'There was a ghost.'

'You mean he actually *saw* a ghost?'

'Oh, yes, all the time,' said Taisia, with the wide-eyed certainty of the true believer. 'He thought I didn't know about it, but he told me about it himself, that night when I went over to borrow sugar. Gennady was away for the week, at a gravel conference in Chelyabinsk, so I was in no hurry – just as well, as Danyl had lots to say. He'd seen this woman, you see, ever since March – a woman standing watching him from the side of the tracks as he went by in his train, at places all over the network, all over the country. And there was something about her clothes – he wouldn't say what exactly, but it troubled him, that's for sure. And then he fell asleep, so I couldn't dig any more. I made a point of dropping round to see him the day after, but he couldn't even remember me being there. He couldn't remember anything but the brand of vodka he'd been drinking. But there was something in his eyes – something you wouldn't expect to see in the eyes of a man like that, the most experienced driver on Russian Railways. Something like – like *fear*.

'Yes, yes – fear. And that was why he went to church so much, towards the end. But that Pastor Loktev! I don't trust him much – never have, though the whole of Yashkino seems to think he's the Good Lord come again. Anoushka Petrovich didn't like him either, I'm pretty certain, though she hadn't enough sense to break things off with the church.

'But *he* did. Danyl trusted Pastor Loktev, hung on his every word, as if Loktev himself could guarantee divine forgiveness for all his mistakes in the past. It's his own sins Loktev needs to look towards, if I'm any judge! Anyway, no pastor could cure fear like Danyl's. Only – only death could do that.'

She stopped talking then – almost a relief to Olga's ears, after the unexpected torrent of words – and looked down at her pale, stubby fingers still wrapped around the scissors she'd been using to trim her flame-crisped hair. She shivered, as if suddenly remembering how cold it was, and how long she'd been standing without her gloves or headscarf on.

'I'll hold those,' said Olga, holding out her hands for the scissors. Taisia smiled gratefully and began to wrap her head-scarf around her once more – but then her eyes fixed on a spot behind Olga, back up the track towards Olga's hut.

'What's that?' whispered Taisia, grasping Olga's arm in fear.

'What's what?' replied Olga, twisting out of Taisia's grasp to follow her gaze, then narrowing her eyes as she picked out a dark, moving shape amid the funnelling snowflakes.

'*It's the ghost*,' said Taisia, urgently. 'The ghost that Danyl Petrovich used to see. It's come back to haunt us – or, no, it's come back to haunt his train!'

'Nonsense,' said Olga. 'You said the ghost was a woman, *nyet*? Well, that looks like a man, and a live one, too – but where's he going? He won't get far that way. There's only brambles and bushes and the old rails they replaced four years back, plus a few hundred tons of snow.'

'*Da, da* – but wait! Who's that behind him?'

Olga stared through the cascading snow, making out a first and then a second shadowy shape running – or rather wading – in the first man's wake.

'That's – that's Vassily and Nevena,' she said, a sinking feeling that spread rapidly downwards from her chest. It was ridiculous to be jealous at the sight of Vassily and Nevena together, she told herself. But her self didn't reply – it didn't have a chance. Taisia broke through Olga's introspection with two simple words that roused her from her reverie: *The killer.*

Of course – of course! Why else would Vassily and Nevena be chasing somebody through the snowstorm? While Olga had been wasting her time talking to Taisia, Roslazny's sergeant of police must have discovered some deadly secret at Café Astana or elsewhere, prompting the killer to take to his heels. And now it was time for Olga to do the same, running back towards the path that led to the village, and then turning right towards the place where the figure had disappeared into the forest that spread across Siberia like a vast green-white carpet. She just had time to see the hut door opening and Polina's unpleasant, toad-like visage appearing, before she turned and dived into the forest, following the footsteps and pushed-aside foliage until she came upon Nevena and Vassily and, ahead of them, a man's figure unmoving on the snowy ground, his head hard against a discarded breeze-block.

'Ludis,' she cried, between heaving breaths, as Nevena and Vassily turned to look at her in astonishment. 'Ludis Kuskov, trying to escape! Who else but a killer would attempt such madness? So it was him! So it was him, after all.'

9

Ms Direction

'Amazing how heavy a man can be,' muttered Vassily, puffing and wiping his forehead.

But Fyodor was too far gone to answer. He merely nodded, then allowed himself to collapse onto the floor of the Roslazny police station. The others, too, had found the act of dragging Ludis Kuskov's unconscious form for half a mile more than sufficiently challenging, and Nevena, Olga and Taisia Aristov soon followed Fyodor's example – Olga taking care to sit a little apart from the others, as a way of telling them she knew her exile had yet to be lifted. Kliment alone seemed unaffected, helping his father to put cushions under Ludis's head and then, with the aid of a reviving Nevena, attempting to bring Ludis back into consciousness.

Finally, after Vassily had managed to coax a few drops of Rocket Fuel past his lips, Ludis spluttered into awareness. But no sooner had his eyes opened than a haunted look passed over them, and he cried: 'Soltsne! Soltsne! I'm coming, Soltsne – I'm coming!'

Then, realising he was still in Roslazny, he fell back into Kliment's arms and wept, the others looking at each other in confusion until Taisia elbowed Vassily and said: 'His son. That's what he calls his son, Vanya.'

Vassily's eyes softened at the gentle nickname, 'little sun'; and while he didn't exactly treat Ludis as if he'd been proved innocent, he was at least willing to hear him out and discover why he had fled the village in such a suspicious manner.

They helped Ludis to sit up, pressed a mug of Vassily's coffee into his hands, and encouraged him to talk between the bouts of nausea he'd earned from the blow to his head. Ludis told them how his ex-fiancée, Inessa, had run off with all his savings three months previously, leaving him barely enough to get by; how his seven-year-old son, Vanya, needed special care that his local school, in Leninsky, couldn't provide; and how Ludis had sold his house, car, and everything but his spare kidney to scrape together enough to pay for Vanya's education, but without success – forcing Ludis to go to his uncle for additional support.

'But Uncle Danyl was wonderful about it,' said Ludis, 'especially as I'd expected him to disapprove. He was always banging on about the need to stick to your guns and see things through.'

Nevena snorted, causing Olga and the others to look at her.

But she only shrugged. 'It'd be the first time I've heard a man talk like that! They're more likely to cut and run whenever they can. That's my experience, anyway. I mean – well, it was my mother's.'

Vassily, thought Olga, would have his work cut out with Nevena, if she stuck around; but Ludis was still talking.

'Anyway,' he was saying, 'Uncle Danyl was wonderful about Vanya, like I said. He told me to bring all the bills with me today and he'd take them on the train with him, pay them all later. But when you started asking all about Vanya,' Ludis continued, nodding at Vassily, 'I couldn't stop thinking about him back at home. It's only my old mother there with him, and she won't know what's happened to me. And sometimes when she falls down she can't get back up again – and what if Inessa came back, while I'm stuck here? She might want more money – and then there's Vanya. Inessa's crazy enough for anything. She might even try to take him away. So, you see, I had to try to get home – I just had to! I wish I'd done it, too!'

He sat bolt upright in his distress, his eyes wide and staring, prompting Vassily and Nevena to step forward with comforting words, while Kliment and Fyodor Katin fussed in the background, boiling the kettle again and finding a tin of soup to put on the stove. Taisia Aristov, meanwhile, was still where she had been ever since they'd rushed back from the tracks: sitting by Vassily's fire, warming her hands and smoking so many cigarettes that Olga thought she must have been filching some of Vassily's own dwindling supply.

Sitting in freedom, that is, rather than in a prison cell – for Olga had decided to keep her knowledge about Taisia's arson attack to herself. She didn't think an old woman's kind-heartedness to a neighbour worth troubling Vassily about in the middle of a homicide case. Besides, if Vassily could keep things to himself, so could Olga. He had talked to her when necessary just now, as they struggled to drag Ludis's body back to the station – but there was still a tangible awkwardness in his conversations with her, an awkwardness that tugged at Olga's heart, though of course some of that hesitancy might stem from the circumstances: he could scarcely discuss the murder investigation with her, after all, because hardly anyone knew that was what it was. Nevertheless, things between her and Vassily were assuredly not as they had been, and it was clear to Olga – Vassily's behaviour had *made* it clear to her – that the mere fact of her co-presence in the police station did not mean she was back on the investigative team.

Olga walked to the window and gazed out of the grimy panes at the trees across the way, weighing Ludis's words in her mind and concluding that no, he couldn't be the killer. His distress over his son was too heart-wrenching to be the product of acting.

No, of course he wasn't the killer, she thought, rather more bitterly. That would have been too easy, too straightforward, and altogether too pleasant a way for the universe to vindicate her in front of Vassily Marushkin and Nevena Komarov. There Olga would have been, standing over them in the snow with secret knowledge in hand, and explaining in simple, even condescending terms how she'd thought it was Ludis all along – or, perhaps more accurately, how she'd thought it *could* have been him ever since she found his bag full of unpaid bills in Café Astana, creating the clearest possible motive for putting an end to his childless uncle and claiming whatever inheritance was coming his way.

But it wasn't him and, looking back, she realised that his guilt had never been a genuine possibility. Ludis Kuskov was too obviously truculent, too tangibly sharp around the edges, to have been a real killer. Like Pasha said, murderers have to act nice – or, at least, they do if they want to remain at large. And so Ludis Kuskov was taken back to Café Astana and surrendered once more to the tender mercies of Igor Odrosov's hospitality.

If it wasn't Ludis, and it wasn't Taisia Aristov, who *was* it? The murderer was still with them – and judging by the scribbled, chalky mess on the police-station blackboard, Vassily and Nevena hadn't made any real progress in terms of tracking him down, either.

And it had to be a him now, thought Olga. It had to be either Gennady Aristov or Pastor Loktev, however spotless they might appear. For who else knew Danyl or Anoushka Petrovich, here in Roslazny? And nobody had come in, or gone out, since the train wreck: the snow still bound them all together, like an icy pressure-cooker, wrapping them round with frozen walls and rendering even the most desperate attempt to escape – like Ludis Kuskov's – an exercise in cold futility. Could the villagers make it to the inevitable thaw with their bodies – and minds – intact? But how long would it be? A day was possible, or two, or even three – but what about a week from now, when the food really began to run out and the killer became ever more desperate? Two deaths had already taken place, and two charred bodies now lay side by side in Popov's back-up freezer. But Olga had seen four, not two, branches fall outside the police station. Who else might die before lockdown came to an end?

She bent lower and peered out, gazing at the very spot where she'd seen the boughs snap and tumble to earth the week before. An unpleasant thought came to her mind: what if yet more branches had since cracked under the unexpected weight of snow, unseen by her? What if yet more deaths could be expected?

But it was hard to see the trees through the constant blizzarding, and she was just rubbing the condensation from the window when a soft voice spoke in her ear.

'Olga,' said Kliment, quietly, but still loudly enough to make her jump. She controlled the urge to swear loudly in her surprise, and turned to Vassily's son: a tall, round-headed boy with his father's height and dark hair but his mother's deep, reflective eyes, standing close to her and fixing her with his earnest gaze.

'Kliment,' she said, feeling a genuine smile sweep over her face. However she might feel about Kliment's father, she was unable to maintain any kind of reserve towards his entirely innocent offspring.

'I'm sorry about Papa,' he said, as if divining her mood. 'And Nevena – Dama Komarov, I mean. They don't want to be unkind – I'm sure they don't! It's just—'

'It's all right, Kliment,' said Olga, grasping his arm by way of a fuller response. 'It's all right.'

He nodded, looking at her and drinking in her words, but not speaking, so she felt obliged to continue.

'Don't worry about me,' she went on. 'I got along fine before your papa came along, and Nevena, too, and I'll get along fine now. I'm making my own enquiries, you know – don't tell anyone, but I'm running my own investigation on the side. That's how I came across— Well, let's just say I've got some clues I'm working on, and not just on our friend Ludis, either. A person's bag is like a person's heart, that's what they say; and just between us, Kliment, the guestrooms at Café Astana revealed exactly that! So, anyway, I've got plenty to keep me busy. And I've still got Pasha, and Anna, and the boys – and don't forget Dmitri! It would never do to forget Dmitri the hedgehog.'

'I just wish – I just wish you still had your hut, too,' said Kliment, 'and that you didn't have to go away. You *will* still have to go away, won't you? Once the snow melts?'

Olga nodded mutely. She was suddenly overcome with emotion and didn't trust herself to speak.

'That Polina,' Kliment continued, 'I don't like her. I don't like her at all. She was so rude when Papa was talking to her – as if he was insulting her, or something! But all he was doing was asking about her last job, up at Itatka.'

'Your papa talked to Polina?' said Olga, her sadness disappearing as her detective's antennae prickled and stood up. 'About her last job?'

Kliment nodded earnestly. '*Da, da* – and about stuff that happened there before she left. He sent me down to the tracks to bring her up to the station. And then – well, first he asked Polina why she'd called Danyl Petrovich a *pridurok*.'

'Kliment!' said Olga. 'You shouldn't use such language. And did you know it was me who told him that?'

'He didn't say,' said Kliment, awkwardly. 'But, anyway, Polina said she'd just meant he was difficult to work with. Moody, she said, and unpredictable – not how she likes her colleagues, she said. She likes them more professional, she said.'

'More controllable, she meant,' muttered Olga.

'And then Nevena – I mean Dama Komarov – spoke up, and told Papa about some things she'd found in her papers from work – stuff from Russian Railways. Stuff that had gone wrong at her depot before she left. Things . . .' he leaned closer still, speaking more softly until his voice was as gentle as his face '. . . things like what happened here – you know, all the little crimes Papa's been busy tracking down. Fires in old buildings, people stealing garden tools, all that. They started up in Itatka, too, a while before she left.'

'So your papa – so Vassily thinks she was responsible? That she – that she did those crimes?'

'Maybe.' Kliment shrugged. 'I think that's why Papa was questioning her, anyway, to see what she knew about it.'

She...

Yes, thought Olga, the murderer didn't *have* to be a he, for there was a she, wasn't there? A she who'd recently arrived in Roslazny with an inside track on derailment techniques, not to mention a nasty sideline in clog-inflicted hedgehog abuse. A railway engineer like herself, and an engineer, moreover, with a unique, and uniquely abrasive, personality... Yes, thought Olga, it was perfectly plausible that she and Danyl had butted heads in Russian Railways over the years – to the extent, perhaps, of creating a resentment that had simmered behind those unpleasant spectacles until it had erupted in a burning desire for revenge. Why hadn't she thought of Polina in that way before?

But then she tutted. Of course: it was Pasha again, or his theory about murderers and affability (or its absence). She hadn't thought of Polina because she was so obviously unpleasant that it would be a stretch, on Pasha's account, to cast her as a murderer. She was more like a red-herring character in one of the detective dramas Olga loved to watch: someone who looks suspicious in the early stages of the story, but who, it later transpires, couldn't have committed the actual crime.

'But the crimes stopped weeks before she left,' continued Kliment, breaking in on Olga's thoughts and throwing cold water – yet again – upon her racing imagination, so that Olga began to wonder if having a writerly slant to one's mind really was a helpful characteristic for police investigations.

'The crimes stopped before Polina left Itatka, I mean,' went on Kliment. 'So she says, anyway. I think she knew what Papa was getting at with all his questions. She said old man Solotov had told her about the crimes around Roslazny. But she said it was someone else who'd done both. And—'

But whatever else Kliment wished to add was lost, for at that instant a loud presence burst into the police station, kicking Vassily's door aside and charging over the threshold with merry abandon.

'Taisia! Taisia Aristov!' cried the intruder's stentorian voice, booming through the low-ceilinged police station and making them all jump. 'Are you in here, woman?'

The voice, Olga saw, belonged to Taisia's husband Gennady, who now stumbled where he stood, as if tripping on some unseen obstacle. Olga tutted again. To be so drunk at this hour . . . It reminded her of her father Mikhail.

Gennady regained his balance and cast his inebriated gaze around the station until his bloodshot eyes locked onto Olga's. 'Ah – the engineer. I owe you an apology, young woman!' he cried. 'I was – I wasn't myself, when I said all that stuff at the track about the accident. I was – I was upset. It's like I said to Taisia – you can't blame the monkey when the organ grinder's at fault! But that reminds me. Taisia! Taisia Aristov!' he cried again, looking away from Olga. 'Where are you? Popov said you were here – a good man, the butcher, though I wouldn't trust his burgers. Says he saw you coming in here with a group of men. Hope it's nothing dodgy, eh? Eh?'

'Gennady!' cried Taisia, getting up from the fireplace with anger written upon her face, and advancing at speed upon the Falstaffian figure who stood in the open doorway, coat buttons in the wrong holes and a stained, untucked shirttail poking out underneath. 'Stop that nonsense this minute,' she hissed, waving her hands at him as if she were shooing a recalcitrant goose.

'Nonsense? Nonsense? What is it with you, woman,' said Gennady, plucking a half-empty plastic bottle from his pocket

– a bottle filled with a familiar, blue-tinged liquid – 'that you think everything I say is nonsense? I've got feelings, haven't I? I've lost people too, haven't I?'

'*Lost* people? What people?' said Taisia, but Gennady only waved at her in response, mimicking her shooing motion as if he could so easily dismiss his wife from thought.

'Yes, I've got feelings, just like you,' he went on. 'And it's not as if you don't have your own – what's the word? Idio-idio-symphonies? You say I'm annoying, and stupid, and disgusting –'

'I never say any such thing!' said Taisia, trying to shush him again, and looking round at the others.

'– but what about your habits?' Gennady continued. 'Just think of all those fripperies you make me haul around whenever we leave the house, just so you can wear a different headscarf every day! Not that it makes any difference to what's underneath,' he went on, with a wink, beads of perspiration now bubbling out on his extensive dome of a head, 'but you ladyfolk will have your dresses and your hats and your muffs and your mink coats, won't you,' he continued, with a wave of his hand at Taisia and Nevena, 'though we have to spend a small fortune?'

Despite herself Olga glanced at Nevena, with an expression that said: *Muffs? Mink coats! How old does he think we are?*

But Nevena wouldn't meet her eye, and Olga noticed that her lips were tightly pressed together – so tightly that Olga could see thin white lines above and below the rich ruby red of her lips. Olga smiled to herself, a tiny movement that nobody else would notice – for Gennady Aristov, she thought, had pricked Nevena's vanity. A woman who looked like her would hate being lumped in with the elderly, and decidedly frumpy, Taisia Aristov! It would be a frosty day in Hell, mused Olga, before Nevena would be seen dead in anything that Taisia might wear.

'Yes, you'll have your wardrobes and your furs,' Gennady continued, 'though it costs us our last kopek. Our last kopek! Though some of you've got more sense than others,' he said, more solemnly. 'I won't speak ill of the dead, and I don't need to!'

'No, you don't,' said Taisia, crossly. 'You've said more than enough already about the oh-so-wonderful Anoushka Petrovich.'

'She was – she was – oh, she was—' Gennady Aristov suddenly broke down, hot tears rolling through his thick fingers as he barred them across his red-rimmed eyes.

'Oh, get out,' said Taisia Aristov, in disgust, whipping her headscarf up and over her scorched hair once more. 'Get out, before you show me up any more. I'm sorry, Sergeant,' she added, 'and thanks for the cigarettes! You'll forgive my husband,' she called, over her shoulder, as she marched Gennady towards the door. 'He can't handle his vodka like he used to – though I can still handle him!'

And then, with a final struggle as Gennady caught his foot on the crooked door and almost brought Taisia down with him, they were gone, staggering out into the snow, presumably in search of Café Astana and Gennady's bed.

'Well,' said Olga, eyes wide and staring at the empty corridor. 'Well . . .'

'So, Gennady Aristov,' said Vassily. 'Looks like we can rule him out, eh? Now we know why he was so upset at the crash site – you remember I told you that, Nevena? It's because he was carrying a torch for poor old Anoushka Petrovich. It's hardly a motive to bring the train down, though.'

But Nevena didn't answer: she was still staring, like Olga, at the place where Gennady and Taisia had been, as if trying – and failing – to make sense of what had just happened. Or had she noticed something the others had missed – some clue in Gennady's words or Taisia's – something strange and unsettling, like the phrase that Olga still could not quite bring to mind? Olga made a mental note to ask Nevena what she'd noticed, if Vassily ever gave them a chance to speak alone together.

'That just leaves Pastor Loktev, then,' said Olga, after a moment. 'And—'

'And you've got something on him, haven't you?' said a voice, alive with suppressed excitement. 'From when you broke into Café Astana?'

Olga turned and stared at Kliment, aghast: how could he reveal her secret like that? He caught her eye in the dim light and turned bright crimson, putting his hand over his mouth as if he could retract his words but of course he could not.

'You did *what*, Olga?' said Vassily, turning his gaze on her once more. 'You broke into Odrosov's guestrooms – on your own? As a – as a private individual? And rooted through other people's belongings, at your own risk?'

'Yes, but—' began Olga.

Vassily wasn't to be deterred. With a voice of thunder he recounted to her the criminal charges that could be brought against her if anyone else found out, and told her in many different ways how idiotic it was of her to take such danger upon herself – she could have gone to prison for years and years, and then what would Anna and Pasha do? And the boys?

And *Dmitri?* And there was, too, the possibility that the murderer might have been in the guestrooms himself. (*Or herself*, thought Olga).

'What if the killer had been waiting upstairs – waiting for *you*?' he cried, jabbing his finger at her in the air. 'You wouldn't have lasted two minutes! Hanging around downstairs is one thing, but wandering around upstairs? That's quite a different matter.'

Olga refrained from pointing out how she had personally saved Vassily from another murderer earlier that year, and instead waited for his anger to vent itself.

'Don't worry, Vassily,' she said, when that finally took place some time later. 'You don't have to worry. I'm quite happy to leave investigating to the police from now on. You're doing such a good job, after all. We can all sleep soundly in our beds, knowing you're on the case. You and Nevena, that is, of course,' she added, with a sideways glance at her friend, who at least had the decency to look at the floor.

'Kliment, it's been a pleasure,' said Olga, quite pointedly. 'And now perhaps you'll walk me home, Fyodor? It's not quite safe out there – not yet. But no doubt our good sergeant will put that right before long. Good night!'

When she got outside, navigating the deep snow with her arm in Fyodor's, she breathed out a long sigh, expressing – she realised – both satisfaction and dismay at once. She was proud of herself for keeping her cool when Vassily had so obviously lost his, but at the same time desperately sad that things had come to this, with a seemingly irreparable gulf between them – not to mention Nevena's seeming willingness to go along with Vassily's rudeness, or at least her perceived inability to do otherwise.

There was one silver lining, though: it would make it easier to leave Roslazny when the time came. And until then, she knew several people whose love was steadier and sturdier than Vassily's.

'Come on, Fyodor,' she said. 'Take me home to Anna and Pasha and the boys. Take me home.'

10

Pastor Don't Preach

Olga was a morning person or, at least, had become a morning person after nearly two decades of continuous hard labour in her trackside hut. She'd had no choice in the matter: it was a case of either getting up on time or not getting paid. Russian Railways was no warm-hearted, laissez-faire, casual-minded operator, like the ones she'd heard of in the West where bus replacements could be laid on at a moment's notice if the driver felt a little below-par on any given day.

Yes, Olga was a morning person, but she still took the chance of a lie-in when she could get it. And that Sunday morning in Roslazny presented an opportunity that might never come again: no trackside engineering duties to attend to, no railway schedule to monitor or unpleasant superiors to mollycoddle. She didn't have any writing to do, either, for her first book was finished, while her second, *Take the Next Steppe*, couldn't really be started until she reached Mongolia. She couldn't even pick up the phone and harry her publishers, as she had done on an increasingly regular basis since the summer, trying to ensure that her masterpiece *Find Your Rail Self: 100 Life Lessons from the Trans-Siberian Railway* would finally see the light of day. All she could do was lie there and listen to the (thankfully distant) sounds of Anna's boys at play, and imagine another sound, subtler still, of hissing flakes laying themselves each upon the next until another infinitesimal, frozen veneer was placed above the Siberian snow.

But then the peaceful sounds became rather less peaceful: she heard a clamour of rapidly approaching voices, reproachful cries, and – last of all – the deafening tinkle and clatter of broken glass as Boris's football flew at speed through Olga's window, followed swiftly by Boris's horrified face and Pasha's head towering above, bearing a look that shaded from extreme irritation to puzzlement.

Once the initial uproar had subsided to a certain degree, and once Anna had been called upon to administer suitable admonishment and punishment, Olga pulled on her *shuba* fur coat and went outside with Pasha to inspect the damage from another angle. She couldn't really see the point of doing so – surely a broken window was a broken window – but Pasha insisted, and once she got outside she saw why.

'It's been newly painted,' she said, utterly mystified, and so it had. There, at the place where the sash met the wooden base, the window now gleamed with liberally applied white gloss.

'It doesn't open,' said Pasha, tugging upwards on the jagged-edged pane. 'Didn't it used to open?'

Olga nodded but didn't answer, staring at the window and thinking that now, at last, she knew why her room had smelt of paint.

'You're sure it wasn't you – maybe after some secret vodka one night?'

Pasha shook his head and pointed at some paint splashes,

visible between floes of melted snow. 'This was done by a leftie. Look – you see that?' He mimicked the action of painting until Olga realised he was right – and right-handed. So Pasha really hadn't painted it – but then who had?

She didn't have long to ponder the mystery, however, for a visitor soon made himself known.

'Olga, quick!' cried Vassily's son Kliment, poking his head through the snowy bushes that surrounded Olga's house. 'I can't stay long,' he went on. 'But you'd better come to Café Astana. The priest's been threatening the old man – Gennady, I mean. Gennady Aristov. Igor overheard him earlier on, and came to tell Papa just now. I wanted to let you know, since I – since I blew the gaff on your investigation. Wanted to make things right, with a clue! But I've got to go – Papa thinks I'm looking for a lost glove. See you there!'

His head then disappeared as rapidly as it had appeared, leaving three adults and three boys staring at his absence.

But it was Anna, not Olga, who broke the silence, urging Olga and Pasha to come inside and help her ready the boys for a walk to Café Astana. 'Of course you've got to find out what Kliment's going on about, Olga,' she said. 'For your investigation, I mean. But we'll come too! We need more food, for one thing, if Odrosov's got any left,' she added, beginning to wrestle Ilya into his Eskimo suit. 'And, besides,' she concluded, 'the boys are driving me crazy. We might as well be cooped up in Café Astana – it's a change of scene, at least.'

Pasha, who looked rather careworn, agreed with alacrity, and shortly afterwards the party of six made their way towards the centre of the village, braving the Arctic, snow-laden winds and wading through substantial drifts as if they were a perfectly normal feature of September in Roslazny. You can get used to anything, in time, thought Olga. Look at Putin – wasn't that the problem, that they had got used to people like him? She rather thought it was.

'Look, Mamochka!' cried Boris, making Olga jump, as they passed the graveyard of St Aleksandr. 'All the stones are under the snow.'

'What stones?' said Gyorgy, nearly cylindrical with jumpers and coat, his voice muffled by the scarf Anna had tied around his chin.

'The gravestones, dummy,' said Boris. 'For all the people who died here.'

'Why? What happened to them?' said Gyorgy, his eyes round with sympathy for the victims of some vast imagined disaster, prompting Olga to burst out laughing.

'Not all at once, Gyorgy!' she said, patting his thickly padded head. 'They didn't all die at once! They just ended up here because they passed away in Roslazny, over the years. Like . . .'

She'd been about to say, 'like Danyl and Anoushka,' but she'd remembered she didn't know where they would be buried. They'd had no children, but perhaps their friends and neighbours would take them away and bury them in Yashkino, where Danyl had made his home after leaving Roslazny – friends and neighbours like the Aristovs and Ludis Kuskov and Pastor Loktev.

But now, it seemed, those very friends and neighbours had begun to turn on each other. What had Kliment said? Pastor Loktev had threatened Gennady?

'Nothing of the kind, my dear sergeant,' said Pastor Loktev, with a smile, as they walked through the door at Café Astana.

He was speaking, of course, to Vassily Marushkin, who stood towering over Loktev at one of the little round tables Odrosov had placed by the door.

'Nothing of the kind,' he said again, getting to his feet. 'Would our beloved friend Gennady be sleeping upstairs in peace, as he is now, if he thought he was in danger from me, or anyone else here? I never heard such nonsense in all my life! I admit I may have – I may have told Gennady that he needed to watch his alcohol intake,' Loktev continued, in a softer tone. 'That's why he's asleep again, at ten in the morning. It's shameful, really. But I said what I did for Taisia's sake! She puts up with a lot, let me tell you,' he added, nodding towards the corner behind the bar, where Taisia's ever-present headscarf could be seen bending over an unappetising, half-empty plate of Svetlana's onion and offal pie.

'Still, Pastor,' said Vassily, patiently, 'I'm afraid I've got to ask you to step out with me. With us, I mean,' he added, glancing at Nevena, who stood beside him like a newly acquired shadow. 'Igor here heard you using some very – some very *unchristian* language towards Gennady earlier today. And as it's quite *public* here' – he went on, glancing at Olga's party, who were still standing by the door, but also at Taisia, and at several other noisy groups clumped around the bar – 'I think it would be best if we talked at the station.'

Loktev's face changed, solemnising away from his previous expression of almost jaunty unconcern, and the pastor stepped out from behind his table and drew closer to the policeman, so close that their chests almost met.

'I would *very much* prefer that we stayed here, *tovarisch*,' said Loktev, in a tone of deep solemnity. But calling Vassily a comrade was an ill-judged move, and now Vassily drew himself up to his considerable height and ordered Loktev to the Roslazny police station in terms of the greatest clarity – and at sufficient volume to penetrate even the hangover-infused haze of Café Astana on a Sunday morning.

Loktev looked around him, seeing pair after pair of wary eyes fixed upon him in the relative silence that followed Vassily's orders, until he seemed to bow under their scrutiny. Olga almost felt sorry for him: it must be remarkably unpleasant, she thought, to feel every hand turned against you, and every man, woman and child suspecting you of wicked doings in the Siberian night.

As yet, nobody knew for sure that Vassily was now investigating a double murder rather than a railway accident, but on the other hand it was no secret that Danyl's train had come off the rails in unusual, even suspicious, circumstances. And it was no secret, either, that Vassily's face had become gaunt with strain, charcoal rings under his eyes stark and clear against his pale skin – and what other reason for this could there be, while food and power still held out in the village, but a pressing and perplexing mystery that remained unsolved?

Even Nevena, thought Olga, was showing signs of stress, but in the opposite direction from Vassily, showing not a haggard symphony of white and dark, pale skin and dark stubble, but a sultrier mix of red-tinged cheeks, tumbling hair and glittering eyes – looking, in fact, thought Olga, very like someone who was about to come down with a fever. She'd seen Anna looking the same way, and Pasha, too, when things were difficult with the children. Vassily was working her too hard, thought Olga. Doesn't he realise she's a tender plant?

Tender plant or not, she marched quickly enough on her

long legs beside Vassily when he turned to leave, following the pastor as he shook his head, accepted defeat, and headed for the door with surprising rapidity. Kliment scurried after her, and then Vassily motioned Olga and party out of the way – but Olga caught Vassily's arm as he passed and whispered in his ear, telling him that she really had seen things in Loktev's bag, as Kliment had revealed – strange things, things that might explain why he had threatened Gennady.

Olga had told herself she didn't care if she was off Vassily's team, but that was one thing while walking home at night with Fyodor, and quite another while looking a suspicious and potentially murderous priest in the eye.

'Olga,' said Vassily, impatiently, pulling away in exasperation, 'I told you, we can't have you blundering around when things are so dangerous – so finely balanced.'

'Come on, Vassily,' said Nevena, stepping in on Olga's behalf – which she appreciated – but putting a restraining, possessive hand on Vassily's sleeve as she did so, which she did not. 'If Olga saw something, surely we should hear her out – if only to add it to the board? We're keeping a record on that blackboard,' she added, somewhat unnecessarily. 'The blackboard Olga set up for us in the first place – remember, Vassily?'

Vassily tutted in exasperation, staring from one to the other – the first time for a while, Olga realised, that he had actually looked straight at her.

'Come on, then,' he snapped at last. 'We'll all go together. Might as well get it over with.'

Olga whipped round to Anna, Pasha and the boys and flashed a quick smile at them. Anna smiled back and Pasha nodded, though a little warily, Olga thought, as if not quite satisfied with Vassily Marushkin. But she dismissed the thought and jerked her head over her shoulder, as if to say: I've got to go. I've got to go and catch a killer! And then she walked out into the darkness, hot on Vassily's heels.

It was a short walk to the police station from Café Astana, but a long trudge in the oppressive weather. Olga had hoped to snatch a moment with Nevena to ask her about Gennady Aristov and other things, but Vassily – as she might have guessed – stayed close by Nevena's side throughout. There was no sign of easing in their wintry lockdown: the snow had redoubled, then redoubled again, whistling along the empty streets and funnelling down upon them in weighty, sluicing torrents, so that, once again, their arrival at the police station was more of an exhausted collapse than a measured entrance.

Loktev went in second, after Kliment, and spent some time – as they all did – beating the snow from his clothes and shoes until he looked less like an ambulant ice-sculpture. But while the others busied themselves with stoking up the fire, putting the kettle on, and taking care of Rasputin, Loktev stood quite still, staring at Vassily with fierce concentration until the Roslazny sergeant-in-charge was ready to talk.

But it was Loktev who did most of the talking. 'You *idiot*, Marushkin! You utter, pigheaded, *pridurok* of a policeman!'

'Start again, Loktev,' warned Vassily, but his ominous tone went unnoticed.

'Don't you realise you've jeopardised everything – *everything*? I've been working on this case for over a year!'

'What are you talking about?' said Vassily. 'What case?'

But Loktev wasn't listening. 'Oh, I'll have to get you all vetted,' he said, pacing around the station with his eyes on the floor. 'You'll have to sign the State Secrets Act. You, too,' he said, turning to point at Olga, then Nevena and Kliment, 'and you, and you! It's a terrible thing, Marushkin, to get civilians involved in things like this.'

'Civilians?' said Olga. 'What the hell are you talking about?'

'Don't you dare talk to me like that, Grazhdanka! Don't you realise I'm FSB?'

Olga's jaw dropped open. 'FSB?'

The FSB, or Federal'naya sluzhba bezopasnosti Rossiyskoy Federatsii, was the successor to the KGB, and every bit as feared.

'FSB,' said Loktev, grimly. 'And Gennady Aristov found out. That's why he and I had words. He stumbled across me while I was – well, it doesn't matter what I was doing, but from that moment he knew I wasn't your everyday pastor from Itatka.'

'So the FSB are running churches now?' said Kliment.

Loktev uttered a yelp of laughter, but one that ended as suddenly as it had begun. 'No, my young friend, not quite. But sometimes we pretend to be who we are not so we can monitor public figures from time to time – and that includes everyone who's capable of wreaking mass havoc upon the public. Hydro-engineers, nuclear power-station workers, you see? Airline pilots, *train drivers* . . . We keep an eye on them in case they get any funny ideas. You know, extremist cults, or foreign influences, or *suicidal tendencies* . . .'

'Ah,' said Olga, suddenly understanding. 'So the things I saw—'

Just in time she stopped herself revealing to an agent of the world's most feared security service that she had been rooting through his private property during an illegal search of his guestroom at Café Astana. She felt his scrutinising gaze beating in upon her, searching her eyes so intensely that she felt an overpowering urge to confess this and every other piece of wrongdoing she had ever encompassed. But somehow she managed to refrain from telling him of what she'd seen in his briefcase: printouts of websites that Danyl Petrovich must have visited, not knowing that the FSB was watching – websites that revealed, perhaps, a desire to end his life by rope or poison or bullet and escape his ghosts, both real and imagined. Olga thought back to the photograph she'd seen of Danyl in the newspaper article, and those eyes of his staring fiercely out at the reader. What was it Nevena had said that night in Café Astana? Local heroes often had secrets? Well, now she knew, she reflected with a pang of sorrow. Now she knew.

'Yes, Grazhdanka?' said Loktev, in a quiet voice. 'The things you saw?'

'Oh,' she said airily, even venturing upon a gentle chuckle. 'Well, I mean – you just didn't seem like a pastor to me, that's all! Not that I've met very many.'

After what seemed like a long while, his eyes moved away from her as he resumed his pacing about the room. 'Yes, we've been watching Tovarisch Petrovich for quite some time, ever since our data people picked him up in a routine scan, looking up strange things on the dark web . . . Had to watch him, after that – but couldn't tip off the Russian Railways people that we *were* watching. For political reasons – you understand? So there we were – but the solution was obvious: undercover work. Spend a bit of time inserting yourself into the local scene, and Bogdan's your uncle. I drew the short straw, and went out and bought myself some of the blackest clothes you'll see outside a Goth nightclub.'

'Anna will be pleased,' murmured Olga to Kliment. 'She never liked the idea of pastors, anyway.'

'It's no laughing matter,' barked Loktev, as Kliment smiled. 'Like I said, you all know too much! Fifty years ago it would've been as easy as four or five revolver cartridges. It still is, sometimes, though you didn't hear that from me. But in this case it's not worth the time for the cover-up. But I'll tell you a story . . .'

Loktev's story – presumably intended to serve as an admonition – remained unheard, both then and afterwards. Events overtake even the FSB from time to time, and so it proved on that chilly Sunday evening in Roslazny. For no sooner had Loktev uttered those words than the door clattered open and Fyodor Katin burst in.

'You're making altogether too much of a habit of this, Fyodor Katin,' said Vassily, quite angrily – but Fyodor's next words cut him off.

'It's Gennady,' cried Fyodor, wiping the sweat from his eyes and the lank hair from his forehead. 'Gennady Aristov. We just – found him. Upstairs, in his – in his room.'

He bent forwards to catch his breath, and then stood up again, looking Vassily straight in the eye. 'Yes, it's Gennady. He's – he's dead! Gennady Aristov – is – dead.'

11

Man in Black

'What d'you call this?' said Mikhail Pushkin to Igor Odrosov in Café Astana the day after, pushing his plate away from him with disgust.

'What d'you mean, what do I call it? It's *kurnik*. You never saw chicken pie before?'

'But look at the size of it. That's what I'd give a baby!'

'You can't give *kurnik* to a baby, Mikhail,' put in Fyodor Katin, who had reluctantly put aside his objections to Mikhail and friends on account of hunger.

'Supplies are running low,' said Odrosov, ignoring Fyodor and leaning forward on the counter with a serious look on his face. 'Look at that weather outside! No deliveries for a week. What can I do? I've had to make certain cut-backs – you know how it is.'

'Why isn't it half price, then?' piped up Zia Kuznetsov, Olga's aunt, who was sitting next to Fyodor, on the other side of Olga's father, Mikhail.

Odrosov turned down the corners of his lips, and at the same time shrugged his shoulders. 'I've got bills to pay like everyone else, Zia Kuznetsov.'

'No deliveries means no bills, *nyet*, Igor?' said Mikhail. But Igor Odrosov had suddenly remembered something that urgently required his attention in the far recesses of the kitchen. He turned sharply on the heel of his *ichigi* Kazakh boot and disappeared, his daughter Svetlana uttering a distant cry at the unexpected interruption of her mid-morning cigarette and magazine break.

Mikhail Pushkin tutted, shook his head, and passed a dirty-nailed hand over his unshaven chin. 'Got us over a barrel, hasn't he?' he said, pulling the plate of chicken pie back towards him.

'Let's just hope the food doesn't run out altogether,' said Aunt Zia, tucking into her own modest portion.

'The food – or warm bodies to eat it?' said a voice, making them jump.

'Polina Klemovsky!' said Fyodor Katin, turning sharply to see the bespectacled railway engineer standing next to them. 'You startled us.'

'You'd think you'd hear her coming in those, eh?' said Mikhail, nodding down at Polina's yellow-painted clogs. 'But she's quiet as a mouse. Makes you wonder what else she gets up to, creeping around the village . . .'

'Quiet, you!' said Polina, giving Mikhail a playful rap on the arm with her handbag, and sitting down beside him on a vacant stool. 'It wasn't me who despatched that old fool – what was his name? Gleb? Gerasim?'

'Gennady!' said Fyodor, crossly. 'His name was Gennady Aristov. Show some respect for the dead.'

'Well, whatever his name was, he obviously annoyed the wrong man,' said Polina, subtly rolling her eyes at Mikhail and

Zia. 'I mean, getting your head bashed in with a pan like that. Doesn't happen without some pretty serious aggravation.'

'Crime of passion, you think, Polina?' said Mikhail, trying not to laugh. 'At his age – and size?'

'Old people have feelings too, you know,' said Zia, quietly, but Mikhail didn't listen, and Polina didn't care.

'Passion?' she said, allowing herself a brief flash of the grimace that served her in place of a smile. 'No. No, not with that face, or that belly. But there was *something*, that's for sure . . . Money, maybe? I can just imagine someone like him getting into debt. Leather jackets, gold rings, flashy car to impress the girls who'd never look twice at him, wheels or no wheels . . . Maybe it was a debt collector – that's happened before. Well, who knows? Can't imagine our police finding out, anyway.'

Mikhail snorted. 'Vassily Marushkin, you mean? Hopeless. Though Anatoly Glazkov was even worse . . .'

As Mikhail embarked on a long-winded narrative about events in Roslazny earlier that year, accompanied by Polina's occasional cackling and Zia's murmured agreement, Fyodor Katin quietly polished off what lay on his plate and removed himself from the counter. He found an alternative seat by the window without much trouble: Café Astana was quieter now that Igor had started cutting portions so drastically, with most of the villagers holed up in their own houses, eking out whatever supplies they hadn't splashed out on Pasha's lockdown party, and lying low to minimise their own risk of being bumped off. But Polina and Mikhail were making enough noise for the whole village, in Fyodor's opinion. Few things were more irritating than inappropriate jollity, he reflected – above all when murder had been done the day before, and just above their heads to boot.

Fyodor wasn't at all surprised by the friendship that had sprung up between Mikhail Pushkin and Polina Klemovsky. Birds of a feather flock together, he thought, allowing himself the guilty pleasure of a rare cliché. Fyodor tried to tolerate everyone who lived in Roslazny, but he drew the line at people laughing and joking about Gennady's murder. After all, with the exception of the Petroviches, and the deaths that had taken place earlier that year, Gennady's was the first murder that had taken place in Roslazny since 1998, when Sofia Eldarov was found behind the bathhouse with a Cossack sabre through her heart. Other places might well have killers stalking the streets – places like Berezkino and Itatka and Leninsky and, of course, Tayga – but Roslaznyans had long prided themselves on the relative safety of their half-empty pathways. And now here were Mikhail and the ghastly Polina laughing and cracking jokes! Tolerance and fellow feeling were all very well, but what about right and wrong? Didn't they matter, too?

And what about Danyl and Anoushka Petrovich? Gennady's brutal murder had confirmed the villagers' growing suspicion that the derailment might have been more than a mere accident. Questions were now being raised at the highest level, and by minds as acute as Popov the butcher's and Igor's daughter Svetlana's, as to whether Vassily Marushkin's accident investigation ought not to become a homicide inquiry – and urgently, too, to avoid yet more corpses piling up in Popov's back-up freezer.

'I've only got so much space to go around,' Popov had said, 'and what am I to do with my Mangalica pigs, my goat legs, my horse heads? Are they just going to rot on the ground, costing me half a year's wages – and the trouble of burning them, too?'

Reminders of the frozen weather that encircled them like a glacial moat were issued to, and duly ignored by, Roslazny's resident meat merchant. 'It's only September!' he said. 'Soon the snow will be gone, and my meat will be as rotten as that cow-swill they serve up in Tayga. But what about the killer – or killers? Where will they be then?' And, of course, nobody could answer him.

Where was Mikhail's daughter at a time like this? thought Fyodor. Shouldn't Olga be here, investigating and asking questions? And Vassily, too – though perhaps not at the same time, since Nevena Komarov had thrust a wedge of sorts between him and Olga. But regardless of romantic complexities, he couldn't help asking himself: where *are* they all?

He looked across at the door, as if they might suddenly burst in and shame Polina and Mikhail into silence – but nobody came. There were only the endless snowflakes, beating upon the dirty glass and shaming it by contrast with brilliant, never-ending whiteness.

As a matter of fact, Olga Pushkin was at that very moment walking towards Roslazny's police station once more, summoned, to her surprise, by the so-called Pastor Loktev. It was to Olga's surprise because she had been ruthlessly excluded from the previous day's investigations of the crime scene at Café Astana, with Loktev instructing Vassily to bundle Olga off home as soon as the news of Gennady's death had arrived with Fyodor Katin.

'There's enough bloody civilians around this place as it is, Marushkin,' he'd barked. 'Goodbye, Devushka Pushkin! Go along with the good Kliment, now, like a worthy citizen should, and don't bother your pretty head about these distressing things.'

But despite Loktev's patronising words – which had made her blood boil, quite apart from his insulting use of *devushka* rather than *dama* – there she was the morning after, invited, she suspected, because Loktev had failed to make much progress in spite of his bravado, and was now in need of all the local knowledge he could lay his discomfiting hands upon. Since Loktev outranked Vassily, there was no way for Vassily to overrule him in the matter of Olga's involvement; and so there she was, with the ubiquitous Nevena Komarov and the station's permanent inhabitants: Vassily Marushkin, Kliment Marushkin, and Rasputin the ferret, who had already succeeded in unsettling the phoney priest.

'Just keep that thing away from me,' said Loktev, drawing his flowing clerical robe around his legs in a manner so reminiscent of Aunt Zia that Olga had to stop herself laughing, despite her sympathy for anyone who objected to hedgehog-eating ferrets.

Loktev heard her barely suppressed snort, however, and swung round to look at her. 'Don't you know that some people just don't like small animals, Devushka Pushkin?' he said.

'Sorry, Pastor,' said Olga, recognising to her surprise that his eyes bore a look of genuine anguish. She was hardly Rasputin's biggest fan, but even her marked dislike paled against Loktev's transparent aversion.

Recognising this, Vassily scooped Rasputin into his arms, then smiled gratefully as Nevena took him into her elegant arms, chirruping softly to the ferret as she whisked him away to his box in the cells, glancing backwards at Loktev as she went.

Olga's heart lurched, but there was no time to dwell on this new demonstration of Nevena's incorporation into the Marushkin household, for Loktev, looking relieved now that Rasputin's snapping jaws had been removed from the equation, turned to Vassily once again. 'Right, Marushkin, I'm running out of patience,' he said. 'Let's get on and solve this case so I can get the hell out of here, away from this godforsaken place and its mangy, disease-ridden rodents!'

'In this weather?' said Vassily, manfully ignoring Loktev's hurtful words about Rasputin, and jerking his thumb at the snow-covered windowpanes. 'You'd be lucky to get to Tayga! You saw what happened to Ludis Kuskov.'

'We sometimes have ways around things like that,' said Loktev, tapping his nose with a long, thin finger. 'But in the meantime it suits me to be here. I spent a year following Danyl Petrovich in case he killed himself, and then – plot twist! He got killed by someone else. Or so you say, anyway, Marushkin.'

'We've still got that hoe in evidence,' said Vassily, speaking quietly but deliberately. 'And my photos of the ballast in a heap by the side of the track. And if the train wasn't derailed on purpose, why was Gennady Aristov murdered? Doesn't make sense. I mean, what are the chances of two sets of murders within a week in a tiny place like Roslazny? They must be connected.'

But Loktev's moustache puffed outwards in a doubtful *moue*. 'Not necessarily. It's possible they're connected – likely, even. But it's not necessary, logically speaking. Someone may have been waiting for an excuse to kill Gennady, for reasons that had nothing to do with the derailment. Reasons to do with Anoushka Petrovich, for instance.'

But Vassily shook his head. 'The only person who was likely to kill Gennady over his feelings for Anoushka – assuming he really did have feelings for her – was Gennady's wife, Taisia. And seeing as *she* was apparently pretty fond of Danyl herself, as Olga now tells us,' continued Vassily, 'I can't imagine her doing away with Gennady for the same thing in reverse. If they all liked the other person, couldn't they just split up and recouple? And, besides, she was with us when Fyodor came to tell us Gennady was dead. And she was with Olga before that,' he added, gesturing at her.

'I agree,' said Loktev, to Olga's surprise. 'Like I said, it's unlikely – and not just because of motive. Think of the technique involved. To despatch the old-timer like that, with no noise and no fuss, and without leaving a single clue – and then to lie there in the room, too, moving the corpse so I thought it was breathing when I popped in yesterday morning . . . That's nothing short of genius. Does the word "genius" come to mind when you think of Taisia Aristov?'

When reconstructing events surrounding Gennady's death, Loktev had volunteered that he'd put his head into the room he shared with Gennady before Vassily had arrived at the café the morning before. Fooled by Gennady's steady movement and rasping, regular breathing, Loktev had walked out of the room again, little realising that someone else had been lying on the floor beyond the body and moving it with Gennady's walking-stick (later discovered under the bed) to simulate the movements of sleep. No doubt they had heard the sound of his approach on Odrosov's creaky floorboards, said Loktev, and been inspired to maintain the pretence of Gennady's breathing for a little longer.

'Genius, or preparation, or – or *possession*,' Loktev continued, pacing rapidly up and down the police station's reception area. 'Either a natural-born criminal, or someone who's worked their way up through endless leg-work – or somebody who's *crazy*, somebody so overwhelmed, so absorbed and consumed by a long-held desire and the need to put it into practice that they can't put a foot wrong. Doing everything like a sleepwalker, with unconscious grace.'

'Somebody who's crazy,' cut in Nevena, who had just returned from the cells, wiping her hands of cast-off ferret hair. 'Crazy like – like a bag of rats?'

'*What* did you say?' said Loktev, glowering at her from under his shaggy brows – but again Olga was struck by a hint of genuine fear.

'Oh, just a turn of phrase,' said Nevena, with the hint of a smile. 'Anyway, it's a shame you didn't realise Gennady was already dead when you walked into his room.'

'Would you have done any better?' snapped Loktev, turning sharply away from her. 'But no – no, you are right,' he went on, in a more reflective voice.

He walked up to Vassily's desk and placed his hands on the uneven surface, fingers outspread. 'I should have known. Yes – yes, you are right. Must be losing my touch. Probably the effect of spending a week in this wretched place, added to a year spent pretending to preach the Gospel . . .

'Anyway, we'd better bring Taisia Aristov in again,' he continued, banging a fist on the desk, 'and see what she knows. Put the old thumbscrews on, eh, Marushkin? This place is so ancient you've probably still got some lying around.'

'Well, we do have some old gear in the back office,' began Kliment, but Vassily hushed him to silence with an exasperated glare, while Loktev uttered another of his unpleasant, barking laughs.

'Very good, very good!' he cried, rubbing Kliment's head with mock affection. 'This one'll go far, Marushkin – mark my words! He'll go far. We'll inspect your back office now and see if you have anything that can be of service to the FSB. But first your son must go to Café Astana and bring back Taisia Aristov. You can do that, *detka*?'

Kliment frowned – like most teenagers, he disliked diminutives – but after a nod from Vassily he obeyed Loktev, donned fur hat and police-issue winter coat, and set off into the cold.

Olga was surprised, in a way, that Vassily let him go: wasn't there still a murderer out and about, prowling the frozen streets of Roslazny to see whom he might devour, and a murderer, moreover, with no hesitation whatsoever about adopting the most violent means to his vicious ends, derailing an entire Russian Railways freight train and battering an elderly man to death with one of Odrosov's flat-bottomed pans, later discovered among Gennady's bloodied blankets?

Then again, Olga reminded herself, Russians liked to raise their children the hard way, whether it was the ruthless sleep-training regime Anna was currently implementing for baby Ilya, or Olga's experience of Mikhail Pushkin's no-nonsense parenting following the death of her beloved mother, Tatiana.

So maybe Vassily was just doing his best for Kliment – doing his best to toughen him up and prepare him for the world beyond Roslazny. And, given what Olga knew of the world, even within Roslazny, perhaps that was no bad thing.

She still wasn't sure, though, if she would be able to send a son out into the snow with such apparent resignation. And she was sincerely relieved when Kliment reappeared a little later, walking into the station behind Taisia Aristov, who was wearing a fur coat, her ever-present headscarf, and a pound or two of freshly fallen snow.

'There you are, Kliment!' cried Olga, getting up from Vassily's desk and helping Kliment and Taisia off with their coats. 'And Taisia, too.'

'And where else would I be?' replied Kliment, with a grin. 'But what were you doing at the desk? Don't tell me Papa's getting you to do his paperwork again!'

'Ha – no chance,' said Olga, darting a smile at him, and remembering how she'd foolishly offered to help Vassily sort out his admin backlog earlier that year – only to admit defeat an hour or two later, overcome by the sheer weight of unfiled paper. But then her smile faded: it wasn't Olga, but Nevena whom Vassily asked to help him these days.

'Not his paperwork, but mine,' she went on, dropping her eyes to the sheets of paper that lay on the desk amid the debris of Vassily's breakfast. 'The pastor has asked me to write a point-by-point summary of my investigations to date, including the things I found in Café Astana – as you announced to everyone yesterday . . .'

Kliment had the grace to look shamefaced, with tinges of crimson embarrassment surging into his pale cheeks.

'It's all right, Kliment,' said Olga, quickly. 'Really, it is! You already gave me a clue to work on, remember? When the so-called pastor had words with poor Gennady Aristov? No, our accounts are quite balanced. You and I will never argue!'

'But where is everyone else?' said Kliment. 'Where are Papa, and Pastor Loktev and – and – and—'

'It's all right, Kliment,' she said again. 'You can say Nevena's name. She's an old friend of mine, even if . . . Well, let's just say I knew her long before your papa did.'

'I know, but—' began Kliment, only to be interrupted.

'Hello?' said Taisia Aristov, quite sharply. 'It's bad enough being forced out of my warm guestroom and dragged through the snow by this overgrown infant, without being ignored at the other end into the bargain – and me sitting here with my poor feet like blocks of ice, and my chilblains, and my arthritis flaring up again! And with – and with my poor Gennady's body hardly cold,' she added, with a sob that, thought Olga, might or might not have been genuine.

Then she turned her gaze upon Olga. 'I thought better of you, Dama Pushkin – I thought we had an understanding. You, more than anyone, know why I did what I did,' she said, making her meaning clear by glancing at Vassily's fire. 'It was for love of Danyl Petrovich – a good man, in the end, despite his flaws. But his goodness didn't save him, any more than it did my Gennady.'

'Yes, your Gennady!' boomed Loktev, striding back into the front office, with Vassily and Nevena hard on his heels.

'Oh, you scared me, Pastor!' said Taisia, hand over heart. 'But why are you – who do you think you're talking to, in this rough manner? What would the church elders say?'

Loktev gave another bark of laughter. 'Of course, of course – I keep forgetting who knows the truth and who doesn't. Hard to keep up sometimes, *nyet*, Marushkin? Listen, Taisia,' he went on, turning to her and placing a warning hand on each shoulder, 'I'm not who you think I am. The details don't concern you. What *does* concern you is telling us the truth, right now, once and for all.'

'Yes, and—' began Vassily.

'I'll handle this, Marushkin,' said Loktev, cutting him off quite unceremoniously, and guiding Taisia sideways, still holding her shoulders, until she fell into one of the chairs that Vassily kept by the desk. 'It won't take long – will it, dear Taisia? We've known each other a while now, so it shouldn't take long at all. Otherwise, what might happen to Irina Palatnik? Yes, yes, Irina, the woman you betrayed, isn't that right? Isn't that what you confessed to me, back in my dear little church? And now you are bound to her, in case she reveals *your* secret in turn. How interesting. How interesting.'

Taisia had drawn in her breath sharply at the mention of Irina Palatnik – Loktev had clearly hit on a sensitive topic – and Olga had to admit that the pseudo-pastor had wasted no time in getting down to business. Nevena Komarov was staring at him with a curious look on her face, mingling admiration with a kind of unease, as if afraid of the terrible revelations his questions might reveal. Even Vassily, she saw, was watching Loktev with grudging respect; and whatever reservations Olga and the others might have had regarding Loktev's methods, they couldn't deny that he was conducting a master class in effective interrogation. He moved from point to point with all the fluid capability of a concert pianist navigating a familiar étude, traversing challenging passages with practised ease. Under his skilful forcing, Taisia had no choice but to reveal, in the end, that she'd known all along about Gennady's feelings for Anoushka – that she'd known, indeed, for over six months.

'Men need their hobbies, *da?*' she said, shrugging her shoulders. 'Some like watching football, some like pickling gherkins – some like carrying on with the neighbour's wife. What difference does it make? I had a soft spot for Danyl myself, as I told Dama Pushkin here' – nodding at Olga – 'but nothing came of it, and so what if it had? What's marriage, anyway, but a promise to stick around most of the time, and watch the same programmes on the box at night? I'd never have done anything to harm Gennady! He was old, and fat, and stupid – but he was mine. No, he wasn't much, was Gennady, just an aggregate salesman, but he was – he was mine,' she went on, this time with something resembling a genuine tear in her eye.

'Besides,' she said, with a touch of heat, 'I couldn't have killed him even if I'd wanted to! I was with the butcher, Popov, at the bar, for hours and hours. He's a good man. Shame about his wife. He told me how he makes sausages from goats and horses together. He combines the meat, I mean,' she clarified.

Vassily nodded. 'Popov said the same,' he said to Loktev. 'Well, he didn't mention the sausages, but he said Taisia here never shifted from the bar.'

But that didn't satisfy Loktev, whose eager nose had scented something more behind her round face and earnest eyes. And now Olga realised that he had saved his true virtuosity for the realm of the imagination, a bravura leap into the unknown that yielded surprising results – an insight beyond even the most fertile of writerly inventions.

'Enough! We know already, Taisia Aristov!' he cried, beating a thin-fingered fist upon the desk until Vassily's breakfast dishes trembled and clattered down upon each other. 'We know – so tell us! Confess it all, as you used to do when I was still Pastor Loktev. Confessing is good for the soul – and, in your case, good for getting you out of a hole, too. We know that you burned the bodies!'

Taisia gasped and stared at Olga with dismay in her eyes, but Olga shook her head hurriedly, a mute disclaimer of all involvement. Olga had, in fact, committed a minor act of perjury by excluding Taisia's arson from her written statement, but there was no way to tell Taisia this in front of Vassily and Loktev.

Fortunately, however, Loktev soon relieved her of the need to do so.

'Oh, it's obvious,' he said. 'Look at her hair! Cut off on one side, but messily, leaving a few scorched strands behind the ear. She probably set the fire with petrol – a rookie mistake, that, it burns too fast. It flared up and caught her hair, and she cut it off to hide what she'd done.'

Olga and Taisia stared, dumbfounded, at this display of deductive brilliance, but Loktev was still talking.

'Come on,' he went on. 'I know there's more – much more! Nobody would go that far to protect the reputation of some drunken neighbour. No, no – there are more secrets under that headscarf than burned hair alone. Come on! I know already. Just get it off your chest, and I'll see about keeping you away from the federal prisons. Otherwise, who knows what I might tell Irina Palatnik, next time I swing by Yashkino?'

'All right – all right!' cried Taisia at last, after Loktev had continued in this vein for some time. She was half standing, as if to challenge his aggression, but then dropped back into her chair and buried her head in her hands, so that her voice when she spoke came to them in dampened, muffled tones. 'All right – so you know. You know I was blackmailing Danyl Petrovich. A train driver who drinks too much – who wouldn't try to make a bit of spare cash out of that? What's the point of making me tell you?'

'Ah,' said Loktev, sinking into a chair across from her and steepling his fingers like a TV villain. '*Ah* . . . Yes, I see. Irina Palatnik has been blackmailing you your whole life. So when you realised Danyl was a drinker it was the obvious next step for you to do the same.'

'*Taisia*,' said Olga, in tones of deepest disillusion.

Taisia shrugged, and shot her a sullen look.

'But you only did it to protect yourself,' Olga continued. 'I suppose you were worried about something incriminating being found in his pocket. And now that I think of it – that photo we found in Danyl's pocket, Zlata M – you were—'

'You were *relieved* when you saw it,' put in Nevena Komarov, her deep blue eyes fixed on Taisia's face. 'Yes, you were relieved. I remember now. How strange to be relieved at seeing some photo from the past come out of a dead man's pocket – unless you were worried something worse might appear . . . A blackmail letter, perhaps?'

'How did you know there was more?' muttered Vassily to Loktev, staring down at Taisia, who still sat, head in hands, unmoving, as if dark silence could conjure her a route away from accusing voices.

'I didn't.' Loktev grinned. 'But it's always worth going the extra mile, Marushkin – you never know what you might find. Just like in your back room, there.'

'The old gear, you mean?' said Vassily, puzzled. 'It's just ancient stuff from my father's day.'

'Don't be too quick to discount old things,' said Loktev, quite serious for once beneath his cleric's whiskers. 'I saw something of your father's that interested me greatly – one old thing that could still be of use. And a second is Taisia herself,' he continued, waving at the head still buried in ten stubby fingers. 'Keep her in, Marushkin! A night or two in your cells would loosen anyone's tongue. Who knows what she's seen, about this godforsaken hole? There could be a vital clue buried under that headscarf. Let's see what we get – and, remember, always go the extra mile.'

'That's what I say,' muttered Vassily, but so quietly that Loktev, now bustling off towards the back office once more, did not hear.

'Marushkin, sling that old hag in the cells, and come!' he called down the corridor. 'Bring your son, too, once you've locked up – and the women. Why have one guinea pig, when four will do?'

Events now moved swiftly towards a conclusion as disastrous as it was unforeseen, though Olga had no notion of their acceleration. She felt, if anything, that things were moving more slowly than she would have liked, and her primary sensation, when walking to the Roslazny police station on the following morning, the Tuesday, was one of frustration.

She was a little hesitant, if she was honest with herself, about returning to Vassily's inner circle – not least because his reason for accepting her into the fold once more was rather opaque. She hadn't been able to muster the courage to ask him directly what had changed his mind, but he had hinted at the value of her unsanctioned explorations in Café Astana, alongside her conversations with Taisia Aristov, Ludis Kuskov and others. This puzzled Olga a little: was Vassily able, legally speaking, to make use of any of these unauthorised enquiries? And, if so, why had he expelled her from the investigation in the first place?

His attitude towards Nevena Komarov had also caused Olga some mystification. At times he seemed quite enchanted by her, fussing around her to ensure that her every whim was anticipated and met with celerity. At other times, though, he seemed almost subdued – overwhelmed, perhaps, by the depth of his newfound feeling for her, wondered Olga, or maybe, just maybe, he was wrestling with guilt occasioned by Olga herself. They'd almost come to an understanding, hadn't they? They'd been close, spent time together, laughed and cried together, had almost *died* together, but always Vassily's lost wife Rozalina had come between them and prevented anything more serious from happening.

Yes, Rozalina – but her memory hadn't stopped Vassily dancing attendance upon Nevena Komarov, had it? thought Olga, bitterly. But, then, Olga didn't look quite like Nevena, did she? Nobody looked like Nevena, least of all Olga.

Still, at least Olga was better-presented than Taisia Aristov on that particular morning, she thought, before reproaching herself for unkindness. If she were Taisia's age, and had spent a night in Vassily's cells, she, too, would probably look as if a bear had dragged her through a hedge backwards. She gazed at Taisia's bedraggled hair, crumpled clothes and dark-rimmed eyes, and felt the beginnings of pity stir within her. Taisia might have blackmailed Danyl Petrovich, but someone else had blackmailed her first – one Irina Palatnik, to be precise, Taisia's fellow-resident in Yashkino and (on Loktev's account) quite a piece of work.

Taisia was always short of money as a result, and since she was too proud – and too old-fashioned – to ask Gennady for help she'd taken a more direct route to solving her problems. And now, said Vassily, she faced up to eight years in prison – eight years that could well witness the end of her earthly existence amid the dreary servitude of a federal jail. Vassily had already fetched the evidence that – barring a miracle – would convict her: the photograph Olga had already seen, with Danyl behind the wheel. In clear daylight, though, she could see what she'd missed before: a bottle of vodka grasped in Danyl Petrovich's left hand. And there were other photos, too, hidden more deeply in Taisia's baggage: images of Danyl drinking behind station buildings, being helped up the steps of his locomotive, and unconscious upon a park bench in summer.

'It's like they say: a person's bag reveals a person's heart,' Olga had said, when Vassily told them of his discoveries – subsequently experiencing a fierce jet of satisfaction when Nevena nodded sagely, as if hearing a well-worn proverb.

Taisia had hardly responded when they brought her a spartan breakfast made up from Vassily's fast-dwindling stores, or when Vassily, a little later, showed her the photos he'd found in her bag, with the notes she'd made on the back.

'You brought them to show Danyl after the ceremony,' said Loktev, with his usual certainty. 'Remind him what's what – eh? Show him what would happen to the so-called local hero, the Russian Railways poster boy, if he didn't keep paying up?'

'Maybe,' said Taisia – but with a shiftiness that was as clear an answer as any. And then, with a sudden access of anger, she stood up and grasped the bars that stood between them. 'You think you're all so wonderful, don't you? Well, whatever I've done, I didn't kill Gennady, any more than I killed Danyl or Anoushka. If I was blackmailing him, why would I derail his train? Stands to reason I'd keep him alive.'

She followed this undeniable truth with a diatribe against police inefficiency. 'You lot are all the same! You do the easy things and let the harder things pass by – targeting little people like me and letting the killers and the oligarchs and the politicians walk free! I've seen it time and again, but I never thought I'd be on the receiving end. Me, a law-abiding *grazhdanka*, who always pays her taxes and puts her bins out on time!'

Olga thought it was a bit much for Taisia, a confirmed blackmailer and arsonist, to describe herself as a law-abiding citizen, but she let it pass.

'So you keep me stuck in here on some trumped-up blackmail charge, while my poor husband's murderer walks free! Poor Gennady, who never did anybody any harm – well, apart from Danyl Petrovich, I suppose, but I don't think Danyl knew, so what does it matter? Gennady wouldn't hurt a fly – he was so simple. Just the other day he asked me what the difference was between real and fake fur, and did women still wear things like his mother had. What can you say to a man like that? Where do you even begin?'

They didn't know how to answer her, and in any case Loktev had urgent tasks for them to complete, so they left her there, muttering to herself about police inefficiency and the injustices of modern-day Russia.

'Let her out later on, Marushkin,' said Loktev, as they went into the front office. 'But not before you get her fingerprints, *da*?'

Loktev's explorations in the police-station back office had yielded a Soviet-era fingerprinting kit that was already antiquated when Vassily's father had taken over the station shortly after perestroika. But the powdered ink, they discovered through experimenting on each other, was still viable, as were the detection pads. With a degree of care and precision Loktev had managed to extract two clear prints from the handle of the half-burned hoe that Vassily had in evidence. The plan for the remainder of the day was to fingerprint the entire village, or as many people as they could before the ancient ink ran out – starting with the remaining well-wishers, Ludis and Taisia, before proceeding to newcomers like Polina Klemovsky, and then all the villagers.

Vassily was particularly attentive towards Nevena that morning – he was plainly in his enchanted mode – and, as a result, had made it clear that Olga wasn't required for the fingerprinting activity around the village.

Reluctant to be dismissed, Olga instead invented a reason of her own for leaving. 'I'd better be off,' she said, gathering her things and darting a brassy smile at Nevena. 'Anna's expecting me back – she and Pasha were up all night with the children, and I'm due to take over and give them a break. Keep me posted, won't you?'

And without waiting for a reply she was gone, thrusting aside the creaking door with practised ease, and ducking her head as she pierced the threaded veil of falling snow that flowed beyond the exit. Then she pulled the door behind her, darkening the passageway as she went.

When she arrived back at the house she saw Fyodor, the Dreamer, standing by the front door and holding it open for Boris and Gyorgy as they scampered in and out, screaming with laughter and clearly relishing the unexpected and prolonged holiday. She hadn't seen them as much as usual these past few days, she reflected, having been so caught up with her investigations, and she smiled as she saw them now.

'Olga Pushkin!' cried Fyodor. 'Look, boys! Olga is here again!'

It took some time for the riotous welcome to die down, especially as it was repeated when Pasha, Anna and baby Ilya came to the door in their turn – but finally all the members of the household, and Fyodor, were snugly ensconced inside Olga's little sitting room and passing round honeyed cakes and mugs of hot, sweet tea.

'I'll almost be sad when everything goes back to normal,' said Fyodor, as the conversation turned – as it often did – to communications with the outside world.

'I agree,' said Olga, but Fyodor hadn't finished.

'I mean, it's like a taste of a different world,' he went on, holding each of them in turn with his penetrating gaze. 'A taste of the past – a simpler time.'

'Oh, yes, a time without anaesthetic,' said Anna, to a suppressed snort from Olga. 'Only a man would think that was better!'

'Yes, modern things have their uses, Fyodor,' said Pasha, who looked thin and drawn – and older, Olga realised for the first time – after yet another sleepless night. 'The army couldn't get by without technology – without radio and sensors and radar and, oh, all kinds of things. I'd probably better not say any more, in case the FSB's listening – or should I say Pastor Loktev?'

'Who's that?' said Boris, suddenly, making Pasha jump nervously.

'Someone's at the door, someone's at the door,' said little Gyorgy, in the singsong voice he adopted when he'd had too much sugar.

'I'll get it,' said Anna, beginning to pull herself to her feet – but Fyodor made her sit down again with a gentle hand, prompting a secret smile between Pasha and Olga, and went to the door himself.

'Vassily Marushkin!' said Fyodor. 'Well, come in, man – the more the merrier! Why – why are you standing there like that?'

'Fyodor,' said Vassily, after a moment, rather tersely, glancing round him towards the living room beyond. 'Olga,' he said awkwardly, stuffing his cap once more upon his tousled black hair.

'What is it, Vassily?' called Olga from her seat; and then, seeing that Vassily really wasn't going to come in, she heaved herself out of her chair – a particularly comfortable one, that had come with the house – and made her way to the door.

'Well, Sergeant Marushkin,' she said, leaning against the doorpost with a cheery smile. The children's welcome a short time before had warmed her heart, and she was in the mood to forget her difficulties for as long as she could. But

Vassily's next words dispelled this possibility utterly and unequivocally.

'I'm sorry, Olga,' he said, 'really sorry, but—'

'But what, Vassily?' said Fyodor, staring at him quizzically. 'You look like you've seen a ghost!'

'Not a ghost,' said Vassily. 'It's our fingerprinting, to be precise.'

'Ah – how's that going?' said Olga.

'Oh, fine – fine,' said Vassily, pulling off his hat again, and scratching his head as if the pressure might help force words out of his mouth.

'But what is it, Marushkin?' said Fyodor again. 'You can tell us, you know – we won't tell anyone else!'

'It's you, Olga,' Vassily said at last.

'What is?' she said, staring at him.

'We drew a blank,' he said.

'Well, it was always a bit of a long shot, and—'

But he cut her off. 'No – we drew a blank *at first*,' he said. 'All we found out is that the hoe was stolen from Artyom Petrov's place, up by your father's. He recognised it as soon as he saw it. But then,' he went on, turning his hat in his hands, 'then we checked the prints we did at first – the ones we did as a practice run, to make sure the kit still worked. And – and we got a match.'

'Not – not *Nevena*?' breathed Olga.

'No, not Nevena,' said Vassily. 'Oh, Olga, the match was you!'

12

Room Without a View

'It's not looking too good, Olga,' said Nevena Komarov, glancing over her shoulder.

'What d'you mean, not looking good?' said Olga fiercely, gesturing at the iron bars that surrounded her. 'It can't look much worse than it does right now!'

Barely an hour before, Vassily Marushkin had taken Olga's arm and marched her through the snow-clad streets, responding to her many questions and entreaties with nothing more than thin-lipped, one-word answers, supplemented by the occasional sideways glance in which Olga detected a certain puzzlement and even – when he thought Olga wasn't looking – a hint of a smile playing around his lips.

Appropriately enough, this half-detected expression on the weather-beaten face of Roslazny's sergeant-in-charge played merry havoc with the emotions of Olga Pushkin. Had Vassily Marushkin come so far – or, rather, fallen so low – in such a short time that he could contemplate her imminent imprisonment not just with equanimity but with genuine amusement? What was Olga to make of her friend, now that he had so visibly shown himself capable of such conduct – behaviour that far out-wintered even Siberia's fell Decembers in its cold-hearted callousness? Were Nevena's lustrous blue eyes such an irresistible draw to him that her own, rather more workaday, green ones deserved such ruthless neglect? She looked sideways at him as they walked, in her turn, but not with a smile.

Seemingly oblivious to Olga's inner turmoil, Vassily had deposited her in the cell next to Taisia Aristov's with a distinct lack of ceremony, pausing only to mutter a few private words to Loktev of the FSB before scooping up the last of Kliment's belongings from the four-plank bed, and tossing them out of the iron-clad door. Then, still unspeaking, he had ushered her inside, clanged the door shut, turned the key, and walked off down the passageway with the relieved air of a parent strapping a recalcitrant child into their car-seat at last, leaving Olga staring after him in dismay and disbelief.

'No, I know, I know,' said Nevena, sympathetically, shaking her head in response to Olga's complaints. She glanced behind her in case Vassily had seen her enter the cell corridor, before relaxing and crossing her legs once more. She was sitting, or rather daintily perching, on the slender bench that ran along the wall opposite the cells – a bench that, in happier times, had served Vassily and his son Kliment as a kind of impromptu wardrobe, but which had now resumed its intended purpose of supporting those who wished to visit prisoners in the Roslazny jail.

'It's just terrible to see you locked up like this,' she went on. 'You, Olga Pushkin, behind bars for derailing a Russian Railways service! It's ridiculous. I can't imagine what Vassily's thinking, depriving his son of prime sleeping quarters for such a stupid reason.'

(Vassily and Kliment, honouring a tradition dating back to the construction of the Roslazny police station in the 1950s, always slept in the cells on account of the superior heating on that side of the building – the joke being that the extra warmth came from the criminals' proximity to Hell.)

'I mean, I know what he's thinking,' admitted Nevena, uncrossing her legs and leaning forward to gaze into Olga's eyes, fixing her with an unswerving sapphire gaze. 'He's going by the book, of course. Ever since he found that ballast removed by the track, he's needed to pin the derailment on someone – if only to make sure he and dear Kliment can stay on here for as long as they like. And ever since he found that half-burned hoe by the ballast, he's needed to find out if there were any fingerprints on it, and if so, whose. It's funny, isn't it, to think of a humble garden tool bringing down a billion roubles' worth of heavy-duty train! A cheap hoe that some yokel farmer used to thin out honeyberry stalks and spread manure over his radishes . . . It's funny, really, when you think about it.'

'Yes, it's absolutely hilarious, Nevena,' said Olga, not troubling to hide her sarcasm, or her gritted teeth.

'Oh, I'm sorry, Olga,' said Nevena, a troubled look flashing over her face. 'I didn't mean to make light of things. I just can't take Vassily seriously when he does stupid things like this.'

'He looked serious enough when he locked me in,' replied Olga, getting up from the uneven, timeworn bed with its threadbare grey blankets, and pacing up and down the cell. 'And banning all visitors, too, as if I were some kind of political prisoner. I just can't understand how he'd think – *why* he'd think – I could possibly do something like that! I thought we were – I thought we were friends,' she went on, pausing, and standing on tiptoe so she could look out of the thin, high, barred window that ran across her cell and its neighbours. But all she could see was white on white, whirling snowflakes set against a sky of bleached, towering clouds that scudded across her narrow shaft of vision.

'The thing is,' began Nevena, crossing her legs, then uncrossing them once more. 'The thing is—'

'What *is* the thing?' said Olga, turning impatiently and staring at her friend with cross eyes. 'Why has Vassily Marushkin done this to me?'

'Look, Olga,' said Nevena, getting up and putting her delicate hands on the bars that separated them, 'you've got to think how Vassily sees things. He's a policeman, *nyet*? Yes, he's a friend, but first and foremost he's a policeman, by training and instinct. So he sees someone like you – a friend, a fellow villager – who, for whatever reason, has got her prints on what turns out to be a murder weapon, and he starts to wonder . . . He would wonder if you might have resented Danyl Petrovich's success, his dramatic rise up the ranks with no account taken of those he trampled along the way, the way *he* made it as an engine driver starting out from your very hut, while you're still stuck on trackside duty – and not just trackside duty, mind you, but duty with an extra dose of unwanted travel to foreign parts. He might think about all those things—'

'You mean he *has* thought about all those things,' said Olga, quite sharply. 'Thought about them, and discussed them with you!'

'Well, yes, I suppose so,' said Nevena, glancing downwards at her feet. 'But I always argue your corner, Olga! I told him you would never get jealous like that – that you'd never take it into your head to derail an entire train just to kill one man! Who would do something like that? Tell me – who?'

Nevena was staring at her with unusual intensity, Olga noticed, and suddenly she became suspicious: had Vassily sent her in to extract a confession? He hadn't returned once since he'd locked her up. Was this part of some master plan to wrap things up as fast as possible and secure his continued residence in Roslazny?

But then Nevena continued talking, and Olga relaxed a little: her friend seemed genuinely curious about the identity of the killer, and clearly on the basis that it wasn't Olga. She was speculating instead about what could possibly have driven a person to such extreme ends.

'Only something very bad – something really terrible – could force someone to do a thing like that,' she was saying, having got up so that she, too, could pace up and down. 'Something very bad – something *evil* . . . Because, of course,' she went on, turning to face Olga with wide eyes, 'it could have been many more lives than just Danyl and Anoushka's – it could have been hundreds of passengers on the Trans-Siberian.

'And there's also the paint,' she added in a much more pragmatic tone.

'The *paint*?'

'Yes – you know, your bedroom window! It was painted shut, so you couldn't have got out to the tracks and back without being seen by your housemates – whom we've already questioned. And then it was painted by a left-handed person, whereas you're right-handed.'

'Well, doesn't that put me in the clear?'

'Not really,' said Nevena, concern written across her features.

'You could still have done it yourself, using your left hand to throw us off the trail. So, you see, it's like I said – it doesn't look too good. I'd better go,' she went on, reluctantly lifting her fingers from the bars of Olga's cell. 'Vassily's busy in the back office with Loktev, so I came out to make coffee, but they'll notice I'm gone soon. Vassily wants my help with the paperwork.'

'Just make sure he doesn't have my name on it,' Olga said, as Nevena walked off, looking sorrowfully over her shoulder at her. 'You're the only one he listens to, these days.'

'Someone a little jealous, are they?' said a voice from the cell next door, making her jump. Having snored soundly through Olga's arrival and subsequent conversation with Nevena Komarov, Taisia Aristov had woken at last.

'Mind your own business,' snapped Olga.

'Touchy! Better not act like that in prison – you'll get your throat cut in no time.'

'I'm not going to prison,' said Olga, firmly – far more firmly, in fact, than she felt. Ever since meeting Vassily, she'd slept just a little more easily at night, reassured by the presence of a policeman among her inner circle of close friends – a policeman who might step in to help her if she ever got into trouble. And she was definitely in trouble now: nobody could doubt that. A month ago – no, even a *week* ago – she'd have felt less anxious than she did now, certain of Vassily's comforting presence and sturdy support. But if he really had turned irrevocably against her, what hope did she have?

Olga shook her head to dismiss the thought, and with it the panic that rose sharply in her chest, then peered out of the window at the tree-tops she could see in the far distance. But there was no comfort there: four branches had broken from the tree, hadn't they, aeons before Danyl's train had crashed? And there had been only three deaths so far. Maybe she'd end up envying Gennady Aristov, she reflected disconsolately, before turning back to her bunk and slumping down upon it. At least Gennady had died in Roslazny. Nobody could take that from him now.

'Grub's up, everybody,' said Kliment that evening, setting down the dinner tray with a clatter.

'Everybody? Everybody?' said Taisia Aristov. 'Who are you talking about? It's only me and this – this *criminal* here.' She jerked her head in Olga's direction, then beckoned Kliment closer to the door of her cell. 'And I don't much care for being grouped in with the likes of her.'

Kliment frowned. 'You're in for blackmailing, don't forget, Dama Aristov – you admitted it to Pastor Loktev.'

'*Pastor* Loktev,' sneered Taisia. 'Loktev of the FSB, you mean. Don't you know they're trained to get so-called confessions out of people who've done nothing? Any lawyer worth her salt would get that thrown out in a second – if we had decent courts, anyway. But *her*,' she went on, jerking a thumb at Olga's cell next door, 'she's been proven guilty by age-old techniques! There it was in black and white, they tell me – her fingerprints on that rake, or pickaxe, or whatever it was she used to bring the train down, and no alibi worth speaking of.'

'I can hear you, you know, Taisia,' said Olga, rattling her fingernails irritably on the thin iron bars that divided them. 'It was a hoe, to be precise. But I keep telling you they aren't my fingerprints on that handle. I never touched it!'

'Oh, well, there you go, Kliment Marushkin!' said Taisia, sitting up and flinging a demonstrative arm out in front of her. 'She didn't touch it! She wasn't jealous of Danyl Petrovich, oh, no – not this one! She never set out one day and dug out that ballast, rock by rock, until Danyl's train came toppling down, and with poor Anoushka inside, too. A crying shame, that was – a crying shame. And if it hadn't been for all that, my Gennady'd still be alive. Oh, yes, I've no doubt of that. She finished him off herself. But, oh, no! You can tell your father to let her out – she's innocent as a dove, this one!'

Olga sighed. She'd heard all this before, as had Kliment – and Vassily, too, when he came by earlier that day, plus Nevena Komarov, Loktev, and any other visitor with the remotest capacity to influence Taisia's relative standing with the police when the weather-induced lockdown finally came to an end. Olga even suspected Taisia of currying favour with Vassily's pet ferret, Rasputin: she'd found her trying to feed him some of her goat stew through the bars of her cell door after lunch. But it was a different story in the long gaps between visitors, when the two women – one nearly old, one no longer young – were left alone in the cells. Then, with nobody left worth influencing, Taisia talked differently, communicating with Olga as if she were a human being rather than a dangerous criminal, and even sharing some poignant anecdotes about her late husband, Gennady.

'He wasn't a great man,' she remarked, after dinner that day. 'He wasn't even a particularly good one, either. But he was mine. Yes! He was mine.'

Taisia had, of course, already expressed this thought on a previous occasion, but Olga didn't feel inclined to say so just then. The poor woman had just lost her husband, after all, even if she was a blackmailer. And wasn't that the key to happiness, anyway, treating things or people who barely passed muster as if they were the key to long-cherished dreams?

She felt less charitable towards Taisia's repetitive repartee by the time it came to lights out on her first day in prison. Day one? It felt like day twenty. Already Olga knew in intimate detail the appearance of all the walls that surrounded them: the mould around the doorframe that led to the front office, the extended crack in the plaster that ran downwards from the edge of Taisia's cell, the yellowed plastic of the single bulb housing that hung suspended over them . . . Olga had spent her whole life in confined conditions of one kind or another, whether it was the house she'd shared with her father Mikhail, her little rail-side hut, or the oppressive machinations of Russian Railways – but this was a different *podstakannik* of tea altogether.

'Bet Mongolia doesn't seem so bad now, does it?' said Taisia, chuckling, when Olga told her of the circumstances that had led up to the crash. And Olga had to admit that Taisia was right: for all she had dreaded journeying to Ulaanbaatar, an extended sojourn abroad was infinitely more desirable than an extended sojourn in a Kemerovo prison. Not even the prospect of new and undeniably rich first-hand experiences – experiences that any worthwhile writer should surely be glad to get under her belt – could allay the cold dread that filled her heart when she contemplated her future.

'Make a book of it – that'll show 'em,' Taisia said, late that night, after Olga had revealed her literary ambitions in a darkness relieved only by the faint shadows of the bars between them. Pressed for conversation despite the lateness of the hour, and tired of answering the same questions about family, friends and romantic encounters past and present, Olga had told Taisia about her bestseller-to-be *Find Your Rail Self: 100 Life Lessons from the Trans-Siberian Railway* – then instantly regretted it on account of the deluge of questions, commentary and advice that flowed from Taisia's lips.

'Just write what you see,' she said, more than once, fixing Olga with glowing eyes. 'A railway-woman's take on prison – that'd sell! I'd buy it!'

But Olga wasn't so sure. Why would her perspective be any more interesting than anyone else's? Wasn't it quite presumptuous to think that it would be, just because of who she happened to be – a railway-woman in prison? Olga thought writing was about more than merely writing down what had happened to you so that the reader could recreate your life, like someone glumly copying a picture. At best, writing like that would be dull, prosaic and banal, while at worst, it could become a kind of chilling uniformity, a subtle ideology urging that nobody could write about anything but their own limited experience. But Olga didn't like to think of literature in that way. Indeed, she didn't think that kind of writing *was* literature. For Olga, literature was about imagination – about transcending the ordinary, not exalting it; neither a surrender nor an embrace, but rather an escape.

'An escape?' scoffed Taisia, mistaking her meaning. 'Fat chance – even from these rusting bars! It's a disgrace, the state of this place – a disgrace!'

Once again, Olga had heard this before, for Taisia had already complained about their accommodation after dinner.

'See what we've got to put up with, young man?' she'd said to Kliment, as he came in to clear up their dinner plates, rapping a knuckle as she did so on a large patch of mould by her head.

'You think *you*'re badly off?' said Kliment, crossly. 'You've got my bedroom, Dama Aristov! Don't you know the cells are the warmest rooms in the place? The heating pipes run through both walls' – knocking, in his turn, on the plaster above his head – 'so you've got double warmth. Comfort, cosiness – luxury! Meanwhile Papa and I are stuck out in the back office, sleeping on the floor, with only the electric heater to stop our tea freezing over. You should be grateful for what you've got,' he concluded, with the primness sometimes affected by the young, 'and not complain too much. Otherwise worse things might happen!'

What could be worse than this? thought Olga, as Kliment turned on his heel and disappeared down the passageway. Locked up, suspected of murder, confined with a self-confessed blackmailer, and deprived of friends and family except during visiting hours (nine thirty to eleven on Thursdays and Saturdays) – not to mention the stinging betrayal of Vassily Marushkin, whose good character had apparently been stolen away by a haunting pair of dazzling blue eyes.

Fyodor would be annoyed, thought Olga. The bad cop was a cliché of police dramas, and he hated clichés – yet here was Vassily, filling the role with ease. The man she'd thought of as different had turned out just the same as all the rest.

'He's not worth it, *solnyoshko*,' said Taisia Aristov, picking her teeth with a nail she'd dug out of the bench. 'He's not worth it.'

That might well be true, Olga admitted to herself, as Taisia fell silent at last, but she mourned his passing, nonetheless.

A world without Vassily at her side, even in the attenuated form of a lovelorn friend bent on an endless, futile search for a disappeared wife, was a colder, more threatening place.

'What's that noise?' said Taisia Aristov early on Wednesday morning.

'What? What noise?' said Olga, reluctantly opening her eyes after an uncomfortable night spent on Kliment's wooden bed. How on earth did he bear it? she thought, reaching down a hand to massage her throbbing lower back. How did he bear it week after week, when she was in agony after just one night in prison?

'That clanging noise, of course,' said Taisia, impatiently, thrusting her face against the bars between them, and staring at Olga with her gooseberry eyes. 'It's that idiot son of Marushkin's, I'll bet, shooting pellets at tin-cans, or teaching himself to count.'

'Nonsense,' said Olga, getting up with a sigh and walking over to the window. She looked up into the crescent light of dawn and saw one fewer icicle than she'd seen the day before, then watched another icicle and a third detach themselves from their moorings and plummet out of sight.

Why must I always see things falling when I look? she asked herself. Boughs, trains, icicles . . . Can just one thing stay upright when my gaze falls upon it?

Aloud she said, 'It's thawing, of course. The weather's turned. And that noise? Probably snow on the roof melting, and falling on something metal outside. A grotty old dish for Rasputin, as likely as not. Though it reminds me . . .'

'Yes?'

'Oh, it's nothing,' she said, turning back to gaze out of the window at the sullen sky beyond, barely registering the consequent grunt of irritation from Taisia.

But it wasn't nothing, really. It wasn't nothing at all. The regularly repeated metallic resonance had brought an old echo to mind: the sound of wheel-tappers at Tayga station, walking past the street-long trains from end to end and rapping each and every shining wheel as they went with purpose-built hammers. A strong, intact wheel would ring clear and true, while a cracked or damaged one, by contrast, would yield only a strangled, muffled clang. If only people could be tapped with purpose-built hammers, thought Olga, such that good ones – like Anna Kabalevsky and her brother Pasha – could be put to one side out of harm's way, and specifically out of the reach of confusing people, like Vassily Marushkin, who seemed good but was in reality, it seemed, not so good after all.

At least there was a third kind: people like old man Solotov, Anna's ex-husband Bogdan Kabalevsky, and Olga's own father Mikhail – people who were so obviously meant to be avoided that a well-placed hammer blow would be quite superfluous. And the same was true of Polina Klemovsky, thought Olga, later that morning, when Vassily brought Polina into the station for a consultation.

'Don't know what *she's* doing here,' said Taisia to Olga, when she heard Polina's harsh, croaking laugh coming down the passageway.

'Ssh,' said Olga, fiercely – so fiercely that Taisia shrugged crossly at her.

'Well, I'm only a poor, grieving widow,' she muttered,

turning back towards the bunk that normally served as Vassily's bed. 'Just a widow – that's all. No reason for anyone to be polite to *me*, oh, no!'

But Olga only pointed silently at the open doorway leading towards the front office where Vassily, Polina and Nevena Komarov were talking, as if to highlight the rare opportunity to gather vital information without Vassily's awareness. Then she pressed her head against the bars nearest the doorway and listened as intently as she had ever listened in her life.

'Later *today*?' she heard Vassily saying. 'They can really get through today?'

'Of course they can,' Polina replied. 'It's thawing fast – can't you see that? And this is Russian Railways we're talking about! We've got the best snowploughs in the world.'

Nevena said something soft in response that Olga failed to catch. Vassily replied in similarly muted tones, prompting Olga to tut in frustration. Why couldn't people speak up when she was trying to eavesdrop on them? But then Polina started to speak again, more distinctly than the others – and though her words seemed innocuous enough, Olga's heart began to beat more rapidly, slowly at first but then with increasing speed until she felt she might faint from excitement.

'That wasn't Russian Railways' fault,' she was saying. 'That was this idiot's, right here! She should have checked with Leonid at Corporate Services, shouldn't she? Then she'd have known when I really got here!'

'Don't say *she* when I'm right in front of you,' put in Nevena. 'It's not my fault they got the paperwork wrong.'

'I'll say what I damn well like!' Polina responded, more hotly than Olga had ever heard her speak before. 'If it wasn't for that mix-up over dates, this other idiot here – what's up, *Sergeant*? Has nobody called you an idiot to your face before? – this other idiot here would never have accused me of setting fire to abandoned buildings and nicking old ladies' unmentionables from laundry lines! And another thing . . .'

Of course, Olga said to herself, no longer listening to Polina's monologue. Of course: someone had tried to frame Polina, not for the derailment but for a host of other, smaller, crimes, both here in Roslazny and in Polina's old stamping ground, Itatka. She'd almost forgotten the hurried conversation she'd had with Kliment at the police station after she broke into Café Astana, when Kliment had related how Polina had told Vassily of strange things back in Itatka: small misdemeanours that had stopped before she left, then started in Roslazny the day afterwards. Olga had discounted Polina as a suspect for the derailment because she was so obviously unpleasant, which ran counter to Pasha's theory that murderers would always seem nice. But what if someone *else* was the murderer, and was trying to frame Polina instead?

Admittedly, they hadn't done a very good job. They'd got the dates of Polina's move wrong, for one thing, so that crimes were going on in Roslazny before she arrived, and had stopped in Itatka before she left. And they'd somehow got Olga's fingerprints on the hoe instead of Polina's, too – assuming, of course, that the Soviet-era fingerprinting kit was capable of telling the difference. (It had crossed Olga's mind that a fingerprinting kit capable of assigning guilt to anyone at all could be a useful tool for a dictatorship.) But regardless of the murderer's mistakes, here was more evidence of a live, cunning intelligence at work – not a wild, undisciplined killer who lashed out willy-nilly, but a man who planned ahead, who thought things through, who *worked* at it. This was someone who took murder seriously – seriously enough to start framing a suspect weeks beforehand, undertaking a grab-bag of petty crimes to cast a dark aura over Polina Klemovsky long before Danyl's ill-fated train ever set off from Novosibirsk. Yes, this was someone to reckon with. Someone to—

Voices broke through her inner monologue – raised voices; and one of them belonged to Vassily Marushkin.

'You can't go down there,' he was saying. 'It's not visiting hours!'

'Do I look like someone who lets rules like that get in my way?' called another voice, before its owner burst into the cell room with a notable lack of ceremony. It was Polina Klemovsky, of course. Who else?

'What are you doing here?' said Olga, coldly.

'Just wanted to get here before anyone from the papers,' said Polina, swiftly raising her phone and snapping a couple of pictures of Olga before anyone could stop her.

'Ah-ah!' she cried, swerving her phone out of Vassily's reach, before pulling her jumper forward and dropping it down her chest. 'I'd like to see you try to get it out of there!'

Vassily started backwards with a look of horror on his face. 'I wouldn't dare,' he muttered.

'That's what I thought,' said Polina, smugly. 'I'll flog these to the highest bidder. And I already know who he is – or rather, who *B* is . . . Don't worry, Olga Pushkin, you'll be famous after all. Just not in the way you thought.'

Olga saw that Nevena, hovering behind Polina and Vassily, was looking at her with sympathy, mixed with evident dislike of

Olga's replacement as track engineer. Behind her, Olga thought she could see Kliment's bowling-ball head, too.

'Don't set too much store by phones, Polina Klemovsky,' said Olga. 'Didn't you know they're a double-edged sword?'

'What d'you mean?'

'Well, I might just have done a bit of filming on the morning of the crash – filming *down by the tracks*. Maybe I picked up something you'd been up to, who knows? Some bit of maintenance you forgot to carry out, perhaps?'

'Rubbish,' said Polina. 'I told you before, I've done nothing wrong. I hardly got here before that damn train went down! If anything, you've just slung a noose around your neck by putting your inadequacies on record. I hope you choke on them!'

'That's enough of that,' said Vassily, clearly shocked by Polina's explicit words. Nevena seemed to agree: Olga distinctly saw a startled look upon her face, and her hand loosened her mother's scarf around her neck.

'Look, I'm serious,' said Vassily, reaching out a firm hand to Polina's elbow. 'If you don't want to join them in the cells, get yourself out front again – now!'

'Better make a move, I suppose,' said Polina, airily, and just as airily brushing his hand off her arm. 'Don't want to linger too long here anyway. Who knows what I'd catch?' With a toad-like grimace at Olga, she turned away from the cells and then, with a final flourish of her yellow clogs, she was gone.

By lunchtime, Olga had acquired something she had never expected to acquire: a sincere admiration for long-term convicts.

How on earth did they manage prison life without going stark raving mad within a week? The unvaried surroundings, the terrible food, the dreary undesired familiarity of tiny details of wood and stone and iron . . . And worst of all, thought Olga, was the conversation: the unavoidable, unceasing, and often unpalatable flood of words that flowed from her neighbour's lips into her own ears as if their shared jail-time could be commuted by another kind of sentence.

How can she chatter away like this, thought Olga, when her husband Gennady is dead by a murderer's hand, and when she herself is facing a long jail sentence for blackmail? Was she so blasé because she herself might be a killer? But no: she had an ironclad alibi for Gennady's death, having spent the afternoon with Nikolai Popov. (Another potential blackmail target, thought Olga, for anyone who knew of his dealings with certain local cat and dog merchants.) And in any case Olga thought that she talked so much because she knew that the alternative was silence, and that in the silence she would be afraid. And the dual-lane dialogue she'd noticed earlier – that, too, was a kind of defensive tactic, wasn't it? A kind of compartmentalisation that she must long have fallen back upon, the churchgoing, headscarf-wearing lady who wasn't above blackmailing a long-term neighbour, and who was blackmailed, in her turn, for reasons unknown. (The one thing Taisia never revealed was the black sin that Irina Palatnik held over her.)

Olga didn't think she could quite rise – or sink – to the level of dividing her time between public good works and private fundraising via roubles in brown envelopes, but she understood the compulsion to fill fearful voids with meaningless words. Seconds became like minutes and minutes like hours, crawling by at a rate so slow as to be almost tangibly painful, and over-shadowed at all times by the dark threat of things to come. But the hardest thing to bear, besides Taisia's frequently repeated anecdotes, was Vassily's absence. Why could he not come and talk to her? If they could just sit down and talk together, with Taisia and Nevena and Loktev and all the others far away, Olga was sure they could sort things out and come to a reasonable – if not a friendly – understanding. Kliment came and Nevena came and Loktev came, but he did not come, and she waited in vain for the sight of his messy black hair and sturdy frame advancing down the passageway.

In the end, her not-quite-solitude was broken from quite another quarter. Not long after Kliment had removed the lunch things from the cells, she heard a thin tinkling sound from the window above her head, followed by a low whistle. Taisia had finally taken a break from exercising her jaw, and looked as if she were asleep again: in any case she was unmoving, so Olga quickly moved aside her bedding and climbed on top of her bunk. By standing on tiptoe, she'd discovered, she could just about see out of the window and down onto the ground, and when she did so she found her brother Pasha standing in the snow and throwing bits of ice at her window.

'Pasha,' she called, pushing open the barred window to its fullest extent – about two inches, just enough to speak through. 'Oh, Pasha! It's so good to see you again! But you'd better not stay too long – Vassily's on the warpath.'

'Don't talk to me about Vassily Marushkin,' muttered Pasha, grimly. 'That man's got a lot to answer for, chucking you in the clink like this – and not even letting us visit, me or Anna or Fyodor or any of the others. The whole village is up in arms,

Olga – we just can't believe it. Our own Olga, accused of murder – of bashing in an old man's head – of derailing a *train*, of all things, after spending so long keeping them safe? Vassily's lost his head – and I know why. It's that Nevena Komarov. She's bewitched him!'

'Oh, Pasha,' said Olga, again. 'Don't you see – it doesn't matter why! It just matters that I'm here, and we need to get me out.'

'We're working on that,' Pasha assured her. 'You've seen the snow melting, of course. Well, we've been putting together a plan of action. Me and Anna and Fyodor Katin. Anna's keeping watch up the road, and Fyodor's back at the house planning who to contact first. We'll have you out in no time, Olga! And then Vassily Kirillovich Marushkin had better watch out. We'll be coming for him next.'

Olga shook her head. What could they do against the authorities? What could even Pasha's love and Anna's piety and Fyodor's passion do, faced with the indomitable might of the state and its numberless arms and agents?

But she said none of this aloud. Aloud, she thanked Pasha, assured him of her relative wellbeing, and asked after Anna's children.

'Oh, they're all fine, fine – missing you, of course. But we said you'd had to go away on the railway again, for work. And then we said— Oh, Kliment!' Pasha continued, in a far louder voice than necessary. 'Fancy – fancy seeing you here! We were just – I mean, I was just out for a smoke.'

Vassily's son Kliment, who had come around the corner with a purposeful look on his face, glanced up at Pasha and gave a quick, distracted smile. 'Hi, Pasha,' he said. 'You're talking to

Olga, I suppose? Hello, Olga!' he added, waving up at the window. 'Don't worry, I'm on your side. I'm just off to the old scrapyard, up by the Blatovs' place, to track down a clue.'

'What kind of clue?' called Olga from the window, and Pasha, too, pressed Kliment to reveal his secrets. But he stubbornly, steadfastly refused: he had let Olga down before, he said, by giving away her clandestine explorations in Café Astana, and had no intention of letting down his source this time – a source, he gave them to believe, with impeccable credentials.

'Just trust me on this one,' he said. 'The person who told me about it can't get there themselves, for obvious reasons – but I can, as long as Papa's kept busy by Pastor Loktev. But I'd better go. That paperwork won't take them for ever. Bye for now – hope to see you out where you belong again soon, Olga.'

And with a cheery wave he set off on his way, tramping down the pathway towards the place where Anna was keeping her (apparently rather inadequate) watch on Pasha's behalf, then disappearing round the corner in the direction of the scrapyard that served as graveyard to the tractors, diggers and other mechanical machinery from the last days of the Roslazny *sozhkhov*.

Olga and Pasha watched him go in rather bemused fashion, then turned to each other and opened their lips; but before they could speak, another and rather more fearsome character hove into view.

'Vassily!' cried Pasha in horror, glancing up the road towards Anna, and realising – too late – that they had picked entirely the wrong spot for her lookout position. Determined to protect against unseen approaches from people coming out of the police station, they had neglected the possibility that the same people might already have gone out before they arrived, before returning from elsewhere like blue-clad boomerangs.

'What on earth are you doing here, Pasha?' said Vassily, with a face like thunder. 'Don't tell me – don't tell me you're talking to the prisoners? You know that's against regulations.'

'The hell with you and your regulations,' began Pasha, but Vassily cut him off.

'Never mind all that now,' said Vassily. 'Just clear off – in a minute. But first tell me if you've seen Kliment. I've been looking all over the place for him – Nevena told me he'd set off on some wild-goose chase on the trail of the killer.'

'Oh, well,' said Pasha, 'I'm not sure, really – I might have . . .'

But Vassily wasn't fooled for a second by Pasha's uncertainty, and soon extracted all the relevant information from him. Pasha had helped to reunite Vassily with Kliment earlier in the year, after all, and could hardly keep them apart now – especially because (as it occurred to Pasha for the first time) Kliment could be walking into a trap set by the murderer himself.

'I won't forget this, Pasha,' Vassily called back over his shoulder. 'Any of this, I mean,' he added, rather more threateningly. 'Now get out of there! Loktev'll be out if he hears you – he's a stickler for the rules, and you don't want to rub him up the wrong way, believe me.'

Pasha watched Vassily go, then turned to face Olga once more. 'I suppose he's right,' he said grudgingly. 'Nobody wants the FSB any more involved in this than they are already.'

'Go, Pasha, go!' said Olga. 'Go, of course! And fast, before that phoney priest finds you. Send Anna my love, and Fyodor, and the children. And don't worry!' she added, as her brother set off. 'I'll be out of here in no time, just like you said.'

Pasha waved and jogged down the road. When he had disappeared from sight, she added: 'But it'll be in a police car, Pasha, I think.'

'That's what *I'm* afraid of,' said a voice behind her, coming from the jail cells.

Olga gasped, and almost fell off her awkward perch between bunk and windowsill. Regaining her balance, she turned and dropped to the floor, then looked up and saw an anxious face staring back at her: the face of Nevena Komarov.

'Listen, Olga,' she breathed, coming closer and holding out her hands between the bars of the cell. 'Listen – things are moving fast. I heard Loktev on the satellite phone, talking to his higher-ups – he's had that phone this whole time, did you know that? Gennady saw him with it – I think that's what they argued about. Anyway, they're looking for a scapegoat to make all this go away. Things are moving fast, and we need to get you out of here. We need to get you out of here now!'

13

From Away

'But, Nevena,' said Olga, trying to process all that her friend had told her, 'how on earth can you get me out, with Loktev and the others hanging around all the time? And – and Taisia Aristov, too,' she added, in a lower voice, suddenly remembering that she had a roommate in the adjoining cell – a roommate who was still sleeping, judging by the resonant snores that filled the air, but who could come to suspicious life at any moment.

Nevena began to respond, but Olga got there before her. 'And in any case,' she continued, 'why would I want to get out? What could look worse, from a criminal point of view, than breaking out of prison? I might as well just call Loktev through now and tell him I did it, that it was me, and I confess my guilt to each and every crime they can think of!'

When Olga fell silent at last, Nevena cleared a space on the bench opposite her cell and sat down, unwinding her mother's green scarf from her neck and folding it neatly beside her. But then she shivered as an icy breeze threaded its way down the corridor, blowing the scarf into a rumpled heap.

'So much for the thaw,' said Nevena, nodding at the window that ran across the cells – a window now covered once more with swirling snowflakes. 'Looks like it's getting worse again. And it'll be worse for you, too, if you stay, Olga. Listen – you don't know what I know. About the case, I mean.'

'How could I know anything, stuck here?' replied Olga, hotly. 'I can hardly pop down the corridor to join your nine a.m. team catch-up, can I? And don't forget, you and Vassily shut me out long before I ended up with iron bars for wallpaper!'

'I know, Olga,' said Nevena, reaching out an elegant hand to caress the metalwork that separated them – a hand with fingers, Olga noticed, that were as pale as the driven snow – as if she could clasp Olga to herself. 'I know, I *know*, and I've felt so terrible all this time . . . But I had to stay close to Vassily, for how else could I try to help you?'

'*Help* me? How do you mean?'

To Olga's surprise, a faint smile began to play around the corners of Nevena's lips. 'Well – you know . . .'

'You've said *know* so many times, but it doesn't *mean* anything without something behind it,' said Olga, becoming irritated again. 'What is it you're trying to say? Just tell me, Nevena, one friend to another.'

Nevena's smile disappeared. 'Olga – *Olga*,' she said, lowering her voice and glancing sideways at Taisia, who, however, was still snoring like Nikolai Popov in the second half of an ice-hockey match. 'You don't have to play the innocent with me any more, you know! I've been around the block a few times. We're friends, *da*? Well, what are friends for, but to close ranks and stand together, like – like family should?'

Olga stared at her for a moment, narrowing her eyes in

sudden suspicion. 'But you don't – you don't think – you don't think I actually *did it*? That I brought down the train, and killed Danyl and Anoushka – and Gennady Aristov, too?'

'Well . . . didn't you?'

'Nevena!' cried Olga, then clapped a belated hand over her mouth. Fortunately Taisia only stirred, falling back into her slumbers once more, so Olga carried on, this time in a lower tone. 'Nevena Komarov,' she said, quite earnestly, 'I never thought I'd live to hear you calmly accusing me of wholesale murder. How – how can you say that? I thought you wanted to convince Vassily of my innocence. What's changed your mind?'

'But, Olga, can you really remember what happened the night before the crash? I remember well enough, because I didn't drink as much as you did. Not that I'm criticising – I know you were off to Mongolia, and hated the thought of it – I'd have downed a gallon too, if I was being sent off to Ulaanbaatar the next day, instead of just up the road to Kemorovo. But because I didn't drink a gallon, I can remember what you talked about – how you resented Polina Klemovsky coming along and taking over your hut, and how Danyl Petrovich had only managed to stay driving for so long, and become a driver in the first place, because he was a man. If I was a detective, I'd say those were two pretty strong motives right there: one to bring down Danyl's train and put him in his place, and two, to frame Polina for it, and put her in *hers*, opening up your job in Roslazny once more . . . And it'd be easy enough, too, for a track engineer to convert motive into action: just grab some garden tools, a hoe and a pickaxe, and move a bit of gravel, and hey presto! Problems solved.'

Again Olga stared at Nevena, slack-jawed. What was her friend telling her now? That she'd confessed to the crimes before she'd even committed them? That she'd concocted some wicked plot to derail Danyl's train and incriminate Polina Klemovsky at the same time, before enacting it with some handy garden tools – and then, presumably, getting rid of Gennady Aristov to keep some secret clue just that, secret?

'Look, Nevena,' she said, 'I'll admit I drank too much that night – how sick I felt, the morning after! And it's true that I can't remember everything that happened. Did I really say those things about Polina and Danyl? I'm embarrassed. But drinking too much Rocket Fuel and ranting about your colleagues is one thing; killing them off in ice-chilled blood is quite another. And what about Gennady Aristov? You aren't claiming I was drunk when he died, too?'

'Olga, people forget traumatic events all the time! It's easier to forget than to remember sometimes – especially when you've done terrible things. Easier just to blank it out, and fill the gaps with something more pleasant.'

Nevena leaned forward once again, and fixed Olga with her dazzling blue eyes, startlingly vivid even in the bleached light of the snow-flecked window. 'Can you really tell me you've never done that, Olga? Are you really sure?'

'Well,' said Olga, looking back into that mesmerising gaze, 'well . . . I – I suppose I don't know. But who – who could possibly know that?' she said, regaining a touch of her former spirit. 'Surely if I *had* somehow erased my own memory, I'd have done it so I wouldn't know – so that I wouldn't be able to tell that I had!'

Nevena flicked her a passing smile, and made as if to speak again. But as she did so a sudden gust rattled the window above

Olga's head, and down the passageway there came the noise of a door closing loudly and unexpectedly, and a muttered curse from Loktev's lips. At the same time a flurry of snow beat against the dirty glass pane that ran across the cells, darkening the pale light that fell over them. In its passing shadow, Taisia Aristov came to life once more.

'Oh,' she said, sitting up and passing a hand over her face. 'Oh – oh, I hate sleeping in the daytime! Makes you feel like death – or a ghost warmed up. Who's there? Oh, it's you, Nevena. What do you want?'

Olga turned to look at her friend, but she had already sprung into action – uttering soothing words and passing Taisia an extra blanket under the door, and going so far as to pluck a bottle of something from her bag and pour a little into Taisia's cup through the bars.

'There – that's better, isn't it?' said Nevena, soothingly. 'You'll soon feel better. All your troubles will seem far away, far away. Far away – far away. Far away. Good. Good! She has left us once more, Olga, and we can speak again, you and I.'

'Nevena!' whispered Olga. 'What did you give her? You didn't . . .'

Nevena laughed her harmonious laugh once again, her fingers white and thin against the red of her lips. 'I didn't – what? Poison her? No! Just a little something to help her sleep. I'm not the murderer here, Olga.'

'Nevena, I *told* you,' began Olga, but Nevena hushed her to silence, her head turned towards the corridor.

'Loktev's still here, don't forget,' said Nevena. 'I slipped past him when Vassily popped out. But don't worry. I've got a plan for him, just like I did for Taisia Aristov. And just like I do for you.'

'You can't just make a plan and magic the FSB out of existence!' said Olga.

'Olga, this is your *last chance*,' said Nevena, standing up and pressing her face close to the bars until, to Olga's eyes, she herself began to look like a prisoner. 'Don't you see? If we don't get you out now, you'll never see daylight again, except through a grimy pane of standard-issue prison glass. You'll be sucked into the district courts, and from there to a federal high-security prison for the rest of your days! I told you, they want to make a scapegoat of someone – and your face fits best of all.'

'But I – I didn't—'

'OK, so you didn't do it,' said Nevena, almost crossly. 'Do you really want to try your luck with the justice system, the way it is – to put your life and freedom into the hands of over-promoted, mediocre old men who only care about climbing further up some greasy pole that leads nowhere in particular? Do you really think you, Olga Pushkin, can triumph against those men when so many others have failed?'

Olga didn't answer. She was looking inwards instead, or rather backwards, to a time not so long ago when someone had told her she'd never be anything but a railway engineer – or, in other words, that she had already achieved everything she could expect to achieve in her miserable little life. Ever since then, Olga had done everything in her power to put those hateful words from her mind, but they had a way of coming back into focus when times were hard – when people tried to send her to Mongolia, or take over her rail-side hut, or exclude her from investigations in her own backyard. They kept coming back because Olga knew somewhere deep inside that she feared failure more than anything – more, even, than an extension of the

confinement she'd suffered all her life. She feared setting out to
do something, applying all her energies to it, and failing all the
same – whether it was driving trains instead of maintaining
tracks, or winning Vassily's heart instead of losing his friendship, or releasing a best-selling book instead of funnelling
money into a publishing scam . . .

Everywhere Olga looked in her life, she saw the spectre of
disaster looming large – so why would her present difficulties be
any different? With Vassily gone from her side, wasn't it only
prudent to take a chance at avoiding the terrors of navigating
the criminal justice system without him? But then again, wasn't
Nevena the reason she had fallen out of Vassily's favour?
And yet here she was, urging her to escape Vassily's jail cells!
It was all too confusing, and Olga buried her throbbing head in
her hands.

As if she had divined Olga's train of thought, Nevena
pressed on regardless. 'It needn't be for ever, you know, Olga,'
she murmured. 'It could just be a breathing space, a quiet time
in some off-the-grid den. Not a disappearance, but a delay – the
time you need to clear your name.'

Olga raised her head and looked at Nevena with troubled
eyes. 'But Loktev knows you're here today, and Vassily too.
If I did go, wouldn't you be in trouble?'

'Don't worry about me,' said Nevena, earnestly. 'I'm pretty
good with stories. I'll make something up – I'll say you took me
by surprise, and hit me on the head with a hammer! I'll pop one
of Vassily's in my bag,' she said, gesturing towards the corridor.
'Or – or I could say you grabbed me, and forced me to open your
door with the spare key or you'd break my arm, or something
like that.'

'All right, but even if that's so, where – where would I go?' said Olga, slowly, almost marvelling at herself for taking the possibility seriously.

Nevena moved back from the bars again, brushed the rust-flakes from her jacket, and smiled at Olga once more. 'Let me worry about that, Olga! Didn't I tell you I've been all around Roslazny in my time? I know just the place – just the place! Somewhere quiet – somewhere *safe*. We can grab some of the police waterproofs and head straight out. But first we've got a pastor to scare off.'

'Scare off? How?'

'Didn't you know, Olga? Sometimes it takes a rat to scare a rat.'

'Nevena – Nevena, ssh!' whispered Olga fiercely, but her friend only doubled up with laughter once again at the thought of Loktev running down the street away from the police station, pseudo-priestly robes lifted up around his ankles – for the FSB agent still affected his clerical garb, to keep up his undercover identity.

'All right, all *right*,' said Nevena at last, allowing Olga to lead her round the corner and into a narrow alleyway that ran north-west, away from the centre of the village. 'You don't have to actually break my arm!'

'I just don't want anyone to hear us,' said Olga. 'Anyway, how did you know that would work?'

'I didn't for sure,' said Nevena, 'but I was fairly certain. You saw how he reacted that time Vassily let Rasputin out? Well, I did a bit of digging last night, when the vodka was doing the rounds in Vassily's back office, and it turns out he had some kind of trauma when he was just a *detka*. Got trapped in a room with a couple of rats, or something. Seems to have hit him pretty hard. All those security types are haunted somehow, aren't they? I suppose we all are, come to that. I know I am. What haunts you, Olga? No – don't tell me. We should each keep our own darkness to ourselves, for now!

'Anyway,' she went on, after a pause, 'it's the only weakness I could find on him, so I thought it was worth a try. And once I'd decided what to do, it was pretty easy,' she went on, ducking beneath a snow-clad plank that had fallen between two buildings. 'Just get at the cage of rats – you know, the one Vassily keeps for Rasputin – then open the door in the back office, and retreat to a safe distance before whisking you out of the door as soon as his back was turned, and then enjoy the added bonus of watching him pelt down the street as if his robes were on fire. That was a real rat race, eh? Ha! A rat race!'

Olga smiled at her friend, trying to share her delight in the feeble pun and, more widely, the success of their impromptu jail breakout. But the exhilaration of the escape – a swift passage down the corridor and out, to be rewarded with a glimpse of Loktev's fast-disappearing shape – had soon faded, to be replaced with the kind of worry more familiar to the inner structure of Olga's mind. Could things really have been that easy? How had Nevena clicked her fingers and conjured Olga out from the Roslazny police station, like a dentist plucking a tooth from a bleeding jaw?

Whether it was because of her father Mikhail's hypocritical tutelage in the ways of Russian virtue – he was far better at preaching than practising – or from Olga's apprenticeship in the Kafkaesque architecture of Russian Railways, Olga had long since internalised the view that the harder something was to accomplish, the more worthwhile it was. And yet here she was, walking up an alley that led away from the jail in perfect freedom, at the price of a few rats running wild through Vassily's station. Of course, Nevena couldn't have organised Vassily's absence – that was just a stroke of luck – but she had certainly managed to incapacitate Taisia and eject Loktev with surprising rapidity. Maybe Vassily had been right, after all, about Nevena's human resources expertise.

She walked rapidly now, too, pushing ahead of Olga and striding through the snow with long, effortless steps, so that Olga had to scurry to keep up with her, her over-large, borrowed waterproofs swishing furiously with the effort. The snow had begun to fall heavily once again, and from a fast-darkening sky: already there was an inch of fresh flakes on top of the old, and Olga knew from the look of the clouds that there would be much more before nightfall. So much for the thaw – but, then, Olga had seen false ones before now, deceptive days when winter's icy grip would clamp down again after a gap of mendacious mildness. You couldn't trust Siberia when it came to weather. You just couldn't.

And what about Nevena? Could Olga trust her to find her a place of refuge? She certainly seemed to know where she was going, forging past lopsided ruins and frozen, spread-fingered barrels with competent ease.

'There's a place out in the sticks we can still get to, weather or no weather,' she said, over her shoulder, good humour now transformed into cold determination. 'The man's away, and I know where the key is.'

Olga nodded, but she was listening to Nevena's confident tone rather than her words: it was blizzarding too hard now to think of anything but following Nevena's footsteps, one after the other, tramping ever onwards as they skirted house after house and street after street before stumbling, clumsy-footed, over the village perimeter and into the white distance beyond. Olga had walked those fields many times in her girlhood and since, marking wider and wider circuits as she grew in strength and confidence – but never in weather like this, never in a snowstorm whose vigour seemed, if anything, renewed rather than vitiated by the brief reprieve it had granted to the villagers. And as they passed the old mound of rocks that Nevena called a *svyatynya* – a shrine – Olga wondered at her friend's sureness, a sureness that far surpassed her own. But, then, what was it she'd said, back in the prison? She'd been all around Roslazny, and knew somewhere quiet – somewhere safe?

Olga frowned, a mere crinkle of her forehead beneath the overhanging, snow-encrusted edge of her fur-lined hood. *She'd been all around Roslazny . . .* But hadn't Nevena said something quite different a few days before? That she never really got a chance to explore places like Roslazny, because she was always off somewhere else on the morning train?

She shook her head and marched on. This was no way to behave, she told herself, scanning a friend's words as if catching a contradiction was a worthy activity. That's what you did for murderers.

But once the idea had caught in her mind it was impossible to dismiss, and with nothing passing in front of her eyes but blank expanses of untouched snow, she found that several new ideas also presented themselves to her attention. For example:

Polina Klemovsky had arrived much later than Nevena had expected, and Nevena had been anxious about it, sitting in front of Vassily's fire when they had met again for the first time – more anxious than Olga would have expected, even for someone used to the kind of constructive criticism offered to errant employees by Russian Railways. Wasn't that a little strange? And wasn't it odd, too, that a spate of petty crime had taken place at Polina's old headquarters before starting up in Roslazny, a hundred miles away – but with dates that aligned with Polina's expected, rather than actual, arrival in Roslazny? Expected, that is, by Nevena?

There was, too, Olga's bedroom window, painted over to render it immovable – thereby giving Olga an alibi of sorts for the night the ballast was removed from the tracks. Painted over by a left-hander – and hadn't Nevena always taken her coffee cup in her left hand when Olga had offered it to her? The old, familiar lines from Pushkin came to her lips:

> *There's a green oak-tree by the shores*
> *Of the blue bay; on a gold chain,*
> *The cat, learned in the mythic stories,*
> *Walks round the tree in ceaseless strain:*
> *Walks to the right – a song it sings;*
> *Walks to the left – a tale it tells.*

A tale it tells, to the left . . . A tale it tells.

And what about the garden hoe, the humble implement that had brought down Danyl Petrovich's juggernaut and robbed him of life? Olga's fingerprints had somehow ended up on its handle, but still nobody knew why. Hadn't Nevena offered her a walking-stick, though, when they returned from Café Astana the night before the derailment? A walking-stick in the night, tall and slim and smooth to her touch – smooth to the touch of her naked fingers, for her gloves had gone missing in the café, while she was sharing drinks with Nevena . . .

'I think my mother, Alyona, might have come this way, in another time,' said Nevena, breaking in on Olga's thoughts. Olga looked up and saw her standing still, gazing back at her with a broad smile upon her lips, and a fierce brightness in her eyes. 'I can almost see her walking beside us – can't you? Just like your mother, Tatiana! And she was so much like her, Olga – I'm sure of it! It's as if we're living through them, and they through us.'

Olga forced a smile to her lips in response, then followed Nevena as she turned and pressed on once more. But soon her steps began to falter, for something about Nevena's off-hand remarks about their mothers had unlocked a secret at last: the unsettling words that had hovered at the edge of Olga's mind, taunting her with their unnerving strangeness and unreachability. But now Olga remembered: it was something Nevena herself had said.

We can all make new lives for ourselves, she'd said, in the police station when they'd first encountered each other in Roslazny, *and become different people in our lives or the lives of others, honouring those who've gone before.*

Become different people, in our lives or those of others . . . But how can we become different people in the lives of others? Was Nevena thinking of the afterlife, in the manner of Anna Kabalevsky? Or, more unsettling still, did she mean become different people *through* others' lives, like the ancient ones who made sacrifices at shrines like the one they'd just passed? Either way, the discovery that the strange and jarring phrase had come from her friend's lips was troubling, and Olga now stared at the back of her friend's Ushanka hat with curious eyes.

As she did so, she noticed a thin line of fabric between Nevena's hat and her snow-speckled collar – a line of dark, silken green. Her mother's scarf, of course – Nevena's mother, that is, not Olga's own dear *mamochka*. And wasn't it a little odd, on reflection, that Nevena still wore the scarf, almost all the time? Olga could understand the desire to keep a few oddments as a memorial, but wearing such an item from day to day? It was almost as if Nevena couldn't quite let her mother go into the unknown vastness that lay beyond, as Olga had had to do.

And then Olga gasped as a series of thoughts dashed tumultuously through her mind, thoughts that brought seemingly disconnected things to her attention: Gennady's remarks upon ladies' fashion in the police station before he died, for instance, and the questions he had posed to his wife, alongside Olga's own admission that she had filmed certain events on the morning of the derailment. And there was, too, a fruit that Nevena had mentioned in passing – an innocent little fruit, but one that assumed ominous dimensions in light of recent events . . . There was something, too, about the photograph they'd found on Danyl's body – the woman called Zlata M. Olga had thought at the time that she looked familiar – and suddenly she remembered why.

She stopped walking, her eyes inclined downwards towards the snow-covered pathway, her lips ajar in wonderment and belated realisation. Then she looked up, eyes keen and staring like Nevena's – but her friend had utterly vanished from view.

She looked to her right, and then to her left, but it was too late. A bar of dull brown flashed across her eyes, and then, soon afterwards, Olga's world faded from white to black.

The first inklings of returning consciousness came to Olga's ears. While her eyes remained firmly shut, she became aware of a slithering, sliding sound that seemed to envelop her entire body – and her body was moving, wasn't it? Yes, it was moving: something was pulling her along – pulling her by her legs – pulling her on her back with a jerky, discontinuous movement that suggested a high degree of effort. Perhaps the movement was causing the slithering noise, thought Olga. Perhaps she was being pulled along some kind of slippery surface, something smooth or viscous or – or frozen.

Frozen – of course! That was it: she was being dragged over some icy, snowbound surface. Olga's eyes snapped open as a dim memory of danger came into her mind, only for her to close them again as the dazzling snow-whiteness that surrounded her sent a dart of pain through her temples. But she began to force them open once more, for the urgent questions that filled her mind were more important than any headache. What had just happened to her? Had the killer come across her and Nevena unawares, first snaring her beautiful friend and then coming back for Olga? But she couldn't remember: she only remembered looking around for Nevena in vain, and then a blow to the head, and a darkness that marked the second time she'd been knocked unconscious that year. I'd better stop making a habit of it, she said to herself, and almost laughed in her absent-mindedness.

But that was no good, Olga realised, despite her head-swimming stupor. That way lay cold surrender to Fate. She opened her eyes fully, ignoring the agony that filled her head, and with an immense effort lifted her head forward until she could see the shape that was tugging her along. Then she almost uttered sounds once more, but this time from surprise rather than ill-placed mirth: for the shape that dragged her was her friend, Nevena Komarov.

Olga frowned and shook her head gently as if she could clear it that way. Why was Nevena pulling her along like a sack of potatoes? Had she hurt herself, or been injured by the killer, so that her friend was dragging her to safety? That was just the kind of thing Nevena would do. Always putting others first, and doing the right thing, whatever the cost. Doing the right thing . . .

But wait – hadn't Olga had some worrying thoughts in her mind, just before the blackness had overtaken her?

Yes – yes. It all began to come back to her, and with the return of dread and fear she found her mind clearing, as if her now-racing heart were forcing all inattention from her thoughts and injecting ice-cold clarity in its place. Of *course* the killer hadn't come across Nevena unawares, or snared Olga in her turn. No: Nevena herself *was* the killer! It had been Nevena all along – Nevena who had tried to frame Polina, Nevena who had brought down the train, and Nevena who had killed Gennady with one of Odrosov's pans, then lain in the darkness moving his body in a hateful semblance of life . . . So much made sense now, though so many things were still unclear – like the reasons why Nevena had broken her out of jail, and where she was taking her, and what she had planned for her when they got there.

But there was no time for chewing over the details of the case there and then. Nevena was plainly in no mood to stop and explain her motivations, even if she'd known that Olga was awake. She had one leg under each arm, and was striding forward once more – but this time not leading her friend to freedom so much as dragging her in fits and starts across a snow-blanketed field beyond the outskirts of Roslazny.

Olga could see that she was struggling despite her wiry, athletic frame; and she saw, too, that Nevena had no idea that Olga had come back to a certain awareness of her surroundings – a fact that Olga could work to her benefit. She stayed limp for another short while, allowing Nevena to drag her along as before. She had to pick her moment carefully, or all would be lost. She waited, in fact, until Nevena approached a low descent towards a bank of spruces that intersected diagonally with their awkward, jagged progress. And then, when Nevena stopped to catch a breath and gather her strength, she jerked upright and kicked Nevena down the low slope that lay before them. Not waiting to see the outcome, but utterly convinced of the need to escape Nevena before she joined Danyl and the others in an early grave, Olga rushed sideways, dashing towards the bank of spruces to gain cover and chart a passage to freedom – or, rather, a passage to imprisonment: even the Roslazny jail cells were better than being dragged towards an unknown destination, like a side of meat taken home from the market.

But there followed only a time of nightmarish dimensions, a period of uncertain duration and geography – a hellish dream in which Olga battled against blizzarding snow, freezing winds, and misleading pathways, and just as much against bitter self-reproach and icy fears of what was to come. How could she have missed all the signs that Nevena Komarov was the killer, the evil-hearted one who had capsized Danyl's train and captured his life, and Anoushka's and Gennady Aristov's, too? How could she have been so blind?

But then a flurry of snow would surge across her staring eyes until they stung and ached and failed to stop her falling painfully across rock and bough and cast-off barbed-wire fences. Then her mind would switch from looking back to looking forward, from retrospection and reprobation to path-finding and fearful prophesying: would she, after all, be the fourth to die, the final death to reflect the snapping boughs outside the police station? She circled back upon herself and found, to her horror, the shrine she'd seen earlier that day with Nevena at her side. Had Nevena dragged her out to make a sacrifice of her?

She gasped as she heard a noise behind her, and then again as she saw a familiar shape in front of her, and a faint light, too, a shimmering will-o'-the-wisp that promised warmth and shelter and safety from the demon that pursued her. She raced forwards past a row of cows, and nearly tripped over a power cable, before finally reaching the *dacha*'s door and pounding, pounding, pounding upon it until at last it creaked open in front of her. She fell back, her eyes momentarily dazzled by the bright electric light that flowed out upon her, cast by a single powerful bulb that hung from a naked cord in the low corridor. Then, when her sight adjusted and she saw who was holding open the door, her face contorted in terror.

'No,' she whispered, seeing before her the shrouded, ghostly visage of Nevena Komarov, framed in darkness by the contrast-ing light beyond.

Olga spoke then more loudly, her voice cracking in horror. 'No – you can't be here – you can't be here! I – I—'

But Olga's strength was wholly spent at last, and her eyes rolled upwards in her head. She fell forward into the open doorway and lay unmoving, with her legs, still outside, gathering snow, like the cows under their winter mantles. Nevena reached down and drew her inside the *dacha*. Then the door slammed, and the fields were dark and silent once more, leaving only a few rapidly disappearing footprints as evidence of her passing. Olga Pushkin, track engineer (second class), aspiring writer and amateur investigator, was lost to the world.

14

The Long and Winding Road

Sergeant Vassily Marushkin half ran, half walked down the path that meandered towards the Blatovs' house on the southwest of the village and, nearby, the defunct scrapyard that served as an informal museum of late Soviet machinery in advanced states of decomposition. Vassily and Kliment had often walked that way in warmer weather: Vassily liked to tell his son about the good (or bad) old days, as the mood took him, and to illustrate his anecdotes with nods towards what remained of Ippolit Kuznetsov's Volga town-car or Artyom Petrov's last-tractor-but-one, now partly buried in the rich Russian earth.

Vassily's interests on that particular Wednesday, however, were far more pressing than Sunday-afternoon reminiscences about the long-forgotten Roslazny *sozhkhov*. Vassily, indeed, was seriously concerned for Kliment's welfare. He wasn't alarmed as yet, because he knew that the killer was nowhere near the Blatovs'. But then again, killers sometimes had silent accomplices – people beholden to them for some terrible reason, or keen to have something over the killer in future, or (worse still) going along with a murderous plan just for the excitement of being involved. Vassily had seen all three types and more in his days working inner-city crime in Novosibirsk and elsewhere – but he'd never had loved ones at stake before. But what about now? What if someone like that were lying in wait for Kliment? he asked himself, his steps speeding up in line with his racing thoughts. What if he were to lose his son again, so soon after finding him, and this time for ever? And how stupid of Pasha, thought Vassily, with an uncharacteristic flash of anger, to let Kliment just walk on alone, rather than pinning him to the ground lest anything should befall him. Didn't Pasha know how precious he was?

But Vassily's panted speculations and reproaches were in vain, for there, as he rounded the corner that led to the untidy heaps of rusting metal beyond the Blatovs', he saw the familiar round-headed shape of his son Kliment, leaning moodily on the snow-covered lopsided remains of a petrol-engined rotavator.

'Kliment!' he cried in relief – a relief that soon turned to anger, before subsiding into annoyance. 'What the hell were you thinking, rambling off on your own like that? Don't you know there's a murderer about – maybe two, or even three? You've got to be more careful!'

'But Nevena told me to come,' said Kliment. 'She said—'

'*Nevena?*' cried Vassily, angry again. 'Don't you remember what I said about her? That you have to' – he looked around him, and lowered his voice – 'that you have to tell me everything she says to you? And that you're not to—'

'Not to go anywhere without telling you, either,' finished Kliment, rolling his eyes. 'I *know*, Papa – I know! But I had to help Olga, didn't I – after what I said before – getting her into trouble, and all that? Maybe she wouldn't be in jail if I hadn't said that, about her going into Café Astana on her own. And Nevena smiled at me, in that – in that way she has,' he went on, looking downwards, with faint red tinges glowing into life on his cheeks, 'and said she'd heard Taisia talking in her sleep – something about a jumper stuffed in one of the rusting lorries down here, by the Blatovs'. Nevena thought maybe the killer had hidden his clothes there – that there might be vital clues to find!'

'*His* clothes?' said Vassily. 'Vital clues? But, Kliment, if Nevena thought that, why wouldn't she walk out there herself?'

'Well, it isn't safe, is it, Papa? For a woman?'

'That makes no difference,' muttered Vassily. 'Not when there's a killer around. Time you learned that. Look at Gennady Aristov – or Danyl Petrovich! And, anyway, that's not why it isn't safe. It's—'

'Yes, Papa?' said Kliment, gazing at him with curious eyes.

'Oh – oh, never mind,' said Vassily, deciding the time was not yet ripe to share everything he knew, and uttering instead some platitudes about the need to be careful in the frosty weather, which had, indeed, started to close in once more, shedding weighty tides of snowflakes upon them and the ghostly, rusting machines that lay scattered about.

'It doesn't much matter, for now,' he went on, putting a reassuring arm about Kliment's shoulders, and marching him up the path that led back to the centre of Roslazny. 'As long as Loktev's still there, anyway. Now let's get back and— Hang on, what's that?'

Kliment shrugged, following the direction of Vassily's eyes and perceiving shadowy figures outside Café Astana. 'Just Alexeyev and the others, probably,' he said. 'Odrosov's run short of Rocket Fuel – Svetlana told me,' he went on, cheeks glowing red once more. 'She said it wouldn't be long before the men started fighting over it.'

'No – no, that's not Alexeyev, or any of his cronies,' said Vassily. 'That's Fyodor, and – and Odrosov himself, and someone else . . . Popov, I think, judging by the belly. And is that Ludis Kuskov behind him? Yes, I think it is. But who's that there, with his back to us?'

'I think – I think it's Loktev, Papa,' said Kliment, whose keener eyes had noticed the pseudo-pastor's clerical outfit. 'Yes – it's him.'

'*No*,' said Vassily, with a vehemence that surprised his son – as did the rough way in which he pushed him aside, careering down the narrow path and almost tripping in his haste over the clumps of drifted snow. 'No – no,' he went on, echoing, if he had only known it, Olga's panicked words at the *dacha*. 'No, you can't be here – you can't be here!'

'But, Papa,' said Kliment, breathlessly, catching up with Vassily as he ran. 'Why shouldn't Pastor Loktev be here?'

But Vassily ignored him. He juddered to a halt in front of Loktev and shook him by the lapels. 'What happened, Loktev?' he said, urgently. '*Where is she?*'

'What's that, Marushkin?' said Loktev, sounding as though he were far away, and wiping beads of perspiration from his pale forehead. 'I've been – I've been unwell . . . I . . .'

'Don't worry, Vassily,' said Popov, patting him on the back. 'Pushkin's still in those cells – but why would this poor man of God know anything about that? He's obviously taken a turn – and I don't blame him, if he's had any of Odrosov's *kurnik*. Fair turn your stomach, that chicken pie.'

'Man of God? He's a bloody FSB agent,' cried Vassily. 'And I wasn't talking about Olga Pushkin, either!'

'Taisia Aristov, then, Papa?' said Kliment, puzzlement dawning slowly over his features. 'I'm sure she's still there, too. Those bars are stronger than they look!'

'No, Kliment,' said Vassily, grasping his son by the shoulders. 'No! It's not Taisia I'm talking of. It's Nevena. Nevena Komarov!'

'But what about Nevena?' said Kliment, still puzzled.

'It's *her*, Kliment. It's her! It's been her all along.'

'Nevena?' said Kliment. 'You mean Nevena's – Nevena's the *killer*?'

'She's the killer,' confirmed Vassily. 'Danyl, Anoushka, Gennady Aristov, the lot.'

'Those people were murdered by that fancy girl?' gasped Popov.

'And you've been – you've been protecting us,' said Kliment, understanding dawning in his eyes. 'Me and – and Olga!'

'I've been trying to,' said Vassily. 'But now she's managed to get rid of Loktev, who knows what she's planning next? Come on – we've got to get back to the station. We—'

Vassily was interrupted by a loud burst of static, and then another.

'Papa!' cried Kliment. 'Your walkie-talkie – they must have got the system back up!'

Vassily tugged the device from his pocket and raised it to his ears, eyes eager, as if he might hear some cheering news of police reinforcements about to descend on the benighted village. But all he heard was a recorded announcement from Russian Railways, warning all emergency personnel in the area that a snowplough would soon attempt to clear the line from Tayga to Suranovo.

'We knew that already,' said Vassily. 'And what use is it, anyway? There's a train wreck in the way.' Then he shook his head: this was no time to ponder the efficiency (or otherwise) of railway operations. He turned and set off eastwards at a run, calling over his shoulder, 'Fyodor, Kliment – come! To the police station, before it's too late.'

'He might've asked me, too,' muttered Popov, under his breath. 'Think a man with a belly can't run?'

But Fyodor drowned him out. 'You're worried for Taisia?' he shouted, running to catch up with Vassily and Kliment. 'You think Nevena might go for her, like she did for Gennady?'

'Not Taisia, Fyodor!' cried Vassily. 'Not Taisia – Olga! Olga Pushkin!'

Olga Pushkin lay on an uneasy bed, a bed that seemed to shift under her like buckling ice-plates on a thawing Lake Baikal. Like a swimmer forcing her way to the surface through jagged floes, Olga struggled to find her way back to consciousness. What had happened to bring about this sickly slumber? She dived into her memory in search of answers – an excess of Rocket Fuel? An accident outside her rail-side hut? – but none were forthcoming from her dazed and unresponsive mind.

With a momentous effort she forced open an eye, seeing an uneven, square-stitched quilt beneath her and, beyond, the light orange flames of a kindling blaze – but it wasn't Vassily's hearth she saw, or her own brick-framed fireplace. And other things, too, were unfamiliar: the long, low roof with intersecting beams, the bits of stained-glass window built into uneven panes, the vast, industrial-sized cooker with doors that would withstand a Panzer tank . . . And walking beneath the long, low roof, like that of a Viking hall, was a woman she recognised but whose name for the moment escaped her. She knew it began with N, though. N . . . N—

Nevena! Of course, Nevena, she thought, opening both eyes. It was her friend Nevena – Nevena Komarov.

She started up on the bed, hoisting herself onto an elbow, but as Nevena turned to her a host of memories flooded in upon her and wiped the emergent smile from her lips. Yes, she remembered now: Nevena meant her harm, had hit her on the head from behind, had dragged her by the legs, but Olga had escaped, and fled into the wilderness, only to fall down at Filippov's door when Nevena's dread face had appeared.

She eyed her friend with wariness, wondering if there might still be a way back, a way to engage with the woman she'd known for decades, rather than the woman she now saw before her – a way to save her life.

'Nevena,' she ventured, several times, easing the familiar name past her lips in the softest, most reassuring tones imaginable. 'Nevena, what is it? What's happened? You can tell me, you know. You can tell Olga. We've known each other so long. That's what friends are for.'

But Nevena didn't answer: she kept pacing up and down, up and down, bowing her head each time she passed the beam that divided one half of Erik Filippov's spacious *dacha* from the other. Olga knew Filippov slightly, a hefty, pink-skinned man whose sturdy Mangalica pigs had become a byword for cold-weather hardiness and savoury meat. He came into Café Astana occasionally to stock up on groceries and petrol, and Olga had spoken to him a few times – but she'd had no idea his *dacha* was such a palace inside! If circumstances had been different, Olga would have snapped some pictures to share with her friend Ekaterina Chezhekhov on the platforms at Tayga station, or to show Anna and Pasha at home, marvelling at Filippov's huge flatscreen TV and gleaming stainless-steel samovar.

If circumstances had been different – but this was no time for souvenirs: not with Nevena Komarov stalking past Olga first in one direction, then the other, glancing sideways at her as she went, and always muttering, muttering under her breath. By straining her ears, Olga could just about hear her – or was she imagining it, a trick of the snow-burdened wind that beat upon the sturdy wall above her head? Was she dreaming, or was Nevena really talking to her mother, Alyona, speaking sentence after sentence as if she could hear and even answer? Or was it something different, something that sent a shiver across Olga's skin – was it that Nevena was really speaking to herself, as if she *were* Alyona? What was it Olga had remembered, on the way out into the *taiga*? That Nevena had talked of honouring those who've gone before, and becoming different people in our life or others? Different people – or *old* people? People we've already known and loved?

'Oh, yes, he had to go,' she heard Nevena whisper once. 'He had to go, my sweetest, and Anoushka, too – they deserved to die, abandoning me like that. They deserved to die. They took the butterfly, that beautiful, precious thing, and crushed it in their hands. And that old man, in the café? He was nothing. A friend of Anoushka's is our enemy, dear little one! He had to go, too. Don't spare them a thought. Don't worry your little head. But spare the pretty child, the one with blonde hair, if you can – oh, spare her if you can! Then we can all be together! We can all be as one, the mothers and the daughters together for ever ...'

Nevena's strange words passed over Olga like a childhood memory, conjuring echoes of her own mother's kindly re-assurances, but mingled with a cold-hearted ruthlessness that had been utterly alien to Tatiana Pushkin.

There was something else, too, besides the eldritch words – something equally unsettling, though in a different register. For Nevena had somehow managed to change her clothes despite the re-energised blizzard, and was now wearing garments that rang distant bells in Olga's aching head: a thickly padded sheepskin coat that surrounded Nevena's familiar green scarf at the neck and, beneath it, a vivid patterned blouse and utilitarian corduroy skirt. It had taken Olga some time to recover consciousness after her descent into unconsciousness at the *dacha* door, and even when she'd finally opened her eyes she found it hard to believe she was really awake. How had Nevena suddenly transformed herself into the woman in the photograph – the photograph that Vassily Marushkin, deceitful soul, had found on the body of Danyl Petrovich? How had Nevena become the mysterious Zlata M, echoing not just her clothes from the past but also the very look in her eyes – eyes that Olga remembered well, for their haunting, sorrowful gaze and the smouldering intensity that lay beneath?

With a sharp intake of breath Olga realised she had done so because they were the same woman: Nevena *was* Zlata M, or rather the closest any woman could be to Zlata M. She was her daughter! And, of course, Olga herself had grasped this out on the snow ... That, and many other things that pointed to Nevena's guilt, now flowed back into her mind.

But wait, said Olga to herself, rubbing her forehead with a clammy hand. Wait . . . Hadn't Nevena always said her mother's name was Alyona? But then again, Olga had never seen it written down. What if Nevena had chosen a different name for her mother, a false name, to hide her identity? A name beginning with A, to hide a name beginning with Z? Not A to B, but A to Z?

Olga watched Nevena pacing up and down, up and down, and wondered what she had planned for her. Clearly, she had been planning all this for some weeks, or months – maybe even years. Equally obviously, Nevena had had some fierce grievance against Danyl and Anoushka Petrovich – a grievance of sufficient depth to warrant derailing an entire Russian Railways train, as well as despatching Gennady Aristov later on. But where did Olga fit in? Unless Nevena was a consummate actor as well as everything else, she really hadn't known that Olga was still in Roslazny. Didn't that make it unlikely that Nevena wanted to kill her? And didn't their old friendship count for anything, or their loss of their mothers in girlhood? Hadn't Nevena spoken to herself, in her mother's guise, telling herself to spare the blonde one?

And Gennady Aristov . . . Gennady Aristov . . .

Olga couldn't shake the conviction that his death was somehow important – and not just to his departed self. What had Gennady seen? What had he seen or said that made his death imperative? Might it be something that made Olga, too, an imminent target for Nevena's elegant yet murderous hands?

She cast her mind back to the last time she'd seen him. It must have been that time he'd burst into the police station, holding court in front of them all with a skinful of vodka. Had he said anything to Nevena – anything that could have sealed his fate?

Olga frowned deeply, and stuck the tip of her tongue out of the corner of her mouth in the way she'd had since childhood whenever a matter requiring particular concentration arose. *What – had – Gennady – said?*

Nevena paused in her pacing and adjusted her scarf, laying it neatly across the lapel of her sheepskin jacket – and as she did so, a bell of remembrance rang in Olga's mind. Yes, yes! Gennady had said something about clothes . . . What were his words? Something about ladyfolk and their fripperies . . . Dresses and hats, he said, and that was commonplace enough, though who wore hats except at weddings? But then he'd gone on: muffs and mink coats.

And Taisia, too, had said something about Gennady – he'd asked her about real and fake fur, and whether women still wore clothes like his mother had. Furs? Muffs? Mink coats? Those were things from the past, from long ago – things like Nevena was wearing now, vanished things from forgotten times, as if they were worn by a woman in a black and white photograph, or by – or by—

'The ghost,' she whispered to herself, but not quite quietly enough. Nevena stopped her pacing and turned to look at her with eyes that glared white in their startled roundness.

'*What* did you say?' she growled.

'Oh,' said Olga, affecting as cheerful a tone as she could muster. 'Oh, nothing – nothing! Just . . .'

She paused: what could she possibly say? What could anyone say, when their recovering mind had just put two pieces of a puzzle together – Gennady's knowledge, acquired she knew not how, that Nevena had a vintage wardrobe hidden somewhere (probably in her still-unsearched room in Café Astana), and Taisia's knowledge that Danyl Petrovich had seen a ghost by the side of the tracks, not once but many times. What had Taisia said? Oh, yes . . .

He'd seen this woman standing watching him as he went by in his train, at places all over the network. And there was something about her clothes – he wouldn't say what exactly, but it troubled him . . . And there was something in his eyes, something like – like fear . . .

Nevena had been the ghost, Olga realised. It was she who had dressed up as her mother Zlata, who had *become* her mother Zlata and haunted the tracks to terrify Danyl.

So what could Olga possibly say to follow the terrible realisation that her friend was not only murderous but utterly unbalanced into the bargain – so unbalanced that there could be no hope of safety, no hope of escape while Nevena still walked freely before her?

No, there was nothing to say. Nevena would overrule her pleading. She would not spare the blonde child, for she knew that if she did, her own freedom – and her strange co-existence with her mother's spirit – could not continue. No: Olga saw it was no longer time for speech, but for action.

Olga waited until Nevena's pacing took her near, then leaped from Filippov's bed and pushed Nevena into the darkness that lay beyond the doorway to her right. She rushed down the *dacha*, pulling Filippov's samovar and TV onto the floor behind her as she went, pulling everything down that she could to delay Nevena's progress and allow her to reach her goal: for

Olga had seen, in her bed-bound surveys of the long, dim interior, a glint of metal by the door that promised keys to a vehicle, and below that the dull gleam of careworn plastic that belonged to an ancient rotary telephone.

Dancing past errant fire-pokers and skipping over bookcases and their contents as they tumbled to the ground, Olga reached the telephone, grabbed the handset, and furiously dialled the number for the Roslazny police station, hoping all the while that the lines were back up by now, and looking over her shoulder with wide, staring eyes at the sight of Nevena Komarov trying to fight her way through the wreckage of Filippov's belongings.

To Olga's desperate relief she heard ringing and the click as someone picked up at the other end. She didn't wait to find out who it was – she merely shouted incoherent words down the line as fast as she could utter them, for Nevena had breasted the TV and was now working to shift the samovar.

'Tell Vassily to come quick – at Filippov's – going to try the car, back to the village – past the track. Come quick! And—'

A deafening clatter and clanging behind her choked off her words, and she saw Nevena's lithe form pushing past Filippov's outsize samovar and heading towards her hideout at the end of the *dacha*. Olga thrust the phone from her, flicked the keys from their hook, and dashed out of the door – or tried to: it had been locked from the inside, and she bruised her shoulder badly. But then her grasping hand found the key, allowing her to burst outside into the cold once more.

She stumbled on the threshold and fell into arm-deep snow – but there, ahead of her and surely within reach, was Filippov's all-weather Lada Niva, nestling under a thick snow-blanket on reassuringly solid tyres. She dragged herself to her feet, glancing behind to see Nevena emerging from the door, and rushed to the driver's side, cursing as she forced the key into the frozen lock and then wrenching the door open and banging it closed and locked behind her as she thrust the key into the ignition – only to look up in horror as Nevena opened the passenger door and stared at her in triumph. Damn that Filippov, thought Olga, in some part of her mind – couldn't he even afford a car with central locking that worked?

The engine started and Olga slammed the gearstick into first, pushed the handbrake down, and popped the clutch with a racing engine and a great whirring of gears. The car lurched forward from its snowy resting-place, all but knocking Nevena to the ground – but she hung on somehow with her graceful, toothpick-thin fingers, and dragged herself back into the car as Olga roared down the path that led back to Roslazny.

Then followed a nightmarish journey of screaming and clawing, screeching gears and protesting machinery, buffeting and crashing as the Lada careered down the narrow road, bouncing in and out of frozen ruts and potholes, and cannoning off bushes and rotting fences, while Olga sought at once to manage the car and a Nevena Komarov hell-bent on taking the wheel, and perhaps both their lives into the bargain. But Olga was stronger than her friend, if only by a little, and it seemed for a while that she would overcome and win her way to freedom and safety. For a little while: but Olga had not reckoned on the railway track, on the twin strands of metal that she herself had maintained for so long. She approached the line too quickly and forgot about the little concrete ramp the railway had built to allow safe passage for cars and lorries – she forgot, and so she veered slightly to the left, down a small depression, and straight into a solid concrete sleeper.

The car bucked in the air like a bear on the hunt, throwing Olga and Nevena forward into the windscreen. It bounced heavily on the ground, and then collapsed on the tracks with a broken axle, coming to rest astride the line with two wheels reaching towards Roslazny and the other two still stranded in the wilderness, the vast, endless *taiga* still carpeted in ever-falling white.

Neither woman had worn her seatbelt, and the impact had stunned them both. But Olga – sturdier again – was the first to recover, and for what felt like the tenth time that day she strove to regain her consciousness and present memory. What was that steaming noise? she asked herself. Oh, yes: the car was ruined, quite destroyed, and the engine was belching ominous fumes. And Nevena, beside her, looked destroyed, too, with a vivid red rivulet running down her alabaster cheek from her forehead, and her face gentle now in repose, bearing a calmer look that Olga knew from long ago – though soon it began to twitch, and come awake, transforming piece by piece, line by line, curve by curve into the deranged monster that Nevena had become.

But there was something else that Olga was aware of, something familiar – not her friend's beauty, but a sound that came to her ears above the hissing engine: a deep, resonant noise that she'd last heard before Danyl Petrovich had died: the powerful horn of a Russian Railways train.

Olga burst into life once more, frenziedly trying to free her door – but it was stuck too firmly for her to shift: the crash must have distorted the car's ageing chassis, trapping them in place.

She turned towards the direction of the railway horn: surely it was just a distant echo, a train beyond Suranovo, or some shunter trying to make its way up the line. But then to her terror she saw a different sight emerging from the snowstorm: the gleaming forelight and downspread bars of a Russian Railways snowplough, forcing its way steadily, inexorably, unstoppably through the drifts that lay all about. The train sounded its horn again and again, warning them that something was wrong, that they should move, escape, free themselves – but this was quite impossible. Nevena, too, desperately tried to claw her way from the car, turning her fury from Olga to the mute, unthinking door by her side, but to no avail. The train came on, ever on, until its dazzling light filled Olga's eyes and the horn pressed in upon her protesting eardrums. It was, she realised, the last thing she would ever see.

She turned away and buried her head in her coat, awaiting the end.

15

Close Calling

'Not that way, Kliment – the other way! Towards the bumper, for God's sake – then get clear as fast as you can.'

Vassily pulled his head back inside the car, glanced at his near-side rear-view mirror, and floored the accelerator pedal as soon as Kliment staggered sideways, ducking his head to escape the fountain of snow, mud and ice that flew outwards and upwards from Vassily's rear wheels.

'Push – push!' shouted Vassily, sticking his head out again, and extending a waving arm to encourage his son to ever greater efforts. It wasn't like him to be so hard on Kliment, but then again it wasn't every day that a woman's life depended on getting some traction out of his ancient Volvo 240 estate. It had been only a few minutes earlier when Olga had called the police station, pouring her summons into Vassily's alarmed ear via the recently restored landline, and prompting him and Kliment into frenzied action.

Leaving the still shaken Loktev to watch Taisia Aristov, and grabbing his car keys, police jacket and son, Vassily dashed out once more into the rejuvenated snowstorm and headed towards his parking spot. The car had started with surprising ease

– usually it was an extended overture with choke and throttle – but Vassily had gone just a hundred yards when his rear wheels fell into a samovar-sized pothole, forcing him and Kliment to waste precious time on trick after trick in the Siberian playbook: driving forward and back again, braking while throttling up, deflating the tyres, and putting cardboard, loose stones and finally snow chains under the spinning wheels, coupled to whatever weight Kliment could apply to the dented tailgate.

At last the car lurched decisively forward, the smoking, threadbare tyres gripping once more, and leaving Kliment sprawled forward on the gleaming snow. Vassily looked in his mirrors again and grimaced, but he knew that stopping now would only risk the same thing happening again – so he waved an apologetic hand out of the window, then put his heavy standard-issue boot on the accelerator again, bracing himself as the still-powerful engine sent the heavy car surging forward down the road that led to the north-west of the village.

He muttered to himself as he went. 'Filippov's . . . Filippov's. I know that place . . . Near where the road meets Olga's track, beyond the train wreck towards Suranovo. What the hell is Nevena doing? I just have to get there and make sure she's all right.'

Vassily hardly dared admit to himself how much he cared for Olga Pushkin, she of the green eyes and stray-stranded hair that curved around her cheek like a caress. He hardly dared admit it to himself, for then he would be distracted from his driving – and if he were distracted from his driving he might have an accident, and then Olga would be utterly at Nevena's mercy.

Nevena . . . He hit the steering wheel with his gloved hands. How had he let things get so out of hand? If Olga paid the price – perhaps even the ultimate price – he would never forgive himself, never. But there was no time to think of that now: he had to concentrate on navigating the Volvo past snowdrift after snowdrift, and all the while trying to remember where the tree-roots and potholes and abandoned bits of machinery lay under the levelling firmness of a white snow-blanket. He had to concentrate on surviving the icy journey so he could get to Olga in one piece, and try to rescue her from whatever Nevena had planned. He had to—

There – there was something ahead of him, wasn't there? A recognisable shape amid the whirling blizzard, something familiar – something very like a Lada Niva. Didn't Filippov drive a Lada? Vassily was sure he'd seen him in one at Café Astana, now and again. But it wasn't moving . . . Had Olga got stuck, then, like Vassily? That was easily fixed! But, no, thought Vassily, as he skidded and bumped his way nearer to the stranded Lada: it wasn't stuck like Vassily had been, but on something that stuck up through the snow – something that glinted silver, even in the wan light of a whitened canopy.

My God, thought Vassily. She's stuck on the tracks! Olga was stuck on the tracks, and the car was a wreck – he could tell, even from a distance, that the front axle had sheared off. There would be no moving the car, short of a crane or a powerful winch.

And *there*, inside the car, Vassily could see Olga at the wheel, but turned sideways, and kicking – kicking at her door, again and again, but with no effect. And beside her – yes, that was Nevena, stirring into life and massaging her temples, then turning to open her own door, but again to no avail.

Vassily pushed his foot down still further, determined to reach the car and free Olga from its buckled frame before Nevena could get to her.

But what was that glint of light to the right – a glint of light through the trees, that grew steadily brighter second by second, and was accompanied, Vassily heard, by a chest-deep rumbling and a shriller, piercing tone, irregularly repeated like a beacon or warning?

A warning, from the right – down the tracks . . .

'My God, the snowplough,' he muttered. Of course: Russian Railways were sending a unit through to clear the tracks, and it must have made good progress to get there so fast. So fast, and with Olga stranded on the tracks . . .

He juddered to a halt by the rails, leaped out of the car, and skidded his way to the boot. Wrenching the door open, he rooted furiously among the flotsam and jetsam of a working police car until his questing fingers lay upon the cold, hard certainty of tempered steel. Turning with an inarticulate cry, he ran to the Lada, gestured to Olga to hide her face, and smashed the window from left to right and up to down. Reaching in, he grasped Olga under the shoulders and pulled her bodily out, staggering as her legs fell down upon him, and falling to earth with her atop him.

From the ground Vassily turned his head and saw that the train had already burst into clear view, its blunt nose still blundering forwards through the snow and its crew now visible, leaning out of its grimy windows and screaming at them to move aside, emphasising the message with continuous blasts of the snowplough's deafening horn, supplemented now with the futile squealing of hurriedly applied brakes.

Vassily realised, too, that a gloved hand was beating upon his shoulder, and swivelled his head to look up at Olga.

'Vassily,' she cried above the din, 'Nevena – Nevena is still in the car!'

Vassily nodded, shouldered Olga gently aside, and ran to the other side of the car, repeating the operation and dragging Nevena from the car, marvelling as he did so at the lightness of her frame, and – despite himself – at her preternatural beauty, displayed now in wintry guise, and dazzlingly white in the reflected glare of the looming snowplough.

She seemed to smile at him – a mere softening of her eyes, as if to acknowledge his bravery at freeing her despite everything, an everything that included his knowledge of her guilt. For an instant she stood still in Vassily's arms, gazing at him so that he knew *she* knew – she knew, and (Vassily sensed) she was happy: it didn't matter any more. Nothing mattered any more to her, Vassily felt: she had passed beyond the world of the living.

But then a bitter gust blew, sending a squall of icy flakes across them. Her hands flew to her throat, bare now and open to the glittering snowflakes that surrounded them, like a second embrace, and her eyes flew to the car behind them.

'My scarf!' she cried. 'My own scarf!'

She twisted out of Vassily's grip and started towards Filippov's ruined Lada, thrusting herself into the shattered window.

'Nevena!' screamed Olga, and Vassily, too, found himself shouting desperately at her to come back, to come to her senses, to stay away from the car, for God's sake, to stay away – but all was in vain. The snowplough ploughed on regardless, taking up the car and crushing it with a horrendous animate impact that crumpled its steel like a collapsing house of cards, enveloping Nevena, still within the shattered Lada, in a deathly embrace, and bearing her on, still onwards, down the track until the snowplough finally came to a disastrous halt.

But something fluttered from the wreck, something thin and snaking and virid, as if someone had cut through the wintry air to reveal a slash of deep, silky summer green. Nevena's scarf drifted down and settled on the snow, lifted once or twice with the remnants of the icy breeze, and then was still.

16

Under a Green Willow

'Pasha,' said Olga to her brother on Thursday morning, 'can you please put Dmitri back in his kennel' – placing her hedgehog in Pasha's reluctant hands – 'and give him some cat food. He's hungry again. When is he not? Oh, and can you tell the sergeant that I'm still not talking to him?'

Pasha smiled at her despite the squirming ball of prickles in his grasp. 'No problem about Dmitri – but don't be so ridiculous about Vassily, Olgakin! He saved your life, you know.'

'Only after risking it in the first place. He used me as bait, Pasha – as *bait*!'

'No, I didn't,' said Vassily, pushing the bedroom door gently open and sticking a head of dark, tousled hair around the edge. 'I was trying to protect you! I thought if I could keep Nevena close to me, you'd be safe from her attention. I admit that didn't work out very well in the end, and I feel terrible, Olga, really I do,' he went on, sidling awkwardly into the room, like an embarrassed teenager, 'but I had to keep Nevena on the loose, and you out of the investigation. I just *had* to . . . It was hard work to keep it up, for I had to pretend to her that all was well, while all the time I was terrified of anything happening to you.'

'You weren't good enough at acting, Vassily,' Olga put in. 'He'd never be a good murderer, would he, Pasha?'

'No,' said Pasha, smiling down at a puzzled Vassily. 'But I think I'll let you explain that one to Vassily yourself, Olgakin,' he went on, slipping out of the door. 'I've got a hedgehog to feed.'

'Oh, it's hardly worth explaining, Vassily,' said Olga. 'Or maybe I'll tell you some other time – if I ever forgive you!'

'Well,' said Vassily, with an awkward smile, 'I hope you do. But you see, Olga, I knew Nevena was tied up with the derailment as soon as she came back to Roslazny the day of the train wreck. What were the chances that Alexeyev would just come across her with his ATV like that, in the middle of the snowstorm? No, that was planned – I knew it. She pretended to leave, then found someone to bring her back after enough time had passed to erase suspicion. And, later on, I saw that she knew the woman in the photo I found on Danyl. Yes, she was involved – I could feel it in my bones.'

'You almost *saw* it in my bones, splintered across the track like confetti,' snapped Olga. 'Oh, Vassily, how could you let her carry on like that? And I thought it was a man, all the time . . . Don't you realise that Gennady Aristov would still be alive if you hadn't let her operate so freely – that Nevena herself might be alive, too?'

Vassily leaned back against Olga's windowsill and sighed, then remembered that Nevena had painted the windowsill as part of her intricate schemes. He jumped to his feet again. 'I *know* that, Olga,' he said, looking down at her with darkling eyes. 'And I'd do anything – *anything* – to go back and arrest her as soon as I saw her. But what would I do for proof?

There was none. We'd have had to release her, and then she'd have disappeared as soon as the snow lifted. There'd be no justice for Danyl and Anoushka, or Gennady, either. And who knows who else she might have killed, in revenge for some other forgotten injury?'

Olga shook her head. 'Nonsense! If you think that, you still don't understand Nevena Danylovna Komarov. It's all in the name: Danylovna. Yes, she was Danyl's daughter! But she was Zlata's, too. And she couldn't forgive Danyl for abandoning them when she was little. Could you have forgiven him, if your mother had gone out like that? No, there was nothing else on her mind, no other crime to avenge, but Danyl's original sin. I wonder if it was that news story on him that pushed her over the edge. You know, the one back in March, about his heroic deed in saving that child from the flames. Wouldn't that make you bitter, seeing your father save a child when he'd heartlessly abandoned you and your mother? I remember she said local heroes have secrets to hide . . . and she knew just what they were.'

'Pity you didn't remember her patronym from when you knew her before,' muttered Vassily – but Olga cut him off with a snort.

'Don't be ridiculous, Vassily! She always used Ivanovna, not Danylovna. She changed it – just like she changed her mother's name. She always said her mother was Alyona, not Zlata – to hide her real identity, of course. If you want to hide a Z, pick an A. But it was all there in her name, all along, only we didn't know where to look.'

As soon as normal communications were restored in the days that followed Nevena's death, Vassily had set his formidable resources into motion, setting two junior policemen to scour the Kemerovo archives for any scraps that might shed further light on the tragic end of Nevena Komarov – or, rather, Nevena Menovsky. For Vassily had also searched for references to Zlata M, the woman pictured in the photograph that Danyl Petrovich had taken to his death and before long he uncovered a brief yet telling clipping from a Kemerovo paper back in 1987.

LOCAL WOMAN COMMITS SUICIDE. FOUR-YEAR-OLD DAUGHTER LEFT BEHIND

Thirty-six-year-old Zlata Petrovich, née Menovsky, hanged herself from her ceiling yesterday, 8 January. The woman's neighbours stated that she had become depressed after her husband Danyl left the family home to take up with another woman, named by local sources as Anoushka Egorov. Zlata Petrovich leaves behind a four-year-old girl, Nevena.

'Yes, even Komarov was made up,' Olga said, leaning back against her pillows and gazing up at her bedroom ceiling. 'I wonder why she chose that name . . . Sounds like *komar*, "mosquito" – did she see herself as a mosquito to Danyl Petrovich, something to buzz around him and discomfit him?'

Olga sighed. 'I suppose I never really knew her at all – how can you know someone, if you don't even know their name? But whatever she called herself, I never guessed she'd try to kill *me*.'

'But she didn't set out to do that, Olga,' said Vassily, easing himself carefully (as if permission might at any moment be denied) into the chair next to Olga's bed, and cautiously lighting one of his Belamorkanal cigarettes. 'It was Polina Klemovsky she wanted to frame, all along – that's why she carried out all those petty crimes in Itatka, and then over here in Roslazny. No wonder I couldn't catch the culprit! But then Nevena had to improvise when she found out you were still around, and Polina had arrived so late, meaning the framing wouldn't work. She must've been shocked that you were leaving so soon, for Mongolia – it didn't give her much time. So she—'

But Olga cut in, carrying on Vassily's train of thought. 'So she stole that bag of garden tools from the Petrovs – you remember she said "honeyberry"? Honeyberries, like at the Petrovs'? How could I have missed that! She stole the hoe from the Petrovs, and got my fingerprints on it, and broke me out of jail to kill me at Filippov's *dacha*,' said Olga, with all the bitterness of a friend's betrayal. 'She knew about Mongolia all along, of course – I see it now. She talked about shoe-sole cake, and deels, and fermented milk – who'd know about those things, if they didn't know about Mongolia? *I* didn't, before I got that letter in the summer. When she first saw me, she asked if they'd moved me to Tayga instead – instead of Ulaanbaatar, of course, she meant. She pretended to help me with my investigation – and yet it was Nevena who hid in Café Astana that time, giving me and poor Igor the fright of our lives.'

'I know,' said Vassily. 'I was so relieved to see you come out alone, and in one piece – but alarmed to think you might've been next to Nevena inside.'

'And don't forget how she got me to go along with her, when I escaped from the police station, making me think I might've derailed the train myself, and convincing me I couldn't trust the police or the justice system – that I had to get out or spend the rest of my life in jail, or worse! And then taking me off into the *taiga* – I was lucky to get away, but unlucky to stumble across her hiding place. But it was unluckier still for Nevena, in the end . . .

'And it wasn't just me she was cruel to,' she went on. 'Think of poor Loktev, and his rats.'

(Loktev, it had emerged, had acquired an intense fear of rodents during his childhood in Kirov, when his father had locked him into a cellar with only rats for company for three days, as a punishment for stealing a plate of *kurnik*. 'I've never quite got over it, Marushkin,' he said frankly. 'But I didn't expect that woman to use it so effectively. Shame she's dead. I'd like to sign her up!')

'Yes – but she also painted over your windowsill, don't forget,' replied Vassily. 'She got the idea from Pasha's renovations, I suppose, or Odrosov's cans of paint at Café Astana. She wanted to give you an alibi for the derailment, I think, or at least to confuse matters so you could get away, somehow or other. At least, I think that was her plan at first – spread so much guilt around that it wouldn't stick to anybody. But then something must have happened to change her mind – to make her resort to more extreme measures. Maybe it happened quite late in the day. It could even have been on the day you escaped.'

Olga breathed in sharply. '*Of course*,' she said. 'My phone!'

'What about your phone?' said Vassily, but Olga had turned to her handbag – a startling blue leather item from the Tayga discount boutique, Madame Kravtsov's – and was pulling items out by the bucketful until she came across her diminutive mobile. She unlocked it, rubbed a smear of lipstick from the screen, and showed Vassily the video she'd taken the week before, standing by the tracks and looking back towards her little hut.

'There!' she said. 'You see that movement? I'd almost forgotten I filmed this. I thought it was just a deer, but could it be Nevena herself, finishing off the job? I even heard something tinkling in the distance that day when I set off towards the tracks . . . The sound of metal on ballast, perhaps.'

Vassily stared at the cracked, dimly lit screen. 'Maybe,' he said doubtfully. 'We'd need to enhance it somehow – maybe in Kemerovo . . . But of course Nevena would know that she'd been there. Did you show it to her?'

'No,' said Olga, 'but I told her about it. And you – and Polina Klemovsky! Don't you remember? That time you all came to see me in prison? The next time I saw Nevena, she'd changed . . .'

'Yes,' said Vassily, musingly. 'Yes, you must be right, Olga . . . She'd changed because she'd decided you were a threat, after all – a threat to her freedom.'

'Her freedom to carry on living in – in her mother's place,' said Olga, a sudden wave of sadness interrupting her words despite all that had happened; and her hand slipped inside her handbag once more, this time not in search of her phone but of the silken touch of Nevena's green scarf. 'That wardrobe full of old furs and dresses in her room in Café Astana – the wardrobe Gennady must have seen. She appeared in her mother's clothes to frighten Danyl, to make him feel he hadn't escaped the secrets that were buried in the past. It's hardly surprising Nevena never married, is it? She'd seen how it could end up.'

'And it's no wonder, too, that Polina said Danyl was moody and unpredictable – or that he took to booze,' said Vassily, thinking of the coroner's report that had, as expected, confirmed high levels of alcohol in Danyl's system on the day of the crash.

'"I'm always next to the line," she said, "wherever I am,"' said Olga, sadly. 'She had to be, to frighten Danyl! But I think there was something else, too: she simply wanted to *be* her mother, to feel like she was still – she was still—'

'Oh, Olga,' said Vassily, seeing the tears welling under Olga's mascara, and reaching out a tentative hand before withdrawing it once more. 'You, too, lost your mother when you were little – I can only imagine what it feels like.'

'No, no,' said Olga, shaking her head, and dashing away her tears with an angry swipe of her hand. 'Well, I mean, yes, that's true. We all come back to our mothers, don't we? A circle that never ends, like a wheel – but some wheels ring true, when struck by a hammer, and others ring false.'

She paused briefly, thinking that this might be worth immortalising as a proverb, before returning to her theme with renewed warmth.

'But I didn't set out to kill my father, did I? Nevena did, after months of terrorising him, standing by the tracks. And she killed Danyl's wife, Anoushka, too, don't forget – and she would've killed many more if it had been a normal Trans-Siberian service! She even told us it would be worth it if Danyl didn't die – you remember? When we were discussing the case together? If he survived, he'd be humiliated, humbled, scared. And she said humans were her speciality . . .'

Olga shivered.

'And she tried to frame Polina Klemovsky,' she continued, after a moment, 'for no reason at all. I mean, I don't exactly have warm feelings towards her, but enough's enough. To prepare so thoroughly – all those crimes in Itatka and here – just to put one stranger into the dock, even though she does wear clogs and kick hedgehogs with them. And then there's poor Gennady, murdered like that, with his head beaten in, and Nevena lying behind him making us think he was still alive. It's so – it's so *evil* . . . She must have had to rush, to get all that done before going to work with you at the police station that day. But she had no problem with efficiency, did she? And there's Taisia, left behind on her own.'

Vassily flashed a dry smile. 'She doesn't seem that upset about Gennady, to be honest,' he said. 'She's more concerned about the blackmail charges against her.'

But Olga wasn't listening, and after a moment she stirred and spoke with distant eyes, frowning with the effort of remembrance. 'What was it Taisia said to me about Danyl? Oh, yes – he was always talking about the sins of his youth. And he told his nephew, Ludis, that men have to stick things through to the end, no matter what. He had a conscience, then, despite what Nevena said.'

'What did she say?'

'That he trampled on others.'

'Don't we all, from time to time?' said Vassily.

'I suppose we do,' said Olga, absently taking one of Vassily's cigarettes from the packet in front of her and lighting it, thinking all the while of something she'd read somewhere – in Solzhenitsyn, she thought, one day in her little rail-side hut when things were slow and she didn't feel like writing, but instead picked up one of the books her mother Tatiana had bought for her long ago. What was it he'd written, that wise old man with the leprechaun beard and far-seeing eyes? Something that resonated with the long hangover in Danyl's life, the inescapable guilt that had followed his youthful, fateful decision to abandon Zlata and Nevena.

Ah, yes – she remembered:

If only it were all so simple! If only there were evil people somewhere insidiously committing evil deeds, and it were necessary only to separate them from the rest of us and destroy them. But the line dividing good and evil cuts through the heart of every human being. And who is willing to destroy a piece of his own heart?

Regardless of the subtleties of Danyl's guilt, life was too hard on women, she thought, exhaling a cloud of grey-blue smoke and staring through it at the cracks that spidered across the ceiling of her bedroom in the house she shared with Pasha and Anna Kabalevsky. It made them suffer and weep and labour as few men ever did, and *because* of men, too, for the most part, who had no such excuse for their wickedness. Was it any wonder that some, like Nevena Komarov or Menovsky, surrendered to revenge and unreality in exchange?

No, it was no wonder, thought Olga, as they laid Nevena to rest in the Roslazny churchyard some days later, after the authorities released her remains for burial. Relatives of the Petroviches and Gennady Aristov had come already to take their bodies back to Yashkino, but nobody had come for Nevena, so she was buried as she had lived her life, alone, carried by strangers' hands from the Tayga morgue to a hearse, then driven through the fields in which she had ended her life, lined with straggling remnants of the snow that her eyes had last looked upon, until at last, in Roslazny, they reached a place where thick, overhanging trees drooped like mourners over the ground.

And there under the sighing boughs, with a pickaxe and a few rusty shovels borrowed from nearby houses, Vassily and the other men carved a gaping hole in the Russian earth, digging down until they could go no further and the soil began to glisten white with the frost that never leaves; and then, with the rough tenderness of the living towards the dead, they carried Nevena's coffin into the hole they had made. The men arranged her gently in the ground before stepping back, wiping the sweat from their brows and pausing to catch their breath. Then, with curt nods at each other and sighs of sweaty weariness, they picked up their shovels once more and began to put the crumbled soil back into the grave, covering the gleaming pinewood with dark Siberian earth as if the heavens had sent black snow down upon it.

But Olga stepped forward and stopped them, taking something from her blue handbag – something that shimmered greenly as she passed it through her hands. Then, with a sigh, she let it slip from her fingers until the earth took it, turning away with a sob as it disappeared into Nevena's grave, and letting the men continue their solemn duty.

Then, following the custom, one of the older villagers began to intone words aloud, croaking rather than singing, but gently, sadly, so that the others felt compelled to join in chanting the familiar, sorrowful words:

> *Pod rakitoyu zelyonoy*
> *Kazak raneniy lezhal*
>
> Under a green willow
> A wounded Cossack lay.
> A raven flew to him

Sensing a tasty morsel.

'Oh, you black raven,
I am still alive!
Fly, please, black raven,
To my young wife.

'Tell her, black raven
That I've married another.
The wedding was peaceful,
Under a willow bush.
My sharp sabre was the matchmaker,
My bayonet was the best man.
The bullet married us quickly,
Mother Earth married us.'

Olga looked up with tear-filled eyes, wishing that more snow would fall, tumbling down through the branches interlaced above and settling at last upon the new-heaped mound, covering its darkness with a layer of pristine, unimpeachable white – but no flakes came from the skies, only a soft, damp breeze filled with the sad decay of autumn.

She turned to Vassily. 'Isn't it just like life to find someone and lose them again? Isn't it just like life?'

17

Back in the USSR

Vassily looked up with disbelief. 'So – I can stay here? In Roslazny?'

'That's what I said, isn't it? Have you got some hearing problem I don't know about? That could change things, you know.'

'No, no,' said Vassily Marushkin, suddenly alarmed. You never knew what might happen when you talked to Captain Zemsky, head of the Tayga police: you could end up assigned to traffic duty on Oktyabr'skaya Ulitsa, or just as easily become embroiled in an impossible cold case that Kemerovo's finest had failed to solve, like the death of Roslazny's Sofia Eldarov back in 1998. For this reason, Vassily tried to avoid speaking to Zemsky whenever possible, but as he was Vassily's direct superior it was difficult to eliminate contact entirely, and impossible following a major homicide investigation. The good news was that Nevena's undoubted guilt was sufficient to keep the Roslazny station open for the foreseeable future: clearing three murders was a rare accomplishment for any rural sergeant. What the bad news might be, Vassily didn't yet know – but he was old enough to understand that there was always some bad news alongside the good, in the end.

'No, no, no,' he continued, speaking as quietly as possible to reassure Captain Zemsky that there was nothing wrong with his ears. 'No, all good up here,' he continued, tapping his head. 'Better than ever, in fact.'

'Well,' said Zemsky, pursing his lips. 'Well . . . Just make sure everything's wrapped up as fast as possible – get the paperwork done today, *da*? I don't want that spook hanging around longer than needed.' Zemsky nodded down the corridor towards the back office, where Loktev had established his temporary headquarters. 'I don't like the FSB – don't like them at all . . . Good work, though, finding out about his Achilles' heel, Marushkin. Afraid of rats – who'd have guessed? Always good to know a weakness, *nyet*?'

'It wasn't me, actually, sir,' said Vassily. 'That was Nevena Komarov, too.'

'Really? Well, I'm impressed. Damn shame she got herself killed – we could've signed her up, eh, Marushkin! We could've signed her up.'

'That's what Loktev said,' muttered Vassily, to a bark of Zemskyan laughter.

Then he watched Zemsky get back into his Audi, heaving a sigh of relief when he finally drove off. Loktev, he feared, would prove harder to get rid of. Admittedly the FSB agent had suffered an embarrassing episode in front of the whole village – but, then, embarrassing incidents were hardly unknown in Roslazny, where scarcely a week passed without some Rocket Fuel-related event. And Loktev had shown no sign of noticing any social discomfort, occupying himself instead with a series of intense and probing debriefing interviews with Ludis Kuskov, Taisia Aristov, and anyone else even remotely connected with the case – a series of interviews so lengthy and prolonged that Vassily began to think they would never come to an end.

In the event, however, the ex-pastor took himself off at short notice and with surprising rapidity, breezing into the reception with bags packed and an unusually cheery smile upon his face.

'I'm away, Marushkin,' he said, tugging at his beard. 'Just got word of another case down Irkutsk way – organised crime on Lake Baikal. Do you know how much you can make off smuggled *omul*? I'm done here, anyway – nothing more to dig up, now that Kuskov's proved to be boringly clean, and Taisia Aristov's been packed off to Kemerovo.'

Olga had come to visit her former cellmate the day before, wishing to say a final farewell before Taisia's transfer to the province's capital. They had shared four walls, after all, and had been through some traumatic experiences together. And Olga also found a certain degree of sympathy for Taisia sneaking into her breast – a kind of recognition, she thought, that people usually have reasons for doing what they do, even if they make choices we mightn't make ourselves, like blackmailing a neighbour, and lying about it, and burning bodies to cover your tracks . . . But who knows what I would do if I were in her cheap plasticky shoes, thought Olga, as the police car took Taisia off, her fingers flapping a forlorn farewell out of the rolled-down window. Who knows what I would do, if I lived behind those mournful eyes and under that greasy headscarf?

'Well, thanks for the hospitality, Marushkin,' went on Loktev, with a slight, sarcastic emphasis on *gostepriimstvo*. 'And for your . . . well, your understanding, if you get me,' he went on, with uncharacteristic quietness in his voice. 'But don't forget,' he added, in his normal acid tones, 'I know where the bodies are buried, Marushkin! I know where they're buried.' Then he swept his priestly cloak around him and was gone.

That left Ludis Kuskov, who emerged from Café Astana with the air of a prisoner freed from a long confinement.

'Come back any time,' said Igor Odrosov, pocketing a thick wad of rouble notes, and pulling the door closed behind Ludis.

'Not likely,' muttered Ludis, through a mouthful of cigarette smoke. 'Cost me a small fortune, and for what? A rickety bed next to a crime scene, and a heap of Popov's cast-off donkey burgers . . . A small fortune? Not so small, after all. It's just as well about Uncle Danyl. I mean, I'm sorry he's gone, but I needed that money. *We* needed that money.'

'You and your son, you mean?' said Vassily, lighting his cigarette from Ludis's. 'You must be desperate to get back to him.'

Ludis nodded. 'I've had enough of fake pastors, crazy women, and bad vodka to last me a lifetime. No offence, Vassily, but I don't know how you stick this place. Why don't you come to Yashkino? Or Berezkino? There's better options than Roslazny, and not far away, either – places with decent roads, proper restaurants, girls who don't try to kill everyone . . .'

Vassily smiled. 'Well, there are more important things than roads and restaurants. And Roslazny's got its merits, too, you know. Oh, yes, it has its good points, if you know where to look.'

Olga Pushkin walked down the corridor that led from the kitchen to the front door and opened it, a smile spreading instantly across her face.

'Sasha!' she cried. 'Sasha Tsaritsyn! I haven't seen you since the – since all that unpleasantness earlier in the year.'

'And here I am again,' he said, grinning at her, 'turning up like a bad kopek whenever there's a story to tell! Igor Odrosov told me you were out this way, so I popped down to ask you a few questions in person. Oh – hello, Pasha!'

Olga turned to see her brother standing behind her, tall and slender, and smiling at Sasha as he stood framed in the pale sunlight that flooded through the open door.

'Well, come in, Sasha,' she said, ushering him in. 'Though I'm not sure I have much to say to a journalist – even a friendly one like you.'

'Nothing for the good readers of the *Kemerovo Herald*? Not even a few crumbs to spice up my next feature? I'll just make it up if you don't tell me, you know,' said Sasha, taking off his leather jacket and following Olga and Pasha through into the living room.

'Then what's the point of telling you?' laughed Olga. 'Come – sit down and catch up with Pasha. You haven't met since the winter, have you? I'll bring tea.'

She stood at the corner, watching her brother and Sasha talking animatedly together, and smiling a secret smile. It did her good to see Pasha lighting up like that – and who knew? Perhaps Sasha could be the one to replace Pasha's lost love, his Ruslan, the boy he'd yearned for so long ago.

But when she returned with the cups, matters had turned serious.

'You didn't know? Oh, she's been asking around for days, they tell me,' said Sasha, sitting forward and leafing through a notebook. 'Let's see – yes, Igor told me she'd been writing things down in Café Astana, and then Popov mentioned she'd been up his way, trying to get his wife to spill the beans on any village gossip. But it was Igor's daughter who said she'd been asking questions about you.'

'Who's this – Svetlana?' said Olga, surprised to hear that Igor's daughter had been demonstrating such industriousness.

'No – Polina Klemovsky,' said Pasha, turning to Olga with a troubled look on his face.

'She's been asking about *you*? But why?'

'I don't know,' admitted Sasha. 'But she's connected to Boris Andreyev, you say? Well, he's just bought the *Tayga Gazetteer*.'

'That old rag? But they haven't printed anything for years!'

'I know – but he must be planning to start it up again.'

'But why? What good's a newspaper to a man like Andreyev?'

'Politics, I should think,' said Sasha. 'He's an ambitious man, isn't he? Then he's probably got his eye on big things – bigger things than running a local Russian Railways depot. And what could be more useful than a paper to sing his praises around the clock? And Polina's one of his minions, you say – well, no doubt she's been assigned to find some juicy local stories. That's what I'd do, anyway, if I were him. I've seen that kind of set-up before – install some informant in a key position, curry favour with some of the looser-tongued locals, and mop up with the resulting info. You can tweak it to any tale, you know.'

'But why has she been asking about me in particular?' asked Pasha. 'She must've heard I left the army – and in a hurry, too.'

'But nobody knows the – the circumstances of that,' said Olga.

'Not yet, anyway,' said Pasha.

'What circumstances?' said Sasha, rolling his eyes at Olga in the resulting silence. 'Oh, come on, Olga – I'm not going to write anything about you or Pasha! I'm a journo, yes, but we've got our limits.'

'I'll believe that when I see it,' began Olga, but to her surprise Pasha cut across her.

'It's all right, Olga,' he said. 'Sasha's earned the truth. He called in the reinforcements back in February – remember? It's only because of him that I found you so quickly, when your life was in danger – right, Sasha? And, besides,' he went on, sending a shy glance at the journalist, 'I think I'm ready to start telling people. Some people, anyway. It's not good to keep things secret for too long, Olga. It's bad for the soul. And Sasha was at school with us, too, just like Vassily. If you can't trust your old class-mates, who can you trust?'

Olga nodded warily, reluctantly, but it was enough: Pasha took a deep breath and told Sasha Tsaritsyn how and why he had been forced out of the army, feeling the tension ebb away from his slender frame as he unburdened himself of his secrets at last, and seeing not disgust or disapproval, but rather understanding and compassion in the bright eyes of Sasha Tsaritsyn.

'Pasha, Pasha,' he said, reaching out a hand and pressing it upon Pasha's. 'How terrible that you had to go through that! I wish I could print it, to show the world how terrible things are for – for – for people like us.'

Pasha nodded but didn't speak, with only a glimmer of reflected light showing the unshed tear in his eye.

'Well, she mustn't print it, if she finds out,' said Sasha, with a firm look on his face. 'Polina Klemovsky, I mean. We have to see to that.'

'But what can we do?' said Olga, but Sasha wasn't listening.

'You say she was talking to Igor about his prices, Olga, and to Anna, about the Kabalevsky hostel?'

Olga nodded in silent affirmation.

'And she knows old man Solotov, too, from way back?'

'Yes,' said Olga. 'But what's that that got to do with Pasha?'

'Oh, nothing,' said Sasha, airily. 'Just wondering if we could kill two, or even three, birds with just the one stone.'

When all was done, Vassily admitted that Sasha, not Nevena Komarov, would be the real superstar of an expanded Roslazny police force.

First, Sasha had slipped Igor Odrosov a handful of roubles, thereby ensuring a place next to Polina at dinner the next day in Café Astana. And there, safe in semi-seclusion on a round table near the front door, he struck up an artful, Rocket-Fuelled conversation in which he shamelessly flattered her journalistic ambitions until she admitted she already had a few stories up her sleeve – stories that would please her boss, Boris, or B as she called him, to a sufficient degree to enable her to get her pick of assignments across the whole *oblast*.

After Sasha had offered to critique her writing – and after he had sworn, on an old copy of *Das Kapital*, that he wouldn't print them himself, a somewhat inebriated Polina had plucked a tablet from her handbag and showed Sasha the text of several stories in development, including one on Olga's imprisonment in the Roslazny police station, complete with photographs showing Olga's startled face behind the bars of Kliment's bedroom. There was another one on Vassily Marushkin, too, telling the tale of Kliment's return, and Vassily's continued search for his wife Rozalina, presumed lost to people-traffickers in the wilds of Russia. These were bad enough, but more troubling still was a story on Pasha that Polina had put together with the aid of a contact in the military archives at Novosibirsk.

ROSLAZNY MAN DISCHARGED FROM ARMY FOR HOMOSEXUALITY, ran the headline, and underneath, next to a grainy picture of Pasha, a strapline that was no better: *GAY PRIVATE PASHA PUSHKIN AT LARGE IN VILLAGE NEAR TAYGA.*

We have taken the unprecedented step of printing this week's edition two days early [began the second paragraph] *because we believe it is a matter of public safety that deviants like this man be identified within the community. No inhabitant of Roslazny, or other villages and towns within Kemerovo Oblast, will wish to remain uninformed of the characters who share their streets, shops, and post offices; no mother or concerned relative will wish the vulnerable to be preyed upon by people of this kind.*

There was more of the same – much more – but Sasha hadn't read any further. He hadn't needed to: he knew what it would say, more or less, though he didn't doubt that the details would be wrong. And even if the details were right, Sasha knew that a whole newspaper – a whole year of newspapers – wouldn't be enough to capture the essence of Pasha's story, the secrecy and solitude and suffering he had endured. He himself had suffered similarly, though without the humiliation of an army discharge. Taken together, it was all he could do to contain his rage at the woman who sat in front of him, gloating over her investigative acumen and never thinking of the human cost it would incur.

'It was childsh – I mean, child's play,' slurred Polina, dropping a familiar hand on Sasha's wrist. 'I knew the man from Itatka – he used to work the records there, and I know all about him and his – his – his mistress,' she finished at last, her eyes almost glazing over before she recovered herself. 'So it was easy. A quick phone call and there I was. Pasha Pushkin dishcovered!'

She grinned at him from behind her spectacles, until he wished he could pour his beer over her tablet.

He did, however, manage to contain his rage – and it was just as well he did, for only one part of his task was complete. Sasha now knew that Pasha's fears were fully justified. He knew what Polina planned to publish and why – but he didn't know how to stop her: not yet. He did know, however, that Polina could hardly be interested in taking over the Kabalevsky Hostel or competing with Igor Odrosov in any way, for she had told him so in as many words.

'Waste my time selling booze and *pirogi* to idiots like this?' she'd said, gesturing with a rather unsteady hand at the Café Astana regulars. 'No, no – that's Sholotov's pigeon. Solothov, I mean. Damn it – Solotosh . . . Solotov. Got there at last! He has the cash. Old friend of my papa, isn't he? Helped me out with a couple of – a couple of *difficulties*, in the past, when I got in trouble with that scheme . . . *Da*, he knows things. So I've got to help him, haven't I? No choice. What do I care, anyway, who runsh – runs – some rotten hostel?'

Sasha had nodded and shrugged his shoulders as if the information was of no interest to him, but meanwhile he was making a mental note of all the salient information – for an idea had come to mind, an idea so exciting that he had to tell Olga and Pasha as soon as possible. He finished his vodka, threw a few notes onto the table, and got up to leave, parting himself with some difficulty from Polina's beseeching hands, and promising to catch up with her as soon as he could.

'It's all about Solotov,' he said to Pasha and Olga, later that night, draining a mug of Pasha's strong coffee and calling for another straight away. '*Bozhe moy!* That woman can drink. Anyway, what was I saying? Oh, yes: Solotov. It's all about Vladimir Solotov! He wants to get his hands on Anna's old hostel: that's one thing. And he's got dirt on Polina, and serious dirt, too, by the sound of it: that's another thing. Put the two together, and what do you get?'

'Two very unpleasant people,' muttered Olga, leaning forward to warm her hands at the guttering gas fire she'd dragged into the living room when the snow had begun.

'Ha!' said Sasha. 'You're not wrong, Olga Pushkin. Yes: two unpleasant people. But maybe we can swap one thing for another. Why not give Solotov what he wants? And then maybe he'll give us what *we* want – dirt on Polina. Something big! And then,' he said, clenching his fingers into a fist, '*then* we can get to work.'

'Give Solotov the Kabalevsky Hostel?' said Pasha. 'And put poor Igor Odrosov out of business?'

'Don't be too sure about that,' said Sasha, sitting back and lighting a cigarette. 'Old Igor's craftier than you give him credit for. Craftier than old man Solotov, anyway.'

'Well, we can't, even if we wanted to,' said Olga, passing him an ashtray. 'It's not ours to give. The bailiffs still have it. Anna's husband Bogdan remortgaged the house, remember, then didn't make his payments. They put it up for sale, a while back – I saw a sign in the agent's office, in Tayga. Don't suppose they've had much interest.'

'I know that,' said Sasha. 'So don't you think Solotov does, too? And don't you think he'd buy it in two shakes of a swan's tail if he could?'

'But Polina said he's got the cash already,' said Olga. 'And I know how, too. Mother always said rich people were tight – that's how they got rich.'

'Yes, he's got the cash,' said Sasha. 'But he's got something else, too, that's not as useful.'

'Oh, come on, Sasha!' cried Pasha, impatiently, glancing at his watch. 'Look – it's after eleven o'clock, and some of us have to get up and look after small children at five in the morning! Just tell us what you're getting at.'

'All right, all right,' said Sasha, grinning at him. 'Keep your hair on! Well, I made a couple of calls, and I found out something quite interesting. Solotov's blacklisted – and so is Mikhail.'

'Blacklisted?' said Olga. 'What for?'

'*Imushchestvo*,' whispered Sasha. *Property.*

'You mean – he can't buy property any more?' said Pasha. Sasha nodded in response.

'*Ah*,' breathed Olga. 'Because of that thing he did, with my father – selling off those plots?'

'You've got it,' said Sasha, nodding again. 'Turns out the agents' union takes a dim view of men hawking land they don't own. They're banned for life, both of them. They couldn't put their name down for a bag of beans, in Kemerovo *oblast*.'

'But what about Aunt Zia?' said Pasha. 'Why couldn't she put her name down? She's always doing stuff for Solotov and Mikhail.'

'Put her name down as the owner of a hostel, Pasha?' said Olga. 'A guesthouse? A *bar*? A place open to the public, with paying customers, alcohol, unseemly behaviour?'

'You're right, Olga,' said Pasha, grinning at her. 'Even she wouldn't stoop to that! OK, they can't buy the hostel. So what do you—'

'Wait a minute,' said Olga. 'Wait a minute. What if one of us put our name down instead and bought it *for* Solotov with his own cash?'

'Well, I can't,' said Sasha. 'I don't live in the area. You know what they're like, round here – you have to prove you're descended from ten generations of serfs before they'll hand over the keys. And there's no way Solotov would let you or Pasha do it, after what you did to your father. Can't see Vassily doing it, either, as it's probably against the law. But maybe one of the villagers would do it. Someone who owes you a favour, maybe.'

'Ha!' laughed Olga. 'Nobody owes me any favours, Sasha – not in this village. But there is – there is someone else we could consider,' she continued tentatively, nodding towards the door that led to the bedrooms. 'Someone with a past connection to that very hostel . . .'

'No, Olga – you can't!' cried Pasha, almost knocking over his coffee in his agitation.

'Why not? It's for a damn good cause.'

'Yes – why wouldn't she do it, if she knew why?' said Sasha.

326

'Well, it used to be her house, for one thing,' said Pasha. 'Until she was robbed of it by that idiot Bogdan. Don't you think she might object to buying it back for somebody else? And she doesn't like Solotov. I mean, nobody does, but she *really* can't stand him. And – and, well, for another thing, she's very ... *traditional*. So I don't know if she'd even want to help us, if we're doing it so that Polina doesn't print that stuff about – well, about me.'

'Traditional ... She's religious, you mean?' said Olga. 'Yes, she is. But she loves you, too, Pasha. Why don't you ask her, and see what she says?'

'But what if she moves out or something?' said Pasha. 'She might take offence. I couldn't bear to see her and the boys on the street again.'

'I can't see that happening,' said Olga. 'Just try her, and then we'll know where we are.'

And so, early the next morning, Pasha asked if he could speak to Anna alone, and then followed his puzzled housemate as she walked back to her room. He trembled as he went, looking around him at the house his sister had bought, the house he shared with Anna and her children, in case Polina's poisonous words might shatter the serenity they had established there, the peace they had built up together through noisy lunchtimes and games in the garden and quiet evenings when the children were asleep and the stars winked into view above the straggly trees that ran along the stream.

As it turned out, he need not have feared. No sooner had he told Anna what was happening than she flung her arms open and enveloped him in a chest-creaking hug.

'Oh, Pasha, Pasha,' she said, holding him very close.

'My poor Pasha, what has that awful Polina written about you? My poor Pasha.'

Gently he pushed her back from him, and disentangled himself from her arms. 'Anna, Anna,' he said. 'You ask what she's written about me, but you don't realise it's all true. That *is* why I was discharged from the army, why Father disowned me and threw Olga out onto the street.'

But she only shook her head, gazing up at him and reaching her arms out to him once more. 'I *know*, Pasha,' she said. 'I've always known, I think – for many years, at least. Not at first – I wanted you for my own! And then you went away, and I met Bogdan. But let's not speak of him. I knew afterwards, though.'

'You – you knew?' said Pasha, dumbfounded. 'How? I still don't know how the paper found out about it, unless it was Aunt Zia. I don't think even Olga knew, until I told her.'

'Because I wanted you,' said Anna, simply, and Pasha nodded, after a moment. That made sense, after all. Nothing pierced more deeply than the arrow of desire.

'Anyway,' said Pasha, putting aside the conundrum of the paper's sources for the moment, 'don't you want me to leave?'

'Why would I want you to leave?'

'Because you're – well, because you're so, you know . . .'

'Religious?'

'Traditional,' said Pasha, quickly.

But Anna only shook her head. 'Oh, Pasha,' she said. 'Do you think so little of us? Do you think that those who stuck to belief in the dark years, the time when faith was a one-way ticket to the gulag, would welcome the return of hatred and judgement, along with freedom to worship? No, no,' she said, taking his hands and gazing up at him. 'Love, only love, is the way. It doesn't matter who you love. It only matters how much you give, and how rich is the giving of it.'

'Anna, I don't know what to say,' said Pasha, blinking away the beginnings of tears. 'I thought I'd have to move out. I was already wondering where I could go to get a bed for the night – somewhere where nobody reads the *Tayga Gazetteer*, for a start.'

'You're going nowhere,' she said, squeezing his arm. 'In fact, I think we need to fight back. Nobody should get away with something like that, not even people like Polina Klemovsky, or that horrible Boris Andreyev.'

'Well,' said Pasha, 'there *is* something you could possibly do, as a matter of fact . . .'

After that, things moved quickly, for Vladimir Solotov proved surprisingly willing to barter away his secrets in exchange for the keys to the Kabalevsky Hostel.

'At last, at last!' he said to Anna, when their negotiations had been concluded. 'Now that old fool Igor will get a run for his money. D'you know he tried to call me a cheat? *Me?* Of all people? When all I did was try to free up the people's land by turning abandoned plots into valuable assets? But let's not think about Odrosov just now – not when there's so much to celebrate. Now, why don't we toast the agreement over a glass of vodka at my place?'

Anna successfully resisted Solotov's advances and returned to the house in triumph. Now that she had gained Solotov's goodwill and swapped property for secrets, she knew precisely how to neutralise Polina Klemovsky. Polina, it turned out, had got bored in her last job but one, at Suranovo, and instead of writing books between trains, like Olga, had set up a pyramid scheme instead, targeting old people living in care homes across the Kemerovo *oblast*, and offering to pay them 30 per cent of their earnings – after a hefty down payment – if they could only persuade five other elderly friends to purchase personalised calling cards.

'Calling cards!' Solotov had said, clearly relishing the humorous aspects of Polina's indiscretion. 'Who uses calling cards, these days? Or for the last hundred years? I mean, it was classic – if only she hadn't got in too deep, and started threatening the old crones, taking cash out of their handbags and nightstands when they weren't looking. That was when her old man gave me a call, and I was happy to come and bail her out. I was happy to come calling. Ha! Come calling – did you hear that?'

Anna had averred that, indeed, she had heard his feeble joke, as well as the hundred or so other puns, innuendos, and double entendres that Solotov lavished on her during the uncomfortable conversation.

'Oh, it was awful, Olga,' she said, later on. 'I was so glad to get away! But I do feel bad about it,' she went on, taking off her hat and releasing a flood of blonde curls over her shoulders. 'Isn't it a bit like – well, like *blackmail* to make Polina change her mind about writing her stories, just because of what we know about her?'

'Well, think of it this way,' said Sasha. 'Polina shouldn't have done those things in the first place, should she? Taking money off all those old people – hundreds of them – and for precious little in return. No wonder she was keeping Solotov sweet: even Russian Railways wouldn't stand for that. And now we know that, we can do anything we like with Polina. Who knows? She might even be persuaded to suggest certain things to certain other people.'

'Certain things? Certain people?' said Olga.

'Well, people like Boris Andreyev, for instance,' replied Sasha. 'She's close to him, isn't she? And isn't he the *pridurok* who wants to send you off to Mongolia?'

'Well, yes,' said Olga, who had been trying not to think about her impending departure to Ulaanbaatar. Boris's PA, Galina, had paid another visit to Roslazny the day before to deliver Olga's new tickets and updated visa, with a departure scheduled for the following week – a stay of execution, but no more.

'Yes, he is that *pridurok*,' she continued, with feeling. 'But how would it help us if Polina suggested things to— *Ah*,' she said, suddenly understanding what Sasha had in mind. 'You don't think – surely we can't— No, it's too much to hope for! Things don't work out like that, do they, Pasha?' she said, turning to her brother for support.

But he merely looked at her, and then at Sasha, with a wondering expression on his face.

Olga Pushkin sat back in her chair and smiled. She could hardly believe all the good things that had happened in the past few days. First of all, Sasha had succeeded beyond all her wildest expectations. Not only had he ensured that Polina would never publish any of the stories she had amassed during her time in Roslazny, but he had also brought it about that Polina herself would 'volunteer' to take Olga's place on the exchange to Outer

Mongolia – forcing her to vacate Olga's rail-side hut and hand the keys back to their rightful owner.

Pasha speculated that Polina must have had some of Boris Andreyev's secrets in her possession, too – for why else would he allow one of his key informants to head abroad? 'That's the problem with politics,' he said, nodding sagely. 'Your friends become your enemies, and your enemies become your friends. It's just a matter of timing.'

'If Polina keeps me here in Roslazny, I'll count her as a friend!' smiled Olga. But the transfer itself was far from amicable.

'I *knew* you were trouble,' Polina hissed, darting close to Olga and covering her with flecks of spittle as she spat the words. 'I knew you were trouble, as soon as you picked up that bloody hedgehog. And now you go behind my back and get all my secrets from that moron Solotov – just wait till my papa hears what he's done! But as for you, Olga Pushkin, hear this: you haven't seen the last of me. Not you, and not Roslazny, either. You'll hear from me again, one way or another. Yes, and when you do, you'll think back to this moment and wish you'd done it differently. Get out of my way!'

And with that she pushed Olga aside and stormed out of the hut in her heavy yellow clogs, storming along the muddy, sleet-lined pathway that led to Roslazny until her footsteps faded into nothingness. Olga watched her go, then turned to Vassily, who had come for moral support.

'Well,' she said, forcing a smile, and trying to forget Polina's undisguised threats, 'that's that, I suppose.'

'That's that, indeed,' said Vassily. 'And now – well, now it's time to take back what's rightfully yours.' He dropped a hand on her shoulder and ushered her inside the old familiar walls of her beloved hut – altered, but not irreversibly so, by Polina's brief inhabitance, and still filled with the same indefinable scent, made up of hot tea, wood-smoke, old paper and the grease of heavy machinery. Within this home from home, this world in miniature moated by silver trees, Olga had mourned her mother, Tatiana, and spurned thoughts of her father, Mikhail; she'd resisted the barbs of chauvinist foremen and misogynistic drivers; she'd puzzled out the pages of Russian classics and written her own masterpiece, *Find Your Rail Self: 100 Life Lessons from the Trans-Siberian Railway*, on cast-off timetables between services and duties; and now she stepped into its known confines once more with a sigh both heartfelt and deep.

And the book itself was another source of delight, for no sooner had the telephone lines been restored in full than Anna fielded a call from the elusive Maxim of Lyapunov Books, keen to reassure Olga that he had been snowed under with work – Olga snorted at his choice of words – but that he had finally cleared the decks and was enthusiastic to move forward with publication for Olga's debut.

'We're starting with a hardback, Dama Pushkin,' said Maxim, down the crackly line, to a jet of pleasure in Olga's breast. 'Just a small run before Christmas, and then a paperback with more copies to come in the spring. Soon you'll be in bookshops from Nizhny Novgorod to Vladivostok!'

Olga had trouble returning to earth for quite some time following this phone call, and passed several days in a kind of dream, trying to come to terms with the fact that one of her most cherished ambitions was to be fulfilled at last. In quiet moments, Olga began to entertain herself with daydreams of an ideal reader, a young and glamorous woman whom she'd named Tatiana, after her mother. She would close her eyes and picture Tatiana walking into a bookshop on Nevsky Prospekt, trailing expensive boutique shopping bags after her, until her eye was caught by the colourful cover of Olga's book. Tatiana would pick it up with a dainty, slim-fingered hand, flick over a couple of pages, bestow a wry smile or two upon its content, and then light-heartedly hand it to a shop assistant, who'd scurry off to bag it up for her. Then she'd add it to her mountain of shopping, head to a café or wine bar, and begin to read it straight away, before darting online to post about a wonderful new writer from whom she was learning so much about life and how to live it.

But then Olga would open her eyes again, and flick the stray hairs that always seemed to curve around her cheeks, and tut at herself. There was no time for daydreaming – not in this life! You had to focus on what was happening in front of you, not on what might happen a week from now, or a month, or a year. Good things were coming, but in the meantime she had a job to do, and lots of other things that had to be done now, not at Christmas in St Petersburg. Hadn't she written as much in her book?

Life Lesson No.74: *We have to focus on the here and now. People on the railways can't lose themselves in daydreams of times to come, because if they do so, the 11.53 from Perm will run into the 11.59 to Suranovo – and if there's one thing you don't want arriving unannounced, it's a two-thousand-ton train filled with impatient passengers. People on the railways have to deal with each thing as it arrives, without indulging their favourites.*

But then she would smile and close her eyes again nonetheless, and begin picturing Tatiana's shopping expedition from scratch.

Speaking of favourites, Olga's dear friend Ekaterina Chezhekhov returned at last from Itatka, full of tales of romantic intrigue that she related to Olga in her husky smoker's voice on Tayga platform, and eager to hear everything – *everything* – that had happened in her absence.

'I can't believe it, Olga,' she'd say, again and again. 'I just can't believe it – after what happened back in January, too! How do these things keep happening to you?'

'To *me*?' cried Olga, after hearing Ekaterina relate her latest brush with danger, this time to do with an accidental incursion into Itatka Mafia territory while on a nocturnal hunt for a bottle of Smirnoff Gold. 'My adventures are nothing compared to yours, Ekaterina. I'm just glad you're still here, and in one piece.'

'Well, I've got to be, haven't I? Who else is going to look after you, my girl?'

'True, true,' said Olga, smiling. 'Though there are a couple of others who help me out now and again. There are a couple!'

A *couple*, she thought, later that day. Was Vassily still part of a couple? By now she had mostly forgiven him for keeping her in the dark regarding his suspicions about Nevena, even though – as she had told him many times over – he could have kept her just as safe, if not safer, by telling her what he was thinking. Men! she said to herself. But now that Nevena's ghost had been laid to rest, another spectre surfaced to haunt her once more: the shimmering, alluring outline of Vassily's lost wife, Rozalina. Now that things were returning to normal, so would Vassily, she expected, return to his long, seemingly unending pursuit of his vanished wife, plucked from him by people-traffickers long ago, and swallowed up in the vast, teeming spaces of Russia.

But Vassily himself had given her new hope in recent days, and that delighted her, perhaps, most of all. It had happened the day after she had found out about her book, or rather the night. Olga found herself at the police station once more, this time to help Kliment with some literature homework while Vassily got on with some equally burdensome paperwork; and once Kliment had finished his essay and gone out for a drink at the recently restocked Café Astana with Fyodor Katin, the Dreamer, Olga sat with Vassily by the fire and did some dreaming of her own.

'If I make a lot of money from *Find Your Rail Self*, I can pay off the house, Vassily,' she said to him. 'And I can go to Tomsk State University and study the classics, and become a real writer at last.'

'You *are* a real writer,' said Vassily. 'You're already that. And not just that – not that a writer is *just* anything, I mean,' he stammered, before laughing along with Olga. 'But look what else you've accomplished this year! You've caught killers, and saved lives, and made a home for Anna and Pasha, and – oh, so much besides. Think of Kliment – you found him, Olga! You brought my son back to me.'

Olga watched him smiling at her, and then turning back to look at the flames of his little hearth, his dark eyes dancing with red and orange and yellow, and she felt her heart move within her. 'I'm just sorry—'

'Yes, Olga?'

'I'm just sorry I couldn't find Rozalina, too.'

Vassily flicked a sideways look at her, then turned back to the fire. 'Well, I've been thinking, Olga,' he said.

'You've been thinking – what?'

'I'm – I'm not sure it makes sense to keep waiting and looking,' he said, clearing his throat again. 'I think it might be time to – time to let her go.'

'To let her go, Vassily? To let Rozalina go?'

She stared at him with painful intensity, not caring if it showed on her face: it was too important a matter to care about mere appearances. But then, when he nodded slowly at her, and even graced his lips with a brief but heartfelt smile, she felt her heart gain in rapidity, and her breathing become shallow, fluttering in and out until a kind of darkness came over her eyes and a fire spread into her limbs, and she lifted her hand to herself as if to grasp her very core for joy.

But her fingers curled into her palm before she touched her breast, her nails pressing white half-moons into her skin as if her heart had warned her to wait, as if it counselled caution and delay despite the immensity of joy that flooded through her veins. And this seemed wise, an intuitive gain, for at that instant Kliment and Fyodor walked in and destroyed the moment with a loud debate over the merits of typewriters versus computers, when it came to writing manifestos. Vassily looked abashed, almost, as if afraid that Kliment might hear of his feelings and regard them as abandonment, or even a betrayal; and so Olga swiftly took her leave, so swiftly that Kliment and Fyodor were surprised.

She spent the night in a fever of sleeplessness, scarcely daring to think that Vassily had been talking seriously – that he'd really meant what he'd said, and that there might be room in his heart for Olga, as well as Rozalina – that there might be space in the world for their love, a flame inextinguishable, a force so strong that one could forget the need to eat and drink and sleep.

But then, in the village the next day, Vassily was nowhere to be seen, and she feared he might have regretted his hastiness – that he might have wished his wonderful words unsaid. At last, though, he found her outside the old church hall, and explained he'd been called away all day – that Zemsky had insisted upon his presence in Tayga to question a witness in an extortion case – but that he'd like her to come for dinner that night, if she was free?

'I'd love to,' she said, and walked beside him down the muddy, leaf-strewn paths – for autumn had returned now that the snow had gone – towards the police station, where Kliment (Vassily said) awaited with a vast pan of bacon and onions and cabbage, and perhaps a tint of vodka, too.

Vassily made some joke about Kliment's cooking as they turned the last corner, and Olga laughed with him, even daring to put her hand on his arm, and feeling it was the most natural thing in the world, and the most delightful.

But then she stopped dead, for another person was there, standing beside Kliment: a blonde-haired woman in a tight-fitting dress, about the same age as Olga or perhaps a year or two older, standing in the doorway of the police station with one hand on her hip, and beaming at Olga and, especially, Vassily with a smile of fierce intensity. Just then a little dog ran out from between her high heels; she darted out to retrieve the creature, which she swept up into her arms, stroking its well-groomed fur and crooning, 'Sputnik, Sputnik, who's a good little Sputnik?' into its pointed ears.

Kliment came up to his father, eyes glowing, and put a hand on Vassily's arm. 'Father,' he said, 'a miracle has happened.

My mother has come back to me! Only – only she's not quite the same, Father. She's lost some of her memory, and they – they *beat* her,' he went on, swallowing as his face reddened with anger. 'So she looks a little different from before – a little different from your photos of the old days. But it's your Rozalina, Father! It's *really her!*'

'Vassily,' said the woman, coming forward with her dog in one arm, and reaching out to him with her other hand. 'It's really you, isn't it? It's really you!'

'Rozalina?' said Vassily, as if he were dragging her name from deep in his memory, or comparing it with the woman who now stood in front of him. 'Rozalina?'

'Oh, we thought it could never happen,' Kliment continued. 'We thought she was lost in the night, swallowed up in some city or town. But she's come back to us, haven't you, Mamochka? And now we can live together for ever. Oh, Father, isn't it wonderful? Isn't it the most wonderful thing that could ever happen to us?'

Vassily looked from Kliment to Rozalina, then back to Olga, and finally to Kliment again. 'Yes, Kliment,' he said quietly. 'It's the most wonderful thing.'

Acknowledgements

In July 2015, in a second-class compartment on the Trans-Siberian Railway between Nizhny Novgorod and Kirov, about five hundred miles east of Moscow, I met a woman called Olga. She was in her thirties, blonde, and extremely tidy. I never found out Olga's second name, but it didn't matter. You don't need second names, on the Trans-Siberian. All you really need is to know when someone wants to get changed, or when they're ready to sleep. With nods and smiles you can go a long way, on the Trans-Siberian.

Still, it's good to talk, or at least try to; and as the Volga rolled endlessly past the dusty carriage windows we did our best to get acquainted. Olga didn't speak much English, and we didn't speak much Russian, but it's surprising what you can do with a smartphone and a dictionary. In our makeshift dialect we swapped itineraries and destinations, families and livelihoods, until we arrived at Olga's hometown, the industrial city of Perm – pronounced, she told us, 'Pirrim'. She got up to go, looking around her in the way you do when leaving a temporary home, in case of abandoned keys or forgotten shoes.

But then she said something that surprised us. 'You English,' she began – and I steeled myself: what might come next? But I needn't have worried. 'You English – you nice,' she said. 'Better than' – she consulted her phone again – 'better than they tell us, in school.' And then, with a final smile, she was gone.

I only knew Olga for a couple of days, but I owe her a significant debt of gratitude. For one thing, it was her face and her name that came to mind when I had the idea for the first novel in the Olga Pushkin series, *Death on the Trans-Siberian Express*. The instant I thought of a crime unfolding around a woman and her remote rail-side hut, I knew the woman in question simply had to be a version of the Olga we met before Kirov. But there was a deeper, wider debt, too – a lasting memory of kindness to set alongside all the other recollections of warmth and hospitality and surprising grace along the endless tracks of the Trans-Siberian Railway. It is a comfort, in these darker days, to recall my encounters with ordinary Russians like Olga, and to cling to the belief that something other than Putin's atavism lies at the heart of this vast country – to the belief that its essence resides less in televised threats of nuclear war than in the soft, enduring words of Leo Tolstoy: 'The sole meaning of life is to serve humanity.'

I started *Blood on the Siberian Snow* during parental leave for my son, Xavier, just as I had done for *Death on the Trans-Siberian Express* with my daughter, Acacia. In trying to combine writing with childcare, I was frequently reminded of the poem *Dreams*, by Fyodor Kuzmych Teternikov. Set to ravishing music by Rachmaninov and fortuitously transliterated with the title *Son*, it begins: 'There is nothing in the world/more longed for than sleep.' But parental leave was a distant memory by the time I finished the book, and I found myself amply compensated for insomniac nights by Xavier's payments of smiles and steps and sentences, offered alongside Acacia's delighted, full-volume storytelling and the gentle cries of our newborn, Irah. Throughout this quite lengthy transition, my wife Claire selflessly endured endless dissection of plots, paragraphs, and dramatis personae, providing her perceptive take on far-flung tales of misadventure, and helping me to ensure that – as Anna Kabalevsky might say – the writing was always *ot dushi*, from the soul. Writing a book may not take a village, but it certainly takes a family.

In making the journey from sketchbook to published novel, I relied heavily on the wisdom, patience, and good humour of my editor, Krystyna Green, and my agent, Bill Goodall. Second novels are as stereotypically difficult as second children are proverbially easy, but Krystyna and Bill's unfailing encouragement ensured a successful transit from A to B. I am also grateful once again to Hazel Orme and Amanda Keats for their invaluable assistance with the manuscript, and to all at Little, Brown for their continued support. And lastly, I must thank my father, John, my sister Sinéad, and my dear friends Andrew, Catherine, and Peter, all of whose unflagging enthusiasm for all things Olga has been a bulwark from the beginning.